"FROM NOW ON THINGS WILL BE DIFFERENT, I PROMISE YOU."

"I'm very happy to hear you say that, Mr. Newcastle. I'm sure you understand now why it was necessary for me to pull away the other night."

"Pull away?" He stared at her in confusion before a flicker of understanding crossed his face. "Oh, you mean when I kissed you? You pulled away? Really?" He looked completely astonished. "I have to give you credit, Miss Blackwell. You're such a lady, I didn't even notice."

"I-I tried to be discreet," she stammered. "I didn't want to hurt your feelings."

"That's damned thoughtful of you. I can't tell you how many women have pulled away from my kiss with no regard for my feelings whatsoever."

She stared at him, openmouthed, not knowing how to respond.

"One woman actually slapped my face. I ask you, Miss Blackwell, what kind of manners is that? It does my heart good to know there are still ladies like yourself."

"Yes, well . . . as long as you agree that nothing like it will ever happen again."

"Oh, I didn't say it wouldn't happen again. I just said next time it will be different. Good day, Miss Blackwell."

Buttons & Beaus

by

Margaret Brownley

A TOPAZ BOOK

TOPAZ
Published by the Penguin Group
Penguin Books USA Inc., 375 Hudson Street,
New York, New York 10014, U.S.A.
Penguin Books Ltd, 27 Wrights Lane,
London W8 5TZ, England
Penguin Books Australia Ltd, Ringwood,
Victoria, Australia
Penguin Books Canada Ltd, 10 Alcorn Avenue,
Toronto, Ontario, Canada M4V 3B2
Penguin Books (N.Z.) Ltd, 182–190 Wairau Road,
Auckland 10, New Zealand

Penguin Books Ltd, Registered Offices:
Harmondsworth, Middlesex, England

First published by Topaz, an imprint of Dutton Signet,
a division of Penguin Books USA Inc.

First Printing, September, 1997
10 9 8 7 6 5 4 3 2 1

 REGISTERED TRADEMARK—MARCA REGISTRADA

Printed in the United States of America

For Warren and Summer,
who are the buttons of my heart

Chapter 1

New York: 1880

"Miss Quackenbush! You simply must open your eyes!" Amanda Blackwell grabbed the wobbling high-wheel bicycle by its saddle seat and reminded herself that patience really was a virtue—even for cycling instructors.

It was hard to believe. Despite the many hours of patient tutoring, Miss Quackenbush didn't know horsefeathers about riding a bicycle. She was clearly the most difficult student Amanda had ever encountered. "You must open your eyes and steer!"

"I *am* steering!"

"With your hands!"

The new model ordinary weaved back and forth with alarming regularity. The India rubber tires permitted a far smoother ride than the wooden tires of earlier boneshakers, but no one would ever guess this by watching Miss Quackenbush bob up and down on her seat like the needle of a Singer sewing machine.

Amanda clenched her teeth in exasperation. Lord almighty, what a sight! The way Miss Quackenbush held her legs straight out made her look like an open pair of pinch-nosed hog clippers!

From the tip of her feathered hat to the shiny toes of her side-buttoned boots, she was dressed in stark black, her high-necked wool dress every bit as unyielding as the stubborn look on her sharp, pointed face.

Amanda was hot and thirsty and this didn't help

her patience one whit, nor did the fact that she was being watched by a man on horseback. *A stranger!*

The brim of the man's shiny tall hat shaded his face, but even from this distance she could feel the intensity of his gaze, and combined with his commanding presence, it was hard, if not altogether impossible, to ignore.

Equally hard to ignore was the mysterious air he conveyed that teased and titillated Amanda's curious nature to the point of agony. For two cents, she'd be tempted to march over to him and demand an explanation!

The man was actually staring, no bones about it, and this was clearly an affront to good manners. Whoever this stranger was, he played by his own rules.

Well, so did she, by George, and her rules clearly stated that no one was to interrupt, stare, or otherwise create a nuisance of himself while she was teaching a cycling class. In her estimation, the stranger was guilty on all counts.

Convinced she was perfectly justified in returning rudeness in kind, she turned her back to him and quickly steered Miss Quackenbush along a narrow footpath leading to Central Park's main carriage drive. Much to her dismay, this didn't discourage the stranger. She soon spotted him watching her from atop a grassy knoll.

She'd been right all along; he *was* following them, and he wasn't just staring, he was, well, *staring*. Why, she could feel his heated gaze as certain as she could feel the warmth of the sun. The nerve of the man!

Ignoring the strand of mahogany-colored hair that had escaped from beneath the brim of her perky hat, she was so intent on losing the stranger, she failed to notice Officer Thorndike upon his horse, blocking the narrow path ahead, until she was practically on top of him.

Amanda was tempted to turn around and head in the opposite direction, but knowing the policeman, he would only follow her.

Old Thorny, as she called Officer Thorndike, was one of several policemen who patrolled Central Park. The locals called them sparrow cops, and for good reason—Sparrows had been brought from Europe in a misguided attempt to enhance the park with a bit of Shakespearean lore. It didn't take long to discover the Bard knew what he was talking about when he wrote of the special providence following the fall of a sparrow.

The birds were pests and had promptly been declared a public nuisance, but that was the least of it. The park was literally plastered with placards warning visitors against doing everything imaginable, from walking on the grass to picking dandelions. Ignoring the signs could be costly. Pulling up so much as a single root of sassafras was likely to cost the offender thirty days in jail.

Amanda would be more inclined to follow the rules had the park board been more concerned with safety. But the majority of rules were meant to instill proper park decorum, and safety was rarely a consideration. Digging up dandelions was considered unladylike and speeding along the main carriage drive, nothing short of vulgar. As far as Amanda was concerned, the park's designers had gone too far with all their rules and regulations, and so had Old Thorny.

Now the old beak glared at her, ready, no doubt, to complain about her whistle, lecture her about trampling the grass, or recite those annoying cycling rules. You'd think it was his God-given duty. As if she didn't know the rules by heart!

"Look who's here," he said with feigned surprise. "Miss Blackwell and Miss Quackenbush."

"You're looking well this morning," Amanda said politely, trying not to irritate him. She couldn't help but think he looked like a cat ready to pounce on some poor, hapless creature.

"May I remind you, Miss Blackwell, that it is eight-twenty-five in the morning? Wheelmen and"—he leveled his eyes on Miss Quackenbush—"wheel*ladies* are allowed to ride through Central Park from Fifty-ninth to One Hundredth streets between midnight and nine in the morning, and not one minute more."

It was all Amanda could do to keep from flying off the handle. But the last time she gave Old Thorny a piece of her mind, she was forced to cool her heels in the city jail.

"I'm quite aware of the time *and* the rules." She resisted the urge to tell him what he could do with that "one minute more" part. If cyclists misjudged the time, what in heaven's name were they supposed to do? Sit and wait until midnight to ride back? True, Riverside Drive was open to cyclists at all times, as was Eighth Street, and summer hours were more lax, but that was beside the point.

"And coasting," Thorny continued. "I believe I spotted one of your students coasting yesterday."

"You must be mistaken!" Amanda said, managing to sound appropriately shocked. Coasting was strictly prohibited, and Amanda was in complete accord with the lawman regarding racing, but they battled continuously over speed limits. What he called speeding, she considered a comfortable clip. The laws of physics were such that cyclists either maintained a certain speed or suffered the consequences of falling off their bicycles. If Old Thorny took the time to get down off his high horse, he'd know that.

"Are you saying I'm seeing things?" he asked.

"Sometimes the light plays tricks with the eyes," Miss Quackenbush interjected.

"What about the ears?" he asked. "I could have sworn I heard Miss Blackwell break the law regarding the indiscriminating use of a whistle."

"Perhaps you heard one of the other policemen chasing sparrows off the grass," Amanda said. "It's been a bad day for sparrows."

"It's been a bad day for cyclists," Miss Quackenbush added.

"And it will be bad day for cycling teachers if I catch either one of you breaking park rules." Old

Thorny turned his horse and rode off. He didn't take kindly to having a cycling school in his territory—and Amanda didn't take kindly to having a humorless policeman watching her every move.

No sooner had Old Thorny turned his back than she held the whistle to her mouth, ready to blow at the first sign Miss Quackenbush was in trouble. She didn't care what the rules dictated. If one of her students was in danger, she intended to blow her whistle, and Old Thorny could jolly well complain all he wanted.

She was relieved to discover that the stranger on horseback was nowhere in sight. Dismissing both men from her mind, Amanda focused her full attention on her student. "Let's proceed."

Miss Quackenbush rode her bicycle like a staggering drunk, weaving from one side of the narrow dirt path to the other. Fortunately it was still early enough that this part of Central Park was relatively quiet. In another hour or so, people would swarm along the footpaths and over the bridges, taking advantage of the unseasonably warm day in early March.

The promenade mall, however, was already crowded. Elderly gentlemen with walking canes in hand and the morning newspapers tucked beneath their arms searched for empty park benches. Hardly a day went by that the writer Herman Melville didn't walk through the park with his little granddaughter in tow, and today he was earlier than usual, his grave, preoccupied expression suggesting another book was in the works.

Soon the dowagers would arrive, gliding gracefully beneath bright-colored parasols, the hems of their Parisian gowns sweeping across the forbidden grass as they stopped to peruse the roasted chestnuts, imported buttons, and gold pocket watches displayed on the carts of peddlers who had managed to sneak past the gatekeepers.

They would be followed by nurses wearing crisp white aprons and little white caps, pushing infants in baby carriages or holding their young charges by the hands. The nurses, hired by the wealthy families who lived in the elegant mansions on Park Avenue, wisely kept the youngsters out of the park in the afternoons, when the matrons of Manhattan's wealthiest families rode along the broad drive in glittering carriages drawn by high-stepping horses.

Amanda resented the fact that carriages were allowed in the park during daytime hours, but not bicycles. The dowagers of Fifth Avenue would do well to get out of their fancy victorias and shiny barouches and pedal. Perhaps the exercise and fresh air would put a healthy glow onto their pallid faces.

Pushing her thoughts aside, she regarded her student with exasperation. The fact that Miss Quackenbush's eyes were squeezed tightly shut was only part of the problem: the spinster couldn't seem to grasp the concept that handlebars controlled the direction of the cycle. Amanda was willing to bet dollars to buttons that pigs would fly before Miss Quackenbush learned to cycle.

Holding the wobbling bicycle upright, Amanda trotted beside it, the hem of her short skirt flapping against her bloomers, and expertly guided the bicycle away from the crowded mall.

"Watch out!" she cried out. "Steer!"

Despite her warning, the front wheel of the bicycle hit a rut. In an effort to avert disaster, Amanda tightened her grip, but despite her quick actions, Miss Quackenbush sailed over the handlebars as smooth as a fly on a fishing line, then tumbled head over heels to the ground.

Chapter 2

The bicycle tipped over on its side, taking Amanda with it. Caught in a graceless heap, Amanda's main concern was for her student. Though this section of the park was deserted, still Amanda blew her whistle on general principles. After she freed herself from the metal wheel web, she quickly crawled to her student's side.

"Miss Quackenbush! Are you all right?"

The woman was all arms and lisle-stockinged legs. She kicked and sputtered, her indignant cries muffled by her dress.

A shocking display of feminine apparel, designed to squeeze, pinch, and otherwise force the female form into an hourglass shape, was revealed. The poor woman was in complete violation of the park rules calling for decorous behavior.

Even more shocking was the spiral spring bosom pad that had popped out of place and landed pointy side up on the forbidden grass. It was soon discovered by a grunting hog that had suddenly emerged from the bushes.

The hefty sow was one of the many hogs owned by the residents living in shanties on the west side of the park. The swine roamed the streets and parts of the park, rooting for trash and generally making a nuisance of themselves. Though the city had once depended solely on hogs to keep the streets clean, the animals created more problems than they solved and many city dwellers objected to them.

The hog snatched the bosom pad in its mouth and tossed it about like a toy. Amanda shooed away the sow with a wave of her hand. "Scat!"

The hog wandered off, taking Miss Quackenbush's bosom enhancer with it, and Amanda fought to pull down the woman's skirt. It wasn't an easy task, considering Amanda had to work around the woman's flailing limbs.

A friendly stray dog scampered over to paint Amanda's face with a wet tongue, unmindful of the fact that stray dogs, like sparrows and swine, were banned from the park.

"Shoo, doggy!" Her voice stern, Amanda pushed the playful ball of fur away. The white-haired dog gave Amanda a melancholy look before spotting a boy with a hoop. Giving a joyous bark, its tail wagging furiously, the little dog bounded off, leaving Amanda to restore Miss Quackenbush's modesty without further interruption.

"Are you all right?" Amanda asked again.

The indignant woman glared at Amanda. "Do I look all right?" she replied in a scolding voice that was mimicked by a jaybird rummaging in the branches of a nearby tree.

Amanda stood, lifted the bicycle upright, and helped her student to her feet.

"Never in all my born days have I been so humiliated!" Miss Quackenbush brushed herself off and glared at a group of schoolboys who were taking a shortcut through the park on the way to the elementary school. The boys had the ill grace to snicker before gleefully running off, probably to spread the word that a former schoolteacher had made an uncommon spectacle of herself.

Her face red as the apples sold at Washington Market, Miss Quackenbush sniffed. With a dramatic nod of her head, she swiped at the black feather dangling in front of her face. "Miss Blackwell! We need to work on my dismounting."

Amanda inspected the bicycle for damage. It never

failed to amaze her how much abuse these machines could withstand. "Your problem is not dismounting, Miss Quackenbush. It's getting on the bicycle and staying on. That's what you need to work on. And you can start by learning to keep your eyes open. Perhaps you would be happier with a tricycle."

"Nonsense." The woman looked insulted. "How would it look if the president of the Knickerbocker Ladies' Cycling Club is seen riding a tricycle rather than a proper ordinary?"

The fact that Miss Quackenbush was the president of the women's cycling organization was less curious than it seemed. Miss Quackenbush had originally thought its members, all former schoolmarms, meant to picket or otherwise protest cycling clubs that excluded female cyclists. It never occurred to her that club members intended to actually *ride* bicycles themselves.

By the time Miss Quackenbush realized her error, she had already accepted the nomination, and was too proud to confess her ignorance at such a late date. The other members would no doubt be shocked if they realized their esteemed president didn't know even the basic skills of riding.

"We're going to show those men a thing or two, just wait and see," she stated firmly, referring to the members of the New York Wheelers' Cycling Club, who steadfastly refused to allow women to join. "We intend to ride in the Fourth of July parade."

Amanda hoped she'd misunderstood. "You do know the parade is only four months away." It had taken Miss Quackenbush several hour-long lessons to build up enough courage to plant her posterior onto the seat. God only knew how long it would take her to learn to steer with her eyes open.

"I'm well aware of when the parade is." The woman rubbed her thigh. "Perhaps I should continue my lesson tomorrow. . . ."

"No, Miss Quackenbush," Amanda said firmly, though she was sorely tempted to end the sessions forever. "We shall continue now. Cycling is like horse-back riding. If you fall off, you must get back on immediately."

Miss Quackenbush arched her eyebrow. "And if I don't?"

Amanda straightened her own lopsided hat. She hated having to threaten the poor woman, but it was for her own good. "See that sign over my shop?" She pointed to an opening through the trees that over-looked the one-story brick building on Eighth Avenue across from the park. A placard proclaimed Amanda's school CAPABLE OF TEACHING ANYONE, YOUNG OR OLD.

"I will add 'with the exception of Miss Quacken-bush.' Then everyone will know you are the most mule-headed and annoying student I ever had the mis-fortune of taking on."

"Ha!" Miss Quackenbush planted her fists on her generous hips. "You only think I'm mule-headed be-cause I didn't take a fancy to that button man you tried to pawn off on me." She referred to the peddler known as Vincent, whose button-filled cart was a fa-miliar sight next to the park entrance.

"You did, too, take a fancy to him!" Amanda said hotly. "If I recall, you practically threw yourself at him. If you would show as much assertiveness in riding a bicycle as you do in tackling a gentleman—" Sud-denly an idea flashed in her head.

She gave the high-wheeler a little shake. "See this bicycle, Miss Quackenbush? We are going to pretend it's a gentleman caller. As you can see, he's very tall . . ." She pointed to the front drive wheel. At thirty-six inches, it was a great deal smaller than the sixty-inch high-wheelers Amanda used for her male students, but it was still daunting. "And he has very wide handles . . . eh . . . shoulders."

Miss Quackenbush regarded the bicycle as if look-ing at it for the first time. "Mercy me. It does have a lot of male properties, doesn't it?"

"Eh, yes, well . . ." Amanda had tried many meth-ods of teaching, but had never before resorted to anything quite so brash. Still, she was determined that Miss Quackenbush receive the cycling badge required by law.

Amanda had a reputation to protect. Miss Blackwell's Cycling School was considered the best of its kind in all New York. Bicycles were the rage in Manhattan, though they were responsible for no small amount of controversy and chaos. Horses were spooked by them, and hardly a day went by that some buggy wasn't overturned when a careless cyclist whizzed by without regard.

Since New York had passed the law requiring a license for anyone wishing to ride a bicycle on the streets, cycling schools had popped up like mushrooms following a rain. But no school was as well respected as the one owned by Miss Amanda Blackwell. She had caused a scandal when she first opened her school to women. Shock waves shot through New York, reverberating through Wall Street and sending the financial district into a panic the day she publicly declared riding a bicycle sidesaddle should be banned.

Any woman graduating from her school was sure to receive the cycling badge that was required by law, and possibly more; if they were single, willing, and heeded Amanda's advice, they might also land a beau—and maybe even a proposal or two in the process.

A born matchmaker, Amanda prided herself on her ability to match her students with appropriate mates. Couples who had met and married because of Amanda's uncanny gift of matchmaking invariably named an offspring after her, and on any given Sunday, half of the little girls in Central Park dressed in fancy frocks and lacy pantalets answered to the name of Amanda.

Amanda had failed miserably on two accounts with Miss Quackenbush. Despite Amanda's best efforts, the spinster couldn't ride a bicycle, and hadn't received so much as a single query in the marriage department!

Though she'd been undeniably tempted at times, Amanda refused to give up. Make no mistake about it. The woman was going to learn to ride a bicycle *and* land herself a husband! Yes, indeed, she was. Or Amanda would know why not!

Now that she had her student's full attention, Amanda assumed her usual no-nonsense stance. "Miss Quackenbush. The gentleman is waiting—" Before Amanda had finished what she intended to say, the spinster had mounted the bicycle faster than lightning, with none of her usual timid ways.

Encouraged, Amanda held the machine steady. "Don't put your feet on the pedals yet. That's it. Let them dangle." She glanced around. In the name of God, she hoped no one heard her.

"All right, Miss Quackenbush," she said, keeping her voice low. They had only fifteen minutes before that nuisance of a policeman chased them out of the park. Seeing no sign of the stranger on horseback, she took a deep breath. "Let's pretend the gentleman wants . . . you know . . . to have his way with you."

Miss Quackenbush's eyes grew as wide as bread plates and her face turned a vivid red. "Oh, my."

Oh, dear. Despite her reservations, Amanda forced herself to continue. "Of course, the gentleman will do only what you want him to do. That's why you must keep your hands firmly on the . . . on his shoulders."

"Yes, yes, yes!" Miss Quackenbush placed her hands on the handlebars. Her pointed face taking on a purposeful expression, her eyes fairly gleamed as she tightened her hold.

"All right now." Amanda placed one hand on the back of the seat and one on the handlebar. "Let's go." She moved the bicycle slowly along the winding path.

Amanda breathed deeply, inhaling the sweet scents of new grass and fresh-blooming violets. What a glorious day! Spring had come early, following nearly four months of a surprisingly mild winter. The sky was clear and the air filled with the sound of twittering birds. Though it was still early, the park began to buzz with activity.

Dogs barked at the various musicians strolling through the park, no doubt keeping the sparrow cops on the run. Just maybe Old Thorny would be too busy to notice if she and Miss Quackenbush stayed in the park after nine.

Amanda and her student skirted the area known as the Children's District. The sounds of a German brass band could be heard playing in the distance.

A small boy in a wheelchair watched Miss Quackenbush wobble by him, his eyes wide with interest. His nurse, a young woman dressed in a bustled black frock with a crisp white apron, gasped in alarm and quickly pushed her young charge out of the way. The boy continued to watch Miss Quackenbush, his eyes bright with interest, until he and his nurse disappeared around a bend.

Amanda searched the park for Vincent, whose "Buttoooooooons!" could generally be heard from here. Where was he? Today the button vendor was suspiciously absent.

How like Vincent to obey the rules when it suited him, which seemed to be whenever Miss Quackenbush was having her lesson, and do what he darn well pleased at other times. He irked Amanda no end. Couldn't he see that despite Miss Quackenbush's strange ways, she would make the perfect wife for him?

"Let yourself feel the motion of the machine. . . ."

"Oh, it's so big and strong," Miss Quackenbush uttered in delight.

"Yes, well . . ." Lordy be, the things she had to do. "Now keep the front wheel aligned with the back wheel. That's it. When you want to turn, pretend you're guiding a man's hand. . . . My word, Miss Quackenbush, gently. You must turn the *shoulders* gently!"

It took all of Amanda's strength to keep the woman from falling a second time. "Let's stop here." Since

Miss Quackenbush had no control over the machine, it was up to Amanda to bring the bicycle to a halt.

"Miss Blackwell, I pay you good money to teach me and I expect a full hour of instruction."

"You always get a full hour of instruction," Amanda replied. *For all the good it does you!* "Very well. We'll try it again." She searched the park for a landmark. "The Ladies' Pavilion is just ahead. I want you to pretend it's a wedding altar. Now as you well know, no gentleman will head for an altar of his own accord. It's up to you to take charge and steer him in the right direction. Are you ready?"

"I'm ready, I'm ready!"

Amanda wheeled the cycle forward, and much to her amazement, her student actually managed to balance herself without wobbling. "That's it, Miss Quackenbush. Why, glory be! I do believe you have it! Now place your feet on the pedals . . . eh . . . next to his."

They rounded a bend and Miss Quackenbush did as she was told. "That's it! Now push down hard!"

"Oh, my!" Miss Quackenbush made a soft swooning sound. "My, my, my!" The bicycle turned away from the direction of the Ladies' Pavilion. "Oh, no you don't! You're not getting away from me this time!"

"That's it!" Amanda cried excitedly. She moved her hands away from the bicycle. "Keep going!"

Suddenly, Miss Quackenbush veered off the path, shot across the lush green lawn, annihilating the numerous placards proclaiming the grass off-limits, and headed straight for the lake.

Amanda streaked across the lawn after her. "Hold on!" She stuck her whistle in her mouth and blew as loud as she could. "Steer! The altar's this way!"

Miss Quackenbush continued to barrel straight ahead at an alarming and, by park standards, *vulgar* speed. A young couple sitting on a park bench looked up in horror, then quickly jumped to their feet and ran. Nannies yanked their charges out of danger's way. Dogs barked and chased after the runaway bicycle, and a hefty hog chased after the dogs.

An artist engrossed in his work glanced up upon hearing the commotion, but before he had a chance to move, Miss Quackenbush's bicycle had ripped through his canvas. His easel flew in one direction, his paints in another. The front wheel of the bicycle ran over a tube of oil paint, and a bright blue stream squirted onto the poor man's startled face.

Apologizing, Amanda sprinted past the outraged artist, blowing her whistle at full blast. Where was that annoying sparrow cop when you needed him?

Suddenly, Miss Quackenbush shot over the handlebars and took a nosedive into the lake. Ducks flapped their wings and quacked furiously, their feet skimming the water. Even the usually serene swans skittered away, frantically trying to escape.

A canopied oar-propelled boat rocked dangerously and another headed for the airy boathouse on the opposite shore. An Italian gondolier swore in his native tongue as he tried to steady his gondola. A fisherman raised his fists in the air, but his curses were drowned out by Miss Quackenbush, who flailed about in the water, screaming like a hog caller in Germantown.

"Woman in the water!" Amanda raced to the lake, yelling all the way. "Hold on, Miss Quackenbush. I'll save you." This was easier said than done since she didn't know how to swim. She searched frantically for a sparrow cop, but naturally none was in sight.

A man whom Amanda immediately recognized as the stranger she'd seen earlier galloped across the lawn on his horse and quickly slid off his saddle. With a running leap, he dived into the water, his tall, shiny hat flying off his head.

Her heart pounding wildly, Amanda stood on the bank with the rest of the spectators, watching the stranger rescue the poor hapless woman. Somehow he managed to calm Miss Quackenbush and she stopped bellowing and went limp in his arms.

Looking like a Greek god, the stranger carried the waterlogged spinster out of the water and laid her gently on the grass. He then proceeded to check her for injuries. "Here, ma'am. Maybe this will help you breathe easier."

He unbuttoned the top button of the spinster's frock with the ease that could only come from practice. Obviously, the man was a womanizer.

Amanda dropped to her knees by her student's side. "Miss Quackenbush! Are you all right?"

Miss Quackenbush ignored her. She was too busy gazing up at her rescuer. "Oh, my! You really do have male properties."

Amanda pressed her fingers together and gave the stranger an apologetic look. He seemed more amused than shocked, his mouth curving in a half-smile that brought a flush to Amanda's face. He looked even more handsome up close, but no less intimidating. He struck Amanda as a man with an insatiable lust for life.

She only wished she knew what he wanted from her. Oh, he wanted something all right; she could see it in the bold dark eyes that seemed to undress her.

With a lift of his brow and a quirk of his mouth, he made it quite clear that not only did he want something, he intended to have it.

He looked amazingly dignified considering his fine tailored suit was dripping wet. He didn't even have the good grace to look startled when Miss Quackenbush grabbed hold of him and brazenly kissed him on the mouth.

"Miss Quackenbush!" Amanda blushed with embarrassment as she beseeched the startled spectators not to judge the woman too harshly. "Please understand, she's not herself."

The stranger looked unfazed, an indulgent glint lighting his eyes. Obviously, he was used to strange women throwing themselves at him, and by the way his brazen gaze settled on Amanda's lips, he appeared to expect her to follow the spinster's lead. She clamped her mouth firmly shut. She was grateful to him for coming to Miss Quackenbush's rescue, but not *that* grateful.

He didn't look the least bothered by the frown she gave him; indeed, he looked amused. "I'm glad I could be of service," he said smoothly, his gaze never leaving Amanda's face. The dark brown depths of his eyes softened to a rich autumn gold that matched the golden highlights in his wet hair. His lips came together and parted in a way that looked for all the world like a kiss.

A kiss! Her mouth dropped open. Her heart beat so fast, she could hardly catch her breath. She'd met her share of womanizers, but none had compared to this man.

Shrugging with schoolboy innocence that didn't fool her in the least, he turned, and spotting a woolen shawl abandoned during the earlier confusion, plucked it off the ground and spread it over Miss Quackenbush.

Amanda swallowed hard and glanced at the faces of the still-hovering crowd. Surely someone had seen his brazen action. But a quick glance at the sea of faces proved futile. The spectators were too busy gaping at the waterlogged spinster, who, judging by her numerous complaints, appeared to have made an amazing recovery.

"Isn't there a law against gawking?" she asked, making a rude face at the crowd. "And whose idea was it to put a lake in front of the wedding altar?"

"There is no wedding altar," Amanda whispered. "We were just pretending there was."

Fussing over her student, Amanda kept an overt eye on the stranger. Lordy, if he wasn't tall. Standing well over six feet, his lean, muscular body was a study in pure, unadulterated masculine splendor. Even after Amanda had managed to pull her gaze away from him, she could still feel the pulsating warmth of his presence.

His male properties, as Miss Quackenbush called them, made Amanda's senses spin faster than the wheels of a racing bicycle.

"There is too a wedding altar." Still ranting, Miss

Quackenbush pointed in the direction of the Ladies' Pavilion. She smiled up at the stranger, managing to look demure. "Our guests are waiting. . . ."

Amanda frowned in worry. Oh, dear, what had she done to the poor woman? The man's inexcusable behavior forgotten in her concern for her student, she turned to him. "You don't suppose she's demented. . . ."

The stranger measured Miss Quackenbush with an appraising look. "She's in shock, but I think she'll be all right. Perhaps you should have a doctor check her over."

Her worries calmed by his strong, confident voice, she nodded gratefully. His concern for Miss Quackenbush was obviously genuine. "You're quite right. She should see a doctor."

"I don't need a doctor!" Miss Quackenbush pushed away the shawl, rose to her feet, and swiped at the dripping wet feather that fell from the crown of her hat to the tip of her quivering chin.

The stranger picked up his hat and placed it on his head. "In that case, I'll be taking my leave. Have a pleasant day, ladies." His gaze met Amanda's for one heart-stopping moment before he turned and grabbed the reins of his horse.

A burning sensation in Amanda's lungs reminded her to breathe. Taking a deep breath, she sighed dreamily. He was clearly the most handsome man she'd ever set eyes on. And she hadn't even thought to ask his name. Not that she cared, of course, but it would have been the polite thing to do.

"I'm much obliged to you, sir," Amanda called after him. He glanced back over his shoulder, flashing a devastating smile before he mounted his horse and galloped away.

Miss Quackenbush plopped herself down on a park bench, a look of utter disgust on her face. "He's like all the rest," she complained. "Mention marriage and he disappears faster than a truant schoolboy." A look of regret flashed in her eyes. "But what male properties!"

Amanda checked Miss Quackenbush's head, and

seeing no obvious injuries to account for the woman's ramblings, she gave her student a gentle shake. "I insist you pull yourself together. It's only a bicycle."

Miss Quackenbush pushed Amanda's hand away. "I'm not talking about the bicycle. I'm talking about the man. Are you blind? Did you not notice him?"

"He *was* handsome," Amanda admitted. She could hardly fault Miss Quackenbush's taste in men, but the woman definitely needed to be more discreet. No wonder Amanda had failed in all her attempts to find the spinster a beau. If this is how she carried on, it explained why men ran the other way every time they saw her coming. "Come on, I'll take you to see Dr. Paine."

"I told you, I don't need a doctor." Miss Quackenbush glared at the spectators still milling around before turning to Amanda, her hands at her hips. "I thought you were holding on to the bicycle."

"How could I possibly hold on? You were peddling so fast, I couldn't keep up."

"I could have been killed."

"Yes, you could have been. That's why I think you should seriously consider switching to a tricycle. There's no shame in riding a three-wheeler. Both men and women ride them."

"Miss Blackwell! May I remind you that I am the president of the Knickerbocker Ladies' Cycling Club?" What a sight she was, her hat ruined, her hair straggling down her back, her sopping wet clothes clinging to her in all the wrong places. She seemed oblivious to the fact that her bosoms were lopsided, one side flat as yesterday's hotcakes, thanks to a certain hog.

Harrumphing, Miss Quackenbush charged up the hill, forging her way past the still-gawking spectators without so much as a glance.

Amanda craned her neck, hoping to spot the man who had saved her student, and perhaps even her own reputation.

Instead, the sparrow cop she called Old Thorny was

galloping toward her on his gleaming brown horse. "Miss Blackwell," he shouted, his face red with fury. "I understand you were blowing your whistle with no regard for decorum."

Amanda glanced around, and it was just as she thought; not one handsome stranger bothered to come to *her* rescue.

Chapter 3

Damian Newcastle paced back and forth the length of his study, hands clasped behind his back. Finally, he stopped in his tracks, his eyes narrowed in concentration, and gazed at the heavily marked building plans tacked to the wood-paneled wall.

A sense of elation unlike anything he'd felt in years washed over him. It didn't look like much on paper. But once completed, the combination office and apartment building would reach unprecedented heights, standing an amazing twenty stories high! It would be a full ten stories taller than the nation's tallest office building to date, the Western Union Telegraph Building, on Dey and Broadway. *Ten stories!*

He chuckled. And they said it couldn't be done! Well, by George, he would show them. Ah, yes! And once he had completed his building, nothing would ever be the same. The economical, not to mention social, climate of New York would change forever.

His blood raced with excitement as he went over his plans again, inch by inch. He couldn't afford to neglect a single detail. Though it wouldn't be as tall as Trinity Church, whose twenty-five-story spire loomed over Wall Street, Damian's building would be the tallest habitable structure in the world. He couldn't believe it, even now, when his dream was so close to fruition. The world!

To build such a tall building was a bold and even daring venture.

Until recently, few people dared to dream that

buildings higher than the customary four or five stories were possible, let alone practical. Had it not been for the recently developed "safety" elevators, they wouldn't be.

No one wanted to climb more than one, perhaps two flights of stairs. As a result, property owners were forced to charge less for upper floors to make them more appealing to tenants. Now the elevator made each floor equally accessible, thus eliminating the need for landowners to lower rent to attract interest.

By George, these superstructures would be a boon for businessmen, especially now that prime property on Manhattan Island was rapidly growing scarce. Already half of Manhattan was developed, all the way from the Battery to the southernmost tip of the park that city planners had optimistically called *Central* Park. At the current rate of growth, it wouldn't be long before their optimism paid off.

Chances were good that in another year or two commercial buildings would spread north of the park and the farmers now populating the area would be forced to move.

Ah, yes, indeed! His high-rise building would make a tremendous impact on the city. No doubt about it. But as grand as all this was, his interest in this particular project was far more personal, the stakes closer to home.

If everything went as he hoped, the success of the building would restore pride and honor to his tarnished family name. Maybe then his young son could return to the school that had so cruelly rejected him, and begin living a normal life. Maybe then Damian could swing public opinion enough to demand a new trial for his father, one that would ultimately lead to the elder man's release from prison.

Yes, indeed, a lot was at stake. That's why he had no choice but to succeed.

Only one minor inconvenience stood in his way: Miss Blackwell's Cycling School.

Originally, his family owned a chunk of the land

that now comprised Central Park, but the city had offered to purchase the land at a shockingly low price, and at the time, the Newcastle Construction Company was in no position to fight City Hall. His father did, however, manage to hold on to a small piece of land outside the park boundaries.

Of course, this was years ago, when the area had been nothing more than swampy wastelands. No one could have predicted how property values would sky-rocket once the park became a reality. In any case, Damian was stuck with a primo piece of property that was a hundred and eight feet deep and less than twenty-two feet wide.

This presented a problem that required the coopera-tion of a certain Miss Amanda Blackwell to resolve. The city's building code stipulated that the height of a building dictated the thickness of its walls. That meant the walls supporting a twenty-story building would have to be at least six feet thick. Unless he was successful in purchasing the adjacent property, he would be stuck with rooms that were little more than ten feet wide.

He had considered purchasing land elsewhere, but none proved as useful for his purposes as the lot on Sixty-sixth and Eighth located directly opposite a park entrance.

He had traveled to Central Park earlier that day to make Miss Blackwell a generous offer on her prop-erty. If Miss Blackwell's student hadn't tumbled into the lake, he would have completed his business by now.

Amanda Blackwell. Just thinking of her brought a smile to his lips. What an appealing sight she made with her soft felt hat askew and her rich mahogany-brown hair tumbling down to her shoulders. Despite the warning issued in the fashion watchdog magazine published by DeMorest that "flying ribbons and fluffy ruffs" should be avoided by any well-groomed cyclist, Miss Blackwell was guilty of both.

She wore bloomers, which Damian approved of for

practical purposes but never personally cared for until seeing them on her, and a white silk blouse. The gathered hems of her trousers inched upward when she moved, revealing well-turned ankles. He wouldn't have noticed the blue ribbon tied in a bow at the base of her neck had it not matched the color of her big blue eyes.

He would never forget how her eyes had flashed when he'd thrown her that kiss, indignation written all over her pretty round face. He chuckled at the memory. Ah, but that's not all that shimmered in the sparkling depths of her eyes. Not by any means. *You can pretend to be shocked all you want, Miss Blackwell, but you were definitely intrigued,* he thought to himself.

She probably would never admit it, even to herself, but he knew when a lady was interested and Miss Blackwell was clearly interested.

She looked even more appealing face-to-face than she had looked in the many photographs that had appeared in the *Tribune* and the *New York Times*. His smile deepened. The woman was every bit as pretty as she was controversial.

The first thing he planned to do the following morning was pay the cycling school another visit. He was definitely going to enjoy doing business with Miss Blackwell, even if her reputation as an astute businesswoman turned out to be true.

Naturally, he intended to use the latter to his full advantage. If she really was all that astute, then she would immediately accept his generous offer. No one in his or her right mind would want to conduct business next to a high-rise building such as he intended to build.

Once he had the deed to her property in his hands, nothing, not his critics or the many enemies his father had made as a result of the terrible catastrophe that had resulted in his imprisonment, would stop Damian from making architectural history!

His thoughts were interrupted by his young son,

who had entered the room unnoticed and was now tugging on the leg of his trousers. "Papa."

Damian smiled down at the earnest face of the tow-headed youngster. "What is it, son?" Christopher had suffered an injury to the spine when the balcony of the Continental Theater had collapsed some three years earlier. The boy had only been four years old at the time. The doctors said the boy would never walk again. This, plus the scandal that followed the tragedy, was more than Christopher's poor mother could handle. The following winter, she'd died of pneumonia, two days before Christopher's fifth birthday.

"Miss Hannah says I have to learn to add before I can design buildings."

"Miss Hannah is right. Mathematics is an important part of architecture. If you don't know how to work with numbers you'll end up building rooms with crooked walls and lopsided ceilings."

Christopher's lighthearted laughter brought a smile to Damian's own face. Though Christopher was basically confined to a wheelchair, he had recently learned to move from room to room by sliding on his behind across the polished plank flooring of the Dutch farmhouse.

Damian regarded his young son thoughtfully, his heart filled with love. The boy had Damian's same brown eyes and brown hair, but had his mother's smile. He reached over to tousle his son's hair. "No one wants to live in a crooked house."

"But numbers are boring," Christopher complained. "It's more fun to read." It's something his mother might have said, and Damian felt a pang inside that made him grimace.

Nothing he could have done, of course, would have prevented the tragedy that had torn his family apart. Knowing this didn't help matters much. He had failed on enough levels since the accident to justify most, if not all, of the guilt he felt. He'd failed his father, failed his wife, and Heaven knows, had certainly failed Christopher.

Since his wife's death, he had done his utmost to protect his young son from the hurtful gossip that refused to go away. The wagging tongues and acid remarks were more difficult to live with than the guilt. Gossip had a way of filtering through the sturdiest walls. It remained to be seen whether or not gossip could travel to the top of a twenty-story building.

"I'll tell you what," Damian said patiently. "You finish your numbers and I'll read you a story."

"Read 'Ragged Dick,'" Christopher pleaded. "Oh, please, Papa, say you will!"

Damian had read Christopher the story of the orphaned bootblack so many times, they both had it memorized. Still, he gave in with a good-natured chuckle. "'Ragged Dick' it is."

Satisfied, Christopher tugged on his father's leg. "Lift me up, Papa. I want to see the building that touches the sky. Then I'll do my numbers. I promise."

Damian scooped Christopher into his arms. When they were outdoors, Damian often carried his son around on his shoulders, but the low ceilings of the farmhouse prevented him from doing so now. Damian moved closer to the wall. "There it is, son."

Christopher's eyes shone as he ran a small hand up and down the drawings. "That's the elevator shaft," he said proudly, "and these are the bear walls."

"They're called bearing walls, son."

"Are we going to live on the top floor?" Christopher asked, though he knew the answer by heart.

His son's enthusiasm never failed to fill Damian with joy. "Indeed we are. You, Miss Hannah, Mrs. Winkle, and I are going to live at the very top." Mrs. Winkle was his trusty housekeeper. Miss Hannah took care of Christopher's physical needs, and a retired schoolmaster by the name of Professor Stone taught Christopher his academic subjects.

Once a day, weather permitting and if Christopher had completed his writing exercises, Miss Hannah drove him to town in her horse and buggy. On occasion, she wheeled him through Central Park to visit the menagerie or feed the swans. At other times she took him to the Metropolitan Museum of Art or pushed him along Fifth Avenue to gaze at the live models in the store windows. On hot summer days they stopped at the dairy in the park to watch the milkmaids milk the cows, and purchase ice cream.

During the winter months, Miss Hannah rented a sleigh and took Christopher riding through the park to the lake to watch the ice-skaters. Once, his nurse had let Christopher ride the merry-go-round, lifting him on the carousel horse herself. But upon learning the merry-go-round was powered by a blind horse and mule kept underground, Christopher refused to ride it a second time. It was this kind of sensitivity that made Damian feel so protective of him.

Miss Hannah had strict orders not to talk to anyone during their outings or to reveal Christopher's identity. It was the only way Damian could protect his son from the vicious gossip that continued to prevail.

"Will I be able to see everything from the top floor, Papa? The ships at sea? And the Great Bridge? And the Egyptian house?"

Damian grimaced at the mention of the Egyptian house, for this was Christopher's name for the New York City prison on Centre Street where his grandfather was incarcerated. An imposing white granite building, the locals called it the Tombs. It was the perfect name for it.

"You can see all those things and more," Damian said, his voice even. The boy had no way of knowing that his innocent question was like a bullet to the heart.

Damian had spent large sums of money to hire the best private detectives the city had to offer, and still he had failed to find proof of his father's innocence. Each day his father spent in that hellhole, something, some small though essential part of Damian, seemed to die.

"And the grizzly bear, too?"

"You'll see the bear and all the animals in the menagerie. From the top floor, you'll be able to see the world."

Building the twenty-story structure was a promise he meant to keep. Just as soon as he finished his business with Miss Amanda Blackwell.

Chapter 4

Amanda arrived at the cycling school early that Tuesday morning to find Vincent, the button man, waiting for her.

Dressed in brown trousers that puddled over his worn leather boots and a flattop plug hat, he gave her a mischievous grin. "Heard Miss Quackenbush took a dive yesterday," he said, his dark eyes twinkling beneath his bushy brows. "I sure wish I'd been around to see that old prune fall off her high horse."

"Shhh," Amanda cautioned, glancing around for eavesdroppers. A short distance away, a boy sat in a wheelchair waiting for his nurse to finish selecting bananas from a fruit vendor.

Amanda had seen the boy a number of times, and each time she smiled and waved. Once the boy had waved back, but his nurse had scolded him. She was a dour woman and Amanda wondered what the boy's parents were thinking to allow her to care for their son.

The boy's gaze lingered on Vincent's cart and Amanda heard him say, "Could we stop and look at the buttons? Miss Hannah, pleeese."

Amanda couldn't hear the nurse's reply, but the young woman didn't slow down one whit and only acknowledged Amanda's smile with a scowl. "Good day to you, too," Amanda muttered to herself. The nurse pushed the boy across the street toward the entrance to the park.

Now that the boy and his nurse were out of earshot,

she continued the conversation. "Why weren't you around, Vincent? Had you rescued Miss Quackenbush, you would have been a hero and won her heart forever."

Vincent said something in his native tongue, his fingertips pressed together as he waved his hand in front of her nose.

"Say it in English, Vincent. You know I don't speak Italian."

"It's a good thing. As for the rest, you know the woman gives me the hives."

"That's because you've never taken the time to get to know her. If you did, you'd know I was right. She'd make the perfect wife for you."

Vincent shook his head. "Have you no heart? Don't you like to see a man happy? Before you came along, the park was filled with happy men." He grimaced as if in pain, and even his sweeping mustache seemed to droop. "Now, thanks to your meddling ways, it's full of married men."

"It's possible to be both married and happy."

"But highly unlikely," Vincent said stubbornly.

"You don't know what you're missing. Miss Quackenbush has—" She tried to think of something about the spinster that Vincent would find appealing. One thing was certain—they were both equally pigheaded.

Vincent's eyes flashed in amusement. "Yes, yes, go on. What has she got besides the disposition of an old mule?"

Amanda had a flash of inspiration. "She has a very passionate nature."

Vincent's eyebrows shot clear to the brim of his stained felt hat. "Now how would you be knowing that?"

She lifted her chin. "I just do, that's all, and had you followed my advice, you would have discovered this for yourself."

"The only passionate trait that old spinster has is the ability to make a man's life miserable."

"It just shows how little you know."

"A man has an instinct about these things." Obviously bored with the subject, he pulled a small package off his cart. "Here are the buttons you ordered. Had to send away special, I did."

Amanda fingered the card of mother-of-pearl buttons. The iridescent colors glowed in the morning sun like little gems. She envisioned them on the shirtwaist she planned to make out of the shimmering silk fabric purchased from one of the fine shops along the section of Broadway known as the Ladies' Mile. "These will be perfect."

"Of course they'll be perfect. Would I sell you any less?" Vincent pulled another card out of the cart. "This is for Donny." He handed her a porcelain button with a colorful sailboat painted on its translucent face.

Donny. Just thinking of the brother she'd practically raised since the day he was born filled her with both pleasure and sadness. A tall, handsome boy of twelve, he still had the mind of a child, and something as simple as a button could keep him occupied for hours. "It's beautiful," she whispered. "Donny will love it. What do I owe you?"

"Ten cents for the mother-of-pearl, but you can pay me later. You owe me nothing for Donny's button."

"Nonsense, Vince. You can't keep giving him buttons. You'll end up at the Randall poorhouse."

"There're worse fates, to be sure. Besides, I like making the boy happy."

She smiled her gratitude. She could never repay Vincent for the kindness he had shown Donny these last three years, not as long as he continued to reject the notion of taking a wife.

Old Thorny rode by on his horse and Vincent inched his cart forward. The law required vendors to keep moving unless actually making a sale, but failed to specify speed. Vendors took advantage of this oversight by moving at a snail's pace. Some vendors managed to move all day without traveling any farther than the length of a city block.

"Maybe the sparrow cop would be interested in Miss Quackenbush's passionate nature."

Amanda gave the button man a playful tap on his arm. Grinning, he started down the street, pushing his cart and yelling, "Buttoooooons. Come and git your buttooooooons."

She turned and let herself inside the brick building of her school. Yesterday's mail was still stacked neatly on her desk next to the newfangled machine she'd recently purchased called a typewriter. The typewriter was supposed to save time, at least that's what the advertisements promised, but so far it had caused her nothing but frustration.

Flipping through the mail, she spotted an official-looking envelope from the Turner, Parker, and Liversworth law firm. Curious as to why a law firm would write to her, she quickly broke the seal at the back of the envelope.

Dear Miss Blackwell, she read. *This is to inform you that Mr. J. Randall Compton has retained my services in his efforts to seek legal guardianship of his nephew, Donald Blackwell. Once Mr. Compton has obtained legal authority over your brother, he will then seek to find a suitable facility that will better administer to the boy's needs.*

She sat down hard on the straight-back chair in front of her desk, and quickly scanned the rest of the letter. Her uncle wanted to take Donny away from her? Her dear, sweet brother whom she loved more than life itself? Suitable facility, indeed! That was nothing but a fancy-dancy name for an insane asylum.

Overcome with disbelief and shock, she felt a fierce rage rise inside her. How dare he?

She had neither seen nor heard from Uncle Randall in years. Years! Not until this past January. Then suddenly, out of the clear blue sky, her mother's brother had appeared on her doorstep and informed her of the death of her maternal grandfather.

Her uncle's sudden arrival had come as a complete surprise, and not a particularly welcome one. Her father had severed all ties with the family nearly twelve years earlier. He had had no choice. Her mother's family had made no secret of the fact that they blamed him for the untimely death of his wife.

In an effort to put the past behind her, Amanda had invited her uncle to stay for dinner. She'd made her share of mistakes, but this was by far among the worst.

Her pompous, overbearing uncle did nothing but find fault the whole time he was her guest. He completely disapproved of Donny, blaming her for Donny's poor manners and childlike behavior. Her uncle then had the audacity to criticize her for sending Donny to his room for throwing his dinner plate on the floor. "What the boy needs is a good whipping," he'd said.

"Over my dead body," she'd told him, and the two had argued furiously.

To be honest, Donny had acted worse than usual, but she suspected Uncle Randall made him nervous. Still, nothing Donny had done could possibly justify her uncle's desire to put him in an institution.

Their argument had escalated into a terrible row and Donny, reacting to the loud voices, started banging on the walls. Instead of staying to help her calm Donny down, her uncle ran out of her apartment faster than a fleeing pickpocket. The coward! And she hadn't heard from him since.

Until now.

She reread the letter, this time studying each sentence before going on to the next. Her hand shook so hard, the words were almost a blur. Some of the legal words puzzled her and she read the same terse paragraph three times before making sense of it.

Her uncle accused her of being unfit to raise a child with Donny's special problems. Unfit? She jumped to her feet. Unfit! Her uncle was the one who wanted to whip the boy. Unfit indeed!

"How could he do this to me?" she cried out, slapping the letter facedown on her desk. She loved that boy, loved him with her heart and soul, with everything she had.

She'd only been eleven when she'd found her mother dead on the floor of their apartment, the tiny infant by her side. At first Amanda had thought the bloodied creature with the umbilical cord wrapped around his head was dead, but a slight movement had convinced her otherwise.

Acting solely out of instinct, she'd picked him up, freed him from the cord, and wrapped him in a warm blanket. It didn't occur to her until years later that she had saved his life.

She'd cared for him from that very first day, always putting his welfare before her own, even when her grief-stricken father had had little to do with him. Her mother had died giving birth to him, and Amanda swore she would raise Donny to be a God-fearing man who would grow up to make his mother proud. Her death would not be in vain.

During those early years, Amanda had spent hours reading to him, singing lullabies, and doing all the things her mother once did for her. It never occurred to Amanda that she was but a child herself. Partly because of her youth and inexperience, but mostly because of the promise she had made to her dead mother, she ignored the warning signs that all was not right with Donny.

Though physically Donny appeared normal, walking just before his first birthday, he didn't utter an intelligible word until he was five. But she refused to believe anything was wrong. Instead, she concentrated on his sweet nature. She reasoned that a child who greeted her with such a bright smile whenever she walked into the room couldn't possibly be slow or otherwise abnormal.

It took her years to face the truth; not until she was seventeen and Donny six did reality hit her.

At the time, Central Park was still a swampland, and she had taken Donny to Riverside Park. The playground had been filled with children that long-ago day;

children much younger than her brother who were able to speak in full sentences.

She would never forget the horror of hearing them taunt Donny. They'd called him a dummy and a blockhead and worse. But the most heartbreaking thing of all was the fact that Donny didn't even recognize the cruelty. He continued to smile as if nothing had happened.

That's when it finally sank in; Donny wasn't just slow. He was never going to be like the others, not ever, no matter how much she wished otherwise. Never had she been so devastated. Sobbing uncontrollably, she'd taken Donny by the hand and pulled him away from the playground.

Upon reaching the apartment house where they lived, she'd lashed out at her father, blaming him for her brother's slow mind. Her father had always been loving and kind to Donny, but had kept a distance between them. This was why Donny was slow—she was convinced of it.

Her father had sat in stony silence as she ranted, letting her give full vent to the anger and frustration that had built up over time. When at last she collapsed at his feet, exhausted, he'd broken down in tears. He hadn't even cried at her mother's funeral, but he cried on that long-ago day, and begged for her forgiveness.

"I'm so ashamed," he'd sobbed. "I think deep inside, I blamed Donny for your mother's death, and I'm so ashamed. He's not to blame. None of us are."

She'd fallen into her father's arms and together they'd shed tears of grief and sorrow for her mother. And for Donny.

That night, her father had held Donny in his arms, apologizing to him, and her brother showed no resentment or anger. Instead, Donny smiled as if the years of indifference had been of no more consequence than a speck on the wall. Her brother's inability to harbor a grudge was one of his most endearing qualities.

During the weeks and months that followed, Amanda became obsessed with finding a cure for

Donny. She'd pounded on the door of every doctor in New York, begging them to examine Donny. She had no money to pay them, but was determined to get the money somehow, even if it took her the rest of her life.

Some physicians took pity on her and examined Donny free of charge. None of the doctors offered much in the way of help, except to suggest she have him committed to an asylum, and this she steadfastly refused to do. But the doctors were adamant; Donny was incapable of understanding speech and much of what was happening around him. It had been a devastating blow, especially when she had been so utterly convinced he understood everything she said to him.

Before long, she'd given up on the medical profession, but not on Donny. Never Donny. Fiercely protective of him, she'd continued to nurture and care for him and gradually learned to accept the strange but fascinating world that was his and was now intricately inter-woven with hers.

To lose Donny would be to lose a part of herself.

Damn her uncle! He wasn't going to get away with his threats. She would fight him every step of the way!

No one—not even her uncle and his fancy lawyers—was going to take Donny away from her!

Chapter 5

A single knock on the door of her school was followed by the appearance of a handsome lad of no more than fifteen or sixteen, dressed in a dark woolen uniform. "You wish to send a telegram, ma'am?" he asked Amanda politely.

Earlier, she had cranked the telegraph call box by the front door, intent upon sending a telegram to her uncle and his lawyers, stating in no uncertain terms her uncensored opinion of them. But she had since come to her senses. For once in her life, she decided not to act impulsively. She needed time to think.

"I've changed my mind," she said, handing the messenger a coin for his troubles.

"Thank you, ma'am."

After the messenger had left, she pulled the placard from the window, turned it over to show her school was open, and slapped it back in place. "Take that!" she muttered, and because her students were due to arrive soon, she took a deep breath in an effort to calm down and glanced around to make certain everything was in order.

Her bicycle school really had outgrown the small two room single-story brick building. One side served as a combination office and classroom. It was here that she instructed her students on bicycle safety and the city's ever-changing and, in her opinion, overly strict cycling regulations.

She owned a vast collection of bicycles, most of them constructed out of the new metal tubing rather than wood. Tricycles, boneshakers, and ordinaries stood side by side in the adjoining room, which also doubled as a repair shop. At the request of some of her older male students, she also owned a couple of velocipedes, which required the rider to propel himself with his feet on the ground.

Her handyman's name was William Williamson, but due to his habit of carrying a bicycle upended over his head, he had been teasingly called Moose by a group of youths, and the name stuck. Moose changed tires and generally kept the bicycles in good repair. On occasion, he assisted Amanda during the lessons, helping to hold bicycles steady for beginner students.

Amanda longed for the day when she could afford to build a school large enough to hold classes inside during inclement weather, with a separate workshop for Moose. With year-round classes possible, she would no longer have to supplement her income in the winter months by giving ice-skating lessons.

She gave a deep sigh. Lord almighty, if it wasn't one thing it was another. Now it looked as if her dreams would have to wait until after the custody battle over Donny was resolved. What little money she had managed to squirrel away might well be needed for legal expenses.

She was busy wheeling the bicycles outside when she caught sight of a man on horseback. Something about him made her take a closer look. Her heart skipped a beat. Unless she was seeing things, it was the same man who had rescued Miss Quackenbush from the lake.

He looked as magnificent today as he had looked the day before. His powerfully set shoulders filled his brown woolen frock coat. His strong, sturdy legs molded against the sides of his horse, straining the fabric of his tan-colored riding britches. He sat in his saddle with the same commanding air he'd shown yesterday, and even the liveried driver of one of the city's wealthiest patrons slowed down to allow him the right of way.

More curious about the man than ever, she parked the boneshaker she had wheeled outside next to a tandem. Her head down, she pretended not to notice him and was surprised at how difficult it was to pull her eyes away, even for the briefest moment. But her initial pleasure in seeing him was followed by a chilling thought that almost knocked her off her feet: what if this man was working for her uncle?

Dear God in Heaven, what if it was the attorney, Liversworth, himself, coming to take Donny away?

The thought, coming out of the blue, shook her to the very core. It was entirely possible. What other reason could he possibly have for spying on her? Though she didn't know his name, he didn't seem like the kind of man to dally away his time without some compelling reason.

And what about the unshakable feeling she had that he wanted something from her? The feeling that told her he intended to have it?

Convinced her suspicions were right, she spun on the heels of her high-buttoned boots and rushed inside. Slamming the door shut, she leaned against the polished oak wood and willed her knees not to buckle. Dear God. What was she going to do?

Catching a glimpse of herself in the mirrored wall, she frowned with impatience. Wasn't this just dandy? A lawyer shows up on her doorstep and she panics. Well, enough of this. Donny's future was at stake and she intended to keep her wits about her if it killed her!

She peered through the curtains, taking care not to be seen. The man had dismounted and was tying his horse to the iron hitching post in front of her school. He glanced up, and she quickly drew back.

Her heart in her throat, she dashed across the room and busied herself at her desk. It was only by sheer force of will that she managed to maintain her composure when the stranger walked through the door, his tall hat in hand.

One look at his confident face and she was more convinced than ever this was Mr. Liversworth himself.

She only hoped he didn't resort to using the same obscure language in person as he used in writing his letter.

"Good morning, Miss Blackwell."

"That remains to be seen," she replied coolly. Inside, he appeared taller than before, his broad shoulders practically spanning the width of the doorway. If he thought she was intimidated by his size, he would be absolutely right.

But if he was the least surprised by her cool reception, he certainly didn't show it. Score one for his side. Well, she could be just as calm, just as collected. Yes, indeed, she'd show him, and until his mouth quirked upward in a devastating smile, she almost succeeded.

"Obviously you don't believe in jumping to conclusions," he said. "I like that."

She jumped to conclusions all the time, but she wasn't about to correct him. Convinced his casual comments were nothing less than a legal tactic, she clamped her lips together and lifted her chin. If he thought she would fall for his little tricks, he'd better think again!

And he'd better not do anything so foolish as to throw her another kiss. The next time she would take him to task.

Her gaze lingered on his slightly upturned mouth. "Don't tell me you're an expert in this, too," he said.

Her lashes lifted and she met his eyes, which were more brown today than gold, matching the color of the thick, wavy hair that tapered neatly to the turned-up collar of his shirt.

"I beg your pardon?"

"The unicycle." He pointed to the one standing in a corner. "Don't tell me you ride that, too."

"No, I keep it mainly for display."

"Wise decision," he said, though he inspected the cycle with interest.

Another tactic, she decided, designed, no doubt, to put her off guard.

The fine cut of his dark woolen suit confirmed her

suspicions: the man *was* a lawyer. Well, if he thought his letter had frightened her or in any way intimidated her, he was wrong! His letters she could handle; it was his presence that was causing her a great deal of tribulation.

Overcome by a fierce need to protect the brother she loved more than life itself, she stared at the stranger with unflinching eyes, her chin jutting out ward. "I'm a busy woman, so kindly state your name and business. And if you know what's good for you, you'll speak in plain English!" She'd had quite enough of his legal language for one day!

He looked taken aback, his dark eyebrows practically touching in a double arch. His expression suddenly changed. "That's a good tactic, Miss Blackwell. Always put the other party on the defensive. No wonder you have a reputation as an astute businesswoman."

Uncertain as to whether he was complimenting her or finding fault, she eyed him cautiously. The nerve of the man, accusing *her* of tactics. She almost lost her composure completely when his gaze slid lazily down the length of her. Apparently he had more than a few tricks of his own for disarming the other *party*. Well, it wasn't going to work. He could leer at her all he wanted.

Judging by his own formal dress, she doubted he much liked her bloomers, and she suspected the look of approval on his face was just a ploy. She resisted the urge to step behind her desk, away from his scrutiny. Her main concern at the moment was to protect Donny. "I don't care if you are an attorney, you don't scare me in the least, and you can tell *that* to my uncle!"

"Whoa!" He held up his hands as if in self-defense. "I'm not an attorney, and to my knowledge, I've never even met your uncle."

She eyed him with suspicion. He wouldn't out-and-out lie, would he? "If you're not here on behalf of my uncle, then who are you representing?"

"I guess you might say I'm representing myself."
When she continued to look doubtful, he shrugged his
shoulders. "I'm in construction."

Now she really was confused. If what he said was
true, then why had he been watching her in the park?
"I thought . . ."

"I know, I know. You thought I was an attorney,
coming to do you harm. You can rest assured, my
only mission is to do you a service."

Still not sure she could trust him, she regarded him
warily. Had he really thrown her a kiss, or had she
simply imagined it? Surely no man would be that bold
and brazen, especially in public. "If what you say is
true, then I owe you an apology."

His eyes softened as if he found her amusing.
"Apology accepted."

She looked at him curiously. "I also owe you my
gratitude. It was a brave thing you did yesterday, res-
cuing my student."

A smile curved his mouth, and she saw that his
teeth were dazzling white and even next to his bronze-
colored skin. His deep tan suggested at first glance
that he was one of the new class of millionaires who
spent their winters in the south of France. But after
studying him more closely, she was convinced she'd
misjudged him on several scores. The tan was too
weathered, the web of lines at his temples too rugged
to be explained by a mere holiday. He was definitely
not a lawyer, and now that she recalled the speed with
which he ran and his powerful dive into the lake, it
seemed more likely he was in construction, no matter
how much his fine clothes suggested otherwise.

"It was hardly brave of me, Miss Blackwell. The
lake is less than four feet deep in that area."

"I wasn't referring to the lake. I was referring to
Miss Quackenbush."

His eyes danced with merriment. Since he apparently was no threat to Donny, she allowed herself to
relax—at least as much as was possible, given the fact

that he was the most handsome man she'd ever laid eyes on.

"I'm glad I could be of service. I take it she's fully recovered?"

"Fully." She smiled. "I apologize for your clothes. I would be more than happy to reimburse you for damages." Judging from the fine wool fabric and tailored cut of his coat and trousers, the offer would cost her dearly.

"That's not necessary. Actually, I have another reason for being here. Do you have a moment?"

On her guard again, she realized her senses had sharpened to the point where she could detect his faint manly scent. Ignoring her quickening pulse, she boldly met his gaze. Was it only her imagination or was there danger in his smile? Danger in the energy that emanated from him? "I'm expecting students to arrive at any moment." Her voice was edged with uneasiness as much as regret. She didn't want him to go.

He stared at her as if she baffled him. Obviously, she wasn't what he'd expected. "If you'd prefer, I could come back at another time. Would this afternoon be more convenient?"

She was tempted to put him off, but if he really was a threat to Donny she had to know about it now. "Are you interested in taking cycling classes?" she asked, praying with all her heart his business with her was that innocuous.

He glanced at the open door leading to the storage room. "I hadn't thought about it. I'm not convinced a bicycle is superior to a horse."

"Perhaps not for transportation purposes, but certainly for recreation. I suspect the bicycle will give the horse a healthy bit of competition with the improvement of roads."

He smiled as if he found the idea amusing. "Even with good roads, I should think cycling a lot of work."

"Physicians agree cycling is the superior sport for promoting physical welfare. Did you know . . ." She was willing to bet he had no interest in the statistics she cited, though he nodded his head politely. She didn't care. Just as long as he understood her underlying message that her reputation as a businesswoman was well deserved. "Over fifty-two thousand people own bicycles, and I predict that number will triple in another year or two."

"You made a believer out of me, Miss Blackwell," he said. "You don't happen to be selling bicycle stock, do you?"

"What I'm selling is a bill of good health. Cycling can add years to a person's life. Obesity could become a thing of the past." He lifted a dark brow and she wondered if he had taken offense. "I wasn't suggesting that you . . ." Her gaze traveled down his lean, well-muscled body. He definitely wasn't a lawyer.

"I didn't think you were," he said, sounding more congenial than sincere. "But your point is well-taken. Perhaps for exercise purposes, I should sign up for lessons."

She bit her lower lip. The prospect of teaching him to ride a bicycle was daunting, to say the least. She pierced him with a probing look. "If you didn't come here to inquire about cycling lessons, may I ask why you are here?"

"I own the property directly next door to you."

Surely she'd misunderstood. "You mean to the north?"

"No, I believe that's owned by the city. I'm talking about the property to the south."

"But that's not possible. That property belongs to . . ." Her voice trailed off in midsentence, her mind in a whirl.

"My apologies. I should have properly introduced myself. I'm Damian Newcastle."

Dear God. She stared at him in disbelief. It couldn't be! Just hearing the name made her throat close in protest. "Newcastle," she gasped, hating the vile taste his name left in her mouth. "Then you must be . . ."

"Phillip Newcastle is my father."

Amanda felt all at once hot and cold. She'd thought

she'd gotten over the hatred and rage, but there it was again, coursing through her body until she was literally shaking. She couldn't believe it. This man was Phillip Newcastle's son. Phillip Newcastle! The man responsible for her father's death.

Chapter 6

"Miss Blackwell? Are you all right?" Damian Newcastle stepped forward, his forehead shadowed with concern, and though he lifted his hand to her shoulder, he stopped short of touching her.

Still unable to find her voice, she could only nod. Did this man really think he could walk in here and announce he was Phillip Newcastle's son and not get a reaction from her? If she were a man, he'd be flat on his back by now, his nose bloodied and broken.

She sat down and held on to the edge of her desk for support. The shock of coming face-to-face with Phillip Newcastle's son was almost too much to bear. She couldn't believe it. She'd thought once the trial was over and Phillip Newcastle had been sent to prison, it would be over.

Now, after nearly three years of trying to put the past behind her, she realized the nightmare would never end. The hatred she felt for the man responsible for her father's death—for the entire Newcastle family—was as strong now as ever.

"What are you doing here?" She hardly recognized the hard-edged voice as her own. Now that she knew who he was, the proud turn of his head suddenly struck her as a tad too arrogant.

"I've come to make an offer on your property."

She stared at him in disbelief. "An offer? You wish to purchase my property?"

"I'm prepared to pay a generous price." When she made no reply, he continued. "I plan to build on my property. But as you know, the original piece of land was divided into two narrow lots, which you and I own." He glanced around her small though tidy classroom. "I'm sure you must find the property as limiting as I do. The money I'm prepared to pay you should be more than enough to purchase a more suitable location for your school."

She could no longer contain her anger. How dare this man waltz into her school and act as if he were doing *her* a favor. Eyes flashing, she rose to her full five-feet-five height. "Do you honestly think I would consider doing business with the likes of you?"

His jaw tightened, but his eyes never left her face. "My money is as good as anyone's."

"Your father is in prison for gross neglect. What he did was nothing short of murder."

"That's your opinion, Miss Blackwell."

"Not just mine, Mr. Newcastle. Many think as I do."

"Come, come, Miss Blackwell. You don't strike me as the kind of woman who allows herself to be influenced by popular opinion. In any case, I didn't come here to discuss my father." He spoke in a polite, even voice that contradicted the dark look on his face. "As I said, I'm prepared to make you a generous offer on your property. If you prefer, I could have my lawyer contact yours. That way, you won't have to deal with me directly."

Another lawyer. She tossed her head angrily. "You are the most arrogant, egotistical, ass—"

He held up a hand. "Your opinion of me is none of my business," he said, undaunted. "So please don't trouble yourself on my behalf. Just tell me whether or not you'll consider selling, and I'll be out of your hair."

"The only way you'll get your hands on my property is over my dead body!"

His eyes narrowed. "I think it's only fair to warn you you're making a mistake."

"Threatening me is an even bigger mistake! Now if you would kindly leave."

"I'll leave, Miss Blackwell. But not until you hear me out." He took a step forward, and it was only by sheer determination that she stood her ground. He seemed surprised at her resistance and scrutinized her with a sharp gaze that was even more intimidating than his veiled threats.

"Before you turn down my offer . . ."

"I already have."

The lines deepened between his eyebrows. "I think you should know I intend to build a twenty-story building next door."

"Twenty stories?" she stammered. Had she heard him right? *Twenty stories?* What did he take her for? A fool? "It's not possible to build a building that high."

"I can assure you, Miss Blackwell, it's not only possible, but quite feasible. When my building is complete, it will rise nearly four hundred feet above the street."

"Why?" she asked.

"Why?" The question clearly astonished him. Indeed, he looked so taken aback, she almost laughed in his face. "Why not?"

"A twenty-story building doesn't sound very practical."

His gaze swept down to take in her bloomers once again. "Ah, yes, Miss Blackwell. I can see you're a most practical woman. How remiss of me not to have taken that into account before approaching you on business. Let me assure you, the new safety elevator has made such a feat both possible and practical.

"It's now possible to travel to the top floor of a twenty-story building in less time than it takes to climb a single flight of stairs. That makes every floor equally accessible. As I'm sure you can imagine, this will be a boon for landowners. It will be possible to multiply income without having to purchase more land." He spoke with a barely contained passion that was oddly contagious.

"Think about it, Miss Blackwell! This is history in the making!"

Stunned to find herself momentarily carried away by his enthusiasm, she masked her confusion with an outer calm. "Generally, history is made when war is declared."

He laughed a warm, mellow laugh that seemed to burrow its way deep inside her. "Let's hope it doesn't come to that. All I want to do is buy your property, not send for the army."

"I thought I made my intentions clear. I'm not selling."

"Ah, yes, your *English* is quite plain," he said, and she didn't miss the irony in his voice. "But it's only fair to warn you that trying to conduct business next door to a twenty-story building will be nothing short of a nightmare. Visitors will travel from all over the world just to see what many have already suggested could well become the eighth wonder. You'll no doubt find the increase in traffic distracting to your students. Therefore, I ask you to reconsider. I think you'll find the offer I'm prepared to make for your property both generous and fair."

"I wouldn't care if you were building a bridge to the moon, Mr. Newcastle. My property is not for sale."

"You haven't heard my offer yet."

"I'm not interested."

"And I thought you were a businesswoman."

"And after yesterday, I thought *you* were a gentleman." *Among other things.*

"What was it about yesterday that made you think I was a gentleman, Miss Blackwell?"

"Why . . ." The man was obviously trying to unbalance her. "Y-you rescued my student," she stammered. So she wasn't imagining things; he *had* thrown her a kiss.

"Oh, yes, of course. The rescue."

She was greatly relieved when Moose arrived. Her mechanic apparently felt the tension in the air, and arranged himself in such a way that Mr. Newcastle was forced to step away from her desk.

Moose was a strapping man with smooth ebony skin and frizzy black hair. He had a gentle disposition, but no one would ever guess it by the way he raked Newcastle over with his eyes before turning to Amanda. "Mornin', Miz Mandy. Got any bicycles need fixin' or visitors need puttin' in their place?"

"Mr. Newcastle was just leaving, but we do have some flats." She pointed at the tricycle that was visible through the open door leading to the next room.

Mr. Newcastle looked about to argue, but apparently changed his mind. Instead, he gave a cheerful nod. "Good day, Miss Blackwell. Nice meeting you, Mr. . . ."

"Everyone calls me Moose."

"Mr. Moose." He glanced at Amanda. "Should you change your mind . . ."

Moose shook his head. "Miss Blackwell don't never change her mind."

Mr. Newcastle regarded the imposing-looking man thoughtfully before replacing his hat. "I like a woman who makes up her mind and sticks with it," he said. He strolled to the door, looking like a man who had succeeded in getting exactly what he wanted—and possibly even more.

Of all the . . . Hands at her waist, she watched him leave. The fact that he didn't have the good grace to admit defeat annoyed her.

She was especially irritated at the way he deftly turned her faults into admirable traits. Indeed. If she wanted to be stubborn and jump to conclusions, that was her business. It had taken her years to hone her faults, and she certainly didn't appreciate anyone making light of them!

"Looks like I didn't get here none too soon," Moose said, grinning. "I could have cut the tension with my tin snips." He drew the implement from the deep pocket of his canvas trousers and snipped the air.

She forced a smile. Moose was more than a loyal

employee; he was a good friend and he worried about her. "I can take care of Mr. Newcastle," she said with more conviction than she felt. At the moment, though, the builder was the least of her problems.

"That's what I was afraid of, Miz Mandy. When you get that look on your face, there's no tellin' what's gonna happen." He chuckled to himself and walked through the open doorway to begin work.

Amanda plucked her whistle from atop her desk and hurried to help Moose with the task of moving the bicycles outside. She wheeled a bicycle with a sixty-inch drive wheel through the narrow doorway to the graveled area on the side of the building. Though the wheel alone stood almost as tall as she did, she handled the bicycle expertly, with little difficulty. But her mind wasn't on the bicycles or even her students, who were due to arrive at any moment.

She was too busy watching the lone horseman circling his way around the park. Mr. Newcastle cut a proud figure sitting astride his handsome black gelding. Never had she seen a man sit on a horse with more presence or pride. One would never guess from looking at him that he had the reputation of a snake.

Anger erupted inside her like a volcano; how dare he think she would do business with him. She held on to the bicycle for support. What a day this had been! And her students had yet to arrive.

First the letter from her uncle's attorney, then the visit from Mr. Newcastle. It was almost too much to bear. One wanted her brother, the other her property. She felt as if she were being circled by vultures.

Shuddering, she glanced at the sky. The black clouds gathered in the northern sky reminded her of the look on her father's face seconds before he'd died. Never would she forget the anguish, the horror, and the helplessness that flashed in his eyes the instant the balcony pulled away from its moorings and crashed down on top of him. The balcony that had been built by the Newcastle Construction Company.

It had been well over a year since she'd had the

nightmares, but the memories continued to assault her, haunting her in unexpected ways.

Moose rolled a high-wheeler next to hers. "You all right, Miz Mandy?"

She pulled her gaze away from the clouds and turned to face him. "I received a letter today from a law firm. My uncle's trying to take Donny away from me."

Moose's forehead creased. "He's gonna have a fight on his hands, Miz Mandy. And I'm just the one to give it to him. Don't you worry your head none. They ain't no one gettin' our boy."

His fierce determination made her smile. She felt better already. "Thank you, Moose. I needed to hear you say that."

"Every word I sez is true." Moose drew a wrench from the back pocket of his trousers and adjusted the seat of the sixty-incher.

Moose was right. No one was going to take Donny away. She took a deep breath, her gaze traveling to the property next door. The narrow strip of land was covered with waist-high weeds. "Moose . . . is it possible to build a building twenty stories high?"

"Twenty stories?" He whistled softly. "I don't think so, Miz Mandy. But then I didn't think they could build a bridge to Brooklyn, and look what they've gone and done. The way they're going, the bridge will soon be open to traffic." The bridge he referred to had no official name, but most people called it the East River or Roebling Bridge. A few called it the Brooklyn or Great Bridge.

Amanda found no comfort in his words. It wasn't all that long ago that some thought spanning the turbulent East River was nothing more than a pipe dream. The river was actually a tidal strait and, with its constant flow of high-mast ships, ferries, and steamers, was considered one of the busiest stretches of salt water in the world.

Amanda studied the empty lot next door, and tried her hardest to envision a building twenty stories high.

Lord almighty, she didn't want to believe it, but if a bridge could be built that could withstand the high winds, blizzards, and ice jams that periodically stopped ferry traffic to Brooklyn, then perhaps a twenty-story building wasn't all that impossible.

Chapter 7

Late that same afternoon, Amanda stepped off the horsecar a block and a half away from the four-story brownstone tenement building she called home, and took a shortcut through the dreary alley locals jokingly referred to as the King's Highway.

Overhead, clotheslines stretched from one building to the next, reminding Amanda of the horrendous tangle of telegraph and electrical wires that still crisscrossed the business district, despite the city's efforts to encourage underground wiring.

Linens and clothing flapped in the wind, revealing intimate details their owners would normally not make public. Amanda "read" the clotheslines like most folks read the headlines in the morning newspapers.

A single glance told her Mrs. Whittaker's bout of rheumatism had improved, allowing the elderly woman to do her wash for the first time in two weeks. The dingy grays on the line beneath Mrs. Whittaker's could only belong to the new bride, Carolyn Webber, who had last week shocked the other tenants by turning her husband's long johns a vivid scarlet color.

A row of shiny satin corsets no doubt meant the prostitute in apartment fifteen had again come out of retirement. The diapers of the newborn Fennessy baby filled two lines, and the frayed shirt cuffs on line nine were a sign the Hollowells had fallen on hard times. Amanda made a mental note to take them a basket of food.

She scanned the second-floor windows, looking for

Donny. He often watched for her to return from work, but today the windows were vacant except for a curtain here and there, blowing in the breeze.

She climbed the steep steps leading into the building. Old Mr. Adams sat on the floor of the dark, dingy hallway, his back against a stained wall. His stubbled chin resting against his chest, he snored loudly, an empty whiskey bottle by his side.

Dressed in a blue uniform with shiny brass buttons, Adams looked even less like a doorman than when Carolyn Webber had first pulled him out of a gutter and given him the job, paying his salary out of her own pocket. It was yet another one of Carolyn's attempts to turn the lowly tenement building into one of those fancy French flats that had everyone talking.

Amanda wasn't certain how much class a drunken doorman added, especially since he spent most of his time in a stupor, but his presence had provided the landlord with yet another reason to raise the rent.

Amanda hurried up the stairs, aware of the hushed, though obviously angry, voices of the Webbers filtering through the thin walls that separated their apartment from Amanda's.

Another argument. It seemed all the Webbers had done since their marriage three months earlier was argue. It nearly broke Amanda's heart to hear them fight. She'd had such high hopes for them when she'd first introduced Carolyn to Arthur. Arthur hadn't been able to take his eyes off Carolyn, who, in turn, had looked like she'd been hit by a bolt of lightning. Glory be, now listen to them.

Amanda knocked on each door as she passed, a signal to Donny she was home. Donny had a hard time grasping the concept that apartment twenty-three was theirs. He considered the entire building his home and wandered in and out of each of the twenty-eight apartments at will.

Fortunately, no one seemed to mind and most of the residents embraced him as one of the family. This was one of the reasons Amanda had decided against moving into the more fashionable Working Women's Apartment building, even though it would have been more convenient to her school.

The landlord was even willing to accept her brother if she kept him quiet and he didn't bother the other residents. But Amanda had decided to stay where she was, for Donny's sake.

She let herself into her apartment and set her packages on the plain wood table that her father had built with his very own hands. After hanging her cape on the wooden peg next to the door, she turned on the gas jets and lit the wall lamps, finishing the chore as Donny walked in.

At five feet six he was only an inch taller than her, but he was growing so quickly, his canvas trousers barely met the tops of his boots. Donny had blue eyes the same as hers—less lively, perhaps, but equally intense, and ringed with dark lashes.

His fine straight nose and high forehead were Blackwell trademarks. His hair was much lighter than Amanda's, almost ginger in color, but unlike hers, his was as straight as straw, falling haphazardly to the collar of his shirt. Now he gave her the familiar crooked smile that never failed to touch her heart.

"Hello, yourself."

She grinned. It was an expression he'd picked up from their father. "Hello, yourself, back." She reached up to tousle his hair and gave his cheek an affectionate pat. His face was still smooth as a baby's and she dreaded the day he sprouted whiskers. How in the world would she ever teach him to shave? At times, the increasing disparity between his mind and his rapidly growing body filled her with dismay. "It's time to wash up." She rubbed her hands together to demonstrate.

He returned her smile with a silly grin. "Wash up."

After he'd disappeared into the necessary room, she turned toward the single window overlooking the alley. Pushing aside the white lace curtains, she lifted the sash and stuck her head outside. It was a long stretch, but she managed to grab hold of the clothesline and work it around the pulley until the wash she'd hung out that morning was within easy reach.

The rusty grinding sound was followed by the scrape of a window opening across the way. Mrs. Aviary poked her head outside, greeted Amanda, and called to Ellie-May Hopkins, who lived in the apartment opposite Amanda's.

A matronly woman with a beaklike nose and a sharp, jutting chin, Mrs. Aviary wore her gray hair parted down the middle and pulled back into a tight bun. She frowned at the pair of man's long johns hanging from the widow Mrs. Brook's line. "See that, Ellie-May?" She pointed out the underwear with her index finger. "What did I tell you? Have you ever seen anything so outrageous in your life?"

Ellie-May looked properly indignant, which was no easy task given her curly mop of red hair, coppery freckles, and ever-present giggle. "To think she's carrying on beneath our very noses." Shrugging her shoulders, she tittered like a little mouse.

Amanda jumped to the widow's defense. "I'm sure there's a logical explanation." She liked Mrs. Brook; the woman had been extremely kind and patient with Donny. She fervently hoped the matronly woman *had* found herself a beau. Heaven knows Amanda had tried her best to introduce the widow to every suitable bachelor she could find.

Besides, it was no one's business what Mrs. Brook hung on her clothesline—or anywhere else, for that matter.

"There's a logical explanation, all right," Mrs. Aviary said, her voice thick with censure.

"Oh, dear." Ellie-May giggled, then eyed Amanda suspiciously. "You haven't matched her up with anyone, have you?"

"No, but it's not for lack of trying."

Mrs. Aviary's face was pinched in disapproval. "That's what I thought. I just wish you would have some respect for the newly departed. Why, Mr. Brook hasn't been dead but a year."

"You're right," Ellie-May added. "Poor Mr. Brook would turn over in his grave if he knew a strange man's long johns were hanging in plain sight on the very same clothesline that once held his overalls."

Amanda ripped the last of her wash off the line. "I don't think Mr. Brook would care a goose egg at this point."

Mrs. Aviary glared at Amanda. "Well, I care!"

Not wanting to get into an argument, Amanda drew her head inside, accidentally dropping one of her black lisle stockings in her haste. She stuck her head out the window again, just in time to see a foul-smelling hog disappear down the alley with her stocking in its mouth. "Hey, come back here!" she shouted, shaking her fist, but it was no use.

She glared at the two women, who were still clucking with disapproval over the widow's clothesline. Disgusted, she slammed her window shut against the cold wind blowing off the North River and the hot air rushing from the direction of Mrs. Aviary's window. Meanwhile, the argument between the newlyweds in the next apartment ended with the slamming of a door.

Donny reentered the room and grinned. He glanced at the still-vibrating wall that separated their apartment from the Webbers'. "Perfect match."

It was a phrase Amanda had used many times to describe her more successful matchmaking efforts, but hearing it come from her brother surprised her. Sometimes she was convinced Donny understood more than anyone gave him credit for. But the doctors had insisted he understood very little. They'd explained that Donny simply repeated phrases he'd learned to associate with certain people, things, or situations; he was incapable of any real verbal understanding.

I swear the doctors are wrong, Amanda thought. But then she immediately dismissed the idea. Certainly the doctors knew more about Donny's capabilities than she did. To think otherwise served no useful purpose and only depressed her. It was far better to accept the truth.

It had taken her many years to reach this point, and now that she had, she would never again torture herself by imagining things that simply weren't possible. Donny didn't understand, no matter how much she wished otherwise.

Donny set the table without a word, leaving her alone with her thoughts as she prepared their supper. He arranged and rearranged the silverware until he was satisfied that every knife, fork, and floral pattern on the china were in perfect alignment.

Seeming to thrive on routine, Donny did everything, from dressing himself to eating, in a certain order.

Amanda selected a package of leftover roast beef from the ice chest and sliced it. She had purchased a loaf of bread from a pushcart outside the park and fresh butter from the dairy.

Donny never spoke during mealtime, and generally Amanda filled the silence by reading aloud from the newspaper. Tonight, however, she had too much on her mind. What a day! First that letter from her uncle's attorney, then the visit from Damian Newcastle.

Mr. Newcastle was more disturbing than worrisome. He couldn't hurt her, especially since she had refused to sell him her property. Her uncle, however, was another matter.

After supper, Donny brought out his game of dominoes and spread it across the table. The game had become a nightly ritual since Mrs. Brook had given Donny the ivory set that had once belonged to her husband.

Once Donny had grasped the concept of matching the little dots, he never seemed to tire of the game and declared himself a winner no matter what the outcome.

"Dominoes!" she said, sliding her last piece in place.

"Dominoes!" Donny announced, unfazed by the number of game pieces still in his pile.

Amanda reached into her reticule for the button

from Vincent. "Look what Vincent gave you. Another button. This one has a sailboat painted on it."

"Buttooooooons!" He mimicked the vendor's call as he took the button in both hands and turned it over with great care.

"You're right, Donny. Vincent sells buttons." Still riled over the argument she'd had with the vendor, she added beneath her breath, "The pigheaded fool!" Why couldn't he see that Miss Quackenbush would make the perfect wife for him?

Donny was watching her with an odd expression on his face, and once again she fell into the trap of thinking him capable of some sort of understanding. Sighing, she pushed the thought away and concentrated on placing the little ivory game pieces into the wooden domino box.

"After you get ready for bed, I'll tell you a story," she said, not wanting him to think she was annoyed with him. "Bed," she repeated, placing her hands together by her cheek and feigning sleep. Every night, Donny chose a button from his vast collection. He kept his buttons in a little tin box that had belonged to their father. Shortly after his death, Donny had claimed it as his own.

Every night Amanda made up a story to go with one of the buttons. How she loved spinning tales of adventure and magic and, yes, even romance. In her stories, all things were possible and happy endings were an absolute must.

Of course, Donny couldn't possibly understand the tales she spun. Even so, he always fell into a peaceful sleep afterwards, his hand clutching whatever button had inspired the story. Perhaps he sensed the stories made her happy. Or maybe he found the sound of her voice comforting. More likely it was his rigid need for repetition that made him insist upon a nightly story. Whatever the reason, he never failed to bring her his button box just before bedtime.

Tonight he changed into his night attire and his pointy nightcap with more speed than usual, and had already brought out his buttons even before she had finished stacking the clean dishes on the shelf.

Amanda put away the last of the plates, discarded her apron, and followed him into the little room off the hall that was his. The room was tiny, barely big enough to hold the feather bed and bureau with its attached arched mirror.

Pulling off her shoes, she laid her head on the plump pillow next to his. She began the story as she began all her stories. "Once upon a time . . ."

He smiled at the familiar words and gazed at the button in his hand. "Once upon a time."

". . . there was a young man named Donny who decided to see what lay on the other side of the ocean. So he built himself a sailboat, a magnificent sailboat, complete with billowing sails and magical oars."

She wove her adventurous tale until Donny's eyes flickered shut and his soft, even breathing told her he was asleep. She placed the button on the bedside table and drew the warm wool blanket over his shoulders.

"Sleep tight," she said softly, though once he was asleep, she suspected he could sleep through anything. It was a good thing. Hardly a night went by that the tenement didn't reverberate with angry voices, slamming doors, crying babies, and an occasional burst of laughter.

Sitting on the bed next to him, she listened to the pulse of life that traveled through the thin walls, and a wave of loneliness swept through her. If only she could have one complete, adult conversation with her brother, she would be the happiest person alive.

It wasn't his fault, of course, that he couldn't do the things she wanted him to do. None of it was his fault. Still, to love someone as deeply as she loved Donny and not be able to talk to him about the future or even how he spent his day was almost too painful to bear.

During the time she was busy at work, she felt content with her lot in life. It was only at night, after

Donny was asleep, that she was overcome with an aching loneliness that gaped inside her.

If only she could have a normal life. The kind of life that included a husband, a kind and loving husband, and children, lots of them. And a home, yes, in the country, a home filled with love and laughter. And a garden. Yes, she wanted that, too, a garden bursting with fragrant flowers and butterflies and the call of songbirds.

Not that she hadn't had her share of marriage proposals, even some that looked promising. But once she explained her commitment to Donny, the prospect of playing papa to a simpleminded boy made even the most lovesick suitor take off faster than a runaway carriage.

It was just as well. She couldn't marry anyone who didn't want Donny. So what if she remained a spinster the rest of her life? No doubt she would be saved a lot of heartache down the road. And aggravation!

Certainly the angry voices of bickering couples drifting through the walls of her cozy apartment on a daily basis made the whole concept of happily ever after seem like an impossible dream.

But sometimes, like tonight, the loneliness seemed worse, the aching more acute, the need more urgent than ever. And it was at such times that she wondered what it would be like to have a beau of her own.

Chapter 8

The following evening, the clanging of a fire alarm sounded outside the apartment building and Amanda rushed to the open window of her bedroom. Fire was a constant fear, and already the fire trucks had been called out to the King's Highway twice that month, once when the new bride, Carolyn Webber, set her husband's trousers on fire while pressing them.

Her hands on the windowsill, she leaned outside, sniffing the air, but there was no smell of smoke, and she sighed in relief. Soon the bell-ringing fire truck, drawn by two white horses, clattered past her apartment without stopping.

Expecting a visit from an old family friend and attorney by the name of David Ludwick, she finished working her hair into a neat bun and walked out to the kitchen area to fill the teakettle.

While she waited, she pulled a book of poems from the overflowing bookshelves in the parlor and curled up in the worn chair that had been her father's favorite.

The book was inscribed to her father, and she knew the handwriting was her mother's. Seeing her father's name on the page brought back so many wonderful memories of him.

How she missed him. Had it really been three years since he died? Three years and she still couldn't break the habit of listening for his familiar footsteps outside the door.

Though he was never far from her mind, she'd

thought about him almost constantly since her confrontation with Damian Newcastle.

She'd lost count of how many times the memory of her father's face flashed into her head when she least expected it. It was never the face she wanted to remember, the kind, gentle face that had played such an important part in her childhood. Instead, she saw only the horror that had marked his face seconds before he disappeared beneath tons of debris.

She shivered against the sudden chill that seemed to sweep across the room. She reached behind her for the knitted shawl and drew it around her shoulders just as a tap sounded at the door.

She hadn't seen Mr. Ludwick since her father's funeral, and was therefore shocked to see how thin and fragile he had become. He'd left the city for a time because of his heart, but had returned recently, and she had assumed his health had been restored. Had she thought otherwise, she never would have asked him to come.

"It's been a while, child."

She kissed him lightly on his parched sunken cheek, and taking his thin, fragile arm, helped him into the room. He walked with a cane and held his hand at his back before lowering himself slowly into a chair. The pained expression on his face told her the effort cost him dearly.

Once seated, he leaned forward, both hands on his cane. "How's Donny?"

"Donny's doing well."

"It does my heart good to hear it."

They caught up on all the news while she filled the teapot with boiling water and set two cups and saucers on a tray.

Following the collapse of the balcony that killed her father, David Ludwick had insisted the city conduct a thorough investigation. Ultimately the tragedy, which had killed more than forty people and injured some twenty others, was blamed on shoddy work and inferior materials, and the man responsible, Phillip Newcastle, was sent to prison. She would always be grateful to David Ludwick for the part he played in bringing the man to justice.

"I hear you're quite the businesswoman," he said. "Your father would have been proud."

She smiled at the mention of her father, but a frown replaced her smile as she watched Mr. Ludwick fight to catch his breath following a fit of wheezing coughs.

"Are you all right?"

He brushed aside her concern. "I regret my poor health has prevented me from being there for you." He tucked his cane by the side of his chair and took a flask out of his pocket.

"I'm the one who should be apologizing. Donny and the cycling school take up all my time, and I'm afraid I've neglected my old friends."

"I'd hoped perhaps you had good news to share with me. You promised, you know, that I would be the one to give you away at your wedding."

"I remember." She smiled wistfully. "But I don't think I'll be getting married for a great many years, if at all."

Mr. Ludwick unscrewed the top of his flask and took a sip. "Because of Donny or because you're too damned independent for your own good?"

She smiled. "A little bit of both."

"Your father used to say it would take a special man to tame you. So tell me, why did you want to see me?"

"I have a problem." She handed him the letter from her uncle's attorney, and while he read it, she poured their tea.

He dropped the letter onto his lap and she waited for another coughing spell to pass before handing him a steaming china cup.

He added a dollop of liquid from his flask before sipping the hot beverage. "What do you plan to do?"

"Fight him, of course."

"You'll need an attorney."

"That's where I'm hoping you can help."

He set his cup on the table and handed the letter back to her. His watery eyes were filled with regret and she felt a sinking feeling inside. "I haven't practiced law in nearly three years."

"But you're a brilliant lawyer. You took on City Hall. No one thought you'd actually manage to convict Phillip Newcastle."

"We were lucky. That scoundrel Tweed had just escaped from prison and the public was outraged." Tweed was convicted of having plundered six million dollars from the city. "The mayor and his political friends needed a scapegoat to cover up their own blunders, and Newcastle fit the bill perfectly."

"He was guilty," she said.

"Gross neglect is not necessarily a punishable crime. Newcastle went to prison because it was politically convenient to convict him. Any lawyer could have done what I did."

"You're too modest."

He wheezed as he laughed. "I've never before been accused of modesty." He took another sip of tea. "I'll talk to your uncle, if you like. Perhaps we can compromise."

"Compromise how?"

"He might agree to let Donny live with him, rather than in an institution."

"Absolutely not!"

"Your uncle is very wealthy. He could provide medical care."

"Donny doesn't need medical care. He needs love."

"I understand, Amanda, but do you have any idea what your chances are of fighting him in court? He'll eat you alive."

"That's why I need your help."

Mr. Ludwick shook his head. "I regret this, Amanda, but I can't represent you. My health simply won't permit it."

"I'm so sorry, Mr. Ludwick. I would never have asked you to come out at night had I known."

He lifted a hand. "Have no fear, child. A little night

air isn't going to make any difference one way or the other." Following another coughing spell, he continued. "I can't help you myself, but I can give you the names of some attorneys who might be willing to take on the case."

She handed him paper and pen and he carefully wrote out the names and addresses of three law offices that handled such cases. He then finished his tea and left, his hacking coughs echoing along the walls as he walked down the dark hall and stairs and into the mist-filled night.

The very next day, Amanda canceled her classes to meet with the attorneys that had been recommended. All three law offices were mere blocks apart. The three attorneys basically told her she didn't have a chance in the world of victory if she went to court, but Mr. Cranston J. Peabody said it in the most direct, easy-to-understand, though unsettling terms. "You're an unmarried woman with an unsavory reputation." He peered at her over the rims of his spectacles, his hands folded on his desk. "The judge will rule in your uncle's favor."

"I don't have an unsavory reputation," she argued. "I'm a successful businesswoman."

"Miss Blackwell . . ." The attorney leaned forward. "You have tossed convention to the wind with your school. A good lawyer could prove you're an unfit guardian simply because you're a working woman." He stood and walked to the front of his desk, facing her with his arms crossed. "Look at how you're dressed! And what about the night you spent in jail? Are you foolish enough to suppose your uncle doesn't read the newspapers?"

Never was Amanda so incensed in her life. She stood and glared at him. "For your information, Mr. Peabody, I work because it's the only way I know to put food on the table. I wear bloomers because they are far more practical for cycling than any other garment. As for spending the night in jail—"

"I don't care why you spent the night in jail. The

fact that you did will be used against you in court. I'm sorry, Miss Blackwell. You simply do not have a leg to stand on."

"And you, Mr. Peabody, don't have the backbone God gave a worm!" She left Mr. Peabody's office in a huff.

She decided to visit the renowned law offices of Parkerson, Bailer, and Stipplehoff, located on Broadway. Mr. Stipplehoff listened to her case and didn't seem the least bit concerned about the night she'd spent in jail, but he did require a large retainer before he would even consider taking on her case. She left his office feeling utterly depressed. She could never come up with that much money.

Then something occurred to her; Damian Newcastle had offered to buy her property, and though she had been opposed at the time, she wondered if perhaps she'd acted too hastily. She needed legal counsel to help her fight her uncle. Like it or not, attorneys cost money, and at the moment, her options were all too limited.

She hated the thought of selling her father's property, but that was nothing compared to Moose's reaction when she told him her plan. He put down the bicycle he was carrying, stared at her in disbelief, and shook his head. "I never thought I'd see the day you'd sell your papa's property to a Newcastle."

"What choice do I have, Moose?"

"I don't know, Miz Mandy, but from what you told me about your pa, I'd say he's gonna turn over in his grave."

"And what do you think he's going to do if I let my uncle take Donny away without a fight?"

"What's this about a fight?" Vincent asked, pushing his button cart toward them.

"Maybe you can talk some sense into her," Moose said. He turned and walked inside, shaking his head and muttering to himself.

"What's wrong with Moose?" Vincent asked.

Amanda explained what she was thinking of doing.

"I don't know, Mandy. The talk on the street is Mr. Newcastle has some strange ideas."

"He says he's going to build a twenty-story building."

"What I heard is that he's going to get his father out of prison."

She gasped in horror. "How could that be? His father is guilty."

"I'd say there's probably more guilty men outside of prison than in." He gave her a sympathetic look. "I wish I could help."

"You've been an enormous help to me already. Do you remember how we met?"

"I'm not likely to forget. There you were, sitting on a park bench, pretty as a picture and crying your eyes out."

She smiled at the memory. The day after her father's funeral, she'd ridden a horsecar up Eighth Avenue to check out the property her father had left her in his will, seeing it for the first time. Weeds were waist-high, providing a shocking contrast to the lush green grass and well-tended flower gardens of nearby Central Park.

Having no idea how she was going to support Donny and herself, she'd crossed over to the park, and that's where Vincent had found her. "You insisted I tell you what was wrong."

"And you told me." He chuckled. "Did you ever! You practically talked my ear off!"

"I don't know why you didn't run the other way."

"If I'd known you were goin' to try and match me up with that crazy Miss Quackenbush, I would have."

"But you didn't. Instead you listened and then you gave me that button." The button was beautiful, with an exquisitely detailed picture of a high-wheel bicycle hand-painted on its smooth porcelain surface. It was the most beautiful button Amanda had ever set eyes on.

"It was a magic button," he said.

"Indeed, it was," she agreed. She'd admired the way

the sun danced upon the smooth, polished surface. She recalled how the slightest movement made it appear as if the gold spoked wheels were actually turning.

That was the day she had first conceived the idea of opening up a cycling school.

"I wish I had another one of those magic buttons," he said. "Hell, I'd give you the whole kit and kaboodle if I thought it would help."

"I know, Vincent. Thank you. And as for Miss Quackenbush—"

"There you go again." He pushed the cart away, yelling at the top of his lungs to drown her out. "Buttoooons. Come and git your . . . buttoooooons."

Undaunted, she called after him, "Miss Quackenbush will make the perfect wife for you!" She should have saved her breath, for the vendor paid her no heed.

"Stubborn fool!" Muttering to herself, she hurried to help Moose finish moving the bicycles outside.

She was going to need a lot more than a magic button to get her through the meeting with Damian Newcastle!

Chapter 9

She debated whether to handwrite the note to Mr. Newcastle asking him to meet her, or to type it. In the end, she decided that a typewritten note appeared more official, even though it would probably take forever to get it right.

Taking a deep breath, she sat in front of her desk and fed a clean sheet of paper into the carriage. She set to work, giving each key a sharp tap. *Dear Mr. Newcattle* . . .

What a nuisance; she had misspelled his name. She ripped out the paper and started over. *Dear Mr. Mewvattle.* The third time she misspelled the word *Dear*, and when she tried to backspace, the keys became tangled.

Frustrated, she gave the Remington a good shake. What a worthless piece of junk! What she was tempted to do was dump the typewriter onto the nearest rubbish pile!

It was a strange-looking contraption, decorated with gilt flourishes, its metal frame a glossy black. Though it had been costly, she had hoped the advertisements were true and the machine really would prove superior to handwriting.

So far the newfangled machine did little more than clutter her desk. Taking a deep breath, she started over, but had no more success than before.

Oh, fiddle! She pushed herself away from the desk and paced about the floor. She was so upset, she could hardly think. At this rate, she'd never get the letter written!

She only hoped Moose was wrong about her papa turning over in his grave. *Oh, Papa! You do understand, don't you?* she thought.

Papa. Just thinking about him brought a lump to her throat. Her father had been a lamp peddler. He'd never made a lot of money, only enough to suit their modest needs. She'd kept her father's books and handled his correspondence, and this, along with taking care of Donny and the household chores, had occupied most of her time. But her father always managed to scrape up enough money for tutors, and she was never allowed to grow lax in her education.

At first he had insisted on the sort of education that befitted a young lady. But being, above all else, a practical man, her father soon saw the futility in making her take sewing and music lessons when clearly she was more interested in mathematics and literature.

The day he'd landed the Newcastle account, they had celebrated with a bottle of imported wine. Even Donny had sensed it was a special occasion and had danced around the parlor, shouting, "Newcastle!"

Her father had supplied the electric light fixtures for the Continental Theater. He was so proud of the exquisite crystal chandeliers, he had personally supervised the placement of each one, then attended the opening night gala to see for himself that nothing went wrong with the lighting.

He had insisted she accompany him as his "assistant," but it shocked her when he wanted to take Donny. They had never taken Donny anywhere, not socially, but her father argued they couldn't keep Donny hidden away forever. "He's not a criminal, Amanda. He's part of this family."

Little did she know disaster would strike that night, leaving her to face the grim prospect of supporting herself and her brother.

After meeting Vincent in the park and coming up

with the idea of a cycling school, she'd started her business with little more than two borrowed boneshakers and a canvas tent.

That was a little more than two years ago. She'd worked long and hard to make her school a success. It hadn't been easy. For the first few weeks not a single student enrolled in her school. Many local businessmen were openly critical of her. Cycling was considered a male occupation, used for business and healthy recreation.

Critics declared cycling dangerous for women and far too undignified. These same critics were clearly scandalized when Amanda stood in Union Square, taking her place next to the many political dissidents and urging both men and women to try her school at no cost.

At last they came. Matronly women bored with sewing circles and whist games arrived first, followed by young debutantes from Fifth Avenue who came with their liveried grooms or matronly chaperons in tow.

Word of mouth took over, and soon even working women began to sign up for the complimentary lessons Amanda offered. Actresses weary of trudging long distances to horsecar stops, train stations, or the Ninth Avenue el on their way to and from the theaters on Broadway signed up for lessons, as did the many women copyists who spent hours at the Metropolitan Museum duplicating the great works to sell at flea markets.

Soon Amanda's students included women from all occupations. Tent and shroud makers, bookbinders and feather curlers signed up. Some of the saleswomen from the department stores along the Ladies' Mile took classes in the early morning hours, before the stores opened, then recommended Amanda's school to their customers. Soon, Amanda could no longer accommodate private classes, except for special circumstances.

Since the first lessons were complimentary, Amanda didn't earn so much as a single penny in those early weeks. At the time she wondered if she ever would. But her students came back for their second lesson and a third, and as more and more women earned their cycling badge and began riding their bicycles through the streets of Manhattan, Amanda's reputation grew accordingly.

Moose was the first man to sign up for a free session, and he offered to work on her bicycles to help pay for future lessons. Amanda needed money to purchase more bicycles, but she needed a handyman and assistant more and jumped at Moose's offer.

The turning point, however, was when she offered to teach a group of Irish immigrants how to ride their bicycles in formation the length of Fifth Street in celebration of St. Patrick's Day.

Dressed in green knee-length pants and matching stockings, and carrying the flags of their native country, the Irishmen had ridden their cycles in the parade, weaving in and out on cue. They were a glorious sight and the crowd had gone wild.

The next day, the police commissioner had summoned Amanda to police headquarters to discuss teaching police officers to ride in formation for the annual policemen's parade in May. Not to be outdone, the Paid Fire Brigade hired her to prepare firemen for the annual firemen's parade.

It seemed to Amanda that New York was fast becoming a city obsessed with parades, and this, of course, was good for her business. Even the torchlight parades at night drew vast crowds. When a group of postal workers signed up for classes, Amanda fully expected them to have a parade of their own.

As incredible as it seemed, New Yorkers even made a parade out of going to church on Easter Sunday. Women dressed in Parisian gowns and fancy hats and men wearing top hats and yellow kid gloves paraded annually down Fifth Avenue and pointedly ignored the churchgoers who, thanks to Amanda and her school, had the good sense to ride their bicycles to church.

Today, as many men as women were enrolled in Amanda's school.

Yes, indeed, she had worked hard to make her school a success. It was one of the reasons she hesitated in moving her school to another location.

Property with easy access to Central Park's network of cycling paths was scarce, and there were few entrances to the park, though it was rumored additional access was under consideration, especially now that the portion of Fifth Avenue facing the park was becoming so popular with the wealthy

"Oh, Papa." She pushed aside the memories of the past and sat at her desk again. "I really don't want to sell the property you worked so hard for." *And certainly not to Mr. Newcastle.* Her father had planned to build on the property and manufacture the lamps he had designed especially for incandescent lighting. It wasn't just the property she was selling, it was her father's dream.

Still, she had a practical nature and she would do what had to be done—even if it killed her.

She set to work typing, and completed the message with little more than a dozen or so strikeovers. She then pulled the paper from the carriage, signed her name, and arranged for it to be delivered to Mr. Newcastle by messenger.

Having completed the disagreeable task, she went home, determined to put the unnerving prospect of coming face-to-face with Damian Newcastle again out of her mind.

The following day, she rode the horsecar toward the park, resigned, though not altogether convinced she was doing the right thing. She had purposely timed herself to arrive at the school for her meeting with Mr. Newcastle exactly twenty-five minutes late.

It never hurt to keep the opposition waiting. She'd called the meeting, determined the place and time. Arriving late would firmly establish her as the one in control.

For all the good it did. She arrived expecting to

have Mr. Newcastle's full attention, only to find he was nowhere in sight.

Where was he? And how dare he keep her waiting? Not that she *had* been waiting, of course, since she'd only just arrived herself, but that was beside the point. Already she had invested a great deal of time and effort in this meeting.

That morning she had exchanged her usual cycling attire for a fashionable two-piece teal-blue business suit, with a wraparound skirt and a fitted jacket. Though she seldom paid much attention to her clothes, she fussed nervously with the lace at her sleeve.

It was now thirty minutes after the hour. Was it possible he had grown tired of waiting for her and had already left? More likely, he was simply playing games with her. For two cents she would be tempted to forget the idea of doing business with him and leave.

If it weren't for Donny, she'd do just that.

Telling herself that moving her school wouldn't be all that bad, she tapped her toe impatiently, her hands planted firmly on her waist. Forty minutes! It was now forty minutes past the hour and still there was no sign of Mr. Newcastle. Enough was enough!

She spun on her heel, key in hand, and was just about to let herself into the school when she heard the clip-clopping sound of a horse. She craned her neck to see through the trees. It couldn't be Mr. Newcastle's horse. This horse was barely moving, and it took what seemed like forever before it came into view. Upon recognizing Mr. Newcastle, her mouth dropped open.

He was forty-six minutes late, and what did he do? He took his own sweet time, that's what!

If that wasn't outrageous enough, when he finally— *finally!*—rode up to the school, he didn't appear to be the least bit apologetic for keeping her waiting.

"Miss Blackwell!" His eyes twinkled as his gaze slid down the length of her, seeming to absorb every detail of her dress—or more precisely, the way her dress molded around her hips and waist. He dismounted, but held on to the reins of his horse. "You weren't going to give up on me, were you?"

"You're late."

"As my father would say, time only counts when you're in prison. What can I do for you?"

She lifted her chin and reminded herself that the moment she lost her temper, he would likely declare victory. "About the offer you made on my property—"

He rubbed his chin. "Are you referring to this property, here? The one you said you'll sell over your dead body?"

"Perhaps I was a bit hasty."

"Testy, more like it. So tell me, Miss Blackwell, is your property now for sale?"

"That remains to be seen. You never did tell me how much you're prepared to offer. Not that my mind's made up, of course. I'm just curious."

"You waited for forty-five minutes out of mere curiosity?" he asked.

"We had an appointment, Mr. Newcastle. I waited out of courtesy."

His eyes sparkled as if he were privy to some private joke. "My hat's off to you, Miss Blackwell. A person would be hard-pressed to find a more courteous woman than yourself. To answer your question, I was prepared to pay you the goodly sum of three thousand dollars."

"Three—" The property was worth at least fifteen hundred more, and even at that price, wouldn't begin to cover all her expenses.

He suddenly burst out laughing. "Congratulations. Not many people could manage to keep their composure in the face of such a generous offer."

"I wouldn't use the word generous," she said evenly. "Insulting would be more accurate."

His laugh deepened. "Insulting, my ass. There isn't a businessman anywhere who wouldn't jump at my offer. Once I've put up my building, your property won't be worth a tinker's damn."

"Five thousand," she said.

"Four thousand, and not a penny more."

"I'll think it over."

"No, you won't. You'll let me know now or the offer no longer holds."

"I don't like to be pushed," she said. "If you wish to purchase my property, you'll have to wait until I'm ready."

"I can't wait, Miss Blackwell. You've already kept me waiting long enough. I need time to draw up new plans to incorporate your property before excavation begins. Any delay would be costly at this point."

"Surely you can recover the costs down the road. You said yourself the new elevators will allow you to charge as much for the upper floors as the lower." She did some quick mental math. "I would say you could pay me what I ask and recover your costs in ten months' time, given the right tenants."

"Good heavens, Miss Blackwell, you're absolutely right. It *will* take ten months to recover my costs. This is terrible."

She stared at him in confusion. "But—"

"Never mind," he continued, his voice smooth as cream. "It's not your fault. I should have checked my figures. I'll tell you what. If you give me a decision today, I'll give you the full three thousand dollars. Wait until tomorrow and it'll be twenty-five."

"Twenty-five hundred?" she gasped. "Why, that's highway robbery. Besides, you offered four thousand dollars—"

"Sold!"

"Oh, no you don't!" she shot back. "Either you pay—"

"I know, I know, five—"

"Six!"

"Six!" He looked incredulous. "Surely, you jest. I daresay you can buy quite a respectable piece of land for four. And build a school to boot! I'll tell you what. I'll even help you relocate."

"How generous of you."

He grinned, and she had the sinking feeling he was enjoying himself.

"Do we have a deal?" he asked.

The idea of selling her father's property to this man made her feel physically ill. There had to be another way.

"Well, Miss Blackwell? Are you or are you not going to sell?"

"Over my dead body." She turned on her heel and stomped through the open door of her school.

"Don't take any drastic actions on my account," he called after her.

"I wouldn't think of it!" Gritting her teeth, she slammed the door shut, but even that failed to block out the warm, velvety sound of his laughter.

Chapter 10

"Miss Quackenbush!" Amanda lay flat on her back, looking up at the sky through the spinning wheel of a topsy-turvy high-rise bicycle. In the course of an hour, the schoolteacher had broken every rule in the park at least twice. Amanda knew more about Miss Quackenbush's undergarments than she knew about her own.

With an impatient shove, Amanda pushed aside the forty-pound bicycle, stood, and brushed herself off. "How many times must I tell you? You must turn the front wheel in the direction you're falling."

"I was trying to, Miss Blackwell, but it's hard to turn the wheel in *both* directions at the same time."

Amanda stood the bicycle upright, checking that no bolts were loose, and took a deep breath.

"I realize the natural tendency is to turn the steering wheel in the opposite direction of the fall. But you must teach your limbs to go against their natural inclination."

Distracted by the feeling she was being watched, she spun around, only to discover her suspicions were right. She should have known! Damian Newcastle sat astride his horse, watching her from a grassy knoll.

Lord almighty, not only was he watching, he actually had the audacity to look amused. The nerve of him!

Furious, she turned her back on him and checked the seat of the bicycle. Despite several unfortunate spills, the seat was adjusted perfectly, but this didn't keep her from giving it a firm tap. Why, oh, why did he continue to watch her when she had made it perfectly clear she wanted nothing more to do with him? "Let's try again, Miss Quackenbush."

The poor woman picked herself up off the ground. She was covered in grass and leaves but paid no heed to her appearance. She grasped the handlebars, rested her left foot on the mounting peg, and hopped along on her right foot. The confounded black skirt she insisted upon wearing billowed in the wind, further hindering her.

Amanda chased after her. "That's it. Now put your leg over the seat."

The schoolmarm lifted her leg, holding it midair, arabesque style, her stomach leaning against the rear of the seat. Amanda had never seen anything quite like it. "Anytime you're ready. Put your leg over the seat." She blew her whistle. "Now!"

The bicycle fell with an undignified flumping sound, but this time Amanda was able to jump out of the way. Miss Quackenbush was less fortunate, and now sprawled facedown on the grass in a shocking pose that broke every park rule regarding propriety, save speeding.

She had even managed to uproot a few dandelions along the way, and that act alone would have landed them both in jail had Old Thorny been around.

Amanda chanced a look over her shoulder. Damian Newcastle no longer looked merely amused, he was actually bent over with laughter. He looked even more handsome today than usual, but this, of course, was of no concern to her.

Seething with mixed emotions, Amanda turned back to her student and quickly covered the woman's exposed legs.

"Congratulations, Miss Quackenbush. I do believe that was the most graceful fall yet."

For two cents she would be tempted to march over to Mr. Newcastle and tell him exactly what she thought of him. "Let's try again."

By the time Miss Quackenbush's lesson was over, Amanda was in the worst possible mood. Since she had some free time between lessons, she decided to finish typing the letter she had started two days earlier. It turned out to be a terrible idea. For one thing, the typewriter refused to cooperate.

Already, she'd spent hours trying to produce a half-page business letter addressed to her uncle's attorney, Mr. Liversworth, a letter that would have taken her, at the most, a half hour to compose by hand.

Now she reached for another fresh sheet of paper. "All right," she growled at the machine. "You get one more chance. Do you hear me?"

This time, she pecked at the keys carefully, using only her forefingers. *Dear Mr. Liversworth. You are a . . .*

She removed the wooden lead pencil that had been clenched in her teeth and called to Moose. "Is *imbecile* spelled with an *s* or a *c*?"

Moose appeared at the doorway of his workshop, his forehead pleated like a folded fan. "Now, Miz Mandy, you agreed that name-callin' ain't gonna do you one bit of good."

"Are you saying *imbecile* is too strong?"

Moose gave a nod. "Not quite as strong as that word you used earlier—"

"You mean *asinine*?"

"Yep, that's the one."

"It suits my uncle to the T."

"That might be so, Miz Mandy, but right now he has the upper hand. Callin' him names ain't gonna help your cause none."

Moose was right, of course. As much as she was tempted to tell her uncle exactly what she thought of him, he'd only use it against her. What she needed was a lawyer, but so far her attempts at finding one willing to take on a man as powerful and rich as her uncle had proven futile, especially since selling her property was no longer an option.

She yanked the paper out of the typewriter and

crinkled it into a ball. Once again she missed the wastepaper basket, and the crushed paper joined the growing pile on the floor. She was tempted to toss the newfangled writing machine on the floor after it.

She worked a fresh sheet of paper into the roller. This time, she'd get the letter right if it killed her.

Dear Mr. Liversworth . . . She pecked at the oddly placed letters on the keyboard using only one finger. It seemed as if the letters of the alphabet had been placed on the keyboard at random.

Strangely enough, the letter *B* was positioned between the letters *V* and *N,* and the *A* was beneath the *Q.* It made no sense whatsoever. The salesman who had sold her the typewriter had warned her about typing too fast and making the keys stick. What a laugh! The keys stuck, all right, but not because of any speed.

A loud thud shook the very foundation of her cycling school. It rattled the windows and jiggled the gas lanterns hanging from a row of metal hooks. Alarmed, Amanda rose from her desk and hastened to the door.

Outside, a long line of horse-drawn wagons extended past her property and down the street for as far as the eye could see. Each wagon carried a piece of heavy equipment.

Enormous hoisting machines fitted with wires and pulleys rose high above the ground. Steam engines, wheelbarrows, and other equipment she couldn't begin to name were lined up in front of her school.

Men dressed in canvas pants and what looked like firemen helmets worked together to roll the equipment down wooden ramps propped against the back of the wagons.

Curious, Amanda stepped outside. Despite the confusion, she had no trouble spotting Damian Newcastle, who watched the proceedings from astride his horse.

Moose joined her, shaking his head. "Lawdy mussy! It looks like our neighbor is about to have hisself a barn raisin'."

"I think Mr. Newcastle has a bit more than a barn raising on his mind," she said. Leaving Moose to watch the school, she stormed toward her neighbor's property.

Though Mr. Newcastle was obviously in charge of the proceedings, he looked strangely removed from the others. Still, his commanding presence was obvious, even though he communicated with little more than an occasional soft-spoken command or hand signal, letting the men work for the most part undisturbed.

He looked straight at her as she approached and she had the strangest feeling he took some sort of perverse pleasure in rattling her. He said something to one of the workmen and rode his horse toward her, meeting her halfway.

He tipped his tall, silky hat and leaned against the horn of his saddle. "Morning, Miss Blackwell. I hope my men didn't disturb your lessons." Though he sounded sincere, the light shining in his eyes suggested he liked the idea of her being disturbed.

"Not at all, Mr. Newcastle," she said with cool disdain. "Sorry to disappoint you."

He raised a dark brow and tilted his head. "Surely you're not suggesting it's my intention to disrupt your classes."

"The thought never entered my head," she said evenly. "But I am curious as to what it is you *are* doing."

"As I explained, I'm building a twenty-story building. Yes, indeed. I'm going to stack those stories one on top of another like a deck of playing cards. It won't exactly reach the sky, but it will scrape it a bit." He looked devilishly sure of himself, and his eyes were bright with a challenging gaze that stoked her to cold fury.

So he was going to play her for the fool, was he? "If you think you're going to intimidate me into selling my property—"

"Intimidate you? Why, Miss Blackwell, it wounds me to hear you suggest such a thing. Granted, it would have been easier had you and I come to terms, but it's not by any means a necessity. I intend to build with or without your cooperation."

"The right price will buy all the cooperation you want."

"Now that's a tempting offer," he said. "All, eh?"

Refusing to play his game, she ignored his innuendo. "Your property is little more than twenty feet wide," she reminded him.

"What I lack in width, I intend to make up for in height." He lifted his arm, painting an invisible rainbow against the clear blue sky with a sweeping motion of his hand. "Now that hydraulic piston elevators have been perfected, there's no limit to how high a man can build. Perhaps in the future, buildings fifty stories or higher will be commonplace. Especially now that the new elevators can travel twenty times faster than the old."

Amanda shuddered at the thought. She'd ridden the Otis elevator in the five-story E. V. Haughtwout and Company store on Broadway. The elevator had been advertised as traveling eight inches per second, and she was convinced that going any faster would have an unfortunate influence upon a person's digestive system, if not the rest of the body. "Such elevators are dangerous."

"Riding those confounded high-wheel bicycles is dangerous, Miss Blackwell."

"You can't possibly compare the two. A building that high is bound to be affected by the wind. What if there's a fire?" People had died in a Manhattan fire earlier that year when firefighting ladders proved inadequate to reach the third floor. "How are the people on the upper floors to escape?"

"I can assure you I'm doing everything in my power to prevent such a disaster. Everything, every scrap of steel, wood, or brick will be fireproofed."

"And if the building collapses beneath its own weight? What insurance do you have against that?"

"My building will not collapse. I give you my word."

"Your *word*, Mr. Newcastle? I'd sooner believe the word of a thief."

"Well, if it will put your mind at ease, I've been called a thief on occasion."

He never failed to astonish her. "That's nothing to brag about."

"I'm not bragging," he said amicably. "But since you'd rather believe a thief, my reputation might make me seem more credible." He touched his finger to the brim of his hat. "Now if you will excuse me, Miss Blackwell, I have work to do." He rode his horse onto the street, stopping to watch as several men guided a derrick from the back of a wagon.

Watching him, it was hard to know what worried her most, the twenty-story building with its speeding elevator or the man himself.

In the weeks to follow, Amanda tried her utmost to ignore the construction site. But it was difficult to do, especially since the number of workmen, wagons, and heavy equipment continued to grow to the point of blocking the street to through traffic, causing her students no small amount of inconvenience.

But if ignoring the site was difficult, ignoring Damian Newcastle was altogether impossible. She was so attuned to him, she knew by instinct when he was on the site and when he wasn't. No matter how hard she tried to deny her interest in him, she couldn't seem to keep herself from gazing in his direction each time she stepped outside.

More worrisome yet was her annoying habit of straining to hear his voice over the constant rumble of iron wagon wheels that labored over the rough cobbled road on the way to the construction site. Even the elevated railway didn't make as much clatter.

She was almost at her wit's end. Sometimes her school shook so hard, she was convinced it was about to collapse. But in all honesty, it wasn't only her irksome neighbor who had her nerves in a dither.

She'd had no further correspondence from her

uncle, and her letter to his attorney had thus far gone unanswered. Not a day went by that she didn't expect one or the other to walk into her school or pound on the door of her apartment. But time passed without a word. Lord, it was hard to know what was worse, the waiting or the noise.

For poor Moose, it was clearly the latter. He was so rattled by the constant thumps and clattering sounds outside the school, he developed a tic in one eye. She insisted he have Dr. Paine look at it and he left early that Friday, promising to stop at the doctor's office on the way home to the Lower East Side where he lived with his mother and seven siblings.

After Moose left, Amanda spent the rest of the afternoon convincing herself that another confrontation with Mr. Newcastle would serve no useful purpose. The man didn't make a move without considering every consequence. She'd seen the drawings, the endless plans. Had watched him stand on the street corner counting the number of horsecars, carriages, bicycles, and hacks so he could project how his building would affect traffic. He knew precisely what he was doing.

Outraged by his obvious ploy to drive her to distraction, and toying with the idea that perhaps her uncle had paid him to do so, she decided to hold her tongue. At least for now.

A short time after Moose had left for the day, she sailed past the construction site on the way to the horsecar stop. Her parasol open, she held her hand just above her nose. She kept her eyes focused straight ahead as if nothing of any consequence was happening.

Mr. Newcastle made no effort to detain her, but she could *feel* his eyes on her, feel an inexplicable warmth travel up and down her body. He was staring at her. She was almost positive. Anxious to make her escape, she quickened her step, though she did mange a furtive glance in his direction upon reaching her destination.

He *was* staring, just as she'd thought, and he made

no bones about it. The nerve of him! Her face burning and her heart pounding, she hurried up the steps of the waiting horsecar, took a seat, and fanned herself with a black lisle glove.

How much longer could her poor nerves—or beleaguered school—stand the strain?

Chapter 11

The situation grew worse with each passing day. Damian Newcastle continued to enjoy himself at Amanda's expense and seemed to go out of his way to gall her.

Every time he caught her eye, he flashed her an engaging, heart-stopping smile and politely doffed his hat. She refused to smile back, though she was sorely tempted to laugh at his arrogance, and the strain was beginning to take its toll.

"Well, I never!" Miss Quackenbush complained one day, after Amanda had snapped at her.

Even Vincent commented on Amanda's uncharacteristic ill temper. "If you don't like my buttons, just say so." He snatched the card of hand-painted porcelain buttons away from her and pushed his cart away.

"Now don't go getting yourself in a dither, Vincent. I love your buttons."

Vincent ignored her efforts to make amends, but not Mr. Newcastle. Oh, no! Instead, he stood openly watching her, legs apart, eyes glittering, like a conquering general.

"Is there a problem, Miss Blackwell?" he called, upon seeing Vincent storm down the street at a speed that was a far cry from the vendor's usual snail's pace.

She was tempted to slap that arrogant look from his face, but of course that would only reveal her true state of mind, and she'd die before she gave him *that* satisfaction.

She replied in her usual noncommittal way. "Not a one, Mr. Newcastle."

Though the alarming amount of equipment that accumulated next door continued to amaze her, it was Damian Newcastle who drove her to distraction. How could he not?

Raw energy and pulsing vitality emanated from his tall, lean body. He exuded a masculinity that filled her with a strange and unfamiliar longing. Though he primarily supervised the work, he sometimes stopped to haul a piece of heavy equipment across the site, revealing muscles that left her feeling weak and her feminine heart fluttering. Never before had she paid such attention to a man's muscles. Or the way his trousers fit. Or how his shirt molded to his back. Now suddenly she was obsessed.

She spent hours watching him, though she waited for Moose to leave before peering out the school window. She was discreet, but obviously not nearly enough, for it soon became apparent her handyman knew exactly what she was doing.

She was even more careful not to be caught staring at the site whenever she was outside, though some of her female students took no such precautions.

"Oh, you simply must introduce me to him," Miss Mary Beth Hallermark pleaded in her soft Southern drawl.

A robust woman by the name of Margaret Porterville, whose father owned the Porterville Textile Mills, clapped her pudgy hands together, her little bow mouth quivering over her stack of soft rounded chins. "She's saving him for me. Isn't that so, Miss Blackwell?"

"He's not good husband material," Amanda said firmly. The two women didn't have the sense God gave a flea. They continued to show up for their lessons in frilly skirts and layers of jewelry despite Amanda's warnings about bicycle safety. Nevertheless, she felt obligated to look out for their welfare. "He's a Newcastle."

Miss Porterville swooned, her long lashes fluttering up and down. "Oh, but he's so handsome."

A third student, Mrs. Davidson, who had been practicing mounting her bicycle unassisted, stopped and scowled. The wife of a lawyer, she had managed to marry off six of her eight daughters and had the gray hair and wrinkles to prove it. She considered herself an expert on the subject of men and matrimony. "Handsome men seldom make proper husbands. My daughter Elizabeth refused to listen to me and what did it get her? A no-good panderer, that's what."

"So what *does* make a good husband?" Miss Hallermark asked.

Mrs. Davidson didn't hesitate to answer her. "A man who wipes his feet at the door shows real domestic promise, wouldn't you agree, Miss Blackwell?"

"I suppose—"

"And," Mrs. Davidson continued, "a man who spreads his handkerchief on his lap while drinking tea will probably be prudent with his money as well."

"Prudence is nice," Amanda agreed, "but integrity and honesty are more important." She scowled at Damian. "And I can assure you Mr. Newcastle fails sadly at both counts!"

Disappointment crossed the younger women's faces. "How do we go about finding husbands with the proper qualifications?" Miss Porterville asked.

Mrs. Davidson stared down the length of her generous nose. "I'll tell you the same as I told my daughters. Look pretty and don't say anything that sounds too intelligent."

"That's ridiculous," Amanda said hotly. "An intelligent man likes a woman with a brain."

"I didn't say a woman couldn't have a brain if she wanted one," Mrs. Davidson argued. "Just as long as she keeps it to herself."

"Horsefeathers!" Amanda said, glaring at the woman. She didn't generally allow herself to argue with her students, but how could she in good conscience allow such rubbish to go unchallenged?

Mrs. Davidson didn't take kindly to having her

opinion questioned. "If men like intelligent women, then why aren't you married?"

"Because intelligent women like intelligent men and they're hard to find."

Miss Porterville shrugged and pouted her lips prettily. "I still think Mr. Newcastle would make a perfect husband."

Tired of trying to talk sense into her students, Amanda blew her whistle. "All right, ladies, mount your bicycles!"

Soon after the three women had finished for the day and Amanda had returned to the school, a woman by the name of Mrs. Defore arrived for her free lesson.

A practicing hypochondriac, Mrs. Defore lived in one of the large mansions on Fifth Avenue with her wealthy banker husband, eleven children, and assorted servants.

Everything from the ridiculous sausage curls to the layers of silk ruffles that fluttered from her high-necked shirtwaist was done to excess. She insisted upon learning to ride on her own custom-made high-wheeler, which was garishly decorated in glittering sequins.

"We'll start slowly," Amanda explained. The woman looked wide-eyed and red-faced, but whether it was from fear of cycling, a too-tight corset, or due to one of her numerous ailments, it was hard to say. "Hold on to the handlebars and walk the bicycle. This will help you grow accustomed to the motion of the machine. That's it."

The hem of the woman's skirt caught in the spokes and Amanda gently tugged at the fabric, freeing it.

"I suggest you wear something less elaborate for your future lessons. Something like what I'm wearing."

"Oh, my." The woman's gaze dropped to Amanda's bloomers, her eyes widening in dismay. "I don't know if Mr. Defore would approve."

"Perhaps a skirt that's discreetly divided would be

more to your liking. It'll be so much easier to mount a bicycle if you're wearing proper clothing."

Mrs. Defore looked uncertain. "Do you mean to say you're not going to teach me to ride sidesaddle?"

"Absolutely not." The very thought made Amanda shudder. Nothing dismayed her more than seeing a woman perched half-cocked upon a saddle, and it didn't matter whether it was the saddle of a horse or the seat of a bicycle. Riding sidesaddle should be outlawed, along with sausage curls and glittery sequins.

Mrs. Defore looked visibly upset. "My husband would never approve of me riding astride. Besides which, I'm not sure my liver can handle the strain."

"You'd be amazed how flexible a liver is," Amanda said. "As for your husband, surely he wouldn't insist you do something so dangerous as ride sidesaddle."

Mrs. Defore fanned herself with her hand. "He wouldn't approve of me acting unladylike." She wrinkled her nose in distaste. "Besides, I could never bring myself to spread my legs."

Amanda resisted the urge to point out that as the mother of several offspring, Mrs. Defore had, indeed, found occasions to spread her legs.

"It'll get easier with practice," Amanda said.

"But spreading one's legs is so unwomanly."

"Quite the contrary, ladies. I would say spreading one's legs is quite womanly."

At the sound of Damian Newcastle's voice, Amanda spun around, her senses reeling like wool on a spindle. Whether she was furious at him for intruding upon a lesson or at herself for allowing him to affect her, she didn't know, but her senses were definitely out of control. "If you don't mind, Mr. Newcastle, this is a private conversation."

"Ah, so it is. Please accept my humble apologies." He bowed slightly from the waist. "I thought I'd let you know we're going to begin digging tomorrow morning. I've informed my construction crew not to interfere with your school, if at all possible."

Not wanting to make a scene in front of Mrs. Defore, Amanda nodded politely, glared at him fiercely, and held herself aloof. "How thoughtful of you."

"If you experience any problems, speak to me directly." He tipped his hat. "I'll let you ladies get back to your . . . lesson." He turned and casually strolled away.

Taking a deep breath, and willing her heart to stop beating up on her rib cage, she turned back to her student.

Mrs. Defore watched Mr. Newcastle walk away, and looked about to swoon. Obviously, her taste in men was every bit as questionable as her taste in apparel and glittery bicycles.

"Are you ready, Mrs. Defore?"

"Absolutely. If that nice man thinks spreading one's legs is womanly, who am I to argue?"

Excavation began at dawn the following morning. For Damian, it was the culmination of months of red tape and frustration, definitely a dream come true. Though it filled him with pleasure to finally see progress, his work had only just begun.

His men would have to dig down seventy feet below street level, through layers of silt and clay known as bull's liver, through hardpan and enormous boulders, before hitting bedrock.

Using a method developed in Europe and perfected by John Augustus Roebling in the building of his great bridge, Damian had arranged to have metal caissons sunk into the ground and filled with concrete. Once his building was complete, nothing short of the end of the world would bring it down. He'd bet his life on it.

He was also willing to bet his life on a few other things, like the fact that his intriguing neighbor was nowhere near as oblivious to him as she would like him to believe.

She could have saved him a lot of trouble by selling him her land, but he was committed to building regardless, even though he was now forced to make certain concessions.

Four thousand dollars was a fair offer, though had she played her cards right, he would have gone considerably higher. But the truth of the matter was, Miss Blackwell had no intention of selling to him, and as soon as she thought he might meet her asking price of five thousand, she'd immediately upped it to six.

She might have convinced herself she wanted to sell, but she hadn't fooled him. People anxious to sell don't show up forty minutes late for a meeting. Little did she know he'd been watching from a distance, waiting for her to arrive before making his appearance.

Well, the decision had been made and they both had to live with it. The woman was as stubborn as she was pleasing to the eye, and as much as he hated to admit it, he found the combination irresistible.

Chapter 12

During the days that followed, Amanda's interest in Damian Newcastle grew to obsessive proportions.

Excavation was now in its second week and showed no sign of stopping. Hazy white smoke rose from the ungainly steam engines from early morning until after dark. The rumbling sounds of ox-driven wagons and windlass trucks continued to shake the windows and walls of her school as loads of dirt and broken rock were hauled away.

No longer able to curtail her curiosity, Amanda arrived at the school early that gray Monday morning for the sole purpose of checking out the site before Mr. Newcastle or his men arrived. What she saw took her breath away. One of the trenches was so deep, it was impossible to see the bottom.

"So what do you think, Miss Blackwell?"

Jumping at the sound of his voice, she turned. "It's a hole, Mr. Newcastle," she said, her voice deceptively calm. "What am I supposed to think?"

He lifted a dark brow and regarded her with a mocking smile. It was obvious he enjoyed catching her red-handed. "I thought perhaps you might be impressed."

Her senses screamed with awareness, not only of the man, but of the dangerously gaping hole as well. She stepped back and almost lost her balance.

He grabbed her by the arm, his fingers forming a circle of warmth that reached through the thin fabric of her sleeve. "Steady. I wouldn't want to have to dive in after you."

Shaken by his touch as much as by the danger at her feet, she pulled away from him. "I didn't expect you to be digging so deep."

"We're not finished. We have to dig to the bedrock and that's at least another twenty feet down."

"But . . . but why must you dig so far down?"

"A twenty-story building requires a firm foundation, otherwise, as you have so graciously pointed out on several memorable occasions, it will topple over in the first strong windstorm." His eyes locked with hers.

"So you actually mean to put up your building?"

A look of surprise crossed his face. "Do you think I would go to all this trouble if I wasn't serious?"

"I thought you were trying to make my life miserable so that I would change my mind."

His eyes smoldered. "Am I making your life miserable?"

"Certainly not," she said, trying to cover the slip of her tongue. "Nothing you do has any bearing on my life."

"What a relief that must be for you. You do know, of course, this is only the beginning. The reason I offered to buy your property was more for your convenience than mine."

She looked him square in the face. "As I told you at the start, my property isn't for sale. I haven't changed my mind, Mr. Newcastle, about selling my property or anything else."

"Does that mean you haven't changed your mind about me?"

"Not in the least. I still have the utmost disregard for you."

He raked her over with his eyes. "And I was so certain that once you got to know me, you'd discover my finer qualities."

She gave him a sidewise glance. "Sorry to disappoint you."

"Oh, I'm not disappointed. Actually, you're to be

complimented, Miss Blackwell. You're not afraid to make a snap judgment and stick with it. I like that in a woman."

"I don't deserve *all* the credit, Mr. Newcastle. Your abominable behavior has since affirmed my initial impression."

A smile touched his lips. "You're one of a kind, Miss Blackwell. Not only do you know your own mind, you give credit where credit's due." A wagon pulled up to the site and Mr. Newcastle turned to wave to the driver. Amanda jumped at the chance to escape.

"Come again, Miss Blackwell," he called after her. "It's always a pleasure."

The following week, things went from bad to worse. The noise levels continued to increase and Amanda was forced to conduct her cycling classes in the park, and this, of course, meant daily battles with Old Thorny.

After one such harried lesson, she rushed inside the school to find her uncle waiting for her.

A portly man with gray-flecked hair, neatly trimmed sideburns, and a wooden leg, he greeted her with a congenial smile that never quite reached his close-set eyes. "Good morning, Amanda."

"Uncle Randall."

"Would you mind closing the door? It's a bit difficult to talk over the noise."

"Of course." Amanda did as he asked, then walked over to her desk. She flipped through the stack of mail, but only to hide her nervousness. "What brings you here?"

Her uncle sat on a chair next to her, his wooden leg extended outward, and twirled his derby in his hands. "I've just returned from abroad. I had hoped the little matter my attorney wrote you about would have been resolved in my absence."

Amanda's temper flared. "The little matter?" She

dropped the mail on her desk. "You wish to put my brother in an asylum and you call that a little matter?"

"Now, now, Amanda. There's no sense flying off the handle. I'm sure if we put our heads together, we can resolve this in a civilized manner. You do want that, don't you? Yes, of course you do."

"I think I made it quite clear in my letter I intend to fight you on this."

"Oh, is that what you said?" He sat back in his chair. "Your letter had so many strikeovers, it was hard to read. If you don't show more care, you'll wear out your x key."

Amanda didn't appreciate his concern over her typewriter keys *or* her brother. "Now that you understand my intentions, I'll have to ask you to leave. I have a full day of lessons."

"I won't keep you any longer than necessary." He made no attempt to leave. "I must insist that you allow me to find Donald a suitable home."

"Donny *has* a suitable home."

"Come, come, child. Your brother has special needs that neither you nor I can fulfill."

"You're talking about putting him in an asylum."

"I've spoken to many highly qualified physicians about Donald's condition and they all agree he would be better off in an appropriate facility."

"They came to this conclusion without examining him? How amazing."

Ignoring her comment, he continued, "I'm telling you, Amanda, this is the best solution."

"How do you know what's best for Donny? Where were you when Donny was an infant? And what about all the years since? You've hardly said two words to him!"

"I regret your father's decision to cut off your mother's family."

"You gave him no choice."

"I don't wish to argue with you," her uncle said. "What happened in the past is all water under the bridge. My only concern at the moment is Donald's well-being."

"Donny's well-being is my responsibility, not yours."

"May I remind you, his mother was my sister? That makes me responsible."

"You've ignored him for twelve years."

"That was your father's wish, not mine. Had I known the seriousness of Donald's condition, I would never have allowed your father's wishes to stand in the way of my responsibilities to my sister's son. We can resolve this issue right now or—"

Angered by his threatening tone, her lips thinned. "Or what?"

"Or we can resolve it in court. It's your choice. Which will it be?"

The man had her over a barrel and he knew it. Justice favored money and power and her uncle had both. Still, she refused to give up without a fight.

"I'll see you in court," she said, managing to sound amazingly confident for someone who had just declared a war she had no chance of winning.

"Very well." Her uncle lifted his leg with his hands and stood, pressing his hat onto his head. "You'll be hearing from my attorney."

It rained for the next week and Amanda was forced to cancel her lessons. After the fifth day of staying at home, she grew restless and out of sorts.

If she played one more game of dominoes or told yet another button story, she would scream, she was certain of it. The only cheering thought was knowing that the rain caused a delay in Mr. Newcastle's building plans.

Worried that another letter from her uncle's attorney might have been delivered to the school, she decided to leave Donny in Mrs. Brook's care and take the Eighth Avenue horsecar to Central Park.

Dressed in her father's rubber boots, which were several sizes too large, and an old hooded cape, she set out. It was still raining steadily, and instead of waiting for a policeman to assist her across the street, as a woman would normally do, she waded unaided through the curb-high water, taking care not to slip on the treacherous cobblestones.

A man blocked her way onto the horsecar, his angry voice startling her as he addressed the driver, who sat hunched over on the open platform. "Six passengers disembarked, sir. Nine remain. That's more passengers than the law permits."

The fleshy driver obviously didn't appreciate the man's criticism. "Are you saying I should leave people standing in the rain rather than burden the horse?"

"The laws are very clear, sir! No more than twelve passengers at any one time." The man backed away from the steps and, seeing Amanda still standing in the rain, tipped his hat in apology and hurried down the sidewalk.

Though the man was a stranger, she admired him tremendously. She, herself, had spoken out against animal cruelty, specifically the disgraceful practice of clipping a horse's hair to the skin, making the poor animal more susceptible to the cold. She had also lodged a complaint with city officials about the recent appearance of dogcarts in Central Park.

Let a poor sparrow even think of landing on the precious grass and all hell broke loose. But no one cared horsefeathers if a dog was made to pull a cart full of children!

She climbed inside the car and, after taking a quick count and determining she was only the tenth passenger, dropped her fare in the tin box and took a seat, the wet straw crunching beneath her feet.

The rain continued to pour as the horse pulled the car along the metal tracks. The animal labored against the wind, its metal-shod hooves slipping on the water-slick street.

Thank goodness she'd had the foresight to have the roof of her school checked that past summer. Confident her school would withstand anything short of major flooding, she walked from the horsecar stop, cutting across the muddied street at an angle and side-stepping a large puddle of water. The rain slanted harder and she lowered her head and buried her hands inside her muff.

It was sheer luck and quick action that kept her from walking into the gaping hole that had opened up between the Newcastle property and her school. She scrambled backward a fraction of a second before the ground gave way in front of her.

Her eyes wide with horror, she clung to the flatbed of a half-buried dray. Squinting against the rain, she watched helplessly as a wheelbarrow sank into the oozing mud, then disappeared altogether.

At the rate the hole was growing, it was only a matter of time before her school was swallowed up. Clinging to the dray for dear life, she trembled with anger. This time, Damian Newcastle had gone too far!

Chapter 13

Damian was convinced it would never stop raining. He had spent the better part of the day in his study, walking back and forth like a caged lion. His pacing did nothing to alleviate his restlessness, though the carpet had, no doubt, grown more threadbare beneath his restless feet.

Shrugging with impatience, he stopped to stare out the window. The sky was as dark and gray as ever and the rain showed no sign of letting up.

He had expected the excavation to be complete by now and the foundation started. The rain was costing him dearly in both time and money.

He'd ridden out to the site the day before. What an unbelievable mess. Mud was everywhere. It would take days for the equipment to dry and even longer to clear away the debris that had washed down the gutters.

The quiet was broken by Christopher's unhappy voice in another part of the house. "I won't!" Christopher's cry was followed by Miss Hannah's hushed voice. Normally, Damian wouldn't stand for Christopher's outburst, but he realized the long siege of inclement weather had put everyone's nerves on edge.

Christopher had spent the morning staring out the window. Any attempts on either Damian's or the tutor's part to engage Christopher in his studies was met with uncharacteristic resistance.

Damian had finally ordered the classes stopped. There was a time to learn math and a time to stare out the window. As Damian could attest, today was clearly the day to stare.

The only problem with staring, of course, was that the most unsettling thoughts kept popping into his head. That was one of the reasons he sighed in relief when a horse and buggy pulled up in his drive and Detective Harold S. Grape stepped out. He never thought he'd see the day the infinitely annoying detective would offer a welcome diversion.

Considered by many to be the best private investigator New York had to offer, Grape had failed thus far to live up to Damian's expectations.

Damian opened the door himself and ushered the man into his study. Detective Grape was a fleshy man with lily-white skin, a limp mustache, and a meek manner that seemed inconsistent with everything Damian had heard about him.

Rumor had it that Grape had single-handedly flattened a roomful of thugs, and more than one criminal had reportedly given himself up upon learning that Grape was hot on his trail.

Now Grape stood in front of the fire, warming himself and managing to look as harmless as a newborn puppy. "I don't know what's worse, spring rains or summer heat waves."

Damian couldn't imagine anyone venturing out on such a day without good reason. "Have you news?"

Grape sat down and methodically struck a Lucifer match, lighting his pipe before he replied. "None that you're going to want to hear."

Damian's impatience snapped. "Spill it out!"

Grape waved the match until the flame disappeared, then tossed it into the fireplace. Standing next to the hearth, he cradled the bowl of his pipe in a delicate hand that didn't look capable of wiping out anything bigger than an ant. "I've conducted a complete investigation and I can't find anything that proves your contention."

Damian clenched his jaw. He paid this man good money. Grape damned well better find something!

"Somebody sabotaged that theater," he said tersely. "That's why the balcony collapsed. It didn't fall because of poor design, neglect, or cheap materials. It fell because somebody wanted to ruin my father."

Grape didn't so much as flinch in the heat of Damian's angry outburst. "We haven't turned up a single piece of new evidence, certainly nothing to support your contention."

"Then you haven't looked hard enough."

"Damn it, Newcastle! What am I supposed to do? What was left of the theater was gutted by fire. If, indeed, the balcony was sabotaged, every shred of evidence has long since been destroyed."

The fire had occurred just days after the collapse of the balcony, and was yet another piece of a perplexing puzzle.

The two men glared at each other, the detective puffing on his pipe, Damian slamming a fist against his open palm. At the rate the investigation was going, his father would be dead and buried before Damian was able to gather up proof of his innocence.

Grape clamped the stem of his pipe between his teeth and patted his coat, finding a writing tablet in the left pocket. He pulled it out and flipped through the pages. "We've checked out the guest list and completed a thorough investigation of everyone who attended the theater opening."

He eyed Damian, apparently looking for a reaction before he continued. "We questioned your father's business acquaintances and both past and present employees of the Newcastle Construction Company." He slid the notepad back into his pocket. "We've come up with zero. *Zero!*"

"How can you be sure none of these people were involved?"

"Because we're missing the big M. It's called motive. If someone wanted to see your father behind bars, there has to be a reason. But hell if I can find it."

"My father has his share of enemies. Every businessman does. What about the money he found missing from the city's building account?"

"My men are working on it, but so far we haven't found a thing that looks even remotely suspicious."

"Did you check out all the names I gave you? It's got to be one of them. It's the only thing that makes sense."

"Nothing makes sense. I've worked on this case for over two years and nothing makes sense."

Damian stared out the window. "So where do we go from here?"

"That's what I'm trying to tell you. We have no place to go. We're beating a dead horse."

This was the last thing Damian wanted to hear. "You're the detective! Find something!"

After Grape had left, Damian reread the transcripts of his father's trail. He methodically compared the known facts with the detective's monthly reports. He knew the transcripts by heart, but he read them periodically on the chance he might have missed something. Today, as always, he found nothing new. Feeling more restless and frustrated than before, he tossed the portfolio aside and continued his earlier pacing.

So what should he do now? Hire another private investigator? He decided to call his father's lawyer first thing in the morning and see what he suggested.

That decision made, his mind turned to other matters. He walked over to the plans on the wall and stared at them. Damn it, there was no getting around the city building codes.

He'd been so certain his latest plan to eliminate the six-foot-wide walls would be approved. No such luck. Now he was back to square one.

He had two choices: either he lived with six-foot walls or he purchased Miss Blackwell's property.

Miss Blackwell. He shook his head and chuckled. Just thinking about the look of indignity on her face when he offered her thirty-five hundred made him laugh. Never had he seen such dangerous sparks flash in a woman's eyes like they'd flashed in the eyes of the auburn-haired beauty. If he offered her the six thousand she asked for, he wouldn't put it past her to hold out for ten.

He wondered how Miss Blackwell spent her time on a day like this. Would she stare out the window, too, as he was prone to do? Somehow he doubted it. It was hard to imagine her standing still long enough to stare at anything.

Never had he known such a woman. He could see her in his mind's eye as clearly as if she stood in front of him at that very moment. Ah, yes, he could see her in those confounded though fetching bloomers of hers, her little jaunty hat askew, her hair windblown and her cheeks flushed from the sun.

Her energy amazed him. It wore him out just to watch her trot next to her students, flashing her engaging smile or blowing that shrill whistle. It also gave him pleasure to watch her walk down the street, all prim and proper, her parasol flung over her shoulder, as she pretended not to notice him.

It amused him no end to watch her and he never missed an opportunity to do so. He had to give Miss Blackwell credit; she never gave up on a student and only under the most trying circumstances did she lose her patience. Not one student, not the honorable mayor himself or the clerk at Finnigan's dry good stores, escaped her watchful eye or stern warning. Damian chuckled as he recalled overhearing her tell Reverend Jesse James that if wanted to learn to cycle, he'd better do less praying and more pedaling!

Miss Blackwell was formidable, all right. And stubborn. As much as she irritated him on occasion, he admired her tenacity. Especially in regard to Miss Quackenbush. Never had he seen such an uncoordinated body in his life. Who would ever think there were so many ways to fall off a bicycle? The woman's limbs seemed to have a mind of their own. Still, Amanda persisted, patiently putting the poor woman through her paces and receiving precious little in return for her efforts.

Still, as much as he admired her tenacity, he'd prefer it if she were more open-minded.

Hating the Newcastles was as fashionable as the annual Easter parade, but nothing anyone said or did bothered him more than seeing the hatred for his family flash in Amanda's eyes the day he first revealed his identity.

Damn, he should have moved away from the city and changed his name when he'd had the chance! But no, he had to stay and fight. That was his father's way and it was now his way, too.

Meanwhile, he had to live in his father's shadow. He was Phillip Newcastle's son, and as far as people like Amanda Blackwell were concerned, that was the beginning and the end.

Ah, but what he wouldn't give to have her look at him without suspicion and hatred, like she did that day in the park when they first met and she didn't yet know his name.

Like she did on occasion when she thought no one was looking.

More than a little surprised that he cared one way or the other what she thought of him, he moved from the window to his desk.

Earlier he'd built a tower out of playing cards. The fragile tower rose nearly two feet high. It wouldn't take much to topple it, nothing more than the slightest nudge.

He picked up the last card in the pack and, moving his hand ever so carefully, used it to bridge the top of the tower.

He pulled his hand away slowly. Suddenly an idea flashed in his head. By George, why hadn't he thought of this before! He pounded his fist against the top of the desk, sending the playing cards flying in every direction.

"Christopher, Mrs. Winkle, Miss Hannah, come quick!" His son, housekeeper, and nurse were accustomed to these sudden outbursts. Now, as always, they dropped everything and rushed into Damian's study, eager to find out the source of his excitement.

The housekeeper entered the room, drying her hands on her spotless white apron. Her prim high-neck dress and tightly wrapped bun were deceiving. Mrs. Winkle liked nothing better than to drink English ale and share bawdy stories with the farmers at the local tavern.

"What are you carrying on about this time?" she demanded, her clipped English accent barely concealing her fondness for her employer.

Miss Hannah followed close behind, pushing Christopher's wheelchair. "Papa has a brilliant idea!" Christopher announced, his face bright as the midday sun. Nothing livened things up more than one of his father's ideas.

"I would say *brilliant* is a perfect word for it," Damian said approvingly. "Now if you would be kind enough to take your places, I shall regale you with the details."

"What does regale mean, Papa?"

"It means to entertain or bring amusement," Miss Hannah replied.

"Thank you, Miss Hannah, and that's exactly what I intend to do, rain or no rain." He waited until the two women had taken their seats and were properly attentive. Miss Hannah sat on the sofa, facing the fire. The housekeeper arranged herself in an upholstered chair, next to Christopher's wheelchair.

Like a commander about to address his troops, he stood before them, hands clasped behind his back. "Now as you well know, I am in the process of building the tallest habitable building in the world."

"We're going to live on the top floor," Christopher added.

"Indeed we are," Damian said heartily. "The problem I've had is finding a way around the city building codes. As you see here"—he pointed to the model of his building that rose from the mantel—"the code states the height of the building dictates the thickness of the walls. That means that in order to accommodate a twenty-story building, the walls would have to be at least six feet wide. That would leave us with a building no more than ten feet in width. About half the length of this room."

"My word," Mrs. Winkle exclaimed. "Why, that's hardly room enough to turn around in."

"My sentiments exactly. That's why I had hoped to purchase the adjacent property. Unfortunately, the owner refused to cooperate."

"More's the pity," the housekeeper commiserated.

"Ah, but it appears there is an alternative solution." He picked up two playing cards from the floor and moved to the mantel. He stood the cards on end with the utmost care and held them in place with the tips of two fingers. "If I stand an iron bridge truss on end just like this, my problem will be solved."

Miss Hannah's eyes never wavered from the playing cards. "Will that work, sir?" she asked politely. It was obvious she had no idea what a truss was.

"I guarantee it. The building code doesn't limit the height of the foundation. If I set something resembling a bridge truss on end, the foundation will extend the entire height of the building. That means I won't have to worry about the thickness of the walls."

"Will the building be safe, sir?"

"Indeed it shall be. It shall be every bit as sturdy as the East End bridge." The bridge was still in construction, but already it had proven itself capable of withstanding gale-force winds.

"Will we still live on the top floor?" Christopher asked, the freckles on his nose bunched in worry.

Damian lifted his son from his wheelchair and held him in his arms. "Absolutely. And from the top floor, you'll see the whole wide world."

Damian wasted no time before beginning work on his plans. His bridge truss idea would cost a small fortune in steel and rivets, but he would no longer be restricted by the current building code or have to concern himself with purchasing Miss Blackwell's property.

This latest plan would gain him additional space, and over time, that alone would pay for itself. By George, this was going to work!

His thoughts were interrupted by the clattering sound of wheels on the cobbled drive. Frowning at the interruption, Damian rose from his desk to peer out the window at the hack. Who beside Detective Grape would be so foolish as to come calling on such a dismal day?

Damian watched in curiosity as a cloaked figure dashed from the hack and ran across the cobbled court to his front door. Calling to his housekeeper to bring a pot of hot tea for the traveler, Damian hurried to open the door before his guest had a chance to knock.

He couldn't believe his eyes. "Miss Blackwell!"

"I knew it!" She glared at him, her eyes lit with anger. "I knew your building would bring me nothing but trouble. You're no better than your father." She raised her arms and lunged forward, striking him on the chest with her fists.

Taken by surprise, he grabbed her by the wrists and yanked her close. She tilted her head back. Breathless with rage, she regarded him with cold fury, but he was momentarily distracted by the tiny raindrops on her lashes.

"Take your hands off me, you brute!"

"I would be happy to do so, Miss Blackwell, if you would kindly return the favor."

Confusion clouded her face, and for one heart-stopping moment she looked soft and vulnerable. Feeling something stir inside, some part of him that had lain dormant for a very long time, he was greatly relieved when she pulled her hands away from him and resumed shouting. He found Miss Blackwell much easier to handle when she was being her usual spitfire self.

"Do take a seat and make yourself comfortable," he said. "You can shout just as loud sitting down as you can standing up." He left her standing by the entranceway and went to toss another log into the fireplace. "My housekeeper's making tea."

Her eyes widened incredulously. She couldn't have looked more shocked had he asked her to take off her clothes. Seeing that she was soaked to the skin, he decided that wasn't a bad idea. He yanked the quilt off the couch and tossed it to her. "You'd better take off your wet clothes before you catch your death of cold."

She sputtered and threw the quilt on the floor.

He shrugged and turned back to the fire. "Have it your way. The tea should be here momentarily."

"I'm about to lose my school and you want me to have tea!"

Not sure he'd heard right, he straightened. "What are you talking about? Why are you going to lose your school?"

Her eyes flashed with blue fire and he was sorely tempted to step out of the way of the flying sparks. "It's falling in the hole! I know you wanted my property, but to steal it from right under my very nose . . ."

He couldn't believe his ears. "Are you saying . . . ?"

She gave a curt nod. "That's exactly what I'm saying. And if you don't do something fast, I'm going to lose everything!"

Cursing beneath his breath, he grabbed a rubber coat from a wall hook and shoved his hands into the sleeves. "How long since you were at the site?"

"An hour, maybe less."

A lot could happen in an hour. He turned to his housekeeper, who had just walked into the room carrying a tray. "Mrs. Winkle, please tell my son I have business in town." Without another word, he dashed out the door.

Chapter 14

What a mess! The situation was far worse than anything Damian could have imagined. He and his foreman stood ankle-deep in floodwater, grimly assessing the damage.

It was still raining steadily, but the wind had died down. He'd stopped at the Kirkpatrick Boardinghouse on the way to the site to inform his foreman, Caleb White, of the problem. Several members of the construction crew lived at the same boardinghouse, which allowed White to gather his workforce quickly, and he and his men arrived at the site shortly after Damian.

Amanda was waiting at the curb in front of the school when Damian rode up on his horse. Her face hidden by the hood of her cloak, she calmly pointed out the area of most concern. She spoke in an unemotional voice that was a far cry from the one she'd used earlier. Under the circumstances—and given the fact she was standing knee-deep in water—she looked remarkably calm. He didn't know whether to laugh or to applaud her, but she had his admiration.

After organizing his workers, he tramped back through the mud and raging waters to reach her side. It had started to rain harder, and since his arrival, more dirt had washed into the gaping hole. "I'll have someone take you home."

"I'm not leaving," she said quietly. "Tell the men they'll find hot coffee inside."

She started to turn, and he laid his hand on the rain-soaked sleeve of her hooded cape. "It could be dangerous," he said. "I don't want to have to worry about you."

She glanced up at him, her face pale in the waning gray light of day's end. It would soon be dark. "Then don't." She lowered her head against the rain and walked the short distance to her school.

Cursing under his breath, he stood guard until she made it safely inside before grabbing a shovel from the back of a wagon and hurrying to join the others.

All night long, the men took turns coming to her school. Amanda kept a pot of fresh coffee brewing and the fire going in the coal stove so the men could warm themselves.

Damian had persuaded a local baker to deliver trays of fresh-baked cinnamon rolls and loaves of bread to the school, and the workers ate hungrily.

They were a strong and sturdy group of men, of many nationalities. Most had immigrated from Ireland, Germany, and Scotland and went by colorful names such as Big Pete and Blade. One man spoke with a thick accent, and though she would never attempt to spell his name, it sounded like *Checkers-wally-brush*.

Amanda particularly liked Caleb White, whom she recognized as Damian's foreman. She had seen him many times on the site, of course, but never before had occasion to talk to him. His impish charm and blue-eyed, blond-haired good looks landed him close to the top of Amanda's list of eligible bachelors, and she had already set to work, mentally, trying to come up with a suitable mate for him from among the young women of her acquaintance.

"You seem very young for so much responsibility," she said.

"I'm not that young," Caleb replied. "I'll be twenty-one come June."

"Twenty-one?" Amanda considered all the women enrolled in her school. The majority were matronly women married to railroad and mining tycoons, many of whom had built fine houses on Fifth Avenue. But some, like pretty Miss Priscilla Parkerdale, were in need of suitable beaus and would no doubt find Mr. White to their liking. "I suppose you'll be taking yourself a bride soon."

Caleb grinned and helped himself to a cinnamon roll. "Not me, Miss Blackwell, I'm not the marrying type."

"Is that so?" Amanda regarded the young man with a practiced eye, and noting with approval his efforts not to drip on her floor, she moved him up a notch on her list of potential husbands. No man worth his salt admitted to being the marrying type, so she wasn't fazed in the least by his protests. She could name at least a half-dozen happily married men who had previously declared marriage out of the question.

"Do you have your bicycle badge?" she asked.

He brushed the sticky sweet frosting from his hands and reached for his coffee cup. "I've been meaning to get it."

"I would be happy to arrange lessons around your schedule. Perhaps"—she glanced at her calendar—"before you start work. Of course I could always arrange to teach you after work, if it's not too late, but traffic is worse then."

"It shouldn't be too late. Mr. Newcastle insists that once we start building, we'll work only eight-hour days."

"That would be wonderful," Amanda said. The labor unions had been making demands for shorter work weeks, but with little success. The vast majority of employers routinely expected employees to work sixty or seventy hours a week, some even longer, and few were willing to cut hours back to the recommended forty-hour week.

"Mr. Newcastle firmly believes that working too many hours impairs judgment. He says that's how mistakes occur." He leveled a steady gaze at Amanda. "He's a good man, that one. I'm lucky to be working for him."

"Not everyone would agree," she said, though without her usual rancor. Loyalty counted, and though she considered Caleb White's regard for his employer misplaced, she mentally moved him to the top of her eligible bachelor list.

"That's true, Miss Blackwell. But they would be wrong."

Sensing an argument brewing, she quickly changed the subject. "Unless you object, I recommend the early morning hours. That way we can ride in the park. Since I've taken on more students, time is limited, but I could schedule our lesson for six in the morning." Though she and Caleb had strongly opposing opinions on Damian, she was more convinced than ever he would make a good husband, and she decided to set to work at once finding him a bride.

Caleb drained his coffee cup and stood. "Six seems a mite early . . ."

"Six-thirty? Of course that means you'll only get a half-hour lesson . . ."

"Six-thirty would be fine."

Amanda wrote his name in her notebook. If she ever got used to the odd placement of keys on the typewriter, she'd type the list of her students. "There," she said. "That makes it official." The hard part was going to be trying to convince Miss Parkerdale to change her lessons from a civilized two in the afternoon to the unearthly morning hour. But since Miss Parkerdale was taking evening classes at the YWCA, Amanda couldn't think of any other way to get the two together.

Caleb walked to the door and turned, his face serious. "He likes you."

Amanda had no idea whom he was referring to. "I beg your pardon?"

"Mr. Newcastle . . . he likes you. Once you get to know him, you'll like him, too." He left quickly, closing the door after himself.

Surprised and strangely touched by the young man, she was even more determined to introduce him to

Miss Parkerdale. Why, the two would make a perfect match! She had no idea how she knew this; she just did. She only wished she had thought to ask Mr. White his opinion of redheads.

The door flew open and Damian Newcastle stepped inside. For some odd reason, his presence seemed to absorb the air, and she had a difficult time catching her breath.

He pulled off his dripping raincoat and hung it over the back of a ladder-back chair. His face pinched with exhaustion, he walked over to the stove and held his hands over the heated grate. "We've placed planks over the hole and piled sandbags along your property line. Your school's safe."

She sighed with relief. "Thank you." Her eyes locked with his for an instant before she turned and reached for the coffeepot on the stove. The room seemed impossibly crowded and the soft light of the gas lamp only added to the feeling of intimacy.

"I apologize, Amanda. I should have known something like this could happen."

His apology surprised her, which is probably why she murmured something absurd about no harm being done. His sardonic manner she could handle, but not his gentleness and certainly not his sincerity.

Shaken by her conflicting emotions, she handed him a mug of hot coffee, her hand shaking. He accepted the mug from her with a grateful nod, his fingers brushing against hers. She shivered and stepped back.

"You're cold," he said, and his look of concern almost ripped away the last of her defenses. "Stand closer to the stove. I won't bite."

"I'm all right," she said, though she took his advice. She wasn't afraid to stand next to him. Of course she wasn't. Not in the least!

He wrapped both hands around the mug as if seeking the warmth it offered. She only wished he wouldn't look at her as if he could read her mind. "What you did for my men tonight, taking care of them . . . it means a lot to me." His gaze traveled over her face.

It had been a long night and she was tired, which probably explained why his soft, velvety voice was as enticing and soothing to her taut nerves as a sweetly sung lullaby.

"I only did what anyone would have done given the same circumstances, Mr. Newcastle," she murmured.

"Damian." This time his voice had a seductive quality. Lord, that's all she needed. "Call me Damian."

Unable to catch her breath, she met his gaze. She didn't want to call him by his given name. She wanted to call him Newcastle so as not to forget for a single moment who he was and the part his father played in her father's death. He moved closer and her heart began to pound. She chanted in desperate silence. Newcastle, Newcastle, Newcastle!

She was determined to keep repeating his name until it had the desired effect. She didn't care how hard her heart pounded or her lips ached, she was not going to do something she would later regret.

He studied her face questioningly, then dropped his gaze to her mouth. She bit down hard on her lower lip. Buttons to dollars! If he was going to look at her like that, he might just as well kiss her and be done with it!

"You need to get some sleep," he said.

Sleep. Yes, that's what she needed. He startled her by pressing his palm against her face, but not enough to make her pull away. Instead, she held herself rigid. For all the good it did her! Almost against her will, *entirely* against her will, she found herself succumbing to the warmth of his touch, and before she knew it, her eyes closed. Her mind scrambled for some measure of sanity. Newcastle, Newcastle . . . "Newcastle!"

She shouted his name and he jumped back, startled, knocking the daguerreotype of Donny off the desk. "What the—"

"Oh!" She covered her mouth with her open hand, staring at him over her fingertips. She felt so unlike herself, all fluttery, both hot and cold at the same time. "I was thinking out loud," she offered by way of explanation. "I prefer . . . to call you Mr. Newcastle."

He gave her a strange look. "Well, if you feel that passionately about it——" He stood the frame back up, his gaze lingering on Donny's image. "Now that's a fine-looking lad."

She felt a sense of sisterly pride. "That's my brother, Donny."

"Your brother?" He studied her as if to check for a family resemblance. "How old is he?" He sounded genuinely interested, his voice normal, thank goodness, with none of its earlier seductive silkiness.

She hesitated a moment before answering. "Twelve." He was as tall as any twelve-year-old, but it was hard for her to recall his true age. Mentally, he was but a young child.

Damian looked puzzled, as if he wondered why it took her so long to recall her brother's age. "Does he live with you?"

She nodded. "That's why this school is so important to me. It's our sole means of support."

"I know your school's important." The gentleness of his voice, not to mention the understanding in his eyes, made her practically melt. "It must be difficult for an unmarried woman to raise a child and run a business. Even a woman as resourceful as yourself."

"It's not easy," she admitted. Nor was it easy standing so close to him, and though she stepped back, she tried not to look obvious.

"What made you open up a cycling school?"

She reached for the button she kept on the corner of her desk for good luck. "Vincent gave me this button on the first day we met." She dropped the button into his open palm.

"Vincent? The button vendor, right?"

"Yes. He's been a good friend. The button turned out to be an answer to a prayer. That's what gave me the idea to open up a cycling school."

Damian held the button to the light. "What a relief

he didn't give you a button with something more ominous painted on it, like a pistol."

She lowered her lashes. "Do you think I might have opened up a shooting school?"

"Knowing you, yes." He pressed the button back into her palm and she quickly pulled her hand away.

"Oh, for goodness' sake," he said, setting his cup down. "Let's get this over with so we can both relax."

"Get what over—"

Before she could finish her question, he pulled her into his arms and pressed his mouth to hers.

It was the most shocking thing that had ever happened to her—and the most thrilling. After taking a moment to adjust to the pleasing feel of his lips on hers, she promptly kissed him back.

He lifted his head and looked at her in surprise, a slow smile curving his mouth. "Well, now. That's more like it."

He covered her mouth again, this time taking complete possession of her lips. Warm flames of ecstasy spiraled through her and her pulse leaped with excitement. She rose to her toes, leaning into his kiss, and tried with all her heart to ignore the flicker of sanity that tiptoed on the edge of her consciousness. *Newcastle, Newcastle, Newcastle.*

She even got up the nerve to wind her arms around his neck, but that did nothing to still the voices inside.

How dare he take advantage of her?

Oh, but his lips feel so utterly delicious.

This is insane!

But, dear God, what would happen if he put his hand—

It must stop! Absolutely must. I must make him stop. And I will—of course I will.

Later!

For now, at least, she was content to linger in his arms just a wee bit longer. . . .

He pulled his mouth away first, though he took his own sweet time in doing so, waiting till they were both out of breath and gasping for air.

"Do you still insist upon calling me Newcastle?" he asked.

Sanity returned full force. She pulled out of his arms, grabbed the tray of baked goods and shoved it at him, forcing a barrier between them. It took her a moment to realize the strained look on his face had nothing to do with the pastry; the edge of the tray had hit him beneath his waist.

"Oh." Her gaze dropped to the point of contact and she blushed. Glory be! The man was fully aroused! A pleasurable shiver rippled through her, making her tremble from the top of her head to the tip of her toes. When she finally managed to pull her gaze away, she found him watching her, his eyes aglow. Lord, if her heart didn't take to spinning like a weather vane in gale winds.

"Won't . . . won't you have a cinnamon roll, Mr. Newcastle?"

He stared at the tray as if it were a loaded gun before finally taking a roll.

She set the tray down—dropped it, actually—and turned back to the stove, hiding her burning face. Lord, he wanted her and she wanted him and it wasn't right. He was a Newcastle. *A Newcastle!*

She frantically shoveled coal through the open door as if she'd been given the sole responsibility of moving a locomotive up a mountain.

"Are you going to ignore what just happened between us, Amanda?"

Though he spoke softly, she jumped and spun around to face him, holding the shovel leveled at him like the barrel of a shotgun. His palms facing her, he looked ready to dive under the desk. "Be careful with that thing."

She had no intention of hitting him, but neither did she intend for him to step one inch closer. The look in his eyes told her that any future kisses would lead to something more. She didn't trust herself to check the area beneath his waist. Nor did she dare answer his question.

"I'd prefer you call me Miss Blackwell."

"If I promise to call you that, would you put down the damned shovel?"

She dropped the shovel into the coal bin. "Would you like some more?"

His eyes smoldered with heated interest. "More?"

She quickly reached for the coffeepot so he would not misunderstand her meaning. "More coffee?"

"What a relief. I thought you were offering more cinnamon rolls." He held out his cup and she filled it, spilling coffee on the floor.

"Perfect, as always," he said.

Her lashes flew upward and she caught the revealing lights in his eyes before he had time to hide them. He knew, damn it, knew what he was doing to her, and he was enjoying every minute of it. But then, come to think of it, so was she.

She set the pot back on the stove and stood with her back toward him. She was shaking, still, but otherwise she was remarkably controlled. Now all she had to do was face him and tell him in no uncertain terms that he was not to kiss her ever again.

"It sounds like the rain is letting up."

It was just the opening she needed. She spun around to find him watching her. Well, let him watch. See if she cared. *I won't look below his waist. I won't!*

"Amanda . . . eh . . . Miss Blackwell, so tell me, are we going to carry on as if nothing happened?"

It was never a good sign when a man wanted to talk about a kiss. It meant he was putting too much stock in it. Now she had no choice but to set matters straight. She couldn't let him think his kiss was anything more than a friendly interlude. "You . . . you better go. I'm sure you must be exhausted." There! She'd done it! If he didn't know before he couldn't mess with Amanda Blackwell, he knew it now!

He lifted a dark brow. "Is this how you treat every man who kisses you?"

"Only the ones who kiss me without my permission."

A slow grin inched across his face. "I can hardly

wait to see how you kiss when you grant permission. Next time, eh?"

"There won't be a next time."

"There'll be a next time, Amanda. You can count on it."

She didn't know what to say, and much to her horror her gaze inadvertently dropped down to the area no lady should be caught looking at.

"There'll be a next time for that, too," he added.

Her lashes flew up and her mouth dropped open. Liquid fire pulsed through her veins and she felt a traitorous spot of color flare on each cheek.

He chuckled. "I think I better go before you throw something at me." He reached for his raincoat. "Or worse, before you offer me more cinnamon rolls."

"I wouldn't think of throwing anything. And lucky for you, I don't own a shooting school."

"I doubt you could have done more damage with a shotgun than you did with that damned pastry tray." He laughed softly. "I love it when you look at me that way. All angry and indignant. Some say there's a very thin line between love and hatred. I wonder how thin that line really is."

"Not thin enough."

"Come, come, Amanda. Does my being a Newcastle really matter that much to you?"

Something suddenly occurred to her, something that shocked her so much, she could hardly answer him. "You don't know, do you?" She'd simply assumed— "You have no idea who my father was!"

"Your fa—" He knitted his brow, his gaze boring into her. "Do I know your father?"

"My father was at the Continental the night the balcony collapsed."

The color literally drained from his face. "I see." He looked shaken. "Was he—"

"He died that night."

"Amanda, I didn't know. I'm so sorry."

"I don't want your sympathy."

"What do you want from me, Amanda? Tell me."

"Nothing." She fought to keep the tears at bay. "I want nothing from you. Your father's in jail and that's all I can ask for. Please, just leave me alone."

The door flew open and Moose entered, stomping his feet until a small puddle formed beneath him. "I heard the school was in danger." He glanced at Amanda before shifting his gaze to Damian. "I guess the rumors were true."

"You needn't worry. The school is safe," Damian said, his steady gaze never leaving her face. "And so is its owner." He donned his raincoat and headed for the door.

Moose pulled off his dripping rubber coat. "Lordy mussy, what's that about your safety, Miz Mandy? Were you in danger?"

Amanda took a deep breath and willed her heart to stop its erratic dance. "Only for the briefest moment."

Damian studied the paper in his hand. He moved closer to the gaslight on his desk, but there was no mistaking what he saw. The name Harold Blackwell practically jumped off the paper, number twenty-three on the list of victims.

He'd read over the names shortly after the accident, and had kept the list hidden away in the portfolio along with Grape's monthly reports, the transcripts of the trial, and the newspaper clippings.

Now, with the sound of Amanda's voice still ringing in his ears—and the pain on her face etched in his memory—he read each name in turn.

He should have known, by God. He should have known the first day they'd met that Amanda Blackwell had good reason to hate the Newcastles. She wasn't the kind of woman to make a judgment based on public opinion.

Damn! Would it never end? One blasted night, one horrifying moment, and his world had changed forever. His son was in a wheelchair, his father in prison, and his wife dead.

He didn't even want to think what that night meant in terms of Amanda.

Feeling drained and exhausted, he slid the list back into its portfolio. Amanda. She had practically exploded at his touch, and her lips . . . God, her lips. He exhaled. "Deny it all you want, Miss Blackwell, but there *is* something you want from me."

Surprised to find himself recalling Amanda's burning kisses with an aching sense of longing, he turned off the gas lamp. But even in the darkness he could see her, feel her, smell her sweet fragrance. It wasn't a good sign. If he didn't watch himself, the little spitfire was likely to steal his heart. Indeed, she almost had!

How could he possibly have known how wonderful she'd feel in his arms? Or guess how she would set his heart aflame and his blood coursing through his veins like hot lava?

Now that he knew she was related to one of the victims, she was a complication he didn't want and probably could ill afford.

He climbed the stairs, stopping by the first bedroom to check on Christopher before walking down the hall to his own room. Stripping out of his still-damp clothes, he threw himself across the mattress, naked.

The springs of his bed creaked beneath his weight and the shutter outside his window banged, but his mind was miles away, riveted back in time to the night the balcony collapsed.

What an unbelievable nightmare. Nothing, not even the passing of time, erased the memories of that night.

He'd searched frantically for his son, pulling bodies out from beneath wood and masonry until his hands bled and his back ached. He had personally touched each and every one of the victims, and one or two had even died in his arms, murmuring their last words. Which one, dear God, had been Amanda's father?

He couldn't begin to guess, but one thing he did know: he was more determined than ever to find the person or persons responsible for the collapse of the balcony.

I won't rest, Amanda. Not until the hatred for my family is gone from your eyes.

Resisting the temptation to think of what he'd rather see in her eyes instead, he rolled out of bed and slapped cold water on his face. He couldn't sleep until he'd talked to that damned private investigator to whom he'd paid good money.

This time Grape better have something to report!

Chapter 15

The rain stopped that Wednesday night and by Friday the last of the clouds had disappeared and the waterlogged city began to dry out beneath the spreading warmth of a clear blue sky.

On Monday morning Damian watched his men mop up and felt a thrill of excitement. He'd spent the weekend going over his new idea with his foreman. With any luck, they would be ready to start working on the iron foundation the following week.

He knew the risks, knew better than anyone all the things that could go wrong. If his idea of shifting the primary weight from masonry walls to a strong metal skeleton frame worked, it would revolutionize the entire construction industry.

Still, his methods were unproven and anything could happen. This is what had kept him twisting and turning every night for the last week.

What if something went wrong? He couldn't live with himself should another tragedy occur. It was this worry that kept him pacing a circle around his property in the wee hours of the morning while the city slept.

It's what kept him checking and rechecking the mathematical equations he'd worked out to determine stress loads. It's what made him check each concrete block, steel beam, and rivet to assure the highest possibly quality. It's why any man not following the elaborate safety procedures Damian had taken such pains to devise was immediately reprimanded and repeat offenders fired. He trusted nothing and no one.

Still, fear gnawed at him like a dockside rat. He remembered the pains his father had taken before and during the construction of the Continental Theater. Disaster struck, regardless.

Damian sighed and pinched his aching forehead with his fingers. No matter how many times he checked everything, he couldn't rid himself of the nagging feeling he'd overlooked something. And so the agony continued. . . .

Amanda resumed her classes that bright Monday morning with the arrival of Miss Quackenbush.

It was the worst possible way to begin a week. It was true, lessons had been canceled because of rain, but this was no excuse for the woman to forget everything she'd learned, even something so elementary as how to mount a bicycle. Amanda had to start over from the very beginning.

Perhaps some things were, as her father often said, not meant to be. She wondered if forcing such things might be tempting fate. Of course, Amanda wasn't thinking about Miss Quackenbush, though surely the same principle applied.

No, indeed, it was Damian Newcastle who occupied her mind. Damian whose kisses continued to burn upon her lips.

With a tight grip on the handlebars, Amanda rolled Miss Quackenbush's bicycle through the many puddles left by the rain, toward the old arsenal near Sixty-third and Fifth. The ground around the lake was still soaked, and already her cork-soled boots were covered in mud. Fortunately the area around the arsenal was relatively dry.

The large redbrick building had been used for many purposes throughout the years. Most recently, it had housed live critters while the present zoological gardens were under construction. Now the building stood empty.

Small wire cages, each one filled with a different species of rodent or bird, were arranged in neat rows beneath a canopied walk in the zoological gardens a short distance from the arsenal. An assortment of hooved animals, mainly sheep and goats, were contained within the confines of a fenced area. Three buffalo were tied to a nearby tree. The woolly heads, shoulders, and humps seemed out of proportion to the animals' small rumps and wispy tails.

The zoo was comprised of a small collection of animals by most standards, but the animals looked healthy and attracted many visitors daily.

"Careful!" Amanda cautioned. Miss Quackenbush had veered her bicycle alarmingly close to one of the cages. "Steer to the right. The right, Miss Quackenbush!"

Miss Quackenbush jerked the handlebars one way and then the other, showing no understanding of physics and a blatant disregard for logic. Any hope she would be ready to ride in the Fourth of July parade was dashed for good.

"Pedal. Come on, you can do it." Amanda gave the bicycle a push. "And steer!"

Miss Quackenbush wobbled but she kept going. "That's the way!" Amanda said excitedly. "Faster!"

They had just about passed the last of the cages when the front wheel of the bicycle hit a brick border. Miss Quackenbush cried in alarm and sailed over the handlebars, graceful as a three-winged bird. She landed facedown in the mud between two knock-kneed camels.

"Oh, no!" Amanda blew her whistle frantically. "Help! Come quickly! Someone!"

The camels galloped around the enclosure in a strange uneven gait, splashing mud in every direction. In a nearby cage, a grizzly bear stood on its hind legs and let out a frightening roar.

Fearing the fierce-looking animal would crash through the wooden bars, Amanda put as much distance as possible between herself and the bear.

Two zookeepers dressed in brown uniforms and beaked hats came running down the path. The taller of the two men scrambled over the fence of the camel yard and ran to Miss Quackenbush's side. He lifted the squawking woman over his shoulder like a sack of newly milled flour.

"Put me down at once!" she sputtered, her face covered in mud.

The zookeeper handed her over the fence to the other man, who promptly and unceremoniously deposited her on the still-wet ground.

Miss Quackenbush ranted and raved and kicked her feet. "I have never been so humiliated in all my life!"

Mimicking her, the monkeys in the nearby cage chattered wildly, swinging back and forth between the branches of a tree. In another fenced-off section, prairie dogs dived headfirst into little dirt mounds, their hind legs flashing in midair before disappearing.

"Are you all right, ma'am?" the younger of the two zookeepers asked, his mustache twitching as if he were holding back the urge to laugh.

"I am *not* all right!" Miss Quackenbush exclaimed. "That camel spit at me." She glared at the larger of the two camels. The animal eyed her back.

"That's Sheik. He tends to do that on occasion," the zookeeper explained. "I don't think he means to be offensive."

Amanda regarded the camel with suspicion. Judging by the way Sheik was glaring at Miss Quackenbush, she was willing to bet dollars to buttons the camel meant offense and would spit again with little provocation.

Amanda thanked the zookeepers, and after the two men had hurried off, she sat down on a bench and motioned Miss Quackenbush to join her. It was time to have a serious talk. "I think perhaps you should find yourself another cycling teacher."

It was the first time Amanda had ever considered giving up on a student. But she had to consider Miss

Quackenbush's well-being. She could no longer in good conscience let things continue as they were.

"Nonsense, Miss Blackwell. If I get another teacher, I'll have to start over."

"We start over every time we have a lesson, Miss Quackenbush. I'm afraid at this rate you won't be ready for the Fourth of July parade." If these accidents and near misses continued, Miss Quackenbush might well be dead and buried by that time.

"If we sit here jawing all day, I won't be ready for the Christmas parade, either." The woman stood, straightened her crooked hat, and went to search for her wayward bicycle.

Officer Thorny rode up on his horse and stopped to talk to the zookeepers. The pompous look on his face could only mean one thing: he was about to unleash one of his long-winded diatribes on park rules.

"Miss Quackenbush!" Amanda called, scurrying along the path, away from the policeman. "Wait for me."

Unfortunately, Old Thorny caught sight of her before she made her escape. "Just a minute, Miss Blackwell!" I want a word with you! Halt in the name of the law!"

Amanda spent the next two days avoiding Old Thorny *and* Damian. Though Moose effectively kept the irate policeman off her trail, even he was powerless to save her from the strange spell Damian had cast over her.

Each time she caught sight of Damian, it seemed as if the pull between them grew that much stronger. He projected a commanding energy that attracted her attention like a magnet.

Moose was aware something out of the ordinary was going on and made no bones about it. "You can deny it all you want," Moose said, after confronting her with his suspicions. "There's no mistakin' the way you two fawn at each other. I'd say you were a-spooning."

Her temper snapped, but she was more furious at herself than at her assistant. "His father was responsi-

ble for the death of my father! How could you possibly
think I'd be romantically interested in him?"

"If Mr. Damian Newcastle was respons'ble for any
wrongdoin', he'd be in prison with his pa," Moose
pointed out.

She gritted her teeth. She hated it when Moose resorted to logic. "Just because the court couldn't prove
Damian was directly involved with his father's fraudu-
lent business doesn't mean he's innocent."

"It does in the eyes of the law."

Moose was right, of course. Damian wasn't guilty
of any wrongdoing, unless there was a law against arrogance. Or kissing a woman who didn't—well, almost
didn't—want to be kissed. It was wrong of her to hold
him responsible for her father's death.

She owed him . . . not an apology, certainly . . . but
a clarification. Yes, that was it. She would simply explain that under the circumstances, it seemed wrong
to get involved with him. Simple as that. Refraining
from accusations, name-calling, and placing blame, she
would make it clear there would be no more kisses.

Her shoulders thrown back, she took a deep, brac-
ing breath, then marched outside and practically
bumped into him.

"Why, Miss Blackwell. I was looking for you." He
was dressed in an olive-green frock coat, green checkered pants, and a gold silk vest. The brim of his tall
top hat shaded his face, but did nothing to hide his
amused look.

"You were?"

"Yes, indeed. I wanted to apologize for the other
night. I should have known about your father. I hope
you don't think ill of me."

"Well . . . I—"

He held out his hand. "No hard feelings?"

Congratulating herself for handling the awkward situation with perfect poise, she allowed him to shake
her hand. She was profoundly relieved she didn't have
to spell out the reasons why he was not to kiss her
again.

He pulled his hand away and nodded with satisfaction. "From now on, things will be different, I promise you."

"I'm very happy to hear you say that, Mr. Newcastle. I'm sure you understand now why it was necessary for me to pull away the other night."

"Pull away?" He stared at her in confusion before a flicker of understanding crossed his face. "Oh, you mean when I kissed you? You pulled away? Really?" He looked completely astonished. "Well, what do you know? I have to give you credit, Miss Blackwell. You're such a lady, I didn't even notice."

"I—I tried to be discreet," she stammered. "I didn't want to hurt your feelings."

"That's damned thoughtful of you. I can't tell you how many women have pulled away from my kiss with no regard for my feelings whatsoever."

She stared at him, openmouthed, not knowing how to respond. How many women had he tried to kiss, for goodness' sake?

"One woman actually slapped my face. I ask you, Miss Blackwell, what kind of manners is that? I tell you, it does my heart good to know there're still ladies like yourself."

"Yes, well . . ." He was the first person to ever accuse her of being a lady! "As long as you agree that nothing like that will ever happen again."

"Oh, I didn't say it wouldn't happen again. I just said next time will be different. Good day, Miss Blackwell."

Her mouth flapped up and down like a broken-hinged shutter. Fuming, she glared after him. "You kiss me again, Mr. Newcastle, and I'll show you just how unladylike I can be!"

He stopped and turned and the grin on his face was pure evil. "I look forward to it, Miss Blackwell." Doffing his hat, he continued on his way, leaving her to stare after him.

Oooovvooooh. Hands on her waist, she felt the steam coming out of her ears. If he thought for one

moment she would stand by and let him have his way
with her, he'd better think again!

"Miss Blackwell—"

"What!" Amanda snapped, scaring poor Priscilla
Parkerdale practically out of her wits.

"I . . . I just wanted t-t-to tell you I was ready for
my lesson," Priscilla said, apologetically.

"Yes, yes, of course. I'm sorry. I . . . my mind was
elsewhere. Let's get started."

Next time will be different. His words repeated themselves over and over in her mind during the next few
days until she was ready to scream.

Different, how? How many ways could a man kiss
a woman? And why in the world was she wasting so
much time thinking about it? She would never let him
kiss her again, not ever!

Just to be on the safe side, she decided to avoid him
whenever possible. This was easier said than done, but
not nearly so difficult as ignoring him.

Damian was the first person she saw every morning
as she opened her school, and she wouldn't be a bit
surprised if he planned it that way. Naturally, she ignored any attempts on his part to draw her into conversation, but he never failed to make her heart
beat faster.

At the end of every day, he called to her as she
locked up, "Have a pleasant evening." She glared at
him with pure contrariness. She would have any type
of evening she darn well pleased!

Still, she carried the sound of his warm, velvety
voice home with her and then spent the evening thinking about him, remembering his kiss and wondering if
she would ever have the nerve to slap a man in the
face, no matter how deserving he might be.

Things went from bad to intolerable. One moment
she hated him, the next moment she found herself
tallying up his fine qualities. All right, so he was kind
to his men—and they in turn seemed to worship the
very ground he walked on. What earthly difference
did it make? He was a Newcastle and that was all she

needed to know. She wouldn't let him kiss her again if he were the last man on Earth.

To make matters worse, Damian's building was rising faster than tempers on a hot July day. Weeks had passed with little happening, then seemingly overnight a monstrous iron skeleton rose from the ground, reaching unbelievable heights.

The newspaper referred to it as steel-cage construction, and though it sounded like one of those advertisements for women's corsets, she supposed it was as good a name as any.

Damian's building attracted the attention of architects and builders around the world. Oh, yes, indeed, the gaunt steel frame began to tower over Eighth Avenue, dwarfing the trees and nearby farmhouses, and the number of people gathered around the site increased daily.

The tenement buildings and theaters, and even the elevator train with its sixty miles of track, looked like mere miniatures in comparison. No matter where Amanda went, the Newcastle tower commanded the eye with its sheer size. She could even see it from the window of her apartment—providing, of course, she draped herself over the window ledge and craned her neck.

The building hadn't escaped Donny's notice. "Big tree," he said, pulling her downstairs and through the alley so she could see it.

"It's not a tree, Donny. It's a building. A tall, tall building."

Donny repeated the words over and over as if he were trying to grasp the concept. "Tall, tall building."

The infernal noise of riveters brought another round of protests, and the pages of the local newspapers were filled with editorials decrying the project as a blight on the city.

NEW YORK IN DANGER OF BECOMING A VERTICAL CITY! screamed the headlines of the *Tribune*.

One morning she watched the men climb several stories above the ground. Fearing for their safety, she held her breath until each man had reached his destination, and even then, she could hardly relax. Every time a man straddled a beam several floors high, she wanted to faint out of fear for his safety.

She knew most of the men by name. Some had signed up for lessons at her school or simply rented out bicycles. But concerned for their safety, she resisted the urge to call up to them while they worked. She didn't want to do anything to distract or otherwise jeopardize a worker's safety.

Though she hated the building and the noise, she was fascinated by the process, and early one morning she was so engrossed in watching the workers, she failed to notice Damian until he spoke.

"Don't stand so close." He spoke in her ear to make himself heard, and his warm breath on her neck sent rippling waves of heat rushing down the length of her body.

His hand on her arm, he gently drew her away. "Those rivets are close to two thousand degrees. As good as my men are, they have been known to drop one."

Her mouth dry, she gazed up at him. He stood so close, she could see flecks of gold in his eyes as she visually traced the fine lines crinkling out from them. She remembered with startling clarity how his lips felt against hers. It was a memory that grew more vivid in her mind with each passing day.

He lifted his head to gaze at the top of the building, and grateful for the distraction, she followed his lead. "They make it look so easy," she said.

"It's amazing to watch, isn't it? Since no one has ever constructed a building like this before, we're making up the rules as we go along."

"I imagine you're very good at that," she said. "Making up rules."

He grinned, his devastating smile making her heart flutter and his promise that *next time will be different* seem that much more intriguing. "I believe that's something you and I have in common."

He pointed to the men on the third floor. "We decided it works best if the riveters work in gangs of four men each. One man on each team heats the rivets until the metal part glows red. He then grasps the smoking rivet with his tongs and tosses it underhanded to the catcher one floor up."

His voice held an intensity that was mesmerizing. It was easy to see that he was as fascinated with the process as he was with the actual results. "Watch that man up there." No sooner had he directed her attention than a rivet sailed upward.

She held her breath until the catcher caught it midair with his bucket. Only then did she allow herself to exhale. "That's amazing!" she exclaimed.

"We can't see it from here, but the catcher will now pick up the rivet with his tongs and slip it in place with a dolly bar."

No sooner had Damian explained this step when the man he called the driver quickly lifted his pressure hammer. Damian raised his voice to be heard over the loud chattering sound. "The driver smashes the rivet into a wide cap."

"What's *he* doing?" Amanda asked, pointing to a fourth man on the team.

"He's called a punk," Damian explained. "His job is to haul sacks of rivets to the heater and keep the buckets filled with water."

"Why isn't the forge on the same floor as the riveters? Isn't it dangerous to toss hot metal from one floor to the next?"

"I thought the same thing when I first saw them tossing those hot rivets about," he said, his hand still on her arm. "But my men tell me it's easier to toss the rivets to the floor above then to toss them horizontally. I have to admit, I didn't believe it myself at first."

"It's amazing," she said, though her words were drowned out by the pressure hammer.

A bell clanged, indicating the need for another metal girder.

"Would you like a ride to the top?" Damian asked, releasing her arm.

"Certainly not!"

He held his hand out, trying to persuade her. "Come on, Amanda. Where's your sense of adventure?" He glanced upward. "From up there you can see the world."

"I'd rather see the world a little at a time, with my feet placed firmly on the ground."

He dropped his hand to his side and gave a careless shrug. "You're missing the opportunity of a lifetime."

He walked over to the construction site, straddled a metal girder, and waved to the man operating the lift. Slowly, the girder rose off the ground and Damian guided it with his feet. With his windblown hair and devilish grin, he looked as impish as a schoolboy. But there was nothing boyish about the heated look he gave her as he rose upward.

Amanda held her breath until he reached the uppermost floor. Her relief soon changed to dismay when he threw her a kiss. Her heart took to pounding like the pressure hammer and it practically drowned out the riveters. "Of all the cheeky . . . !"

Her composure disrupted, she turned and, mustering up every bit of dignity possible under the circumstances, walked headfirst into an iron pillar. Rubbing her forehead, she glanced back, hoping her clumsiness had gone unnoticed.

Damian grinned and waved and threw her yet another kiss. The shiver that shot through her quite frankly left her breathless and feeling weak.

The man made up his own rules, no question about it, and as much as she hated to admit it, it was one of the things she found so intriguing about him. If he weren't hanging so precariously from the side of the superstructure, she would have been tempted to make up a rule or two of her own—or at the very least, return his kiss!

Chapter 16

The following day, the members of the Wheelers' Cycling Club arrived for their lesson, late as usual. The group was comprised of some of New York's most respected and renowned citizens, including Mayor Ledbetter and the man who hoped to beat him in the next election, William Howard Lockhammer.

"So where is Mr. Lockhammer?" Amanda's voice was drowned out by the sound of a horse-drawn wagon rattling over the cobblestones. She tapped her foot impatiently. She had hoped to run the wheelmen through their routine on the carriage drive in the park, but it was already eight-thirty and bicycles weren't allowed in the park after nine. Old Thorny never made exceptions to the rules, not even for the Wheelers.

"We'll wait another couple of minutes and then we'll begin today's lesson," she said, though it was obvious no one was paying her the least bit of attention.

Clearly the Wheelers were more interested in the high-rise building than in their lesson. The cyclists watched workmen on the tenth floor raise a heavy piece of equipment to the upper level scaffolding with a block and tackle, making the task look amazingly easy.

Mayor Ledbetter clucked his tongue, his beady eyes shifting back and forth over his elongated mustache. His balding head hidden by a red felt cap, he was dressed in the navy blue uniform of the club. Meant for a less robust form, his parole jacket protruded over his barrel-sized stomach. It hardly seemed possible that his birdlike legs, too skinny to fill the white knit stockings, could support his bulky weight.

"I never imagined such a tall building was possible. It hurts my neck just to look at it." The mayor rubbed his neck to illustrate. "If we don't watch out, we'll all be living in terra-cotta canyons. We'll be the laughing-stock of the country. What we need is a statutory en-actment that limits how high these confounded buildings can go."

Reverend Jesse James nodded in agreement. Though the reverend shared the name of a notorious outlaw, few people dared mention it, at least to his face, though certainly not out of consideration for his feelings. Known throughout the city for his fire-and-brimstone sermons, he maintained what he called the Sinners Roll Call. Anyone so foolish as to make snide remarks about his name would likely find himself added to the list posted every Sunday at the back of the church.

He and the mayor seldom saw eye-to-eye. The only thing he had in common with the mayor was his bony knees, which stuck out beneath the fabric of his tight white stockings. "If you ask me, any building rising higher than the Trinity Church cross is sacrilegious."

The mayor was clearly delighted to have yet another argument to add to his own, and he embraced this idea with a vigorous nod of his head. "Yes, yes, Rever-end, that's a good point. I'm sure if you put your mind to it, you'll find something in the scriptures to support this contention."

Amanda had no doubt the reverend would find enough scriptures to sway even the most skeptical dis-believer. He had been known to quote an amazing number of biblical verses that, according to his inter-pretation, strictly forbid women from wearing bloom-ers, riding bicycles, or doing much of anything but bearing children and obeying their husbands.

Dr. Paine adjusted the seat of his high-wheeler. A tall, thin man with pasty white skin and jet-black hair, he nodded gravely. "These tall buildings could pose a health danger. Anyone foolish enough to go to the top floor should be prepared to suffer dizziness and headaches. Maybe even heart failure."

"My word!" the mayor exclaimed. "I never thought of the health risk. Why, you're absolutely right. The air has got to be thinner up there." The wheelmen continued to gawk as they pondered this latest concern.

Reverend Jesse James shook his fist as he was prone to do from the pulpit. "In the name of God, we must put a stop to this madness."

Sergeant Summerset nodded in agreement. As the chief of the United States Signal Service Weather Observatory, he had a vested interest in the building. "I'm sick and tired of having to move my weather station every time someone gets it into their fool head to build a taller building."

"It's a nuisance, all right," the mayor agreed.

"It's a lot more than a nuisance!" the meteorologist argued. "No sooner did I move my station to the Equitable building than I had to move it to the top of the Manhattan Life Building. Do you think it's easy to retrain pigeons?" Summerset's homing pigeons traveled between weather stations, carrying reports of weather conditions up and down the coast.

The weatherman regarded the Newcastle tower with utmost disdain. "Now I'm going to have to move my weather station to the top of that thing."

"Oh, dear," the mayor exclaimed. "You poor man."

Amanda tried to think of something to say that would ease the man's worries. "But you'll be able to see for miles around. You'll probably see a storm coming hours before it reaches us."

Summerset glared at her. "I don't even know if pigeons will roost that high. The hell with the pigeons; I don't even know if *man* can stand it that high."

"You better come in for a physical," the doctor said, looking like a man faced with the prospect of handing out a death sentence.

"You'd be wise not to miss church on Sundays, either," the reverend added. "You'll need all the prayers you can get."

The missing member of the cycling club came rushing up to the school, huffing and puffing like a steam engine. Mr. Lockhammer was a compact man with a walrus-type mustache, thick eyebrows, slick black hair parted straight down the middle, and graying sideburns. He didn't look the least bit concerned at having kept the others waiting.

"You're late," Amanda said, frowning.

Ignoring her, Lockhammer stared up at the highrise and sneered. "Good heavens! Are they ever going to stop building?"

The mayor glared at Lockhammer. He didn't much care for the man who was running against him in the next election and he made no bones about it. "We were just discussing the need for legislation that would limit the height of such buildings."

Lockhammer's eyes blazed hard as steel. "It's going to take more than talk to solve the problem. It'll take good leadership."

"You won't get any argument from me there," the mayor said.

Lockhammer's eyes glittered. "Does that mean I can count on your vote?"

"Count on . . ." The mayor's bushy eyebrows moved up and down like ships on a stormy sea. "Are you out of your mind? I wouldn't vote for you if my life depended on it. If you had your way, we'll all be burrowing under the ground like moles."

"Harrumph! I'll have you know some people think my idea of an underground railroad is brilliant. I'm telling you, it's the only thing that's going to save this city."

The mayor turned almost purple with rage. "And some people think it's a good idea to put an ugly tall statue in the middle of the harbor, but it doesn't make it right!" France's gift to the United States had been a bone of contention between the two politicians ever since it first reached American soil. The enormous arm and three-story-high torch of the Liberty Statue were on display at Madison Square, waiting for the city to raise enough funds to move it to one of the islands.

"We don't need a three hundred foot lady guarding the harbor, and we sure in hell don't need a three-hundred-foot building marring the New York skyline!"

Amanda blew her whistle to stop the escalating argument and took her place in front of the cyclists, hands at her waist. "Gentlemen, if you will kindly form two lines, we'll cross over to the park to begin our drill."

Ignoring her, Lockhammer wasn't about to let the mayor's comments go unchallenged. "You're wrong about the statue, Ledbetter. It would be a symbol of pride for our country. Tall buildings, on the other hand, are nothing but eyesores, built to stroke the egos of small-minded men."

"Really? I thought that was the purpose of politics."

At the sound of Damian's voice, Amanda's legs weakened. He stood taller than any of the other men and had a commanding air that was almost as impressive as the building behind him. His gaze collided with hers before he turned to the pompous politician, and the only thing she could think about was his promise to her that the next time they kissed would be different.

Lockhammer didn't look the least apologetic for his insulting words. If anything, dislike—if not actual hatred—glistened in his eyes as he glowered at Damian. "Make no mistake about it, Newcastle, I intend to see that New York's skyline is kept to a reasonable height!"

"I would say you have to get elected first," Damian replied, and Amanda didn't miss the knife-sharp edge to his words. Damian clearly disliked Lockhammer and he made no effort to hide it. Not that she could blame him, of course; she wasn't particularly fond of Lockhammer herself.

"Gentlemen," Amanda interjected, glaring at Damian. "May I remind you that the Fourth of July parade is only a few weeks away? Now if you will kindly mount your bicycles, we will proceed."

Damian touched his fingers to the brim of his tall hat, then stalked away. Still reeling from Damian's unexpected appearance, she willed herself to breathe.

She turned and faced the cyclists, who had yet to arrange themselves in formation style. Her tolerance pushed to the limit, she blew her whistle hard and gave the group her no-nonsense scowl. "Gentlemen, now!"

This time, the men rolled their bicycles into place and she sighed in relief. It was gratifying to know there were still some things in her life she could control.

Later, after the wheelmen had left, she headed for the area beneath a shade tree where Newcastle stood talking to his foreman.

Damian looked up as she approached, his eyes sparkling. "Why, Miss Blackwell. We were just talking about you."

"That we were, Miss Blackwell," Caleb said.

"Caleb was telling me he's taking cycling lessons. I'm thinking of signing up for classes myself."

Amanda's heart practically stopped. "You want to take bicycle lessons?"

"Yes, unless, of course, you have some objection to taking me on as a student."

She had objections, all right, but she wasn't about to give him the satisfaction of knowing what they were. Instead, she gave him her sweetest smile. "What possible objection could I have?" She tried her best to sound sincere, but the dimple on his cheek deepened. She was greatly relieved when Caleb left. Now she could speak her mind.

"I would appreciate it if in the future you keep your opinions to yourself while I'm teaching a class."

Damian lifted a dark brow. "Now don't go getting

yourself all tied up in a knot, Amanda. This is a public street. I'm quite within my right to answer my critics on public property and you know it."

"You can answer your critics all you want, but it doesn't change a thing. You're putting a great many people's lives in danger. If that building topples . . ."

"It won't."

"No one shares your opinion. Doesn't that tell you something?"

"It tells me you and I have something else in common. Neither one of us is afraid to stray from public opinion." Though he pointed to the iron skeleton overhead, his gaze took a dive down to her controversial bloomers before he glanced at the building. "I have inspected every square inch of steel and cement myself. As I've told you before, Amanda, we use only the best grade of materials."

The best grade of materials. Oh, yes, she'd heard that before. "The best and the safest?" she said skeptically. "Didn't I read in the paper that your father said the very same thing when he testified on his own behalf?"

A muscle tightened at his jaw, but it was the only sign she may have struck a nerve. "My father took every safety precaution possible. Did you know the Continental was the first theater to have asbestos curtains? Ah, I thought not. Then you also don't know that when the city refused to pay for those curtains, my father paid for them out of his own pocket."

"I'm sorry, Damian." The words were out of her mouth before she knew it, and it was hard to know which of them was more surprised.

"Sorry?" He studied her for a moment. "What do *you* have to be sorry for?"

"For . . ." Her mind whirled in confusion. It had been so simple when she could place the blame for her father's death on Phillip Newcastle's doorstep. But things had become more complicated in recent weeks. Now that she had come to know Damian, had seen with her own eyes how his men admired and respected him, it was hard to discount his fervent belief that his father had done no wrong.

But if Phillip Newcastle wasn't to blame for what had happened to her father, then who was?

"Nothing," she said. "I'm not sorry for anything." She turned and hurried away. She had a lot to think about, and that was impossible to do in Damian's presence. He had to be the most distracting man she'd ever met!

"Will tomorrow morning be convenient?" he called after her.

She stopped midstep. "Tomorrow?" She swung around to face him.

"For my cycling lesson."

She gulped, but kept her apprehension hidden. Dear God, let him be bluffing. "I can give you a lesson at eight," she said, knowing full well he started work at that time. "It's the only time available."

His mouth twitched with amusement. "I'll be there."

Chapter 17

The following morning, at exactly five minutes and forty-six seconds before the hour, Damian appeared at the cycling school and tied his horse to the hitching post in front.

Amanda knew the precise moment he arrived because she had been anxiously staring out the window for the last half hour. At the sight of him, her heart thudded. Not wanting to be caught, she quickly raced across the room to her desk and began pecking away at the typewriter.

Damian walked into the classroom with unnerving ease, dressed in a pair of knickerbocker pants. Unlike most men, his powerful legs filled his stockings without a single wrinkle or fold or bony knee in sight. "Morning, Amanda," he said cheerfully, hat in hand.

She looked up, feigning surprise. "Oh, dear, is it time for your lesson already?"

"I'm afraid so," he said with a boyish grin. "Incidentally, I've discovered that typewriters work more efficiently with paper."

Mortified, she rose from her desk. "I'm quite aware of how a typewriter works," she said coolly. "I believe your bicycle is ready." Determined she was not going to let him befuddle her, she led him through the workroom and out the back door.

His bicycle *was* ready. She'd made certain Moose had completely overhauled the largest bicycle she owned. The front wheel measured a full sixty inches across. Even her boldest students had been intimidated by its size. But Damian didn't look the least bit fazed and seemed anxious to begin his lesson.

She stopped him when he placed his left foot on the pedal, prepared to mount. "Not yet," she said in her most efficient, no-nonsense manner. She had made up her mind to treat him as she treated every other student. He would receive neither special favors nor undue attention. "Walk the bicycle first. This will help you grow accustomed to the motion and rhythm of the machine."

Damian wrapped his fingers around the handlebars. "Like this, Amanda?"

She kept her face perfectly composed, but inside she was anything but. "That's right. Now let the bicycle talk to you. That's the way. Keep it perfectly upright. If the bicycle inclines to the right, turn your handle in the same direction." They walked across Eighth Avenue toward the park and Amanda signed the register at the gate before leading him along the winding path. "You're fighting it, Damian. Let it guide you."

"Ah, I see what you mean, Amanda. It's sort of like making love to a woman. A man finds it to his advantage to let her lead the way."

Amanda tried to ignore his brazen comments, but her cheeks flared and her heart pounded. *Next time it will be different.* Unable to keep the unbidden thought at bay, she grew more flustered by the minute.

In an all-out effort to hide her jittery nerves, she took a deep breath, and kept her eyes focused on the path ahead. She would not, could not, let him affect her. She had a job to do, and by George, she intended to do it!

Telling herself everything was under control, even if her pounding heart did make a liar out of her, she inadvertently progressed to the next step faster than was prudent. "I'll hold the bicycle steady while you mount."

Raising one hand to the handlebars, she placed her free hand on the spring in back of the seat. She braced herself, then tightened her hold on the bicycle. It didn't take as much muscle as know-how, but Damian was taller than most, his limbs more powerful.

She worried needlessly, for he mounted the bicycle with unexpected ease. She wished all her students were so easy to teach.

Tilting back her head to gaze up at him, she felt a feminine flutter travel down her body, all the way to her toes. How handsome he looked, perched high— almost majestically—upon the seat, his head framed against the clear blue sky. It was all she could do to keep her mind on her work.

"Am I doing it right, Amanda?"

"Yes, but let your feet dangle. That's the way." Since he had no trouble maintaining his balance, she guided the bicycle along the path, slowly, and accidentally brushed against his leg. The nearness of him made her senses spin, but it couldn't be helped. The safety of her student had to come before any other consideration. "Do you have the feel?"

He glanced down at her, his eyes smoldering with fire. "I believe I do."

She turned to focus ahead. "In that case, place your feet on the pedals."

"Like this?" he asked. Suddenly the bicycle began to oscillate with wild abandon.

"Steer!" she exclaimed in alarm, struggling to hold the bicycle upright. Why, oh, why hadn't she asked Moose to come along?

"I *am* steering!" The bicycle suddenly took off in one direction and Damian dove off in the other. Somehow he managed to wrap his arms around her, taking her with him.

Together they rolled down a grassy knoll, tumbling all the way to the bottom. The wind knocked out of her, Amanda lay on her back. Damian was on top of her, his full weight pressed against her body, his powerful chest flat against her breasts.

Breathing in quick shallow gasps, she tried wiggling her hips, but his long legs were spread on either side of hers, holding her captive. "Damian?" Alarmed by his stillness, she shook him anxiously, searching his face for signs of life.

"Damian! Say something!" When he didn't move or otherwise respond, she frantically reached for the whistle around her neck and blew with all her might. The high-pitched sound pierced the air, and Damian rolled off her quicker than a log rolling downhill.

"Damn!" He covered his ears with his hands. "Are you trying to make me deaf?"

"I was calling for help," she stammered, relief washing over her. He obviously wasn't seriously hurt. She stood and brushed herself off. "When you didn't move or say anything, I thought you were injured." Though Heaven knows he didn't look injured. He didn't even look out of breath.

He watched her with a look of curiosity. "Would you have felt badly if I had been injured?"

"Of course," she said, and because he looked unbearably smug, she couldn't resist adding, "Losing students is bad for business."

"Is that all you're worried about? Your school's reputation?"

She shrugged carelessly. "You're right. I worry needlessly. I doubt your demise would hurt my reputation one iota."

"Probably not," he agreed. "The city would likely give you a medal for ridding it of yet another Newcastle." He winced and rubbed his back, a wicked grin spreading across his face. "Riding a bicycle is a hell of a lot harder than making love, don't you agree?"

"Not if you do it right," she said, her voice deceivingly calm considering the way her emotions were spinning inside.

"Are you going to be as heartless with me as you are with Miss Quackenbush and make me get back on the bicycle?"

If he thought for one minute she could be persuaded by his smile, he would be absolutely right. Oh, he loved this—loved rattling her, saying outrageous things to keep her off balance.

Well, enough was enough! She was the teacher, and as such, it was her responsibility to make certain her student toed the line. "It's the only way," she said, sounding more fiendish than professional.

If he was worried or otherwise intimidated by the threatening tone of her voice, he gave no indication. Instead he gave a casual, good-natured shrug and limped up the hill to retrieve the bicycle. By the time she had brushed the grass off her bloomers, repinned the stray strands of hair that had escaped from beneath her hat, and walked up the grassy slope to the path, he was standing beside his high-wheeler, waiting for her.

"Are you ready, Mr. Newcastle?" she asked.

His eyes seemed to drink her up. "I've been ready."

She inhaled sharply and fought to ignore the magnetic pull that had been evident earlier but was now a tangible force that took all her energy to resist. She was greatly relieved when he mounted the bicycle unaided.

After a rather wobbly start, he suddenly began pedaling around in a perfect circle. "What do you think, Amanda?"

At first she was absolutely astonished, then reality dawned. This whole thing had been a ploy. He was obviously an excellent cyclist. Biting back the impulse to tell him what she thought of him *and* his little game, she decided to give him a bit of his own medicine.

The top-heavy design of the bicycle made riding in circles extremely dangerous. Anything—the least distraction—was likely to topple the rider. Knowing how vulnerable he was, she lifted her open palm and blew him a slow, sensuous kiss, pursing her lips in a way she knew would send him wild. It was a bold and shocking thing for a woman to do.

His eyes widened and his jaw dropped visibly. It did her heart good to see him so clearly astonished. Just as she'd hoped, he lost control of his bicycle. "Yeoow!" He fell in a clattering heap that made Miss Quackenbush's spills look graceful by comparison.

She waited just long enough to make certain he wasn't seriously hurt, then stalked away.

"Amanda, wait." *Damn!*

Leaving the bicycle behind, Damian picked himself up off the ground and limped across the grass after her. His leg hurt, his back hurt. Come to think of it, every blasted bone in his body ached. Next time he rolled about with Amanda, he intended to make damned sure it was on the soft, comfortable surface of a bed. "Amanda!"

Where the hell was she? He stood in place, scanning the park. No one could escape that quickly. Noting the nearby bushes shaking, he grinned to himself. She wasn't going to get away from him that easily.

"Amanda!" He crashed blindly through the tangle of branches, determined to teach her a lesson about who had the upper hand, and found himself hugging a hog—a disgusting and smelly hog! Startled, the animal bolted and Damian landed flat on his stomach, the wind knocked out of him.

Damn! That woman was going to be the death of him yet. Slowly, so as not to further injure himself, he crawled out of the bushes backward on hands and knees, then picked himself off the ground.

Something hit him square on his already sore back. "Ouch!" He spun around, ready to take the maddening woman in his arms and kiss her until she begged for mercy. Only it wasn't Amanda. It was a group of crazed women attacking him.

"What the . . ."

One woman pounded him with her fists and another clobbered him over the head with her parasol.

Bewildered, he held up his arms, trying to ward off their blows. "What the hell is going on? Have you all lost your minds?"

A matronly woman glared at him from beneath a frilly hat. She held her folded parasol over her head, ready to clobber him again at the slightest provocation. "You're a common child thief!"

"You must be mistaken. I . . ." It was then that he noticed the dozen or so wide-eyed toddlers gazing up at him.

One darling blue-eyed rugbug held her arms up. Obviously, she wanted Damian to pick her up. "Da-da."

The child's mother lifted her little one up in her arms and lashed out at Damian. "How dare you!"

"I swear to God, I never saw that child in my life and I certainly never fathered her."

"I should say not!" the woman looked scandalized at the thought. "But you were trying to kidnap her. You called her by name. I heard you with my own ears."

"I did nothing of the sort. I was calling a friend of mine," he explained. "Her name is Amanda."

The little blue-eyed girl trilled again, "Da-da-da!" Another little girl in a white organdy frock and a straw hat left her mother's side and wrapped her arms around Damian's leg.

Damian tried to free himself, but the little tyke held on with all her might. "Don't tell me these children are all named Amanda?" Suddenly seeing the humor, he burst out laughing. He'd heard Amanda was a matchmaker but this was ridiculous. Apparently, her meddling ways had helped populate half of Manhattan.

By the time he'd convinced Officer Thorndike he was not a kidnapper, and had soothed the ruffled feathers of the children's mothers and nannies, he was tempted to wring Amanda's neck. How could she just leave him, one of her students, stranded?

Those crazy women could have killed him. Hell, he could have been trampled to death by the hefty hog! At the very least, he could have been injured. What was he thinking? He *was* injured. What kind of teacher was she?

His hand on the small of his back, he pushed the

bicycle along the path, across Eighth Avenue to Amanda's school. He parked the bicycle outside and hobbled into the classroom. She sat typing, of all things, and showed not one bit of concern for his welfare. The least she could have done is sent a doctor to check on him. "You kissed me!" he said accusingly.

She glanced up, but not before finishing whatever it was she was typing, irritating him no end. This time she'd remembered to put paper in the typewriter. "I did not kiss you. I threw you a kiss."

"Same thing."

"It's not the same thing," she said hotly.

"You made me fall off my bicycle."

"That's exactly what I intended to do. You made a fool of me."

"You left me to the mercy of those crazed women." Amanda blinked. "What crazed women?"

He told her what had happened in the park and then leaned over her desk. "Now, I ask you, Amanda, what kind of teacher would abandon a student?" He grimaced. "Ow."

She rose to her feet, her mouth rounded in concern. "Perhaps you should see a doctor."

He lowered himself onto a chair. "I don't need a doctor. Just a gentle, loving massage will do." He eyed her expectantly. Ah, yes, she was wavering. For all her faults, she had a kind heart and he intended to take full advantage of it. "Ow!" He grabbed the small of his back and leaned forward and groaned. He exaggerated the pain, but not by much.

"Damian!" She hurried to his side and was all fluttery with concern. Well, it was about time. "Are you able to lie on the floor?"

"Maybe—if you help me." He leaned on her, groaning and moaning, until he was facedown on the rag carpet in front of her desk. Aha! He had Amanda Blackwell exactly where he wanted her. After she rubbed his back, he would suddenly become cured and that's when he would pull her into his arms and kiss her, just like he'd promised. That'll teach her to mess with his heart!

She knelt by his side and he shivered as her hand brushed against his shoulder. She leaned over and whispered in his ear. "I'll be right back."

Thinking she was going to turn the sign in the window from OPEN to CLOSED, he sighed happily and grinned to himself. *Take your sweet time, Amanda. I'm not going anywhere.*

She returned a short time later and her hands on his back felt surprisingly strong. "That feels so good," he said softly. "I guess it's not too surprising that someone with the lips of an angel would also have the hands of one."

"That's mighty nice of you to say, Mr. Newcastle."

Damian's eyes flew open at the sound of a male voice, and he rolled onto his back. What the hell was Moose doing here? And where was Amanda?

Moose grinned back at him. "I always knew I had a special touch." He held up his large hands and studied them. "But I ain't never cured anyone this fast. No, sir, not ever."

Chapter 18

In the days that followed, controversy over Damian's building grew to amazing proportions. The *Herald* ran editorials proclaiming the structure of the Newcastle building contrary to the laws of physics. Not to be outdone, the *New York Times* decried the idea of New York becoming a vertical city. Politicians declared themselves either for or against the rising skyline, depending on public reaction, and preachers spurred on by Reverend Jesse James turned the issue of building height into a moral debate.

Every drunk in the city used it as an excuse to guzzle more alcohol, toasting each floor in turn. "Let's 'ave another round for the eighth floor." Then, "Har's to the ninth floor." The jails had never been more crowded.

Still, the steel frame rose daily, like a fast-growing weed. In a very short time, the monstrous steel skeleton had reached its full height.

Though Damian had made his intentions clear from the start, nothing had prepared Amanda for the reality of running a business in the shadow of the mighty giant. It made her dizzy just to look to the top, and sometimes by the end of the day her neck literally ached.

She had nightmares that the mass of steel toppled onto her school, and more than once she had awakened in a cold sweat. Still, the commanding structure captured her imagination, second only to Damian Newcastle.

Hardly an hour went by that she didn't gaze toward the construction site, searching for Damian. Invariably she spotted him on the rafters overhead, or walking back and forth on the ground, his purposeful steps bringing a sense of order to the otherwise chaotic mass of men, equipment, and materials.

She knew the routine of his day as well as she knew her own. He arrived early each morning, long before his men arrived. She knew this because she had fallen into the habit of arriving early herself. Not to watch the goings-on next door—certainly not!—but the parade was little more than two months away and she had scheduled extra classes for the students planning to participate.

The number of students enrolled in her school had increased daily, and she'd had to add evening classes to accommodate the number of people. But she was happy for the business because once the parade was over, most of her wealthy students would leave the city on holiday to escape the summer heat, and would probably not return until summer's end.

After one exhaustingly long day, after her students had left and the last of the rentals had been returned, Amanda stepped outside and locked the door behind her. She half expected to see Old Thorny waiting for her.

Now that the park hours had been adjusted to accommodate the coming summer, the old beak had been on a tirade. The park rules required bicycles to carry lanterns after dark and she always made certain her rentals complied. But there was no pleasing the sparrow cop. Either the lights were too bright or not bright enough. His constant complaints were enough to make her want to scream.

She dropped the key into her reticule and was startled by a nearby movement. She sighed. How foolish of her to think she would sneak away without having to listen to another one of Old Thorny's lectures. "What is it this time?" she asked irritably. "Were the lanterns placed too high or too low?"

The shadowy form stepped into the circle of light cast by a nearby lamppost. "I wouldn't know."

Her heart fluttered in response to Damian's rich, warm voice. "Don't sneak up on me like that. You startled me."

"As well I should. It's dangerous for a woman to walk the streets alone at night."

"Are you referring to pickpockets and muggers or yourself?"

"Come now, Amanda. I know you have little regard for me, but surely you don't consider me dangerous."

Oh, he was dangerous, all right. There was danger in the heated gaze that raked over her, and danger in the soft, all-knowing smile that curved his mouth. There was even danger in the aggressive way he stood, legs apart, as if he meant to prevent her escape.

"I hardly consider you at all," she lied.

"In that case, I'm sure you won't object to my taking you home."

"I don't need your protection."

"Perhaps not. But I'm sure my company would be much more to your liking than sitting in a crowded horsecar would be."

What he offered was tempting. She was tired and the hot, muggy night was stifling. "Hard as it is to believe, you may have a point."

He held out his arm for her, chuckling softly. Swallowing hard and willing her knees to stop shaking, she slid her hand through the crook of his elbow and walked with him to the horse and buggy that was parked a short distance away.

It was less than twenty blocks to her tenement building, but never had the distance seemed so short. He insisted upon walking her upstairs and through the dark hall to her door. He seemed oblivious to the sounds of marital discord coming from the Webbers' apartment or the Fennessy baby crying two doors down.

He waited outside her open door while she lit the gas lamp inside. Donny was at Mrs. Brook's apartment, waiting for Amanda to signal her return with a knock on the door.

A flame flickered and flared and a steady light filled the room, playing against the rugged features of Damian's face. "Would you care to stay for refreshment?" she asked. She was certain she still had a bottle of her father's whiskey or brandy somewhere.

For a moment she thought he was going to accept her invitation, and her heart pounded in anticipation. But then he shook his head and she felt her spirits plummet in disappointment.

"My son is expecting me."

"Your son?" She vaguely remembered his calling out something about his son the day she was at his farmhouse, but with the worry of losing her school and the confusion that followed, she'd not given it another thought.

"His name is Christopher. He's seven years old." A look of parental pride softened his face.

A million questions popped into her head, questions she had no business asking. She had not considered the possibility that Damian was married. "Is your son's mother—" The words escaped before she was able to stop them.

"No, I'm not married, Amanda, so you needn't feel guilty for kissing me."

Was she really that obvious? Heaven help her if she was! "I don't feel guilty at all," she said defensively. "Everyone's entitled to one mistake."

"Is that so? Well, you look guilty."

She took a breath. He was doing it again, confusing her, turning her emotions inside out, upside down, making her want things from him she had no business wanting. "That's because I don't generally pry into other people's business."

"You pry all the time and you know it. Half the population under five years old is named after you, and all because of your meddling ways."

"I don't meddle. I simply help nature along."

He laughed aloud. "Is that what you call it?" Then

he surprised her by growing unusually serious. "My wife died two years ago. Another victim of the Continental Theater accident, I'm afraid."

She stared at him in confusion. *"Two* years ago?"

"She died a year after the balcony collapsed. It killed her to hear the Newcastle name dragged through the mud." His voice broke. "The doctor called it pneumonia, but I'm convinced the real cause of death was embarrassment and shame."

Amanda knew what it was like to be publicly scorned, but this must have been far worse than anything she had experienced. Public reaction to the tragedy and trial were fueled by ruthless politicians out for their own gain and by the bold newspaper headlines that were every bit as ugly as they were relentless. It wasn't possible to go anywhere without hearing people say terrible things about the Newcastles. "It must have been awful for your family. For your little boy, especially. And your wife."

"Yes." His face grew dark with anguish, and she felt his withdrawal as his eyes dulled with pain. Shocked by the depth of raw emotion on his face, the grief and sorrow etched in the lines that were suddenly exposed, she stepped forward, desperately wanting to comfort him. "Damian—"

His gaze sharpened and she suddenly lost her nerve, but only because his inner pain was no longer evident and his usual derisive facade had returned. With one smooth motion, he slid an arm around her wrist and drew her so close she could feel his hot breath on her face. Her eyes lifted to his, only to find him assessing her with bold regard.

"What are you looking guilty for this time?" he said with a low growl.

Her eyes widened and her gaze froze on his lips. "For . . . for . . . not knowing that you had been affected personally by . . . by what happened."

He looked surprised and released her. "Would it have made a difference, Amanda? Would you have felt differently about me had you known?"

"I don't know," she admitted honestly.

He grimaced. "Don't tell me that's pity I hear in your voice."

"Of course not," she said.

"I think it *was* pity," he said. Suddenly his face turned grim. "Let's not have any of that, shall we? The next time you get it into your pretty little head to throw your arms around me, I want it to be for the right reasons."

"I had no intention of throwing—"

"Good night, Amanda." He tapped her lightly on the nose with the tip of his finger and turned away.

"I wasn't going to throw my arms around you!" she called after him, unmindful of her neighbors. At least not the way he meant. *Oooooooh*, he made her so mad. To think she'd wasted her time feeling sorry for him! Never again!

Still, she felt strangely disappointed to see him go, especially now that she had a glimpse of the man behind the polished facade. She called down the hallway after him, "Thank you for the ride home."

She thought she detected his footsteps faltering for a moment before he descended the stairs at the end of the hall. Then they faded away as he reached the ground floor, and she was surprised at the loneliness that echoed in their stead.

She stood in the dark hallway for several moments, willing her emotions to grow calm, before finally walking the short distance to Mrs. Brook's door.

Chapter 19

The next morning, Amanda ran around her apartment, scooping up clothes and other belongings until her arms were piled high. She dumped everything on the nearest chair and glanced at the clock on the bookshelf. "Donny, do hurry or we'll be late."

Donny sat on the floor struggling with his boot, seemingly oblivious to her prodding.

"If you want to see the big building, you'd better hurry." She stood in front of the beveled mirror next to the hat rack and arranged her jaunty felt hat on her head. She ran her fingers over the carved wooden glove box that had been her mother's, and gently lifted the lid. She chose a fresh pair of lisle thread gloves, which were less likely to slip on the handlebars than kid or silk gloves. Today she wore Turkish trousers and a blue serge reefer jacket trimmed with black braid.

Donny was still struggling with his boot by the time she was ready to go. Biting back her impatience, she stooped down to help him.

He searched her face with a frown as if he sensed her displeasure. The doctors had explained that though he often reacted to another person's emotions, he had no real understanding.

But now as she looked into his clear blue eyes, she had the strangest feeling he was trying to apologize for making her late. Knowing it was only wishful thinking on her part, she shrugged the thought away.

She finished tying his boot and handed him his straw hat. The hat had belonged to their father, and after his death, Donny had claimed it as his own, never leaving the apartment without it. It was an old hat, with a misshapen crown and a brim that flopped over one eye.

Several months earlier, the hat had blown away in the wind while she and Donny were crossing Broadway, and as usual when anything unexpected happened, he had a terrible fit right in the middle of the busy intersection.

Thank God for the stranger who had chased after it and saved the day. But the incident was still fresh in her mind and she prayed nothing like it would happen today.

Donny was fascinated with Damian's building. Last Saturday, he had climbed to the tenement's roof for a better view and had nearly scared her to death. The memory of him standing on the dangerously pitched roof filled her with renewed horror. He could have fallen and broken his neck.

She promised to take him to the building if he would stay off the roof. She had no choice but to keep her promise, of course, but she dreaded it. It was hard to predict how he would react in public. Sometimes he would cling to her and not say a word. On other occasions, he'd become agitated and sometimes even uncontrollable.

Moose had promised to keep his eye on Donny while she conducted lessons, but it was a lot to ask of her assistant. Still, she couldn't keep Donny locked away from the world. He needed these outings, no matter how nerve-wracking they were for her, and if nothing too horrible happened today, she might even consider letting Donny attend the Fourth of July parade.

She took a deep breath and said a silent prayer. "Let's go, Donny."

"No roof," he said.

"That's right," she said, and despite what the doctors had said, she hoped with all heart that her young brother understood the concept of danger. "You're not to go on the roof."

Less than fifteen minutes later, Donny sat on the horsecar on the seat next to her, holding his beloved hat on his lap. She held on to his arm. The last time she'd taken Donny on a horsecar, he'd jumped out the window while the vehicle was still moving.

Today, however, Donny seemed perfectly content to sit still and gaze at the rows of town houses they passed. They reached their destination without mishap and Amanda sighed in relief as they stepped off the vehicle. Then, without warning, Donny dashed across the street toward the building site.

Racing after him, she caught him by the arm and shook him gently, trying to get his attention. "Donny! You mustn't run away from me."

"Big, big building!" Donny shouted, jumping up and down in the middle of the street. He clapped his hands and laughed aloud.

Nothing pleased her more than to see him happy, and she didn't have the heart to scold him. Instead, she took him firmly by the hand and let him out of the path of a horse and carriage. "We have to walk."

"We have to walk," he repeated.

His eyes widened as they drew closer to the building and his hand trembled in hers. Oh, no! He wasn't about to have one of his fits, was he? *Please, God, no!* She drew a deep breath. No matter what happened she must, simply must, stay calm.

She wrapped an arm around him, speaking in a soft, soothing voice. Soon his body grew still again, and she released him.

"Big, big building!" he repeated, his face bright.

His childlike enthusiasm never failed to fill her with joy and happiness. "Yes, it is a big building, Donny."

Together, they walked around the base of the building, hand in hand, avoiding the dangerous equipment. No sooner had they circled the building than Donny insisted upon going around again.

After several turns, Amanda decided it was enough. "Come, Donny, we have to go now."

"Big, big building!" Donny shouted, but he spotted

a squirrel, and after chasing it up a tree, was distracted enough for her to take him by the arm and hustle him into the school.

Once inside, he checked out the rows of bicycles, then discovered the typewriter. Amanda worked the paper into the carriage and showed him how to push the keys.

"Buttons," Donny said.

"They look like buttons, don't they?" she agreed. "See this one here?" She pointed to a key. "This is a Donny button." She pressed the letter *D* with the tip of her forefinger. "See." She pointed to the paper. "*D* for Donny."

"Donny button!" Donny pushed the key with his finger and squealed in delight. "*D* for Donny."

"That's right; now press this *O* button."

"*O* button." Donny pushed her hand away so he could press the key by himself.

"Now two *N*'s," she said, pointing. "That's right. Press it again."

"Two *N*'s," Donny said.

"Now a *Y*." she waited for him to press the right key, then pulled the paper out of the carriage. "See what you typed? It says Donny."

"It says Donny."

She smiled and put the paper into the carriage again.

"*D* for Donny," he said, pressing the key. "Now *O* key." Much to her amazement, Donny spelled out his name a second time with no help from her.

"It says Donny," he said after he'd pressed the last key. He then pressed the *D*.

"First you have to press the space bar. Like this. Now you can type a *D*."

She watched him type his name repeatedly. She couldn't believe it. It was all she could do to keep from jumping up and down with joy. She had failed in all her earlier attempts to teach him to write with a quill pen, and yet in the course of a few moments' time, he had learned to type his name. Dear God, it was a miracle!

Leaving him happily typing, she turned the placard in the window to OPEN and then began the task of moving the bicycles outside in preparation for her day.

"Amanda!"

Just hearing Damian call her name sent a rush of heat through her body. Catching her breath and wiping her damp hands against her skirt, she turned, hoping her cheeks didn't look as red as they felt.

Damian carried a small boy in his arms. At first Amanda didn't recognize the child as the crippled boy she'd noticed from time to time in the park—not until she saw the boy's nurse standing next to the empty wheelchair.

Damian walked up to her. "I want you to meet my son, Christopher. Say good morning to Miss Blackwell."

The boy leveled his eyes at her, and she realized now why he'd looked familiar. His resemblance to his father was remarkable, especially now that she saw the two together.

"Good morning, Miss Blackwell."

"Good morning, Christopher."

Christopher glanced at the shiny high-wheeler that was parked next to her. "One day I'm going to ride a bicycle," he said. "Would you teach me?"

Amanda didn't miss the dark look that flashed across Damian's face, and the sudden realization that she had something in common with him was a stunning blow; they both loved and cared for a handicapped child.

"Of course I'll teach you." She knew by the way Damian avoided looking at her that she'd said the wrong thing, but the boy had sounded so earnest, she could hardly deny his request. So Damian, too, had difficulty striking the right balance between being a careful parent and an overprotective one. It was something else they had in common.

"Can you teach me today?"

"I think not," Damian said. His voice was gentle, his expression bland, but she couldn't keep from recalling the anguished look on his face the night before.

She longed to reach out to him, to comfort and be comforted by him, to throw her arms around his neck. Glory be, she wanted to do what she hadn't been brave enough to do when he stood in her parlor!

Clamping her mouth shut, she kept her emotions in check, her feet firmly planted on the ground, and a tight rein on her arms, lest they start acting of their own accord. Today, it wasn't Damian that prevented her from doing what her heart longed to do. It was the memory of her father. Damian was a Newcastle and she best not forget it.

"It's time to go home, son, and do your lessons. Say good-bye to Miss Blackwell."

"Good-bye, Miss Blackwell."

"Come again, Christopher."

Amanda watched Damian walk the short distance to where the boy's nurse waited. Her heart swelled as she watched him lovingly lower his son into the wheelchair. It was becoming more difficult to hate the man for all his arrogance and outrageous ways. Especially now that she had seen this other side of him.

Not difficult—impossible.

Feeling at odds with herself, she entered the school. Donny was no longer at the typewriter. "Donny!" She quickly checked the storage room and Moose's work area. He had seemingly vanished into thin air.

Trying to remain calm, she raced outside and quickly scanned the street and construction site. He could be anywhere. "Donny!" she called frantically. "Donny!"

Damian spun around to face her. "Amanda? What's wrong?"

"It's my brother," she cried, her voice shaking. "He's missing. He was—" Oh, no! She blinked her eyes in disbelief and horror. "Oh, dear God, no!"

Chapter 20

Donny stood on the fourth level of Damian's high-rise, an arm and a leg extended over the edge.

Amanda ran toward the building, avoiding the equipment and leaping over any steel beams in her path. "Quick! Do something!"

Damian went into action, covering the distance with fast, long strides. "Caleb! Quick. Fire up the engines!" His commanding voice boomed out commands as he ran toward the lift. "Big Pete, over here!"

His crew raced around her, shouting out orders and moving equipment. Amanda stepped aside to let the men stretch out a tarp beneath Donny.

Her gaze never leaving her brother's face, she tried to keep calm. If she panicked, he might have one of his terrible fits. "Hold on, Donny," she called, her voice faltering. She cleared her throat and tried again. "Hold on tight. That's a good boy." This time she managed to sound more herself, even if her voice trembled.

"Big, big building!" Donny called back, laughing.

"Damn it! This isn't a joke!" Damian's angry voice rose above the sound of the steam engines. "What's the matter with you, anyway?"

"What's the matter," Donny shouted, trying to imitate Damian's angry scowl.

Amanda grabbed Damian's arm. "He doesn't understand," she cried. "He has the mind of a small child."

Damian searched her face. "Why didn't you tell me?"

"I—"

He squeezed her hand. "We'll save him, Amanda. I promise." He turned to signal the man by the steam engine. Turning back to Amanda, he said, "Keep him calm." Grabbing a chain with both hands, he straddled a girder. "Ready!" he shouted. The chain clanked and rattled as the steel beam began to rise.

Meanwhile, Amanda did her best to engage Donny's attention. "Hold on tight." She demonstrated with her hands. "Tight."

"Hold on tight," he repeated.

"That's a boy." Amanda covered her mouth to keep from crying out when Donny leaned over the ledge. He was evidently trying to find the source of the hissing sound that came from the steam engine.

God knew what Donny would do when Damian tried to reach him. He didn't always respond well to strangers.

The girder stopped on the fourth floor. Damian grabbed hold of an iron pillar and leaped onto a crossbeam.

Donny still hadn't spotted him. He was now seated on the very edge, kicking his feet in midair and chanting, "Big, big building." He let go of the pillar to straighten his hat, and it was all Amanda could do to keep from crying out. Her hand on her chest, she tried to find her voice.

"Hold on, Donny. Use both hands."

"Both hands," he called back. "Big, big building."

"Big, big building," she repeated. Keep smiling, she told herself. She had to keep smiling. And talking.

"No roof."

"That's right. You mustn't go on the roof."

Damian was making slow but steady progress across the steel beam. Amanda felt a sick worry, like a heavy weight, settle in her stomach. She hated to think what might happen when Damian reached Donny's side.

Donny could react in a way that would put both their lives in jeopardy.

"Dear God." Miss Hannah, her voice edged with hysteria, covered her face with her hands.

Sitting next to his nurse, Christopher looked worried. His body slightly forward, he held on tight to the arms of his wheelchair, his knuckles white. "Papa, don't fall!"

Feeling sorry for the small boy, Amanda took his hand in hers and gave it a reassuring squeeze. "Nothing's going to happen to your father."

By some miracle, she managed to convey more confidence than she felt. She glanced at the nurse, finding the woman teary-eyed and close to hysterics. "It's important that we keep calm," Amanda said gently. "Donny doesn't understand what's going on, but he does react to the people around him. If we stay calm, chances are he will, too." In reality, of course, that wasn't always true, but it was their only hope.

The nurse bit her lower lip and made an obvious effort to pull herself together. "I'll do my best, Miss Blackwell."

Amanda glanced up at Donny again. "Hold on tight," she said. "Hold on tight to the big building."

"Big building. No roof."

Damian was now only a few feet behind Donny. Straddling the beam, his long, powerful legs dangling in midair, Damian inched his way along.

Donny turned to look at Damian, but didn't appear panicked or frightened. Instead, he seemed almost mesmerized by the soothing sound of Damian's voice. "Hold on, Donny. I'll have you down in no time at all."

Suddenly a gust of wind blew from the direction of the Hudson River, rustling trees and kicking up spirals of dirt in its wake.

Donny's straw hat flew off his head and he let out a wail, lunging forward. Damian's arm shot out with lightning-fast speed. He managed to grab Donny by the shirt and haul him back to safety.

Amanda nearly fainted with relief, and a collective gasp rose from the workmen who watched from below.

"Thank God." The nurse laid a hand on Christopher's shoulder. "He's going to be all right. Your papa is there now."

Amanda wished it were that simple, but her practiced eye saw what the others couldn't see. "Be careful, Damian," she called. "He's going to have a fit."

In a desperate attempt to do something, Amanda chased across the street after the hat. Just as she reached it, another gust of wind picked it up and carried it even farther away, until finally it caught on one of the neatly trimmed hedges bordering the park. Amanda plucked the straw hat from the bush and ran back, waving it over her head. "I have your hat, Donny. Look!"

But Donny was already thrashing about, his body moving violently. Suddenly, he let out a loud, piercing wail. "What's the matter with him?" Christopher asked.

"He's . . . scared," Amanda said, not knowing how to explain Donny's condition to a small child.

Damian braced his back against a vertical beam and held on to the struggling boy with the iron-tight clamp of his muscular arms and legs.

"Let me have it!" Caleb said, taking the hat from her. He tossed the hat to one of the workers on the first-floor level, who in turn flung it up to someone on the next level. Finally, the riveter on the fourth floor walked along a beam with the ease of a high-wire acrobat and handed the hat to Damian.

Meanwhile, Caleb had reached the fourth story and stood waiting next to the girder lift to assist Damian down.

Donny's fit seemed to last forever, but in reality no more than seconds passed before his body grew limp with exhaustion and he laid his head on Damian's chest. Damian made no attempt to start down. Instead, he held Donny in his arms and continued to talk to him in a low, hushed voice.

Amazed at Damian's ability to handle Donny, Amanda could only stare in wonder. Damian knew instinctively what to do. Though she couldn't hear his voice over the sound of the steam engine, the gentleness on his face told her all she needed to know.

At last, Donny looked up and spotted the hat that was now perched on Damian's head.

"See Mandy," Donny said, obviously parroting something Damian had said. Donny's voice, louder and higher than Damian's, carried over the other sounds. "Put your hat on." It was a phrase he'd heard Amanda say repeatedly.

Damian signaled to Caleb and then showed Donny how to straddle the beam. Together they inched their way to the girder lift where Caleb waited.

When at last the lift touched the ground, the workmen cheered. Amanda blinked back the tears that threatened to blur her vision and whispered a prayer of thanks. She threw her arms around Donny, but he quickly pulled away, distracted by all the people around him.

She turned to Damian. "Thank you," she whispered, choking back tears. "Thank you so much."

"There, now," he said, pulling her into his arms and stroking her hair. It was the *there, now,* that got her. Rather it was the way he said it, all soft and gentle and concerned—with not a trace of arrogance or censure.

There was nothing to be done, of course, but accept the comfort he offered her. But it didn't seem right to be in his arms without *doing* something. So she slid her hands over his shoulders and around his neck. That was definitely more . . . comfortable. Sighing to herself, she rested her head against his chest, and allowed herself the luxury of having a good cry.

She would have been tempted to stay in his arms for the remainder of the day had it not been for the disturbing memory that suddenly popped into her head. *Next time will be different.* Startled by the sudden rush of warmth that tore through her, she quickly pulled away and wiped her eyes.

She'd left a circle of moisture on his shirt, but he didn't seem to mind, if indeed he even noticed. He was too busy watching her and, judging by the amused look on his face, had apparently read her mind!

"Y-your shirt," she stammered, blushing beneath his gaze.

He glanced down and shrugged. "It's not exactly what I'd hoped for, but at least you didn't throw yourself at me out of pity as you were about to do last night."

"I didn't throw myself at you at all," she said defensively.

"You wanted to. Admit it."

"Don't tease," she pleaded. She'd just had a traumatic experience. Her emotions were raw, her defenses down, and she was feeling strangely vulnerable. Besides, he was right and he knew it! But she would die rather than admit it aloud.

"I'm not teasing; I'm perfectly serious, Amanda."

"I'm grateful to you," she said. "Can't you understand that?"

He drew his dark brows together. "I understand it completely. But you do know that gratitude can be a dangerous thing. I know several instances where women have married out of gratitude."

"You needn't concern yourself," she said primly. "I'm not *that* grateful."

Christopher's nurse walked up to them. "It's time for Christopher's lesson," she announced. She turned to Amanda. "I'm so glad your boy is safe."

"Thank you," Amanda said, thankful for the interruption. Miss Hannah wheeled Christopher away, leaving Amanda and Damian alone again.

"What a lovely child," she said, jumping at the chance to change the subject to one she could better control. "You must be very proud of him."

"Yes, I am. Unfortunately, he will never walk again. Nor will he ever ride a bicycle."

"But he will grow up to live a full and normal life." Immediately regretting her remark, she hastened to add, "I didn't mean to make his affliction seem trivial."

"I know you didn't, Amanda."

She noticed Donny chase after Christopher's wheelchair. "Come back, Donny," she called.

Donny stopped in his tracks and stood quietly watching Miss Hannah push Christopher's wheelchair up the slanted ramp that had been especially designed to fit her buggy.

"Your brother . . . do you know what's wrong with him?" Damian asked.

"All doctors can tell me is oxygen was cut off to his brain during birth. When I found him, the cord was wrapped around his neck."

"When you found him?"

"I was only a child when I found my mother dead with the baby by her side."

"How awful for you. First your mother and then . . ." He had been about to mention her father, but obviously thought better of it. Still, the rapport that had been steadily building between them was suddenly halted by an awkward silence.

"Tell me about Christopher," she said softly.

"He's been to the best doctors in the country. While I don't want to discourage him, it's important he face reality. The sooner he learns his limitations, the less frustrated he'll be."

"But he's just a child. How can you possibly know for certain what limitations he might have?"

She had the strangest feeling she'd lost him to some secret torment inside. She was reminded of the times Donny closed her out, turning inward to a place that only he could escape to. Unable to bear the thought of Damian blocking her out, too, she tried to think of how to bring him back.

"Damian?"

The faraway look faded away, and humorous glints took its place. "Surely you would agree," he said, sounding more like his old self, "that everyone has limitations."

Once again she was surprised by how his smile affected her. Lord almighty, her feelings for this man had changed, and it frightened her to think what this might mean. "Some people might say the same about buildings."

Chapter 21

During the next few days, Amanda struggled like never before with her feelings for Damian. If she could just put a name to the strange flutterings of the heart, perhaps she could better control her reaction whenever he came into view.

For certain it wasn't love. Absolutely not! Love was something that came into bloom during a proper courtship; it required time to develop and a willingness by the two people involved for such feelings to occur. Love didn't masquerade as hate, then sneak up later to steal a person's heart like a thief in the night.

In her more rational moments, she was still filled with rage over the death of her father and she refused to believe Damian wasn't in some way, shape, or form responsible for the collapse of the Continental Theater. Damian had admitted in open court to purchasing the materials used in the building, though he denied ordering inferior ones.

Still, she couldn't ignore the fact that since Damian had rescued Donny, something had changed between them, something that went far beyond physical attraction, something that affected every nerve ending in her body.

She was extremely grateful to him, of course, for saving Donny's life. But it was more than just gratitude that kept her tossing and turning at night, more than desire or even the memory of his kisses—though certainly she would never forget the warm, luscious feel of his lips on hers.

For the first time ever, she no longer felt alone. Damian understood something about her that no one else could possibly understand: he understood what it was like to raise a handicapped child.

It was reason to seek him out at every opportunity, to talk and be close to him, to share the part of her life she'd not been able to share with anyone, at least not since her father's death.

Having resolved the issue in her mind, at least temporarily, she accepted Damian's invitation to take the boys to the park that warm Sunday afternoon in late May. At first, Damian had suggested they take a steamboat from the Battery to the amusement park on Coney Island. But Amanda was opposed to the idea. Donny was a handful and there was no telling what was likely to happen at a place as crowded as Coney Island.

Damian had insisted. "You can't keep him locked up. Come on, Amanda, isn't that what you accused me of doing with my son?"

It was true, of course, but Christopher didn't have the same problems as Donny. She did, however, reluctantly agree to an outing in Central Park.

Damian picked them up in his carriage after church, waiting for her at the entrance to the King's Highway. Amanda, wearing a blue silk taffeta promenade frock with an adjustable cape, tucked her folded parasol under her arm as Damian helped her into the carriage.

The hem of her tiered skirt had been shortened to allow ease in walking, but she lifted it a tad higher, revealing a glimpse of a shapely calf that, judging by the look of approval in Damian's eyes, didn't go unnoticed.

Glory be, he was doing it again; he was making her feel all shivery and nervous. She glanced over his shoulder at her neighbors. Someone was hanging out of every window, frantically slinging wash over the clotheslines.

Mrs. Aviary's head had popped out first, followed by the appearance of Ellie-May, Mrs. Brook, Carolyn

Webber, and the three sisters who lived in the corner apartment with their elderly mother. Others had appeared in quick succession. Everyone prudently kept a small basket of laundry handy for just such an emergency. Snooping was unforgivable, of course, but if a person had a legitimate reason for hanging out the window, nobody objected.

Following Amanda's gaze, Damian looked surprised at the activity. "Don't your neighbors honor the Sabbath?"

"Oh, they're not working," Amanda assured him. "They're just being neighborly."

During the short ride to the park, Donny was surprisingly calm and couldn't seem to take his eyes off Christopher. When they reached the park, Donny insisted upon pushing Christopher's wheelchair himself along the winding path that ran past the sheep meadow.

"Oh, dear," Amanda said worriedly. "I'm not sure this is a good idea."

"Stop being an old mother hen," Damian teased. "We'll stay close behind."

Amanda soon realized she had nothing to worry about. Donny did whatever Christopher told him to do.

Donny wheeled the chair onto the grass and Christopher patiently pointed to the placard. "It says STAY OFF THE GRASS, Donny."

"It says stay off grass!" Donny said, but didn't correct their course until Christopher pointed to the narrow footpath.

It didn't seem possible, but Amanda actually found herself relaxing. With her open parasol resting against her shoulder, she enjoyed strolling next to Damian and didn't miss the covetous glances he drew from the young women playing croquet on the east green. When one woman smiled at him in a way that was far too suggestive, Amanda slid her arm into the crook of Damian's and he rewarded her with a twinkling gleam.

"Don't tell me you're jealous, Amanda."

"Certainly not!" she said. The idea! Why, she'd never been jealous in her life. But she kept her arm firmly in place until the east green fell far behind, just the same.

The sun was warm, and there was only a hint of a breeze, but it was enough to stir the flowers that bordered the path, and a lovely sweet perfume filled the air.

"Christopher is a very special child," Amanda said. "Children have been cruel to Donny in the past, but your son is so patient and kind."

"Christopher knows Donny has a special problem. We've talked about it."

She gazed up at him. "You have?"

"You don't mind, do you?"

"No, of course not. I'm . . . I'm touched." They stopped while the two boys inspected one of the many bronze statues in the park.

"That's Daniel Webster," Damian explained. "I wasn't much older than you, Christopher, when my father took me to our nation's capital to hear him speak."

"Can I hear him speak, Papa? Please?"

"I'm afraid not, son. Mr. Webster is no longer living."

They continued on their way. Hearing Donny laugh aloud at something Christopher said made her smile. "Christopher is good for Donny."

"Donny's good for him, too," Damian said. "I think we ought to do this more often."

A group of cyclists headed up the path and Amanda waved. "It's the Wheelers' Cycling Club," she said excitedly.

Damian didn't share her enthusiasm and, if anything, looked downright hostile when Lockhammer came into view. "So it is."

"It's going to be perfect weather for the parade," Sergeant Summerset called as he pedaled by.

"I'm going to hold you to that," Mayor Ledbetter said, stopping to catch his breath.

"Me, too," Lockhammer added, holding on to the handlebars with one hand and mopping his forehead with the other.

"Give the signal," Donny called after the cyclists, clearly agitated. "Give the signal, give the signal!"

Damian frowned. "What's he saying?"

"I think he wants me to blow my whistle." She turned to Donny. "I didn't bring my whistle today, see?" She untied her cape to show him. Still, it took a great deal of time before Donny calmed down enough to continue their walk.

Damian seemed unwilling to let the matter rest. "What do you suppose upset him?"

"I don't know. It's not always possible to tell."

"He's not afraid of bicycles, is he?" he persisted.

"No. He likes bicycles."

"He seems all right now."

Donny lifted Christopher out of the wheelchair, but when he proceeded to follow a group of children up the side of a rocky hill, Amanda called him back.

"Let them go," Damian said.

"But—"

"We'll watch them."

Christopher's delighted laughter rang out from the top of a rocky outcropping where Donny had set him down. The two boys complemented each other perfectly. Christopher had taken on the role of guardian, telling Donny what he could and could not do. Donny, in turn, provided Christopher with mobility, and Christopher squealed with delight as the two boys investigated the winding trails normally inaccessible to him.

Following the other children, Donny lugged his new friend to the mouth of a hidden cave.

Lord, Amanda couldn't remember a time when Donny looked more happy, and her heart filled with joy to watch the two boys together. Amazingly enough, neither of them seemed to mind the other's limitations. "It's a miracle," she whispered. "When they're together, they seem, I don't know, whole."

She could tell by the look on Damian's face that he was thinking along these same lines. "How much does Donny understand?"

"The doctors say he understands very little," Amanda explained. "He learns by rote and repetition. He associates certain phrases with certain actions, which is why we tend to think he understands more than he actually does."

"Does he have any formal education?"

"Only what I've taught him. We hired tutors in the past, but none of them lasted for long."

"I don't suppose it's possible for him to read."

"That's what I thought, but something happened recently that made me realize I can't assume anything. He's learning to type."

"Type? You mean words, sentences?"

"It's incredible, I know. But he can actually type his own name and mine, too. And the other day, he typed the words *horsecar stop*."

"Have you talked to the doctors about this?"

"Not yet. In a way, I'm afraid to."

"Afraid to? Why?"

She lifted her face to the sky, absorbing the warmth of the sun that filtered through the branches of a sprawling white oak. "Because, the doctors always have a perfectly logical explanation for everything Donny does, and it's never the explanation I hope for."

She lowered her gaze to Damian's face. "I want to believe his ability to type real words is a breakthrough. Oh, Damian, it's been so long since I've felt hope. I've been to so many doctors, specialists, there's nowhere else for me to turn. Donny's made no progress in years. Then suddenly he starts to type and meets Christopher and everything changes. I don't want some doctor to tell me—"

He touched a knuckle to her cheek and she felt warm waves radiate from his touch. "I know," he said softly. "You don't want anyone telling you it doesn't mean anything."

"I know I'm being foolish."

"Not foolish at all. It *does* mean something, Amanda. You have to believe it and keep believing it, no matter what anyone tells you."

"I want to," she said slowly. "What about Christopher?" she asked. "Will he ever—"

"Walk?" He pulled his hand away and let it drop to his side. "The doctors say no."

"Doctors could be wrong. It's possible . . . I think sometimes . . ."

"What, Amanda? What do you think?"

"That the doctors might be wrong about Donny. That he really does understand more than we know. . . ." She closed her eyes, tight, surprised that she finally had the courage to voice the feelings she had previously been afraid to put into words.

"It's possible, isn't it?" he asked.

She opened her eyes. "I don't know. I keep telling myself it's only wishful thinking."

"What if it's not?" he persisted. "What if doctors really are wrong?"

"Then I could never forgive myself for losing faith in him."

"Have you lost faith in him?"

"It's hard not to. You should know."

He looked surprised. "You think I've lost faith in Christopher's ability to walk?"

"Haven't you?"

He frowned against the sun. "I haven't lost faith, Amanda. Not in Christopher, not in anything. Not even my father. One day I'm going to prove my father innocent. I have to. It's not the wheelchair that keeps my son confined. It's the unjust charges against my father and the vicious gossip. I had to pull Christopher out of school because of it."

"How awful for you both," she said softly. "I'm so sorry."

"You said yourself how cruel people can be."

She nodded. How well she remembered the way Donny had been taunted at times, by adults as well as children. "Your father was tried and convicted," she said gently. "How can you still believe . . . ? I mean, to keep your faith in someone when the whole world is against you. How is it possible?"

When at first he didn't answer her, she thought perhaps she'd gone too far. But then he spoke, and he didn't sound angry or insulted, or even offended. "I know my father, and I know he would never put anyone's life in jeopardy. Not for money. Not for any gain." He brushed his fingers through his hair. "I wish you could believe that."

She wanted to believe in something or someone as much as Damian believed in his father's innocence, but she didn't know if it was possible. In the beginning, she had trusted her instincts and had refused to believe anything was seriously wrong with Donny. But that had proven to be a terrible mistake, and she had been devastated when doctors told her she had done him irreversible harm as a result of postponing medical treatment. She doubted she would ever have that kind of faith again, in anyone or anything. "I want to," she said honestly. "I really do want to."

"Why, Amanda, I'm shocked." The corner of his mouth lifted upward. "You never fail to amaze me. Do you mean it?"

"I didn't say I believed, exactly. I said I wanted to."

"Well, you could knock me over with a feather. I never thought you'd even consider I might be right."

"Stranger things have happened," she said. "If your father's not responsible, then who . . . ?"

"That's what I've been trying to find out. I've hired private investigators, but so far they've found nothing to support my belief. It's damned frustrating."

"I'm sure it must be," she said. What would happen, she wondered, if Damian were to find out his faith in his father was misplaced and Phillip Newcastle really was guilty? She shuddered to think.

The sound of laughter signaled the boys' return.

"We'd better go before they leave us behind," Damian said.

The number of people increased as they drew closer

to the menagerie. She and Damian rounded a bend and found the boys in front of the monkey cage.

Christopher read the sign aloud. "Don't feed the monkeys."

"Feed the monkeys," Donny said.

"*Don't* feed the monkeys," Christopher repeated. "You have to say *don't*."

"You have to say don't," Donny said.

Donny pushed Christopher from cage to cage, stopping while Damian gave an interesting little talk about each animal. Damian went into great detail explaining the feeding habits of the boa constrictor.

"I'm impressed," Amanda said.

"You mean I didn't impress you with my twenty-story building?"

She thought for a moment. "I think the part about the boa constrictor's digestive system impressed me more."

"What's that, Papa?" Christopher pointed to the three large animals tied to the willow trees behind the arsenal.

"Those are African Cape Buffalo," Damian explained. "They were a gift from General Sherman himself."

"Watch out for the bear," Christopher cautioned Donny, his eyes wide with worry.

"You have to say *don't*," Donny said, and after Damian had helped him turn the wheelchair, he pushed it in the opposite direction.

The boys looked at every animal at least twice, then they followed the path leading to the lake. "Look!" Christopher called, pointing to Officer Thorndike astride his horse. The wheels of the wheelchair rolled over the forbidden grass and the mounted policeman galloped toward them, shouting at the top of his lungs. "Off the grass, off the grass!"

Donny laughed loudly. "Off the grass!" he repeated.

"Off the grass," Christopher said sternly, and this time, Donny pushed the wheelchair back onto the footpath.

But old Thorny wasn't satisfied. He dismounted his horse and faced the two boys with his hands at his waist. "Can't you read?" he said, pointing to the placard.

"I can read," Christopher said proudly.

"You have to say *don't*!" Donny said.

Amanda hurried to catch up to the boys. "The boys didn't mean to disobey the signs."

Old Thorny glared at Amanda. "Well, look who's here. It seems that you and me have a bit of unfinished bus—"

Donny's ear-piercing scream filled the air and Amanda spun around. Old Thorny's horse, Chester, had bitten a hunk out of Donny's beloved straw hat.

Amanda rushed to Donny's side, but Damian had already reached him. He lifted Donny in his arms and laid him on the grass out of harm's way, but it was Christopher who saved the day.

"The horse likes you, Donny," Christopher said. "That's why he bit your hat." Christopher made a chewing motion with his mouth. "Hmmmm, good. Horse likes you."

Donny suddenly stopped trembling. "Horse likes you."

Half laughing and half crying, Amanda nodded in relief. It was seldom that an impending fit could be averted. "Yes, yes, the horse likes you."

Soon the four of them were laughing and even Thorny finally joined in. "Can't think what got into old Chester, here. He never ate a hat before."

"Horse likes you," Donny said, and this brought another round of laughter from the others.

Later, Amanda and Damian sat next to the lake. The boys were a short distance away, watching the little toy boats. "It's incredible, Damian. Christopher can reach Donny when all the experts have failed."

Damian gazed off into the distance. "Maybe that's been my trouble," he said thoughtfully. "I've left my father's fate to the so-called experts."

"Are you talking about lawyers?"

He nodded. "Lawyers. Private detectives."

A little sailboat drifted by and she was reminded of the little boat her father had once made for her. "Do you have any proof of your father's innocence?"

"None. Only what I believe inside. I know what you're thinking, Amanda. You consider me a fool, don't you?"

"I don't think anything of the sort," she said. It was the same explanation she'd given doctors whenever they insisted Donny should be institutionalized. Contrary to what anyone told her, she had always suspected deep inside Donny understood more than they knew. She couldn't explain it, exactly. It was just a feeling she had and, if she was honest with herself, still had—today more than ever.

She took a deep breath. "Sometimes what we know inside is all we have to go on."

"But it's not always enough, is it, Amanda?" he asked.

She let her gaze drift across the placid still waters of the lake. Damian was right. It wasn't enough. Damian would have to produce legal proof before he had any chance at all of freeing his father, and she would have to find some concrete proof of her own regarding Donny's ability to understand. It was the only way to fight her uncle.

Feeling hopeful and encouraged for the first time in years, she smiled up at him. "But it's a start."

Chapter 22

The following afternoon, Priscilla Parkerdale arrived for her regularly scheduled lesson. A bubbly small-framed woman with flaming red hair and sparkling green eyes, she didn't put on airs like so many young women from similar rich families tended to do. Following Amanda's counsel, she never failed to show up in proper riding attire and wore no jewelry or frilly accessories that could catch in the spokes or tangle on the pedals.

She did have one annoying habit: she slept until noon, and steadfastly refused to change her cycling lesson to the early morning hours. For weeks, Amanda had tried to get her to change her mind, with no success. It was downright frustrating.

Still, it was hard to fault the pretty red-haired woman with the engaging Irish brogue. Priscilla was a fast learner and had gotten the feel of the bicycle quickly. She was one of the few students Amanda had allowed to mount the bicycle on the first lesson.

Priscilla was ready for her cycling badge and only her lack of confidence held her back. Amanda was certain, however, that another lesson or two was all she needed. Then Amanda would have no opportunity to bring her and Caleb together. The time had come for desperate measures.

"You're making wonderful progress, Priscilla. But I do believe you need more practice riding your bicycle in traffic." Since it was too late to ride in Central Park, Amanda taught Priscilla to ride on one of the cow paths north of the park. "That is, if you're not too tired."

"Oh, dear." Priscilla actually shuddered.

"Trust me, once you get used to riding the city streets, you won't even think about the traffic."

"I hope you're right. I do want to get my license, but I'm afraid once I do, I'll never get off my ordinary." She lowered her voice. "I suppose that means I'll never find myself a husband. My mother said men don't want wives who are cyclists."

If Priscilla's mother showed more concern for her daughter's sleeping habits, Priscilla would no doubt be betrothed by now, if not altogether married. Naturally, Amanda didn't say this aloud. "If all women were cyclists, men wouldn't have much choice, now, would they?"

Priscilla giggled. "I guess they wouldn't." She lifted her foot onto the pedal and started forward again.

"Steer straight," Amanda cautioned. "I'm right beside you." She mounted her own high-wheeler and pedaled hard to catch up.

"Wheeeee." The young woman's enthusiasm brought a smile to Amanda's face.

They doubled back and followed Eighth Avenue the length of the park, passing farmlands and fields of sheep and cattle, back to the school and the Newcastle construction site. Amanda made her stop and start repeatedly. "Perfect!"

She waited until a wagon filled with bales of hay and drawn by two draft horses had passed before making Priscilla ride in a circle in the middle of the road. Church bells pealed out the hour and Amanda smiled to herself. So far, everything was going according to plan.

At three o'clock every afternoon, Damian insisted his men take a fifteen-minute break from their duties. "That's it for today," she called. She pedaled hard to catch up to her student. "Let's walk our bicycles so I can go over some of the restrictions you'll need to know before I can issue your badge." Priscilla dismounted and walked her bicycle next to Amanda's.

Amanda eyed her student approvingly. Her red hair gleamed in the sun, her eyes sparkled, and her skin was as soft and smooth as a newborn's. How could Caleb possibly resist? "You know, of course, you can't ride in the park between nine in the morning and five at night?"

"What a tiresome rule," Priscilla complained.

"If you ride at night, you must have a headlamp, and it's advisable to ride with a gentleman escort."

"Perhaps I can talk my father's groom into escorting me after dark."

"Yes, well . . ." Amanda waited until they were only a few yards away from where Damian's foreman, Caleb, stood looking over the building plans. Caleb was so serious-minded, he couldn't seem to bring himself to rest even during the mandatory break. If things worked out like Amanda hoped, Caleb was going to have something else to think about beside work. She smiled to herself. Yes, indeed, and it will do him a world of good.

Amanda pretended to lose control of her bicycle. Giving the handlebars a sharp turn, she let the front tire plow into Priscilla's bicycle.

"*Ohhhhhhhhhh!*" Priscilla turned the handlebars frantically, but the unwieldy machine fell on its side, taking Priscilla with it.

Priscilla's frantic cry brought Caleb running fullchisel, just as Amanda had hoped. "Are you all right, miss?" he asked anxiously. He dropped down on one knee, his hand on Priscilla's shoulder.

"I think so," Priscilla said, smiling up at him. Though she looked perfectly capable of picking herself up off the ground, she let Caleb pull her to her feet. Priscilla's sleeping habits were abominable, but at least she knew how to conduct herself in a man's presence.

"Thank you so much," Priscilla said, sounding slightly breathless. Her cheeks flushed a most becoming shade of pink as she gazed into the foreman's face.

Looking flustered, she adjusted her sunbonnet and tried to tuck a wayward lock into place.

"My pleasure," Caleb said, looking rather flustered himself. He was smitten, Amanda was certain of it. "These things can be dangerous."

Priscilla giggled and Caleb turned red. Amanda smiled to herself as she quietly stood the bicycle upright. She'd been right all along; the two were a perfect match.

Just when everything was going according to plan, one of the workmen beckoned to Caleb. Caleb hesitated for a moment before touching a finger to his hard leather hat. "Good day, ladies." His eyes lingered a moment longer than necessary on Priscilla, but Amanda's hopes were dashed when he walked away as if nothing out of the ordinary had happened.

Lord almighty, what was the matter with the man? He didn't even bother to introduce himself to Priscilla, nor did he so much as ask her name.

Was the man blind? Did he not recognize providence when it came knocking at the door? Could he not *feel* the stirrings of his heart? Men!

Though nothing much had happened, you'd never know it by the way Priscilla carried on afterward. If Amanda hadn't been present, she would have thought Caleb had dropped on his knees and proposed.

"Oh, what a handsome, handsome man!" Priscilla squealed the moment she and Amanda were inside the school where they couldn't be seen or heard. She whirled about the classroom in a dainty dance. "And did you see how he looked at me? Oh, you simply must tell me his name."

"His name is Caleb White. He's twenty-one years old and he's very responsible. Mr. Newcastle trusts him completely."

"Caleb." Priscilla let his name linger on her lips for a moment before she caught herself with an embarrassed laugh. She started digging into her coin purse. "I owe you for last week and this week."

Amanda took the money and made a careful notation

in her ledger, but she wasn't thinking about finances. Now that she had successfully arranged for the two to meet, she was more convinced than ever they were meant for each other. Both liked the outdoors. And although Caleb was extremely serious-minded, Amanda was convinced his reserved personality would provide the perfect complement to Priscilla's more fun-loving nature.

Amanda was certain it would be a match made in heaven, and she was anxious to put the second part of her plan into action.

Priscilla eyed the typewriter. "What a wonderful machine. I see you have one of the newer models with a shift key. Do you mind if I try it?"

"Please do." Amanda stood and Priscilla arranged the desk chair in front of the typewriter. Quick as a wink, her fingers were flying over the keyboard.

Amanda was astonished. "Why, glory be, you're using all your fingers."

Priscilla blushed modestly. "I've been taking classes at the YMCA," she explained. "My instructor insists that we can type faster if we learn to use all the fingers, not just two."

"But how do you remember where the letters are? The alphabet is all mixed up."

"It's done that way on purpose," Priscilla explained. "The letters are placed according to the number of times they occur in normal usage. Once you learn the keyboard, typing is as easy as playing the piano. Did you know that Mr. Mark Twain typed the manuscript of his latest book himself before turning it in to his publisher?"

Amanda gasped. "You can't be serious." It was all she could to type a half-page letter. "He *typed* a whole book?"

"That's what my typing instructor told us. And she also said the time would come when every author would be expected to submit a typewritten manuscript."

"That's dreadful," Amanda said. "I should think

writing a book would be hard enough without having to worry about typing it."

"I'll teach you to type with all your fingers if you like," Priscilla offered.

"I'll think about it," Amanda said thoughtfully. "Have you thought about hiring yourself out? I'm certain a lot of businesses would benefit from the use of such a machine. Maybe even Newcastle Construction Company. I'm sure Damian . . . Mr. Newcastle . . . must have a great deal of business correspondence to write."

Priscilla giggled at the thought. "My father would have a conniption. He thinks my time is better spent learning domestic skills. He's convinced that a man would not want to marry a woman who spends her day in front of a typewriter. Since I'm both a cyclist *and* a typist, my chances of getting married are probably nonexistent."

"Horsefeathers! Why, a lot of young men would give anything to marry a capable woman such as yourself. Take Mr. White, for example."

"Caleb? Really? He would want a wife like me?" A look of disbelief crossed Priscilla's face. "How would you know that?"

"For one thing, he's very tolerant, and he didn't seem the least bit alarmed the first day he saw me wearing bloomers."

"Really?"

"Yes. If only he wasn't so terribly shy. It really is a pity."

"But he didn't seem shy to me."

"I do believe you're right. He did seem very comfortable with you, didn't he? I've never seen him act that way before. What do you suppose it means?"

Priscilla blushed. "Means?" She looked to be at a loss for words. "I have no idea."

"I wonder if you would consider . . . Never mind. You already said you wouldn't and I have no right to ask you to do something you have your heart set against."

"Do what?"

"Never mind. It's not that important."

"Please, Amanda, please do tell me what you have on your mind."

"Well, if you insist. I was wondering if you would consider changing the time of your lessons. I know you said it was virtually impossible for you to rise much before noon."

Priscilla shuddered as if the mere thought was too much to bear. "I don't understand. What has any of this got to do with Caleb . . . eh, Mr. White?"

"As I said before, he's normally very shy. He absolutely refuses to join a regular cycling class, so I'm giving him private lessons. But I think it's time he learned to ride in the company of others."

"Yes, I can see where that would be beneficial." Priscilla thought for a moment, her normally worry-free forehead lined. "Are you saying you want me to change my lessons to correspond with his?"

"That would be ideal, of course. Unfortunately, that means you'll have to come at six-thirty in the morning."

Priscilla's eyes widened. "Th-that early?"

"Mr. White simply can't bring himself to take lessons when other people are around and absolutely refuses to ride on the streets. The park is generally empty at that time."

Priscilla looked uncertain. "I understand how he feels but do you really think I could be of help to him?"

"I'm convinced of it." Not wanting to appear too anxious, Amanda paused for a moment before continuing. "It would only be for a lesson or two. Once Mr. White gets used to riding in front of other people, I'm sure he'll agree to a more suitable time."

Priscilla toyed with the coin purse in her hands. "I suppose I could manage it for such a short time. And as you say, it's for a good cause."

"Oh, yes," Amanda agreed. "A very good cause."

* * *

Damian was late arriving at the site that third week in June, having stopped at the Tombs earlier to visit his father. He hated having to report his failure to find new evidence, but what choice did he have? He couldn't lie.

His father had accepted what he had to say without comment, and that had hurt Damian deeply. Hell, it had almost killed him. It wasn't that long ago that his father had actively worked with him, but no longer. It was as if he'd given up.

Now Phillip Newcastle was but a mere shadow of the man he once was. Not only had he shrunk physically, his once powerful legs and arms were stick-thin, and his spirit had diminished to the point that Damian hardly recognized him.

Damian had arrived at the site feeling depressed and frustrated. It didn't help his mood any to find his workers standing around, idle.

"What's going on?" he asked one of his men. "Where's White?"

One of the riveters, a Scotsman named Blade, glanced at the others before answering. "He's . . . eh, rather occupied, he is."

Damian narrowed his eyes. Due to the combination of spring rains, a labor strike at the docks, and his ongoing battles with the building commission, they were already behind schedule. He wasn't in the mood for games. "Perhaps you'd be kind enough to tell me what exactly that means?"

"He's . . . eh . . . getting married today, sir."

"Married . . . ? White?"

"Aye," Blade replied. "To Miss Priscilla Parkerdale."

Damian glanced at the circle of men, wondering if he was the butt of a practical joke. "I didn't even know White was betrothed."

Blade rubbed a hand across a whiskered chin. "He didn't have time for no betrothal. The lady's parents ain't 'xactly dancin' with joy at the thought of their daughter minglin' with a construction worker."

Damian could well imagine. The Parkerdales' circle of friends included the Astors and Vanderbilts.

He drove a fist into the palm of his hand. Another delay! As irritating as this was, it didn't keep him from jumping to the foreman's defense. "Caleb's a good man. They aren't likely to find a more serious, hard-working lad."

Blade nodded. "That's what Miss Blackwell said."

"Amanda—?" He should have known. "And what exactly has Miss Blackwell got to do with this?"

"Miss Blackwell done introduced White to his bride. Said when two people care for each other like White cares for Miss Parkerdale, it don't matter what he does for a livin'."

"That's right," the man named Chipper added. "So White decided to elope."

"Did he now?" Damian muttered. He was happy for White, of course, but he'd be a whole lot happier had his foreman waited until construction was complete.

"We all took turns holdin' the ladder while he convinced the lady to marry him," Blade explained. "Finally, the bride-to-be climbed out o' the window and she and White rode off on a tandem bicycle."

The man known as Big Pete grinned, his two front teeth missing. "Miss Blackwell said she even had a prospective bride in mind fer me."

All eyes turned toward the beefy man, whose scarred face caved into a buttery grin.

"So is White coming back today?" Damian demanded.

Chipper shook his head. "He said he was taking one of those bridal tours."

"He means a honeymoon," Big Pete explained.

Damian threw up his hands. Wasn't this just dandy? His foreman had run off and eloped, and all because of Amanda. "Get to work, all of you!" he ordered. Without another word, he cut across his site to the school.

"Amanda!" He glanced around to make certain no

tots were within hearing range before calling her name again, this time louder. "Amanda! I want a word with you." She was sitting behind her desk, glowering at the typewriter. Reams of black ribbon were puddled on the floor next to her feet. Her hands were covered in black and she had a black smudge on the tip of her slightly upturned nose. Yet one look at her and his spirits suddenly soared.

"Mercy me, Damian. What's the matter with you? Why are you yelling?"

"I understand my foreman has eloped and it's all because of your meddling."

She looked startled, almost horrified. "Caleb eloped?"

"Don't pull that innocent act on me, Amanda. He eloped with one of your students and you know it."

A look of relief crossed her face. "Oh, thank goodness. For a minute I thought . . ."

"Go on," he said. "Don't let me stop you. What did you think?"

"I thought you were telling me he had eloped with someone else. Why, that would have broken poor Priscilla's heart."

"And we can't have anyone's heart broken, can we?" he said, more amused than annoyed. Hell, what's another week's delay? Besides, he was having a hard time concentrating on the subject. He was too busy trying not to drown in those big blue eyes of hers, trying to keep from wiping that smudge off her intriguing nose and kissing her pretty pink lips.

"I would think you'd be happy for him."

"Happy? Happy that my foreman has taken off without so much as a word to me?" It was so unlike Caleb to be irresponsible. Imagine marrying someone he'd only recently met. Obviously, Miss Parkerdale was a bad influence.

"I'm sure he meant to say something. . . ."

"But he didn't."

"Oh, Damian, stop being an old fudd."

"Is that what you think I am? An old fudd?" She

didn't look the least apologetic for the inconvenience she'd caused him by meddling in his foreman's affairs. If anything, she looked downright pleased with herself! "How would you feel if Moose suddenly didn't show up?"

"If he were getting married, I'd feel happy for him."

"And I'm happy for White. But I can't have you going around marrying off my men, and that includes Big Pete."

Her lips clamped together and her eyes narrowed. Obviously, she intended to fight him on this. "My men are off-limits, Amanda. Off-limits. Do I make myself clear?"

Before Amanda could reply, a heavyset woman with spring-tight curls stuck her head through the open door. "Tell me again, Miss Blackwell, which one is Big Pete?"

Chapter 23

It had to stop! If Amanda didn't quit trying to marry off his men, he'd never get the damned building finished! First Caleb and now Big Pete. Why, the giant of a man had spent the last two days walking around in a daze. Enough was enough!

Damian had arrived on his site before six that morning to check the building materials that had been delivered on the previous day. He'd taken over the job himself in Caleb's absence. His work crew wasn't scheduled to arrive for another hour.

He was checking the pallets of brick that would be used for fireproofing against the inventory list when suddenly a movement caught his eye. Thinking one of his men had arrived early, he straightened. "Morning," he called. The person had evidently stepped behind the stack of steel girders.

He called out again but received no response. Suspicious now, he walked toward the back of the steel-framed building. "Is anyone there?"

Suddenly a man jumped in front of him, brandishing a knife. Damian froze in his tracks. The man was slightly built, with dark hair combed back from his forehead and a scar that slashed an ugly line across his cheek. Damian had never before set eyes on the man.

"I have nothing of value on me," Damian said. He was no stranger to muggers, but generally encountered them in the Battery, not here by the park. "Only a gold watch."

"I don't want your bloody watch." The man jumped at the sound of a long, shrill whistle.

"What's that?"

"It's just Miss Blackwell next door. She won't cause you any problems."

The man's gaze slid over Damian's shoulder. Suddenly he turned pale and cursed.

Damian glanced over his shoulder and almost laughed aloud. No wonder the man looked so damned skittish. At least forty uniformed policemen formed two lines down the middle of Eighth Avenue, each perched upon a high-wheel bicycle.

Amanda's voice rang out. "Do you call this a formation?" She clapped her hands briskly. "Straighten your lines, men. Where's your pride?"

Next to her, Donny imitated his sister. "Where's your pride?"

Silent as a panther, and looking almost as lethal, the stranger moved to Damian's side and thrust the sharp point of his snickersnee against Damian's neck.

Damian cursed silently. He was in plain view of forty-some policemen and not one noticed him with a knife at his throat. He was on his own.

"Get rid of 'em."

"Just how do you propose I do that? It's a cycling class."

Amanda's whistle shrilled. "All right, men, I want you to form a circle!"

"Where's your pride?" Donny called, clapping his hands.

The stranger looked undecided for a moment before backing away. "Don't try to follow me." He was gone in a flash. Damian waited a beat before chasing after him, but already the dark-clad figure could be seen racing away on a black horse.

The man was obviously a lunatic. New York was full of them. This was one of the reasons why Damian had taken it upon himself to drive Amanda home on the nights she worked late.

He watched the police cyclists whiz by in perfect

formation. Recalling the look on the thug's face moments earlier, he burst into laughter. Who would ever think having a cycling school next door would someday come in handy?

He put the strange encounter out of his mind and didn't give it another thought until that night, when he drove Amanda and Donny home and caught sight of someone hiding in the shadows.

He snapped the reins and clucked at his horse. He said nothing to Amanda about the hidden figure. There was no reason to alarm her. Besides, she hardly let him get a word in edgewise. "Oh, Damian. Did you see the police cycling team? They're tremendous. I just know the Fourth of July parade is going to be perfect!

"My only concern is for Miss Quackenbush. She insists upon riding in the parade. Glory be, she can't ride worth a fiddle. What am I going to do?"

"I'm sure you'll think of something." He glanced over his shoulder, but the street was deserted. "You always do."

"Yes, well—" She quickly changed the subject. "Oh! I didn't tell you the best news yet. Donny typed up all the signs today by himself. You know, STAY OFF THE GRASS and STAND HERE FOR HACK. I do believe he's memorized every sign he's ever seen."

The excitement in her voice made him smile. "That's amazing."

"And that's not all," Amanda continued. "He can type the names of every statue in the park."

"Does he know what he's typing?"

"If I read the words aloud as he's typing, he remembers them. If I say to type *Daniel Webster,* he does it."

"This is wonderful news, Amanda! It means he understands more than we give him credit for!"

"I know." Her eyes shone like stars as she smiled up at him. All too soon, they arrived at her apartment.

"Would you like to come up?" she asked.

He was tempted; damn, he was tempted. But he'd

promised Christopher he'd make it home in time to read him a bedtime story.

"Some other night," he said. "Christopher's waiting for me." He jumped to the ground, walked around the back of the buggy, and placing his hands firmly around Amanda's tiny waist, lifted her to the ground. "I wish I could stay," he said softly. She looked beautiful, the light of the full moon shining in her eyes.

Enticed beyond endurance by her dewy soft lips, he lowered his head to kiss her, but was stopped by the sound of windows being hastily thrown open. Apparently, the laundry spies were about to strike again.

Tempted to give the old busybodies something to talk about, he nonetheless dropped his hands and stepped back. He intended to kiss her again, and soon, but not in front of an audience.

"Good match," Donny said.

Damian drove off grinning. Amanda was right—the boy understood more than the doctors gave him credit for.

During the next two days, Damian was convinced someone was following him. But who? And why?

Three days after he'd been accosted, he stood on the fifteenth-floor scaffolding and saw a man leave Amanda's school who looked just like the man who'd held him at knifepoint. But by the time he rode a girder down to the ground, the man had disappeared.

His mind was in a whirl. Amanda? Was she the one having him followed?

Were the warm smiles and lingering looks she'd given him recently all part of an elaborate plan to let him think she really did want to believe his father innocent? He didn't want to think it was true. But what if she wanted to avenge her father's death? It was possible, wasn't it?

Damn! Could it really be true? When they'd first met, she'd made no secret of how much she hated his family. Maybe she still felt that way. He didn't want to believe it, but once the thought was planted, it refused to go away. In the end, he had no choice but to check out his suspicions. He had to know, by God, which side Amanda was on. Even if it killed him.

Amanda caught the sleeve of her shirtwaist on a nail as she leaned over the windowsill of her apartment. Tugging gently at the fabric, she craned her head over the flapping bedsheets to better see her neighbor, Mrs. Aviary. "You did what?"

Mrs. Aviary peered at Amanda from beneath a ruffled bed cap and didn't look the least bit ashamed of herself, though Lord knows she should. If anything, she looked perfectly smug. "Now don't go getting yourself all in a dither. I have every right to know who's living next door to me, and I'm telling you Mrs. Brook has a man in there."

"That's no reason for you to be listening at her door."

"Would you rather I ask her outright?"

The scraping sound of a window sash signaled the arrival of Ellie-May. "Did you hear about the Webbers? Oh, it's simply dreadful." She dabbed at her eyes with a lacy handkerchief and Amanda's heart sank.

"What happened?"

"Mr. Webber didn't come home last night."

"Oh, no!" Amanda glanced at Carolyn Webber's window. It was shut tight, the curtains drawn, and not one garment hung from the clothesline.

"I could have told you this would happen!" Mrs. Aviary said, glaring at Amanda. "That woman has a mind of her own. She'll never make a good wife."

"Carolyn is the perfect wife for him," Amanda insisted. Apparently the two of them didn't know it yet. "They're just having a difficult time adjusting to marriage." She set to work pulling her wash off the line. "It could happen to any couple." She felt uncomfortable discussing the Webbers' personal problems with her neighbors. But, by George, she had every intention of discussing it with Carolyn.

Suddenly, she saw a man standing in the shadows of the building across the alley. Something about him made her take a closer look. Peering beneath the clothesline and the corset she had yet to take down, she was astonished to discover it was Damian.

Her heart pounding, she backed away from the window. Damian! What was he doing? Certainly he wouldn't be spying on her, would he? She peered outside again, taking care to keep herself hidden as she pulled the wooden clothespins off the line. Damian was nowhere to be seen.

A knock came at the door, startling her so much she dropped her corset. Watching the pink satiny garment fall to the ground, she glanced around to see if any hogs were in the area. Just let one of those annoying porkers put so much as a snout to her corset and she'd make bacon out of him.

The knock came again, this time louder, and wondering how Damian had made it to her door so quickly, she rushed to let him in.

Chapter 24

Carolyn Webber stood at the door to Amanda's apartment. Wearing a silk dressing gown, her small, dainty feet sheathed in a pair of satin mules, she looked pale. Judging by the shadows beneath her red-rimmed eyes, she hadn't slept much. Even her blond hair, hastily pinned into an untidy bun, lacked its usual luster. She looked absolutely awful. "Oh, Amanda!" Carolyn burst into tears and buried her face in her hands.

"Oh, you poor thing." Momentarily forgetting about Damian and the corset that was no doubt being devoured by a gluttonous hog, Amanda drew her friend into her apartment and shut the door. She then led the sobbing woman to the davenport.

"Arthur didn't come home last night and it's all because of the bed."

Alarmed, Amanda was momentarily speechless. If the bed was involved, the Webbers' problems were definitely more serious than she'd originally thought. "You're not telling me Arthur has another woman. . . ."

Carolyn shook her head vehemently at first, then her eyebrows shot clear up to her hairline. "Oh, dear, I never thought of the possibility of Arthur having another woman. It would certainly explain his bad temper of late."

"Carolyn Webber, now listen to me!" Wishing she could take back her careless remark, Amanda laid her hands on Carolyn's shoulders and shook her gently.

"You're the only woman for him! Now explain the bed situation."

"I bought single beds."

Amanda dropped her hands and pressed them together in her lap. "You did what?"

"Don't look so scandalized. You know single beds are all the fashion right now. Why, all the best families are reported to have them."

"But you're still a bride."

"That doesn't mean I can't be fashionable, does it?"

"Is that the only reason you purchased single beds? To be fashionable?"

"Well, of course. What other reason could there be?"

"Did you explain this to Arthur?"

"I tried, but he wouldn't let me get a word in edgewise. He said even Reverend Jesse James disapproves of single beds."

"And what, may I ask, does that old Bible thumper know about furniture?"

Carolyn pulled her lace handkerchief out of her sleeve and blew her nose. "I asked Arthur the very same thing. He told me the reverend believes single beds weaken the holy bonds of marriage."

Amanda made a sound of disbelief. "If a marriage can be weakened by a two-foot separation, it wasn't very strong to begin with."

"Oh, dear. Maybe you're right. Maybe our marriage was never meant to be." Carolyn's tears flowed anew.

Amanda sighed; it seemed everything she said only made matters worse. "I'm sorry, Carolyn, I didn't mean to suggest . . . Why, lots of people think single beds are a good idea. Dr. Paine says single beds allow a woman to sleep better and she's less likely to suffer hysteria."

"I've never been hysterical in my life," Carolyn sobbed. "Not ever, ever, EVER!"

"Yes, I can see you're always in control." Amanda tried to think of something to say to calm her down. "I'll fix us both some tea." She crossed to her Reform stove, hoping for inspiration. She'd counseled a lot of distraught wives and a few distraught husbands in her time, but never had she dealt with the issue of bedroom furniture.

She set the teakettle onto the hot grill, then glanced out the window, taking care not to be seen. Damian was back, watching her apartment. He was up to something. But what? And why?

Carolyn continued to wring her hands in dismay. "Oh, Amanda. What am I going to do? We argue about everything. If it's not the beds, it's something else. All I'm trying to do is make our home fashionable so that . . ."

Amanda tore her eyes from the window. "So that what, Carolyn?"

Fresh tears rolled down Carolyn's cheeks. "So that his family won't think I'm nothing but a charwoman."

"That's nothing to be ashamed of," Amanda said. "Besides, Arthur knew what you were when he asked you to marry him."

"Yes, but he didn't know his father would write him out of his will."

"It wouldn't have changed a thing had he known. Arthur would still have married you."

"I'm not so certain." Carolyn sniffled and dabbed at her tears.

"Well, I am!"

"But that doesn't mean he plans to stay with me. You know how fast the divorce rate is rising. Why, according to the *New York Times,* last year in Maine alone there were twenty-three divorces for every one recorded just fifty years ago. I shudder to think what the divorce rate is here in New York."

"Arthur's not going to divorce you, Carolyn."

"We don't know that for certain. What I do know is if he had it to do again, he would never walk away from his family to marry me."

"But that's just it. Don't you see? He *did* walk away from his family. He wanted you. So why do you keep trying to give him all the things he walked away from?

Maybe he doesn't want fashionable furniture and fancy clothes."

In the short time since they'd been married, Carolyn had literally filled their apartment with Japanese hangings, rattan armchairs, and walnut furniture. The furnishings would be more suited to the fancy French flats on Eighteenth Street than the more modest apartment that overlooked the alley known as the King's Highway. It was Carolyn's idea to hire the drunk named Adams as a doorman, but even he couldn't make the run-down tenement building look fashionable.

"Don't you see, Carolyn? Arthur married you not because you could give him what he already had, but because he wanted a whole new life."

"I never thought of it that way."

"When Arthur enrolled for cycling classes, he never smiled. He was always so serious. I purposely introduced him to you because you made everyone smile. And you know what? It worked. I actually saw Arthur laugh out loud that first day he met you."

Carolyn smiled and a dreamy look crossed her face as she recalled the day Amanda described.

"Once you married him you got all serious-minded. I haven't heard Arthur laugh in recent weeks," Amanda said gently. "And I suspect you haven't been doing a lot of laughing, either."

"Oh, Amanda! You're absolutely right. We've been so busy arguing over furniture and wallpaper and . . ." A worried frown settled on her forehead. "He's so distant; I'm not sure I can make him laugh again."

Amanda took Carolyn's hand in hers and squeezed it. "You might start by getting rid of those single beds."

No sooner had Carolyn left than Donny walked through the door. "Where have you been?" Amanda asked, knowing he had probably visited every one of their neighbors in turn.

"Hello yourself," Donny said, grinning. He then

dumped his tin box of buttons onto the floor and began sorting them according to size. He never seemed to grow tired of his buttons and spent hours at a time arranging them into various groups.

Amanda wandered over to the window and peered through the lace curtains. Damian was still watching her apartment.

More curious than ever, Amanda drew a black shawl over her shoulders. "Stay here, Donny. I'll be back."

"Where's your pride?" Donny said, lining up his brass buttons.

It was unusually quiet in the hall. Not even the Fennessy baby was crying.

The doorman was propped up against the wall by the front door, sound asleep, an empty whiskey bottle by his side.

Amanda hurried past him and cut across the cobblestone alley where she had seen Damian moments earlier. Wouldn't you know? He was nowhere in sight. Nor, for that matter, was her corset. "Darn hog! I hope you have a stomachache."

Muttering to herself, she checked every conceivable hiding place up and down the King's Highway, startling a scavenging ragpicker in her search. Finally, she gave up and headed back to her apartment. Was it possible she was seeing things? She doubted it. Still, Damian was always on her mind lately. Lord almighty, hardly a night went by that he didn't appear in her dreams.

Just as she reached the second-floor landing, something clamped down hard on her wrist. Startled, she cried out, almost fainting with relief upon discovering it was Damian.

"Are you looking for me, Amanda?"

"Damian! Don't ever sneak up on me again. You nearly scared me to death."

He released her wrist, but continued to scrutinize her.

"What are you doing here?" she demanded.

"I'm looking for answers. Why the hell are you having me followed?"

Amanda stared at him in confusion. "You're a fine one to accuse *me* of following *you.* You're the one lurking in the shadows. Besides, why would I have you followed?"

He lifted a dark brow. "You didn't have me followed?"

"No, of course not."

"And you didn't sic your knife-wielding friend on me?"

"Knife-wielding—?" Alarm rushed through her like an ill wind. This was serious. "Damian, I have no idea what you're talking about."

He stared at her hard, as if trying to make up his mind if she spoke the truth. "I saw the man who held me at knifepoint leave your school."

"Really?" The idea of a man with a knife at the school was alarming, but not really as much as Damian's accusations.

"He's slightly built, stood so high." He held his hand shoulder high to demonstrate. "Dressed in black."

She thought for a moment. "I can think of only one man fitting that description. He stopped by to inquire about cycling lessons, but never signed up."

"Did he leave his name?"

"Not that I can remember. Oh, Damian!" She covered her mouth with her fingertips.

"What is it, Amanda? Do you know him?"

"No, but . . . he could be working for my uncle."

Damian's eyebrows rose. "Your uncle?"

"My uncle is trying to gain guardianship over Donny."

"Why didn't you tell me this before?"

"I don't know. . . . I didn't think you'd be interested."

"Damn it, Amanda! Of course I'm interested." He drew his brows together. "Would your uncle hire a knife-wielding thug?"

"I don't know. It was just a thought. . . ." Her voice faded away. It was crazy. Uncle Randall wouldn't resort to violence, would he? "You don't think *I* hired the man?"

"You blame my family for your father's death. I thought perhaps . . ."

Her eyes locked with his. "If I were out for revenge, you'd know it. I wouldn't be sneaking around behind your back!" Angered by his accusations, and hurt beyond belief, she tried to escape, but he halted her with a firm hand on her arm.

"Do you blame me, Amanda? You said yourself you hated my family. Hated me."

"But that was before. Now that I know you . . . I could never—"

"Many people whom I trusted turned on my family during my father's trial and afterward." A bleak look crossed his face. "You loved your father very much and I know you have a fierce need to protect those you love."

"And *you* love your father," she said, accusingly.

"That's true."

"And you would love and defend him even if he *were* guilty."

"I can't deny that, Amanda. But I would never, *never* try to set a guilty man free. Not even my own father."

Strangely enough, she believed him. "And I would most certainly not hire a knife-wielding thug for revenge!"

"I'm sorry—" he said, surprising her. The eyes that held hers were dark with regret and remorse, and the depth of his sorrow touched her deeply.

No longer angry with him, she nonetheless had to say what was on her mind. "You could be wrong, Damian. About your father's innocence. No one wants to believe a loved one is capable of doing terrible things."

"I know my father and I'm not wrong. One day I hope to prove it to you."

"You don't have to prove anything to me, Damian."

His eyebrow arched with surprise. "You aren't just saying that, are you? I'll know if you are."

She looked at him curiously, relieved to see a quirk of humor tease the corner of his mouth. "How would you know?"

"Like this." He lifted her chin and gazed into her face and she couldn't miss the delicious masculine smell of him as he lowered his head to kiss her. Her heart leaped with excitement and her knees threatened to buckle under her. His lips were warm and gentle at first; then he slid his free hand around her waist and crushed her to him.

Lord almighty, did he ever mean business this time! He ravished her lips hungrily, probing, demanding, giving as much as he took. His lips were like fire intent on devouring everything in its path. But nothing prepared her for the titillating feel of his tongue in her mouth.

She gasped in surprise. Never had a man kissed her so! He lifted his lips from hers and chuckled softly. "I told you next time would be different."

His lips descended on hers again, and this time when he forced her lips open with his thrusting tongue, she offered him all the encouragement he could hope for.

Noises sounded around her, voices blurred together. But the clamoring sounds meant nothing to her in light of the new and utterly delicious sensations created by his hands and mouth.

Their lips parted at last, but only because they were both out of breath. He cupped her face with his hand and gazed into her eyes. "Your lips told me you meant what you said about my father."

Is that *all* her lips said? Obviously, she had a lot to learn about kissing. "Of . . . of course I meant it."

"Now let's see if you're as honest about the other." He nuzzled her neck with his lips before whispering in her ear. The low, sensual tone of his voice affected her almost as deeply as his kiss. "Did you like it, Amanda? The kiss. Did you like it?"

Mesmerized by his silky voice, she could only nod.

"You aren't just saying that to be a lady, are you? You won't hurt my feelings, so tell me the truth."

She pulled away from him. *Ooooooh*, he made her so mad! He couldn't just kiss her and be done with it! Oh, no! he had to use it to taunt her. "No, I'm not just being a lady!" she said irritably.

He studied her for a moment. "I'm glad to hear it. But your eyes—ah, yes, your eyes. They tell me you still feel torn between me and your family loyalties." He dropped a feathery kiss on her forehead. "Don't look so worried, Amanda. I'll wait."

"Wait?" Still feeling the effects of his kiss, her eyes widened. "For what?"

"For the day you can come to me without getting yourself all tied up in knots."

"I'm not tied up," she said defensively.

"Yes, you are. You think that letting yourself love me is disloyal to your father."

"Love!" she exclaimed, shocked. She always knew he was brash, but nothing he'd said or done prior could equal such a bold assumption. "I most certainly do *not* love you!"

"You're just not willing to admit it. But don't worry, you will."

"Would you stop telling me not to worry? And I would appreciate it if you would refrain from telling me what I will and will not do."

"All right, but only on one condition. You promise to stop being so stubborn. Knowing you, you'll never own up to your true feelings just to prove a point."

"You're calling me stubborn?" She stared at him in astonishment. "If anyone's stubborn—"

"Careful, Amanda. You might one day have to eat your words." He pulled her satin corset out of the deep pocket of his coat and shoved it into her hands before starting down the stairs. "You owe me," he called over his shoulder. "I had to wrestle a thousand-pound hog for that thing."

"I wish I could have been there," she called after him. "Where are you going? I've not finished with what I have to say—"

"Don't worry about it. Actions speak louder than words and a kiss speaks loudest of all. Besides, I want to see what all the commotion is about."

Stuffing her corset in the stairwell where she could retrieve it later, she stomped down the stairs after him. "Come back here. Damian!"

She was surprised to find a crowd of people outside her building and she glanced around worriedly, thinking there must be a fire. Had Carolyn burned Arthur's pants again? A water wagon blocked the alley, forcing Amanda to squeeze past a smelly old mare in order to see what everyone was gawking at. She caught a glimpse of Damian, then lost him in the crowd.

All eyes were focused on the astonishing sight of two single mattresses entangled in the clothesline outside the Webbers' second-story window.

Amanda's neighbors hung out of every window and no one bothered with the pretense of hanging up clothes. Mrs. Aviary's strident voice was pitched high with excitement. "I was minding my own business when suddenly I heard Carolyn say she wanted to get rid of the beds and Mr. Webber immediately tossed the mattresses out the window, one right after another."

"That's exactly what happened," Ellie-May said, giggling.

"Never saw anything like it in all my born days," Mrs. Aviary continued.

"Never," Ellie-May agreed.

Mrs. Brook shook her head in dismay. "How are we going to get the mattresses down? That's what I want to know."

Everyone had an opinion. One man suggested they call the fire department. A passing ragpicker stopped to suggest they cut the clotheslines. Others argued that since Mr. Webber had tossed the mattresses out the window, it was his responsibility to take care of the problem.

The neighbors continued to lament about the mattresses long into the night.

Amanda didn't care a fiddle about the mattresses. She had other things on her mind. Long after Donny had gone to bed, she sat at the table and, ignoring the voices drifting through her open window, tried to make sense of the rampaging emotions that kept her on tenterhooks.

She *loved* him? Indeed! What an arrogant thing for him to think. Nothing could be further from the truth.

Whatever would make him say such a thing? Not only was he the most arrogant man she'd ever met, he was also the most irritating.

Of course she had to admit that he *did* make her heart sing like no one else had ever done. And when he kissed her! Oh, Lordy, it was as if she were flying on a cloud. But just because she liked his kisses didn't mean she loved him. Absolutely not!

Chapter 25

It was hot that Independence Day and Sergeant Summerset gleefully informed Amanda it was going to get hotter. "What did I tell you?" He practically jumped with joy as he dangled his thermometer in front of her face. "It's gonna be a blazer, all right!"

"A blazer!" Donny called out, his face beaming beneath his ever-present straw hat.

Sergeant Summerset had predicted the mercury would rise to unprecedented heights, and the few times in the past the meteorologist's predictions had proven accurate, he had been unbearably smug. Today was no different. He ran up and down the parade route, boasting to the waiting crowd and practically crowing with delight every time the mercury on his thermometer inched up another notch. He was beginning to get on Amanda's nerves.

She didn't need the meteorologist to tell her it was hot; the Belgian blocks beneath her feet shimmered with heat and she could feel the warmth of the cut-stone sidewalk through the soles of her shoes. The fabric of her shirtwaist stuck to her back and the tendrils of hair felt damp on her face. Worse was the pungent smell of the dairy and sheepfold that drifted down from Central Park.

Still, the air crackled with excitement. New Yorkers whose business or financial circumstances had prevented them from escaping to the fashionable resorts of Newport, Bar Harbor, Saratoga, or Europe for the summer lined Fifth Avenue, eagerly waiting for the parade to start.

Drums rolled in the distance, followed by the blast of brass horns. Carriages decorated with bright summer flowers and wagons wrapped in colored streamers stood in a line, waiting for the parade to begin. High-stepping horses with braided manes and plaited tails pranced about impatiently, their riders dressed in fashionable riding breeches and plumed hats. Women dressed in fitted bodices and flowing skirts, their hats draped with flying veils, sat elegantly perched upon sidesaddles, their riding crops in hand.

Amanda kept a watchful eye on Donny. It was difficult to predict how he would react to such a large crowd, but so far he seemed more interested in what was going on around him than alarmed, and he actually laughed at the antics of the clowns. But he held on tight to his button box and didn't stray far from Amanda's side.

"The parade will start soon," Amanda said, squeezing his hand.

"Horse likes you," Donny said, holding his floppy-brimmed straw hat as a group of men rode by on horseback.

Together they stood on the sidewalk, and Amanda fanned herself furiously as she waited for the members of the Knickerbocker Ladies' Cycling Club to gather.

Amanda wore a white poplin Carter frock over a blue-and-white sateen underdress. Her face shaded by a straw skimmer decorated with ribbons that matched her dress, she scanned the crowd for her still-missing students.

Miss Quackenbush was the worst possible cyclist, but at least she was punctual. Today she had abandoned her usual black dress and hat in favor of the white divided skirt and blouse the Knickerbockers had adopted as their official uniform.

Not even the black grosgrain ribbon tied beneath her pointed chin made her look any less formidable.

Amanda had tried everything in her power to discourage Miss Quackenbush from riding in the parade, but the fool woman was as stubborn as an old toothache and was bound and determined to make a fool of herself in front of hundreds of people. Amanda had no choice but to take matters into her own hands. If this plan of hers didn't work, her school's reputation could be in ruins, or worse yet, spectators might well be injured.

Moose walked up beside her and playfully tousled Donny's hair. He wore trousers in a bold yellow plaid, a white shirt, and a brown waistcoat.

"Hello, yourself," Donny said, grinning up at the man.

"Hello yourself, back," Moose said, looking pleased. He shifted his gaze to Amanda. "Don't you go worryin' yourself none, Miz Mandy. This is gonna work, I guarantee." He chuckled now as he had a few days earlier when Amanda had first proposed the idea to him.

"How can I not worry? The reputation of my school is at stake." She inclined her head toward the members of the ladies' cycling club, who were threading their bicycles through the crowd. "If they so much has suspect a thing, poor Miss Quackenbush won't be able to show her face again." As annoying as the woman was, Amanda couldn't help but feel sorry for her.

"Trust me, Miz Mandy. There ain't nothing to worry about. Everything's goin' exactly as planned and nobody will suspect a thing." The big black man sauntered away, whistling to himself.

Church bells rang out, the melodious chimes signaling the start of the parade. Children shuffled their feet impatiently and a group of rowdy newsboys had to be chased out of the street.

Women garbed in bustled frocks and flat-brimmed, high-crowned hats chattered among themselves, while their escorts stood to the side, smoking cigars and discussing politics.

One man dodged beneath the curtains of his camera, shouting to his family to hold still.

"Where's your pride?" Donny called out upon seeing the children form a straight line.

Amanda pulled Donny out of the camera's view. The poor man had been trying to take a photograph for the last hour. But his three young sons, dressed in knee-high britches and side-buttoned boots, were too excited to stand still for the length of time required to let the chemicals dry.

A lacquered carriage rolled down Fifth, trailing streamers. Mayor Ledbetter sat by the driver and shouted into a megaphone, welcoming everyone to the parade. "This promises to be the best parade ever to grace the fine streets of our great city."

Loud cheers rose as members of New York's paid fire brigade came into view. The three boys moved away from the camera, their father's complaints falling on deaf ears.

The crowd clapped for the brightly painted horse-drawn fire wagons and the brand-new hook and ladder that had been designed to reach to the top of a five-story building.

"Oh, Donny. Isn't it wonderful?" The smile died on her face. Donny looked startled. "Fire hot!" It was a phrase he'd heard her say time and again to warn him away from danger.

"There's no fire, Donny. It's a parade. And that's a hook and ladder." He'd seen the fire wagons roll by their apartment, but the hook and ladder was something new.

"Hook and ladder," he repeated after Amanda, and seeming to enjoy the words, he kept repeating them, though he still continued to issue stern warnings to those around him. "Fire hot!"

Close behind came the Paid Firemen Brigade Cycling Club in perfect formation, mounted on shiny big-wheel bicycles painted red. The firemen wore bright red shirts, their black trousers held up with red suspenders. Their japanned leather helmets gleamed and the sun danced upon the polished brass trim.

Amanda mentally put the men through their paces.

"Perfect!" she called out, though she decided to make a few changes in the routine before the next parade. She held her breath as the cyclists began to position themselves for a tricky maneuver.

The cyclist at the head of each line turned in the opposite direction right on cue, and Amanda's worries faded away as the firemen followed their leaders with flawless precision, forming two perfect circles.

"Where's your pride?" Donny called, clapping his hands.

Weaving in and out, the cyclists barely missed hitting each other, and hoots of appreciation rose from the crowd when the leader gave three short whistles and the firemen returned to their original formation.

The cyclists rode down the center of the street to the crowd's enthusiastic cheers. No one clapped louder than Amanda, except perhaps Moose.

Damian arrived and parked Christopher's wheelchair next to Donny. "Are you still angry at me?" he asked her.

"Angry?" She gazed up into his smiling eyes. "Certainly not. You don't affect me in the least."

He grinned. "Careful what you say, Amanda. I'd hate to have to prove you're a liar in front of all these people." He tapped her on the lips lightly before turning away.

Now she *was* angry! How dare he blackmail her with his kisses.

She decided to ignore him, but this was easier said than done. Even in the crowd, he commanded attention, and as much as she hated to admit it, he looked utterly handsome in his white cotton shirt and checkered pants, his red suspenders matching his bow tie. Just looking at him, which she did despite her best efforts not to, made her heart beat faster.

Much to her mortification, he caught her gazing at him and grinned, touching the brim of his straw hat with a fingertip. "You look pretty as a picture," he said. He then leaned closer and whispered in her ear, "I love to see you blush."

"I'm not blushing!" she said, fanning herself furiously. "It's hot."

As if to prove her right, the weatherman ran by, gleefully announcing the temperature had risen another degree.

"A blazer," Donny said.

"A blazer," Christopher agreed.

"If the weatherman is right, it's going to get hotter," Amanda added, avoiding Damian's eyes.

"I don't doubt it," he concurred, though a quick look in his direction confirmed her suspicions. He wasn't talking about the weather. The thought sent an involuntary shiver down her spine.

She quickly pulled her gaze away from him. "Oh, look, Donny. A pony."

Christopher's face was bright as he took in all the wondrous sights around him. "It's gonna be the best parade ever!" His eyes widened as another brass band headed their way. "Papa! Look!"

"Papa, look!" Donny echoed.

"Shhh, Donny." Embarrassed, Amanda hastened to explain. "He's only repeating what he hears. He doesn't really understand what he's saying."

"If Donny wants to call me Papa, it's fine with me. I'm sure Christopher won't mind. Will you, son?"

She bit her lip and tried swallowing the lump in her throat. It was hard to stay mad at a man who was infinitely kind to her brother. "Thank you, Damian, for insisting I bring him today. I was very worried about it."

"See? What did I tell you? There's nothing to be concerned about."

For some reason, she found herself battling tears. Lord almighty, what a time to get all softhearted. She forced herself to concentrate on the big brass band that marched by, the music from its gleaming horns drowning out the appreciative applause.

She turned to assure Donny there was nothing to fear, but Damian had reached him first and was quietly talking him through his anxiety.

"Don't be scared, Donny," Christopher said, looking older than his seven years. "It's just music." He clapped his hands and swayed to the rhythm.

Donny laughed and did likewise. "Where's your pride?"

Amanda laughed, too. Lord, what was the matter with her? One moment crying and the next, laughing. Her emotions were out of control.

Damian waited for the band to pass before moving closer to Amanda. "May I leave Christopher in your care? I gave Miss Hannah the day off and it turns out I have some business to attend to."

"Of course," she said without hesitation. Not only was she genuinely fond of the boy, Donny never left Christopher's side and this made her job so much easier. "I can't imagine what business would call you away on a holiday."

Damian gave her a conspiratorial wink. "It just so happens there's a damsel in distress. Heaven knows I can't say no to a lady." His eyes twinkled. Damian stooped in front of Christopher's wheelchair. "Do as Miss Blackwell says." Meeting her gaze, he turned and hurried through the crowd.

Donny set his tin of buttons on Christopher's lap and grabbed the handles of the wheelchair. Christopher seemed to sense how important Donny's button collection was and he held on to the tin box with both hands. "I can't see the parade," he complained.

Amanda hesitated. "Very well. Let's move over there, Donny." She helped him steer the wheelchair closer to the curb, and Christopher made a sound like a foghorn to warn others to step aside. Donny loved the sound and did his best to imitate it. By the time she had staked out a spot next to the curb, both boys were laughing in delight.

"Can you see now?"

"Yes." Christopher's eyes shone brightly. "Oh, look, Donny, a monkey! And look over there, a clown!"

"Don't feed the monkey," Donny admonished.

"You have to say *don't.*" Donny's head turned in every direction, trying to take in all the sights. As long as he held on to the wheelchair, he didn't appear to be frightened or otherwise overwhelmed. Christopher had a calming influence on Donny, and for that Amanda would be forever grateful.

Old Thorny rode by on his horse. Donny pulled his beloved straw hat off his head and held it out to the sparrow cop's horse, Chester. "Horse likes you."

"Yes, Chester likes you, Donny," Old Thorny said. "But you better put your hat on your head." He rode off, calling a warning to spectators to stay off the street.

The men's cycling club started along the parade route. The men went through their routine with no problem, though Sergeant Summerset dropped his thermometer and had to stop his bicycle to retrieve it.

After the routine was complete, Lockhammer was so busy showing off for the crowd and trying to upstage the mayor, his bicycle clipped Ledbetter's front wheel. The mayor sailed over his handlebars and took a nosedive into the crowd.

"Give the signal!" Donny called out, clearly agitated.

"What does he mean?" Christopher asked.

"He wants me to blow my whistle," Amanda said.

"Give the signal!" Donny repeated, but he calmed down when a gaily decorated phaeton rolled by, drawn by two high-stepping white horses. "Horse likes you."

Amanda craned her neck to the empty field where the Knickerbockers waited, the women's bicycles in proper formation. She was so nervous, her heart thumped against her rib cage.

Miss Quackenbush stood in front of the other cyclists, holding her bicycle by the handlebars.

"One day I'm going to ride a bicycle," Christopher said.

Amanda laid a hand on Christopher's shoulder. "I believe you will."

Vincent spotted her as he pushed his button cart

along the parade route. "Don't tell me that crazy Miss Quackenbush is actually going to ride in the parade."

"Shhh." She looked around to make certain none of the Knickerbockers had heard him. "She has to ride. She's the president of the cycling club."

Vincent glanced skyward. "God help us all."

Vincent was about to take off when Moose beckoned to him. "We need your help."

"I can't leave my cart," Vincent protested.

"Miz Mandy will watch it." Moose grabbed Vincent by the elbow and the two men disappeared into the crowd.

Amanda pushed Christopher closer to Vincent's cart and rubbed her wet palms on her skirt.

"Buttooooons!" Donny called as he'd heard Vincent do. "Come and git your buttoooooons!" Amanda tried to hush him, but he continued his loud chant.

"How much are the porcelains?" a woman asked, checking over the merchandise with the aid of a jeweled lorgnette.

Amanda told the woman to come back later, but her voice was drowned out by a German brass band. The ladies' cycling club was next. Miss Quackenbush blew her whistle right on cue. At least she got that part right.

Loud boos rose from the crowd. One man shouted, "Women don't belong on bicycles!"

"They don't belong in voting booths, either."

Amanda wouldn't normally let such statements go unchallenged, but today she ignored them.

"Oh, look!" Christopher called out. "There's Papa."

"There's Papa!" Donny said.

"Oh, no!" Amanda pressed her fingers together. She had no idea Moose had pressed Damian into service, too. But there he stood, tall and handsome, along with Moose, Caleb, and Vincent. She sighed in resignation. Now she had another reason to be grateful to him, and knowing him, he would take full advantage of her gratitude.

The four men positioned themselves on either side

of Miss Quackenbush. Looking proud as royalty, with no apparent concern for her lack of riding skills, Miss Quackenbush blew on her whistle a second time. At Moose's signal, the men bent over in unison and straightened, lifting Miss Quackenbush's bicycle high off the ground. The schoolteacher looked startled, then shocked, as the four men balanced the wheels of her bicycle shoulder high. Fortunately, by the time she found her voice, the crowd's loud cheers drowned out her protests.

In all the confusion, Miss Quackenbush forgot to cue the others. Amanda quickly felt for the whistle she wore on a ribbon and blew two short blasts followed by a long one.

The four men moved forward and the other members of the cycling club followed close behind.

What a commanding sight Miss Quackenbush made, perched high over the heads of the four men. She looked as if she was beginning to enjoy herself. At least she had stopped demanding the men set her down. Instead, she waved her hand and the crowd went wild.

Christopher laughed out loud, his eyes filled with glee. "Miss Quackenbush looks funny."

Amanda couldn't stop smiling and she clapped her hands in time to the music played by the distant band. "Miss Quackenbush looks wonderful."

After the parade was over, the members of the Knickerbocker Ladies' Cycling Club gathered around Miss Quackenbush, congratulating her. Even Mrs. Brewer, who seldom bothered to compliment anyone, was actually gushing.

"That was truly an inspiration," Mrs Brewer said. A matronly woman shaped like a butter churn, she raved on and on, her open parasol bopping up and down as she spoke. "It never occurred to me to invite men to march by our side. What a splendid way to solicit their support."

"It was brilliant!" agreed Mrs. Winston from the shade of an enormous blue hat decorated with a sheaf of peacock fathers. "Now that Mr. Newcastle has publicly endorsed our club, I think we should make him an honorary member."

Amanda nodded in agreement, but the wife of publisher Joseph Blankenship shook her head vigorously. "You do know Mr. Newcastle's reputation is in question?" Her French accent was thick, but her meaning clear.

Mrs. Winston's hand flew to her ample bosom. "Oh, dear, she's quite right."

Miss Quackenbush, looking unbearably pleased with herself, stared down her pointed nose at Mrs. Blankenship. "Personally, I like a man whose reputation is in question."

Mrs. Brewer tittered and Mrs. Winston whipped her fan back and forth furiously.

Miss Quackenbush apparently thought the matter settled. "I hearby decree that Mr. Newcastle, Mr. Moose, Mr. White, and . . ." She cast a shy glance at the button man's cart. ". . . Vincent are honorary members of the Knickerbocker Ladies' Cycling Club."

Amanda was pleased with herself. Not only had she saved Miss Quackenbush's skin, she had accurately predicted the former schoolteacher would take a liking to the button vendor. Now all Amanda had to do was convince Vincent that he and the schoolmarm made a perfect match.

Amanda's job didn't get any easier following the parade. For one thing, Vincent didn't take kindly to finding himself a member of a women's organization and the following morning showed up at the school to complain.

"What's that crazy Miss Quackenbush going to think up next?" he complained. "If word gits out, I'll be the laughin' stock of me profession."

"No one's going to laugh, Vincent. That was a very nice thing you and the other men did for her and she wants to show her appreciation."

"I didn't do it for her," Vincent said defensively. "I didn't want her ridin' her dang bicycle into the crowd." He walked away, mumbling to himself, and then, spotting a group of potential customers, strolled toward the entrance of the park. He threw back his head and called, "Buttoooooons. Get your . . . buttoooooons."

Amanda watched him go, then turned her attention to the construction site. She hadn't seen Damian since yesterday's parade. Not that she cared, of course, but it was curious. It was nearly noon and he was still nowhere in sight. It wasn't like him to stay away from the site this long.

She spotted Caleb and hurried toward him. "Have you seen Damian?"

Caleb looked up from the blueprints. "He left for Philadelphia first thing this morning. Something about his father. He expects to be back in a couple of days. He said he'd see you as soon as he returned."

"His father?" Her mind whirled with possibilities. "Do you suppose he's found what he's been looking for?"

"I don't know. All I can tell you is that he received a telegram early this morning and he left on the first available train."

Amanda felt a rush of excitement. Maybe this was the news Damian had been searching for. She was surprised to discover how much she wanted this. If Damian really did prove his father innocent, there would be nothing, absolutely nothing, to keep her from loving him. That is, if she wanted to, which she didn't.

"Are you all right, Miss Blackwell?" Caleb asked.

"Yes, of course. I . . . eh . . . want to thank you for helping us with Miss Quackenbush."

Caleb grinned. "After what you did for me, it's the least I could do."

The smile on his face filled her with pleasure. Never had she seen a man look as contented and happy as Caleb had looked since his marriage to Priscilla.

"I don't know how to express my gratitude," he added.

"Don't worry about it." She frowned. Now she was beginning to sound like Damian. "It's not necessary."

Growing red as a fresh-boiled lobster, he scraped the ground with the toe of his boot. "Priscilla said it's not proper to talk about such things in polite company . . ."

"Thank God I've never been accused of being polite."

"Then in that case . . . If the good Lord sees fit to bless us one day with a baby girl, we plan to call her Amanda."

"Amanda, eh?" She was still smiling when she left him.

Moose was outside the school, pushing a strange new child-sized tricycle around in a circle. Seeing her, he straightened. "What do you think?"

"I think it's too small for you."

Moose gave her a crooked grin. "It's for your little friend, Christ'pher."

Her interest piqued, she examined the bicycle carefully. It was a strange-looking contraption, its bucket-shaped seat sandwiched between the wheels. "For Christopher? But he can't move his legs."

"Now don't you go worryin' none over that, Miz Mandy. The little fella won't need to move his legs. He can pedal with his hands. All he has to do is grab hold of these here hand levers. There's nothin' to it." Moose demonstrated.

Her smile broadened in approval. "Oh, Moose. What a wonderful idea! A hand-operated bicycle. Do you think this will work?"

Moose grinned. "You know what they sez, Miz Mandy. The proof is in the puddin'."

Chapter 26

The following day, Amanda brought Donny to school with her so he could practice his typing. He spent the morning pecking away at the typewriter, filling endless sheets of paper with the phrases and words he'd memorized from various signs and billboards on the trip from the apartment to the school. *Stay off the grass,* he typed, and *horsecar stop.*

Amanda was amazed at the number of signs he recalled. *Metropolitan Elevated Railway* was next, and he managed to spell each word correctly before pecking out the words *New York Central and Hudson River Railroad.* He typed the names of every theater on Broadway and the sign he'd read that morning outside their tenement building: *To Let.*

Amanda had to laugh when he typed out *hemorrhoids,* a word he'd seen on a sandwich board.

"Oh, Donny. You really are a brilliant boy." She hugged him tight.

He gave her a half smile. "Good match."

A warm glow flowed through her. "We are a good match." She lowered herself by his side and studied his serious face.

"Good match," he repeated. "Good match."

Suddenly something occurred to her. "You want to know how to type it, don't you?" She could hardly contain her excitement. He wasn't just typing words at random. He actually understood the words had meaning. She was convinced of it. "You type it like this." She pecked out the letters. "There. Good match."

"Good match," he repeated. He then filled up an entire page with the two words.

He was still typing when the first of the wheelmen arrived for his lesson.

Dr. Paine looked surprised to see Donny at the school. "Good morning, Donny. You're looking well this morning."

"Hello yourself," Donny said.

"I'm glad you came early," Amanda said. "I've been wanting to talk to you." She handed him a type-written sheet. "Look at this."

The doctor scanned it thoughtfully. "Donny did this?"

Amanda nodded. "I thought he was typing words he'd seen at random. But I think he understands the words have meaning. He just asked me how to type the words *good match*."

"Amanda . . . I've told you before—"

"I know what you've told me, but this has got to mean something," Amanda persisted. "Suppose he does understand what is being said to him? Suppose his main problem is his inability to verbalize?"

"Now, hold on there, Amanda." The doctor scratched his gray head. "That's a mighty lot of supposing."

"It's possible, isn't it?"

"Anything's possible, I suppose, but—" The doctor leaned over Donny's shoulder to watch him type. "Why is he typing Daniel Webster's name?"

"It's the name of the statue in the park."

Dr. Paine rubbed his chin. "Donny, type *Daniel Webster*." Donny did as he was told.

"What did I tell you?" Amanda said.

Still looking skeptical, the doctor tried another tactic. "Now type out the name of one of our country's great statesmen."

"He can't do that," Amanda said. "He doesn't know who the man is or what he stands for."

"Then how can we be certain he's attaching any sort of meaning to the words he types?"

"Watch." She leaned next to her brother. "Donny, type the names of the statues."

Donny immediately went to work. Soon he had typed *Daniel Webster, Shakespeare, Robert Burns, and Liberty*. Watching, the doctor shook his head. "The Statue of Liberty is at Madison Square."

"I didn't stipulate locations," Amanda said.

"You're quite right." Dr. Paine rubbed his whiskered chin. "Don't tell me Donny has every blasted statue in the city memorized."

"Pretty much so. So what do you think?"

"I think it's amazing. Yes, yes, absolutely amazing. But, Amanda, I feel it's my duty to caution you against getting your hopes too high. There's a lot we don't understand about the human mind."

"But you have to admit this is a big step forward."

"I would say so, yes."

"Would you testify to that?"

The doctor's eyes widened. "Testify? In court?"

"My uncle wants the court to give him guardianship over Donny. He plans to put him in a sanitarium. Donny doesn't belong in one of those places. He belongs with me. He's happy with me."

"I see. In that case, I shall be glad to testify, if you think it'll help."

Amanda threw her arms around the doctor's neck, dislocating his spectacles. The flustered doctor blushed with embarrassment. "Oh, my, my, my."

"Good match," Donny said.

The mayor arrived, followed by the other wheelmen, and Amanda and the doctor walked outside, leaving Donny to finish typing his list of statues.

Summerset was walking in a circle with his hands held out, palms up. "I don't understand it. We should be having thundershowers about now."

The reverend nudged him with an elbow. "Buck up. A person can't be expected to guess right all the time."

"Guess? Guess?" Summerset was so aghast, he pulled his red knit cap down to his ears. "You think I guess at the weather?"

Amanda blew her whistle just in time to stop an argument. "All right, men, mount your bicycles and form two lines. We're going to make a few changes in your routine."

Donny ran outside the school, waving his sheet of paper at the doctor. Dr. Paine stopped his bicycle and took the paper in his hand. "Why, thank you, Donny. One never knows when a list of statues will come in handy." He folded the paper and stuck it in his coat pocket, then fell in line behind the other cyclists.

Meanwhile, Donny ran along the sidewalk shouting, "Give the signal. Give the signal."

Lockhammer braked and wiped his damp forehead with his sleeve. It was hot and humid. "Would you tell that kid to shut up!" he growled.

"Hush, Donny." Amanda placed her finger on her lips, but Donny ignored her.

"Give the signal, give the signal!"

"Donny! That's enough!"

Donny looked ready to ignore her, but then he spotted Christopher and Miss Hannah emerging from the park entrance, and he clapped his hands excitedly. "Hello yourself."

"Practice that last routine again," Amanda told the men. "Summerset, take them through their paces."

"It would be my pleasure," Summerset called. "All right, men, pay attention. The wind is coming from the north, so we are going to ride toward the . . ."

Amanda smiled to herself. She should have known better than to ask the weatherman to replace her. She called to Moose. "Christopher's here."

Moose walked outside, the bicycle he'd made particularly for Christopher held upside down over his head. He set the bicycle next to the wheelchair and Christopher eyed it curiously.

"It's for you," Amanda explained.

Christopher's eyes grew big and round. "For me?"

Amanda hunched down by his side. "You said you wanted to ride a bicycle. Now you can."

Christopher's face lit up in delight. "I can ride? Really?"

Miss Hannah frowned in worry. "Oh, dear, I'm not sure this is a good idea."

Amanda patted her arm. "It'll be all right."

"Come on, let's see what you can do," Moose said. Moving with surprising gentleness for someone his size, Moose lifted Christopher out of his wheelchair and lowered him between the wheels and onto the basket seat. "We have a little harness here so you don't fall out." Moose fastened the harness around Christopher's waist. "See? What did I tell you?"

Miss Hannah wrung her hands together. "I'm not sure Mr. Newcastle would approve."

"It's all right, Miss Hannah," Amanda said. "I'll take full responsibility."

"Now grab hold of the hand levers," Moose said. "Attaboy. Extend your arm down all the way. There you go. Now do the same with the other arm. Pretend you're swimming."

Amanda pulled Donny out of the way.

Christopher did as he was told and the tricycle inched forward. Donny laughed out loud, and encouraged, Christopher moved his arms again, this time faster.

"That's it!" Amanda cried excitedly. "Keep going."

In no time at all, Christopher was able to make the bicycle move forward and back, though steering to the right or left was still difficult for him. "Look at me!" he called, a broad smile on his face. "I can ride!"

Donny clapped his hands. "Where's your pride?"

Even Miss Hannah was excited and appeared to have forgotten her reservations. Why, the woman was actually jumping up and down like beads of water on a hot grill. "Mercy me. It's a miracle."

Amanda squeezed the big black man's arm. "It *is* a miracle," she said, her voice thick with emotion.

Christopher whizzed past the members of the cycling club and Donny ran after him.

"Praise the Lord!" Reverend Jesse James declared.

"Sunny days are ahead!" the weatherman announced.

The mayor rubbed his chin thoughtfully, no doubt trying to think of a way to take credit.

Summerset clapped his hands. "This way, men," he called, and the wheelers rode off in the opposite direction.

Meanwhile, Amanda began to worry. "That's far enough," she called, but both Christopher and Donny kept going. She glanced at Moose. "Do you suppose he doesn't know how to turn around?"

"Oh, dear," Miss Hannah said, her forehead wrinkled.

Moose cupped his hands around his mouth. "Stop, Christopher, and I'll help you turn around!" Christopher kept going and Amanda blew her whistle. Either Christopher was too intent on what he was doing or he was out of earshot. As long as he kept going, Donny was likely to follow. "I better go after them," Amanda said, racing for a bicycle.

She'd barely reached the side of the school where the spare bicycles were parked when Miss Hannah let out an ear-shattering scream. Thinking Christopher had fallen, Amanda spun around just in time to see Christopher being pulled off his tricycle by a stranger.

She was so startled by what was happening, she failed to notice a second man wrestling with Donny until she heard his high, piercing screams.

Faster than lightning, Amanda mounted her bicycle on the run. Her whistle in her mouth, she blew hard, then shouted at the top of her lungs. "Stop it! Leave them alone!"

Donny's attacker glanced up as Amanda approached. He hesitated for a moment before making a mad dash for the carriage parked a short distance away. He disappeared inside just as it took off in a cloud of dust, with Christopher inside.

Chapter 27

Chaos ruled in those first horrifying moments following Christopher's abduction.

Amanda raced to Donny's side, jumped off her bicycle, and dropped to the ground. "Donny!" But already he was out of control and his high-pitched screams continued to pierce the air.

Fearing he would hurt himself, she grabbed his arms, but he was flailing around so much she couldn't hold him. She was grateful when Moose arrived and took over for her.

The wheelmen rode up. "We heard all the commotion," The mayor shouted to be heard over Donny's screams. "What happened?"

"Someone kidnapped Christopher," Amanda shouted back. "Hurry! Go after that carriage!"

The mayor looked aghast. "Good heavens!"

Dr. Paine dismounted and dropped down on one knee next to Donny. "I'll take care of him. The rest of you, go!"

She nodded in gratitude. "I'll get your friend back, Donny. I promise."

Amanda mounted her bicycle again. She was the best cyclist of the bunch and knew every alley and shortcut in the area. "Follow me, men!" She signaled with her hand. "This way!"

She headed downtown, taking Eighth Avenue. Moose was close behind, followed by Lockhammer, Reverend Jesse James, and the mayor. The weatherman took up the rear.

The carriage turned onto the tree-lined boulevard known as Broadway. Amanda led the pack around horsecars, carriages, and the numerous horse-drawn commercial vehicles parked along the street. Traffic was heavy and Amanda lost sight of the carriage.

"There they are!" Reverend Jesse James called out, pointing. "Turn left at the next corner."

"After them!" Amanda shouted.

Gathering momentum, the cyclists chased the carriage through the streets of Manhattan. Some of the cobblestone streets were so narrow, it was a wonder the carriage could make it through.

"See if you can cut them off," she called to Moose. He nodded and darted up a narrow alley, taking the reverend and weatherman with him. Amanda and the mayor stayed on the trail of the carriage. Bicycles had an advantage. What they lacked in speed they made up for in maneuverability.

They circled around to Broadway again, and by now, traffic had come to a complete standstill. She could see the back of the carriage ahead. "Hold on, Christopher! I'm coming!" She pedaled her bike over the curb and rode along the sidewalk. A vendor moved out of her way, his pushcart capsizing in his haste. Flowers spilled across the sidewalk, forcing Amanda to swerve.

Traffic began to move again and she felt her hopes plummet. Moose emerged from a side street, almost colliding with her bicycle. "There!" she said, pointing at the fast-disappearing rear of the carriage. "Hurry!"

"This way!" Moose and the others followed her, pedaling fast.

"We got them!" the mayor called out triumphantly.

Sergeant Summerset veered his bicycle onto the sidewalk to avoid the slowing traffic and knocked over a uniformed doorman. The mayor zipped around an ice wagon and barely missed slamming into a horse-drawn hearse.

"Holy mackerel. Get out of the way!" Reverend

Jesse James shouted, just before plowing into a two-wheeled sulky.

Ahead, the front wheel of the carriage clipped a fruit cart, sending apples rolling across the street. Moose rode his bicycle through a gypsy's tent and was chased by two mean-spirited men with rings in their noses.

A peddler crossing a street took one look at the cyclists before diving out of the way, the colorful array of suspenders he carried over his shoulders flying in every direction. One pair of suspenders caught in the spokes of the mayor's bicycle, sending him veering into an open fish market and nose-diving into a lobster tank.

"We lost the mayor!" Moose called.

Lockhammer continued to pedal as if nothing had happened. "What a pity."

The carriage stopped suddenly and Amanda cried out excitedly. "Hurry, Moose. This is our chance!" She knew the area, knew it well. They were within a stone's throw of the King's Highway. Anyone not familiar with the area could easily get lost in the maze of alleys and dead-end streets that wound around the complex of brick tenement buildings.

"Oh, no!" she gasped, braking. Suddenly her way was blocked by an enormous herd of hogs.

The hogs spilled across the cobblestones like an army of invading ants. The swine filled the air with throaty grunts, their thick, bristly hides covered with flies. Snouts close to the ground, the hogs sniffed out the garbage strewn along the way as if they were bloodhounds.

"Shoo! Scat," Amanda shouted. She blew her whistle, but rather than speed the animals along, the high-toned screech only seemed to agitate them.

"Scat!" The weatherman lifted his voice to be heard over the noisy grunts. "These pigs are a damned nuisance. Scat!"

"If the mayor had done his job, hogs would have been banned long ago," Lockhammer sniffed.

Amanda tried forcing her bicycle through the herd, but one beefy hog butted his snout against her front wheel.

Amanda shot over the handlebars and landed on the back of a hefty boar. The wind knocked out of her, she flopped up and down like a rag doll on the deck of a wind-tossed ship.

"Moooooooooose. D-d-do s-s-some—Help me!"

"Lawdy mussy! Hold on, Miz Mandy," Moose shouted.

"H-h-hurry!" she cried. She flopped off the back of one hog and onto another. This time she managed to grab hold of the animal's ears. Suddenly the herd thinned out and Moose made a leaping dash toward the hog. The boar dodged, then turned and ran in the opposite direction, with Amanda holding on for dear life.

"Heeeee . . . lp!"

The hog came to a sudden stop. Unable to hold on, Amanda shot over its head and fell to the ground like a sinker. It took her a full minute to realize she was more winded than seriously hurt.

Blinking, she rolled over onto her back and tried to make sense of her surroundings. When she realized what had happened to her, she practically shouted out with joy. She wasn't dead and she wasn't crazy. She had landed on a mattress—a wonderfully soft, wonderfully safe mattress. But it wasn't until she saw Mrs. Aviary hanging out the window above her that she realized the source of her good fortune.

She was lying flat on her back on one of Carolyn Webber's mattresses. Somehow it had tumbled from the top of the clotheslines to the alley below just in time to block her fall.

Ignoring the pain that shot through her shoulders and back, she sat up. The neighs of a horse drew her attention to the carriage, which had stopped a short distance away, and her heart skipped a beat. The kidnappers' horse whinnied and reared, its front hooves pawing the air. Amanda couldn't believe her good luck. The carriage and horse were hopelessly entangled in one of the clotheslines.

The two kidnappers were frantically trying to free the horse, but soon abandoned the idea and took off down the alley, running.

Amanda half ran, half hobbled to the carriage, her hand on her sore hip. Inside Christopher was huddled on the floor, his face hidden in his hands.

"Christopher!" Never had she been so happy to see anyone in her life. "Thank God, you're all right." Forgetting her bruised body and sore muscles, she pulled herself into the carriage and took him in her arms, smothering his dear, sweet, precious face with kisses.

Christopher clung to her, tears rolling down his cheeks. "I want my papa."

"Oh, sweetie. I know you do. Your papa will come. Just as soon as he knows you need him. Meanwhile, you're going to be just fine." She didn't know whether to laugh or cry, she was that happy. "No one's going to harm you. I promise." She cupped his face in her hands. "You aren't hurt, are you?"

Christopher shook his head. his slight body trembling to her touch. "I was scared."

"I know," Amanda whispered, rocking him. "So was I."

Moose's anxious face peered through the door. Upon seeing both Christopher and Amanda safe and sound, the man grinned. "When I done saw you flyin' through the air like nobody's business, I thought for sure you were a goner, Miz Mandy."

So had she, dear God, so had she.

"Praise the Lord," Moose continued. "It weren't meant to be. When those kidnappers got themselves all tangled in the wash, they brought the whole kit and kaboodle fallin' down on top of them. Though I have to say, I never saw anyone hang their mattresses on the line to dry before. Nope, I never did."

How the mattresses came to be on top of the clotheslines was a long story and one that Mrs. Aviary was at that very moment reciting aloud to anyone willing to listen. "And then the mattress came shooting out the window. And no one knew what to do with them. And there they stayed until today, when . . ."

Amanda smiled to herself. After what had happened today, the King's Highway would never be the same. Lord, *she* would never be the same.

"I think I'd better see if I can find you something decent to wear in all this wash," Moose continued. "That old hog took off with your bloomers."

"What?" It was true. Her bloomers were gone, along with the bottom half of her skirt.

Moose wiped his eyes with the back of his hand, his gaze on Christopher. "I don't think I've been that scared since I wuz in Californ'a and awoken out of a sound sleep by a grizzly bear. No, sir, I don't think I ever wuz."

It had been one of the longest days of her life.

Christopher was safe. Dear God, he was safe. Still, she was hardly able to let him out of her sight. Even now, hours later, she kept tiptoeing to the door of her bedroom to make certain he was still where she'd left him, asleep on her bed, next to Donny, who had refused to sleep in his own room.

She heated water and filled the tin bathtub to the brim, hoping a hot bath would calm her nerves.

Lord, she was sore. Every bone in her body throbbed. She couldn't have ached more had she fallen off a roof or been run over by a herd of cattle. *Ooooooh!* If she ever got her hands on that hog! Biting back the pain, she stepped into the tub and lowered herself into the soothing warmth of the water.

What an unbelievable day! Miss Hannah had been so upset by the experience, Dr. Paine had given her something to help her relax. It was obvious the nurse was in no condition to take care of Christopher, and Amanda had no choice but to bring him back to her apartment.

Donny had been beside himself with joy when she and Moose returned with Christopher. "Good match!"

he'd shouted repeatedly, and the two boys had been inseparable for the rest of the evening. Donny even let Christopher wear his straw hat.

It was almost nine before the two had fallen asleep on her bed.

Dear God, if she lived to be a hundred, she would never forget this day.

Caleb had dispatched a telegram to Damian's hotel in Philadelphia, advising him of the situation, and they expected him back on the late-night train or first thing in the morning.

Moose had agreed to wait at Damian's farmhouse until Damian arrived. He would then inform him of Christopher's whereabouts.

She hoped Moose could persuade Damian to wait until morning before coming to the apartment. It had taken hours to calm the poor child down. Waking him in the middle of the night to take him home would serve no useful purpose.

The hot water relaxed her but she doubted she could sleep. The events of the day kept running through her mind. Who were those men? And why would they kidnap Christopher? For ransom? Revenge? What?

The Newcastles had many enemies. But the thought of someone seeking revenge by kidnapping an innocent child was too horrifying to contemplate.

The bathwater had grown cold and still she remained in the tub. She dreaded having to face Damian. If only she hadn't insisted Christopher ride that tricycle, none of this would have happened.

Shivering, she climbed out the tub, grimacing with pain as she stepped onto the bare wooden floor. After drying off, she wrapped herself in a thick Turkish towel.

She ran a tortoiseshell comb through the wet strands of her hair, then checked the lock on the door. She had checked it several times in the course of the evening. Now, she stood with her ear to the door, listening. It seemed unnaturally quiet that night. Not even the Fennessy baby cried, and the unsettling silence was nerve wracking.

Even the Webbers' apartment was quiet. Peace was restored on the day Arthur had tossed the mattresses out the window, and the two had been acting like lovebirds ever since.

Despite her aches and pains, Amanda giggled to herself. Never would she forget landing on that mattress. It was providence the way the mattresses fell at just the right moment, one to stop the carriage and the other to cushion her fall. Who would ever think that Carolyn Webber's twin beds would save the day?

Chapter 28

Damian rested the back of his head on the leather seat of the two-wheel hansom he'd hired to take him from the Grand Central Train Depot to his farmhouse. What a day this had been! What a night. The trip to Philadelphia had turned out to be nothing more than a wild-goose chase.

The mystery man, who supposedly had information for Damian about his father's innocence, never showed up for their appointed meeting. Damian prayed the telegram sent to his hotel was yet another hoax, but his instincts told him otherwise. A muscle tightened at his jaw. God help the man who harmed a single hair on Christopher's head!

Rocked back and forth by the motion of the vehicle, Damian grabbed hold of the leather strap over his head. The hack flew like the wind through the deserted streets of Manhattan, the horse's iron-shod hooves pounding the rough cobblestones.

Damian had promised the driver a generous compensation if he covered the distance between the train station and the farmhouse in record time. Judging by the way the hack jostled and bounced, and swerved around corners, the driver meant to take Damian up on his offer.

Dogs barked as the hack raced past block after block of brownstone row houses. A ship's horn sounded in the distance. Rowdy voices rose from crowded taverns, all but drowning out the wailing screech of fiddles. A trail of curses followed the hack as it whipped around a corner, barely missing a group of newsboys.

Damian watched the muted gaslights of the city fly by the window, his mind filled with a thousand questions. The telegram had said Christopher was safe following an attempted kidnapping.

Kidnapping! He couldn't believe it. Who would do such a thing? And why? Had his trip to Philadelphia been part of the plot? Had the kidnappers wanted to get rid of him so they could get to Christopher? It was a chilling thought. Apparently the kidnappers knew him, knew how to make him dance to their tune. The question was, why?

At long last the hack turned into the drive of the farmhouse. He grabbed his carpetbag and jumped out before the hack rolled to a stop, shoving a handful of bills into the driver's hand. The burning lights in the front window of the farmhouse filled him with alarm. It was late, too late for either Miss Hannah or Mrs. Winkle to still be up.

The door flew open before he reached it, and Damian's housekeeper beckoned him inside where he found Moose waiting for him.

"We didn't know when to expect you," Moose began.

Without bothering to ask what Moose was doing there, Damian handed his housekeeper his hat and carpetbag and headed for the stairs, taking them two at a time.

"Christopher's not here," Mrs. Winkle called after him.

His hand on the banister, he turned to stare at Moose. "The telegram said he was all right."

"He is," Moose said. "He's with Miss Blackwell."

"Amanda?"

Damian hurried back down the stairs and headed for the door, but Moose stayed him with a hand to the shoulder. "He's safe and it's late."

"I need to see for myself."

"Why not wait till morning?"

"Tonight. I have to see him tonight."

Moose dropped his hand. "I thought as much. I told your groom to ready your horse."

Damian nodded his thanks. "It's late. Feel free to stay the night, if you like. Without another word, he ducked into the night and headed for the stables.

Within moments, he was racing back toward the city. Why the hell was Christopher with Amanda and not his governess? Where was Miss Hannah when all this was happening? Cursing himself for falling for what appeared to be nothing more than a ploy to get him out of town, he snapped the reins, urging his horse to go faster. Kidnapped! Damn, none of this made sense.

He reached Amanda's tenement house and tied his horse to a wooden post in front. The doorman was slumped over, the smell of alcohol strong. Disgusted, Damian kicked the empty whiskey bottle with his foot before dashing up the stairs. A baby cried out, followed by a woman's soothing voice.

It was dark in the hall, the smell of cooked fish strong. He was able to find Amanda's apartment by counting the thin slivers of light beneath each ill-fitting door.

He gave the door a soft tap, and when he got no response, he knocked again, this time harder.

"Who . . . who is it?"

"It's me, Amanda. Damian."

He heard her fumbling with the lock, and the door had barely cracked open before he pushed inside. She surprised him by throwing herself into his arms.

"Amanda! Are you all right?"

"Yes," she said, her voice muffled.

"Christopher—"

"He's asleep." She pulled away from him and nodded toward the bedroom door.

Alarmed by the paleness of her face, he hesitated to leave her side. He ran his hands up her arms and felt her flinch at his touch. "Amanda?"

She bit her lower lip. "I'm . . . just a little sore."

She wore a white linen nightgown that clung to her trim hips and well-rounded breasts, then fell in gentle folds to her bare feet. Her hair tumbled down her back in a mass of damp curls. She looked amazingly attractive for someone who, judging by the exhaustion on her face, appeared to have lived through hell.

"How did it happen? Who took him?"

She quickly explained how Christopher was abducted from the park, but he could hardly make sense of what she told him. He stared at her, completely baffled. "Mayor Ledbetter was attacked by a lobster?"

She burst into tears. "And it's all my fault. If we hadn't put Christopher on that tricycle—"

Feeling sorry for her, he slid his hands around her waist and drew her into his arms, careful not to hurt her. *Did he hear right? A lobster?* "There now, Amanda. Don't cry." He felt an overwhelming need to protect her and erase everything bad that had ever happened to her. "The kidnappers would have found another way to take Christopher. They wouldn't have gone to all the trouble of sending me out of town unless they meant to succeed."

She gazed up at him, her blue eyes brimming with tears. "The kidnappers sent you out of town?"

"I'm almost certain of it. I received a telegram from a man named Kendall Smith saying he has proof of my father's innocence and asking me to meet him in Philadelphia. Needless to say, the man never showed up and the hotel had no record of a guest by that name."

"And you think the telegram was sent by the same men who kidnapped Christopher?"

"I'll bet on it." His gaze drifted to the bedroom door. "Do you mind?"

"Of course not."

He pressed his lips tenderly against her forehead before pulling away and heading to the bedroom. He pushed the door open. Light filtered into the dark room and streamed across the bed.

Overwhelmed by relief and gratitude for his son's

safety, Damian tiptoed to the boy's side and laid his hand on Christopher's forehead. Christopher's hair felt soft as silk beneath his touch.

Damian swallowed the lump that rose in his throat. Dear God, he loved this child more than life itself. Had anything happened to him . . .

Overcome by the thought, he squeezed his eyes tight and forced himself to breathe. Christopher stirred. "Papa."

"I'm here, son." He ran his hand along Christopher's back. "I'm here." Christopher's eyes fluttered shut again and Damian tiptoed out of the room. Now that he knew without a doubt Christopher was safe, he pondered everything Amanda had told him. "A lobster?" he muttered to himself.

Amanda glanced at him when he entered the room, a steaming teakettle in her hand. She finished pouring hot water into a teapot and put the kettle back on the stove.

Moving more slowly than he'd ever seen her move, she arranged cheese and bread on a plate. He took the tray from her and set it on the low table in front of the davenport. The room was sparsely furnished, but immaculate, and a single gas lamp cast a warm, friendly glow across the flower-print walls.

"I have some whiskey, if you prefer."

"I would prefer that you sit down and rest." He waited for her to make her way to the davenport. "Now tell me everything you know." Tossing his hat on a ladder-back chair, he sat down opposite her. "Do the police have any leads to the kidnappers? And where is Miss Hannah?"

She sat back and grimaced, then rubbed her shoulder. Alarmed, he sat forward. "You look like you're in a lot of pain."

"Just a little."

He moved to her side and reached for her hand. She trembled at his touch and her flesh felt alarmingly cold. "The kidnappers didn't hurt you, did they?"

"Actually, I had a run-in with a hog." She told him

how she, Moose, and the wheelmen had chased the kidnappers through town.

Amazed, he sat back. "You never fail to amaze me, Amanda. The kidnappers made a big mistake. You're the one they should have sent out of town."

She pulled her hand away and reached for the tray, but he took the teapot from her and poured the tea himself.

"Those hogs are the meanest creatures I ever did see," she complained. "Though I suppose poor Mayor Ledbetter would argue that lobsters were meaner yet."

"Undoubtedly."

Her eyes flashed. "One of the hogs had the audacity to run off with my bloomers."

"Your bloo—?" His gaze dipped down to take in the rest of her, but her legs were hidden beneath the soft folds of her nightgown. "I'm not sure I understand the part about the mattresses. You said they came flying out of a window?"

"You remember, don't you? The mattresses Arthur Webber threw out the window."

"Oh, *those* mattresses!" Damian chuckled. The whole thing was beginning to strike him as a comedy of errors. "I shall be eternally grateful to Mr. Webber and his wife." He sat back. "You still haven't told me what Miss Hannah was doing during this time. Why wasn't she with Christopher? And where is she now?"

Amanda quickly jumped to Miss Hannah's defense. "None of this is Miss Hannah's fault," Amanda said. "The poor woman was frantic with worry. Dr. Paine had to give her something to calm her down. Under the circumstances, I thought it best if I brought Christopher here."

"Thank you, Amanda. I'll always be grateful for what you've done. Christopher means the world to me."

"And you're not angry that we let Christopher ride a tricycle?"

"I'm not angry."

"Oh, Damian! You should have seen him. He was so happy and then suddenly—" Her eyes glistened with fresh tears.

He took her in his arms, careful not to hurt her. "It's over now, Amanda," he murmured into her silky hair. "Whoever those men were, they're never going to touch any of us again. I promise you." He lifted her chin and kissed her gently on the lips, but when he tried to pull her closer, she cried out in pain. "I think I better get you a doctor."

"I don't need a doctor," she said, clutching her stomach. "I'll kill that hog, so help me I will!"

He drew back, not wanting to cause her more discomfort. "And here I was worried about you riding those damn bicycles."

She smiled up at him, but her face soon grew serious. "None of this make sense. Why bother sending you out of town? It all happened so fast. I doubt if you could have stopped them even had you been there."

It was a good question and one he had no answer for.

"To think something like this could happen in broad daylight." She wiped away her tears and he handed her a cup of tea. Her obvious attempt to pull herself together made him smile. Most women would be incapacitated after such a horrendous ordeal.

She sipped her tea slowly. "Why do you suppose they took him? Do you think it was for ransom?"

"It's possible." Actually, several possibilities came to mind, including revenge. His father had made many enemies, especially after what happened at the Continental Theater, and though he was in prison, it was conceivable that someone might want to exact revenge through the family. It was equally possible the kidnapping was connected to the knife-wielding stranger. For certain it had something to do with the persistent feeling he had of being followed.

"Do you think they'll try again? The kidnappers?"

His elbows on his lap, he cradled his cup in both hands. "I don't know what to think at this point."

"I'm so sorry, Damian." She laid her hand on his back. "I wish I knew what to say."

The gentleness of her touch was surprisingly comforting and all too welcome. "Were the authorities notified?" he asked.

"Yes, but we weren't able to give them much information. No one got a clear look at the kidnappers."

He sat back. "Are you sure you didn't recognize either one of the kidnappers?"

She hesitated. "The one man . . . I don't know. He was dressed all in black. I only got the briefest glimpse of his face, but there was something about him . . ."

Damian rubbed his chin. The man who'd held a knife at his throat was also dressed in black, but without a better description, he couldn't be sure if it was the same man. "Had you ever seen this man at the school?"

"I can't be sure. Everything happened so fast—"

Damian set his cup down and, feeling the need to stretch his legs, stood and began pacing. Damn it all! Who would kidnap his son? Who?

Amanda watched him anxiously. "If you wish, you may leave Christopher here for the night. It seems a shame to disturb him."

"I'd feel better if I took him home with me."

"But it's late and . . ."

"I know, Amanda, but I'd rest easier if he was with me."

Amanda didn't argue with him. Lord, if it had been Donny who had been kidnapped, she would feel the same way. Together they walked into the bedroom and she lit the candle on the night table.

Damian leaned over the bed. "It's time to go home, son." He slid his arms beneath Christopher, scooping him up off the bed, and cradled him in his arms.

Donny sat up with a cry and grabbed hold of Christopher's leg. "Good match, good match."

"It's all right, Donny," Amanda said in a low, soothing voice. "Christopher has to go home now."

"Hello yourself," Donny said, still holding on tight.

"Donny!" she said firmly. "Let go of Christopher."

"Good match!"

"Yes, I know, he's your friend. But he's safe now."

"Safe now."

"His papa is going to take him home."

"Good match."

Damian laid Christopher back on the bed next to Donny. "Would you like him to stay with you tonight?"

"Stay with you," Donny said, the frown leaving his face. "Stay with you."

Damian's eyes locked with Amanda's. "It looks like I'm going to be taking you up on your invitation."

"Don't go, Papa," Christopher said, grabbing his father's hand.

"Don't go, Papa," Donny repeated, taking Damian's other hand.

Amanda smiled. "It's not a very large bed, but you're welcome to stay."

Damian grinned. "It doesn't appear I have much choice." He sat on the edge of the mattress and pulled off his boots. He then settled himself on the bed next to Christopher.

Christopher giggled, then rolled to his back. "Don't go," he said, looking up at Amanda.

"Don't go," Donny echoed.

Damian gazed at her lazily, his hands folded beneath his head. His mouth quirked in a smile that was every bit as irresistible as the coaxing tone of his voice. "I think our boys need us to be together tonight."

She hesitated, but only because her breath caught in her throat. "I believe you're right," she managed at length. She sat on the opposite side of the bed and, grimacing with pain, slowly stretched out next to Donny.

Donny reached into the tin box he always kept with him, fished out one of his treasured buttons, and handed it to her. It was the button with the sailboat.

She took the button from him and began, her voice soft. "Once upon a time . . . there were two very good friends named Donny and Christopher. And one day they decided to sail around the world in their little sailboat. . . ."

Donny fell asleep first, then Christopher, and after finishing her story, she tucked the button into the tin box, then blew out the candle by the bed.

Damian's low voice floated out of the darkness. "Have you ever had a man in your bed before?"

"Certainly not!" she whispered back.

He chuckled. "I love it when you sound all righteous and indignant."

"I never sound righteous," she said, taking offense.

"You do, too," he said, his voice low. "I just want you to know that next time will be different."

Her heart thudded. "Next time?"

"The next time I'm in your bed."

"What makes you so certain there'll be a next time?"

"There's always a next time, Amanda." He turned over and fell silent.

The silence stretched between them for the longest while before she worked up the nerve to ask the question that burned like a flame inside her. "Different? How?"

Chapter 29

Wind howled across Manhattan Island that late September day, whipping up dust and falling leaves and lifting the hems of feminine skirts. Great gusts of wind lifted hats off the heads of their owners, showing no favoritism for class. The bowlers, high toppers, and beavers of the wealthy were shown the same disregard by nature as were the plug hats of the poor.

When pedestrians weren't chasing hats, they hurried along the sidewalks, heads down, ducking into doorways or waiting hacks at the first opportunity.

It was too windy for cycling and Amanda made a handwritten placard to display in her window, listing new class schedules. Normally, she would welcome the unexpected free time, but Donny was spending the week at Damian's farmhouse, and she dreaded the thought of returning to her empty apartment. She didn't think it possible to miss anyone as much as she missed Donny. Unless it was Damian.

She'd seen very little of Damian in recent weeks. Finishing work on the building made it necessary for him to work long hours, and she could hardly wait until the day came that they could spend more time together.

Since the kidnapping, Damian had restricted Christopher's activities, refusing to let him come to town and hiring guards to watch the farmhouse. Donny had missed his friend terribly, of course, and finally she agreed to accept Damian's invitation and let him spend the week with Christopher.

How she hated the fear and suspicion that had become such a major part of their lives since the kidnapping! Everyone was suspect and Damian was forever on his guard. Anytime he saw a stranger enter her school, he bounded over to investigate, and though she was grateful for his vigilance, it only added to her insecurity.

Nothing out of the ordinary had happened since, and it appeared the kidnapping attempt might have been an isolated incident. This was an enormous relief, of course, but she couldn't help thinking the other shoe had yet to drop.

It was nothing she could put her finger on—just a feeling she had. At times she had the strongest sense she was being watched. Lately, as she stepped from a horsecar and walked the short distance to her school, she found herself looking over her shoulder.

Naturally, she didn't say anything to Damian. He was worried enough about Christopher's safety without having to worry about hers. Besides, she had just about convinced herself she was simply being paranoid. Wouldn't anyone be, after living through that kidnapping ordeal?

But upon receiving a second letter from her uncle's attorney, informing her of a November second court date, she decided she wasn't being the least bit paranoid.

Her uncle was having her watched!

She was certain of it. No doubt he was looking for proof she neglected Donny or was otherwise unfit to care for him. She should have known. Dear God, what was she going to do?

So far she'd failed to find a lawyer willing to represent her against a man as rich or as powerful as her uncle without charging her an arm and a leg. And time was running out.

A sudden gust of wind blew her door open and she hurried to close it. She was puzzled by the small knot of people gathered across the street from Damian's building. She reached for her wrap and, pulling it tight around her shoulders, darted outside.

Reverend Jesse James greeted her. "Morning, Miss Blackwell." He shouted to be heard over the wind and held his high topper on his head with one hand. "Be careful you don't catch your death of cold!" He pulled his scarf around his neck and pressed his hands deeper into his coat pockets.

"Good morning," she called back. She brushed away the hair blowing in her face. "What's everyone doing here?"

"If they're smart, they came to pray," the preacher replied grimly.

"Praying isn't going to help much." Summerset held up a wooden contraption that spun in the wind. "I predict the winds are going to get worse as the day progresses." He could hardly contain the excitement in his voice. "Much worse. Eighty miles an hour, at least!"

"Oh, dear." The mayor wrung his hands together. "The building's bound to topple for certain."

"You don't know that," Amanda said. Damian claimed there was still work to be done, but the building looked finished on the outside, the walls faced with intricately cut terra-cotta blocks that hid the red fireproofing bricks beneath.

The sheer enormity of the building never failed to astonish her. It towered over everything around it, making even the tallest trees in the park look like miniatures. The size alone gave the building a look of permanence.

Still, the winds were exceedingly strong and already several trees had been uprooted in the park. Nervously, she gazed at the very top of the building. As far as she could determine, the building hadn't swayed.

"It'll fall," Lockhammer said. "Mark my words."

"St. Peter's will fall before this building does." At the sound of Damian's voice, all heads turned in his direction. He was hatless, his hair blowing freely in the wind. Though he addressed the crowd, his gaze lingered on Amanda's face. "And to prove it, I plan to spend the next twenty-four hours on the top floor. Anyone care to join me?"

Lord almighty, she was no fool. She knew his invitation was meant for her alone, and anger flared like a rocket inside her. He was testing her, testing the two of them, testing the tentative trust that had developed between them. How could he do this to her? She would not go to the top of that building. No matter what she saw in his pleading eyes!

A murmur rose from the gathered spectators. The mayor sputtered in disapproval. The meteorologist measured the wind and shook his head.

"That's madness," someone called from the back of the crowd.

"You're asking for trouble!"

Damian's eyes never left Amanda's face and she read his silent plea, *Trust me.*

She *did* trust him. He had to know that; it was the building she didn't trust. When she failed to respond, something flickered in his eyes and she sensed something like a door slam shut between them.

"Very well." He swung his gaze over the crowd. "I'll see you tomorrow at this time." He darted across the street.

"Damian!" She shouted to be heard over the wind. "You don't have to do this."

He stopped and turned, his granite face revealing little in the way of emotion.

"He won't!" someone shouted. "He hasn't got the nerve God gave a hound."

"He's a bloody coward, o'right!"

"He should be locked up with his father!"

"Stop!" she cried. "All of you!"

"You're a fine one to talk," someone yelled. "I don't see you takin' him up on his offer."

Her eyes met Damian's. Although he was a distance away, she could see the questioning look on his face as he stood waiting for her to change her mind. When she made no move toward him, he spun around and disappeared inside.

Vincent walked over to her, his hands buried deep into the pockets of his fur coat. He wore a red woolen cap and scarf knitted by Miss Quackenbush.

"I bet buttons to dollars he won't stay the night."

"He'll stay." If Amanda knew anything, she knew this.

Vincent gazed at the building. "Then the man's a bigger fool than I thought."

"He's trying to prove to these people they have nothing to fear. Can you blame him for that?"

"There ain't no one goin' to believe him, no matter what he does. He's a Newcastle, after all, in case you've forgotten."

"I haven't forgotten."

Vincent arched a dark brow. "Is that so? Well, you could have fooled me."

The wind increased and the air grew colder.

Summerset practically jumped with joy. "See? What did I tell you?" he shouted to the small group of people who remained huddled a distance away from the building. "I said it would grow more windy and it did!"

Vincent mumbled something beneath his breath and, giving up the thought of selling buttons on such a blustery day, lowered the shutters on his cart.

Shivering, Amanda returned to her school. Her hand resting on the doorknob, she cast one last glance at the building next door before hurrying inside to warm herself by the coal stove.

If the Newcastle tower collapsed, her school would be buried beneath the rubble. Had she one sensible bone in her body, one sensible thought in her head, she'd leave.

In a state of nerves, she paced a path back and forth between the windows. Oh, Damian, why must you do this to me?

She took a deep breath. The building was safe. Of

course it was! Damian wouldn't have gone to the top had it been any less.

Thinking she would lose her mind if she didn't do something, she sat at her desk to practice the typing exercises Priscilla had given her and managed to get the keys in a tangle. No matter how hard she tried to use all of her fingers, she couldn't! Today her nerves were such that she could barely manage two!

Frustrated, she tapped her fingers along the edge of her desk. The wind howled and the shutters flapped and her heart beat with worry for Damian.

Gradually, the light began to fade, but the wind continued to blow and each time a gust shook the building, she jumped in her seat.

She watched the lamplighter make his rounds, his scarf blowing in the wind as he struggled to open the square glass lamps with a long torchlike device. It took him longer than usual to turn on the gas jets and kindle them into flames.

Darkness covered the city, descending on Central Park like a shroud. The Newcastle tower was a solid wall of brick and mortar. A soft flickering light shone from the topmost window and she had visions of Damian, alone, with only the demons of the past to keep him company.

She debated about going home, but she hated the thought of battling the wind even the short distance to the horsecar. Or spending an evening alone in her apartment, with nothing to do but worry. She might as well worry right where she was. At least she could keep her eye on the building.

Hungry, she opened up the basket of food she had stowed in her office. That morning she had purchased fresh bread at the bakery and fruit from a vendor to take home for her supper. One of her students had arrived that afternoon, not knowing lessons were canceled for the day, and had brought Amanda fresh goat cheese.

She had ample food on hand, enough for two people. The thought sent a shiver of anticipation down her spine. She couldn't believe she was actually toying with the idea of taking her picnic basket up to Damian. *On the twentieth floor* . . .

What was she thinking? She would not—absolutely could not—travel up to the twentieth floor. Not even if it were the last place on earth!

The elevator. Of course! She would send the basket up in the elevator. Delighted with her plan, she set to work arranging a generous selection of food in the wicker basket, holding back just enough for herself.

A violent gust of wind rattled the door and her heart practically jumped out of her chest. How could Damian put her through such torture? If he made it through the night, she just might kill him herself.

After she had finished packing the basket, even tucking in a bottle of red wine and a single glass, she donned her cape. Lifting the hood over her head, she slid her arm through the handle of the basket.

Her stomach felt all fluttery and she was shaking so hard she could barely turn the doorknob. This was ridiculous. All she had to do was set the basket in the elevator and leave. It was as simple as that. If she heard so much as one teeny, tiny snap or crackle or any other sound that suggested the building was about to cave in on top of her, she would run out of there faster than lightning.

Her plan firmly in mind, she hurried outside, holding her lantern up high.

The wind cut through her clothes like icy knives. Head bent low, she hurried along the path, paying little mind to the newspaper reporters who stood guard across the street.

It was a struggle to open the heavy door of the Newcastle building against the wind, an even bigger struggle to close it.

Once inside, she leaned against the door to catch her breath. It was like another world. So still and quiet, almost eerily so. The light from her lantern cast shadows upon the white marble walls and floor of the lobby and the gleaming steel cage of the elevator.

Her heart thudded against her ribs. She tried not to think of the tons of steel and brick that rose high above her head. What if Damian's critics were right? She shuddered and the shadowy walls seemed to close in around her. She wet her dry lips with her tongue and wiped her damp forehead with the end of her scarf. All right, now. Easy does it.

Like a cat burglar, she inched her way across the marble floor. She set the lantern down in front of the elevator, along with the picnic basket. She measured the distance to the door leading outside. It wasn't that far away. She could cover the area in two seconds flat. Taking another deep breath, she reached for the elevator switch.

She jumped in surprise at a loud creaking noise. But instead of running outside as she'd planned, her feet had seemingly turned to lead.

Something fell from the ceiling. She screamed and the sound bounced from wall to wall, filling the air with her frantic cries. Panic rose like a volcano inside her. Memories from the past assailed her. Her father's horror-filled face in the final seconds of his life. Tons of brick. Mortar. Dust. Frenzied voices. Screams.

She sank to the floor. "Papa!"

Chapter 30

No sooner had the elevator come to a clanking halt than Damian leaped out and rushed to Amanda's side. He dropped to his knees and cradled her gently in the crook of his arm, pushing the hood of her cape off her head. "Amanda! My God, Amanda, talk to me!"

In the flickering light of the lantern, her face looked pale. Her eyes seemed focused on something that was beyond what he could see. His hand on her forehead, he smoothed away the worried creases, feeling her body tremble next to his.

"Papa," she sobbed.

"It's me, Damian." He ran a finger down her soft cheek, following the trail of silky tears. "What happened to your father . . . it's never going to happen again. I swear."

She blinked and focused her eyes on him, the fear on her face fading away like the darkness at dawn. "Damian?" she whispered. "I . . . I saw something fall from the ceiling, and the noise—"

"You saw the control cables of the elevator drop. As for the noise, the damned contraption makes a dreadful racket. I'm afraid there's no helping it."

Her lips trembled lightly. "The . . . the building's not going to . . . fall?"

"It better not. I have a terrible fear of standing beneath falling objects. We're perfectly safe." He tapped her on the nose, watching the color rush back. "Trust me."

"I do trust you, Damian," she said, sitting up. "It's the building I don't trust."

"So what are you doing here?"

"I . . . brought you something to eat." A gust of wind rattled the door. She grabbed his arm, her gaze riveted to the ceiling. *"Oooooooh."*

"It's all right," he said soothingly. "The building is strong. It hasn't so much as swayed. I thought you knew me better than to think I'd spend the night here if danger actually existed. I have a son to think about."

She lowered her gaze. "How did you know I was here?"

"I saw you from the window and thought you might like some company during your first ride in the elevator."

"The el—" She looked like her old self again. "Certainly you don't think I intended to ride up to the top floor!"

He gave a careless shrug. "The thought did occur to me."

She shivered and hugged herself. "Well, you can get that thought out of your head right this minute. My feet are not leaving the ground."

"It's warmer upstairs," he coaxed. "Much warmer, and the view is spectacular." The dark look she gave him made him laugh aloud. "Come on, Amanda, be a sport. It's perfectly safe. The elevator is equipped with safety brakes. I tested them myself." He held out his hand, but she looked away. "Come on, now, don't be a chicken. I know firsthand what you put your students through. And look how you chased down those kidnappers."

She glared at him reproachfully. "How could you possibly compare cycling with traveling up to the twentieth floor?"

"That's my point exactly. There is no comparison. What I'm asking you to do is far safer."

"Horsefeathers!"

"Now don't go getting your dander up. Think a minute. How many bicycle accidents are there in a year's time?"

"I don't know. Hundreds, perhaps."

"More like thousands," he said. "And how many people are injured going to the twentieth floor?"

"No one's ever gone to the twentieth floor."

"I have. And so has my construction crew and not one person has suffered a single mishap. Come on, now, on your feet." He placed his hands under her arms and lifted her to her feet.

"I can't do this, Damian. Please don't make me."

"That's nonsense. You can do anything you put your mind to. Isn't that what you tell your students?"

"This is different."

He picked up the picnic basket and the lantern and set them on the floor of the elevator. "Come on."

"I'm not getting in that elevator!" she said stubbornly. She folded her arms across her chest and stared at him in open defiance. "Dr. Paine said it's bad for the heart."

"Dr. Paine's exorbitant fees are bad for the heart."

"But Mrs. Swanson fainted on the third floor of A. T. Stewart's department store and she claimed it was the height."

"I wonder what her excuse was for fainting during her wedding night." The socialite had made headlines after being carted off to the hospital following her much publicized wedding. "You'll never forgive yourself if you let this opportunity pass you by."

"I'll live with it." She turned toward the front door, but he grabbed her by the elbow, spun her into his arms, and with one sweeping motion, kissed her.

"Damian, I . . ."

He kissed her again, this time tracing her full lips with his own. He then flicked his tongue in and out of the sweet recesses of her mouth. She gave a womanly sigh and swooned against him, her arms sliding up his chest and winding around his neck. It was all he could do to resist taking her on the spot.

Reluctantly, he pulled his mouth away. Her lips still

swollen from his kiss, she gazed up at him, her eyes filled with liquid softness. God, he loved it when she looked at him like that, all soft and loving. For once the look of desire overshadowed any lingering doubts she might still have.

Sighing with contentment, he nibbled her ear, then feathered kisses down her neck before capturing her lips again.

They were both breathing hard by the time he'd managed to ease her into the elevator. He considered it a tribute to his considerable skills as a lover that she failed to notice he had navigated her into the lift.

Smiling to himself, he again lowered his mouth to hers and slid the door shut behind her back. He spun the wheel and let out a long pleasurable groan, hoping to drown out the clanging sound of the elevator. It would have been easier to mute the sound of cannons.

Her eyes flew open in alarm. She then let out a blood-curdling scream that practically rendered him deaf. "Oh, no!"

"Now, calm down, Amanda. We're almost there."

She threw her arms around his neck; her legs clamped around his middle. "Stop!"

His ears ringing with her screams, he fell back against the steel frame. Damn, if she wasn't cutting into his windpipe. "Let go, Amanda," he gasped. He tried prying her fingers loose, but her hands were rigid as steel.

"Stop the elevator!"

"Damn it, Amanda. I . . . can't . . . breathe."

The elevator reached the top floor and shuddered to a stop. "Let go, Amanda," he squeaked out. "We're there."

Mercifully, she'd stopped screaming, but she held on as tight as ever.

He threw back his head, rolled his eyes, and made a loud gasping sound. *"AAAAARGH!"* His little ploy worked, for she immediately loosened her hold on his neck, though her legs remained firmly wrapped around his hips.

"Dear God!" she cried in alarm. "It's your heart, isn't it? Dr. Paine was right."

"There's nothing wrong with my heart, Amanda. Now, if you will just put your feet on the floor . . ."

Her legs slid down the length of his, but her fingers were firmly embedded in his neck. "That's a good girl," he gasped out. Slowly, he backed her out of the elevator.

Once they were outside the cage, he was able to pry her hands loose from his neck. At last she stood on her own two feet, but she was as unsteady as a newborn colt.

"You can open your eyes now," he said.

Her lashes flickered, but she kept her eyes shut. "Come on, Amanda. Open your eyes. You can do it."

He watched her open one eye and then the other, and laughed at the expression on her face. "I knew you had it in you."

"You are the most . . ." She fell speechless as she looked around the room. Except for a coal heater and a bedroll that was spread out on the floor, the room was empty.

"Are . . . are we on the top floor?" she asked. She sounded amazed, as if she expected something more.

"We are."

She looked around in disbelief. "I don't feel dizzy or anything. Dr. Paine said—"

"Dr. Paine doesn't know what he's talking about."

"But . . . it looks like a regular room."

He grinned. "Look out the window and you'll see how high we are."

"Oh, I couldn't—"

"Of course you can." He took her by the hand and led her across the room, though she fought him all the way. "There, see?"

He had to physically turn her head toward the window to get her to look, but once she did, her mouth rounded in a perfect circle. "Oh, my."

Thinking she was going to faint, he slid an arm around her waist, but she pushed him away so she could step closer to the window. "It's . . . beautiful," she whispered.

"Yeah," he said softly. "Beautiful." So was the view. Actually, the view was spectacular—but it wasn't until that moment that Damian realized how much better the city looked now that he had someone to share it with.

Suddenly, the most ordinary sights seemed to take on a magical quality. The gas lampposts along Fifth Avenue looked like little fireflies flickering in the night. The horsecars and carriages on Broadway resembled children's toys on Christmas morn.

"Look, Amanda. Straight ahead. You can see the lights on the ships." The lights moved back and forth as the ships rocked in the wind. The bright beam of the distant lighthouse swept across the river at intervals, glancing off hundreds of ship masts.

"Oh, Damian." The look of wonder on her face touched a chord inside him. After months of battling ridicule and controversy, battling his own self-doubts, he finally felt it was all worthwhile.

"I never thought New York could look this beautiful." Her voice, hushed with awe, was little more than a tremulous whisper.

"Yes," he said, memorizing every nuance on her face so he could recall this glorious moment at will, in perfect detail, as many times as the future warranted.

She lifted her eyes, her face radiant as she gazed at the starry night sky. Without trees, buildings, or the endless web of telegraph wires blocking the view, the sky looked like a black velvet treasure chest chockfull of bright, shining diamonds.

"I've never seen anything like this. Surely these must be the windows of Heaven. Oh, Damian. No wonder you want to live here. Christopher will love it."

"I think so, too." Her enthusiasm filled him with the utmost joy. "You can get a better view from that window over there." He took her by the hand and this time she offered no resistance. Together they circled the room, stopping to gaze out each window in turn.

"Oh, look," she said, pointing. "That has to be A. T. Stewart's." The marble building of the fancy dry goods store on Broadway gleamed like a polished gem in the silvery light of the waning moon.

After locating the dry goods store, it was easy to pick out the various theaters along the section of Broadway between Madison Square and Forty-second Street known as the Rialto. In recent years, Broadway had replaced Union Square as the theatrical center of the city, and the theaters and hotels were brightly lit by Edison's new incandescent lamps.

A slow-moving procession of lacquered carriages moved along the wide cobbled street. No doubt the carriages were filled with women dressed in elegant Parisian gowns and men wearing those new tailless evening coats that were all the rage.

Even the wind couldn't keep the crowds away from the theaters.

"Come and look at the Metropolitan Museum," he said, drawing her to another window and pointing to the barely visible building on Fifth near Fifty-third Street. Far easier to spot was the Barnum's American Museum. It became a game between them; no sooner would they name everything in sight at one window than they moved to the next window to begin *oohing* and *aahing* all over again.

"Oh, my word!" She gasped at the wondrous sight of arc lights shooting from a hundred-and-sixty-foot tower on Madison Square. "Can you imagine if the whole city was lit with Edison's lights?"

"It's going to happen," Damian said. "Just as one day there'll be other tall buildings in the city, maybe even taller than this one."

"Surely not taller!" she exclaimed in disbelief.

At last they had come full circle, having admired the city from every possible window.

She showed no sign of tiring of the game, and he

chuckled when she picked out yet another landmark that had previously gone undetected.

"Wait until you see the view in daylight."

"It couldn't be any more glorious," she said.

"Ah, but it is. With all the parks and trees, New York actually looks like Paris from this height."

"Paris!" She looked skeptical and he could well guess why. Few people would make such a comparison. "Have you ever been to Paris?"

"Indeed, I have, and I'm telling you, from twenty stories high, it's hard to tell the difference between New York and Paris."

"I find that hard to believe."

"Ah, but it's true."

She turned back to the window. "Oh, look! Isn't that Delmonico's? And the Times Building and Printing House Square. And look over there. That must be—"

Laughing at her enthusiasm, he finally pleaded for mercy. "If we don't eat, I'll die of starvation. Knowing Dr. Paine, he'll say I died of a heart attack just so he can take credit."

She turned from the window, stars shining in her eyes. "How can you think of eating when there's so much to look at?"

"We have all night to gaze at the city," he said. He walked over to the elevator to fetch the picnic basket. "Come on over here, Amanda."

She lingered by a window for another few minutes before joining him on the blanket. Already he had emptied the picnic basket, and packages containing dried beefstick, cheese, and bread were spread on the floor in front of him. He uncorked the bottle and poured the red wine into the single glass.

"I guess we share," he said, handing her the glass and watching as she lifted it to her pretty pink lips. He then took the glass from her and raised it to his own.

"Sorry, I don't have any chairs."

"I like it better this way," she said softly. "It feels

like a real picnic. Oh, Damian! Just think! We're higher than anyone in the whole city."

Her childlike enthusiasm made him grin from ear-to-ear. He handed the glass of wine back to her. Their fingers touched and their eyes locked.

"Are you really going to live here?"

"Absolutely. I promised Christopher I'd build him a building high enough so he could see the world. That's pretty much what I've done." He settled down on the blanket next to her. "Do you think he'll like it?"

"He'll love it. I know he will."

"I don't want him to feel confined in his wheelchair. Up here, the world would literally be at his feet. You'll let Donny visit, won't you?"

"Do you honestly think I could keep him away?"

"That's what I like about Donny. He has his sister's determination."

She smiled, but all too soon her smile faded away. "You're so good to him. I can't tell you how many parents refuse to let Donny near their children. People can be so cruel!"

"I know, Amanda. But it's fear that makes them act unkind. Anyone who knows Donny as I've come to know him couldn't help but love him."

"Oh, Damian!" Her eyes grew misty. "It means so much to hear you say that."

He set the glass on the floor and laid a hand on her shoulder. "I mean it, Amanda."

She wiped away a tear. "I feel the same way about Christopher. I couldn't love him more if he were my own."

"I know." He untied the ribbon at her neck and removed her cape. "And he feels the same way about you." He folded the cape and laid it on the floor next to the blanket.

"The tricycle Moose made for him . . . Oh, Damian, I wish you could have seen him ride it. I've never seen such happiness on a child's face!"

She caught his hand in both of hers, holding it tight.

"I miss Christopher. I miss not seeing him in the park. Do you suppose he can start coming again?"

A sigh escaped him. "I can't take the chance of his being kidnapped. I still don't know who was responsible. Until I do, I have no choice but to curtail his activities."

"It seems such a shame to deny him something that brought him so much pleasure."

"I know." How he hated having to surround the farm with armed guards, hated having to keep Christopher confined, but what choice did he have? Christopher resented the new restrictions on his life more than he did the wheelchair. "I can protect the farm and even secure this building, but I can't protect him in public and certainly not in the park."

"But it doesn't have to be the park," she said earnestly. "He could ride his bicycle anywhere." She glanced around the room. "Even in a room this size."

"I'm . . . I'm . . ." He gazed into her eyes and he felt a stirring deep inside. Fascinated by the gold flecks at the tips of her lashes, blinded to every other consideration by the shining lights in her eyes, he almost lost his train of thought.

"You were saying?"

He drew a ragged breath and reached for a wedge of cheese. "I'm not sure it's safe for him to ride. If he falls, he can't pick himself up like normal children."

"But he is a normal child, Damian. Just because his legs don't work . . ."

"That's my point exactly. His legs don't work. If he falls . . ."

"He could just as easily fall out of his wheelchair."

"But Miss Hannah would be there to help him."

"And I'll be there to help him ride. Please, Damian, I know this would mean so much to him. Maybe when he's older, he'll be able to ride a tricycle everywhere."

He found the thought unsettling. He suddenly realized it wasn't just the threat of another kidnapping attempt that made him resist the idea. He had worked hard to keep Christopher safe from the outside world.

The boy adored his grandfather and was devastated when Damian had to tell him the truth—that his grandfather was in prison.

But that was nothing compared to what had occurred afterward. The newspapers had been filled with hateful accusations leveled against the Newcastles, rocks had been thrown at Damian's carriage, the windows of their farmhouse broken. Christopher had been taunted so badly at school by his classmates that Damian had been forced to pull him out and hire a private tutor.

He was never certain how much or how little the boy understood. Encouraging Christopher's independence was a threat to the protective circle Damian had taken such pains to create.

"Damian?"

"Let me think about it." He bit down on the cheese.

It wasn't an answer, but she didn't force the issue and they ate in silence. No sooner had they finished their picnic than she jumped to her feet and proceeded to circle the room again. Like a child on Christmas morning, she raced from window to window, crying out in delight. "Oh, look! Over there!"

Enchanted by her enthusiasm, he hurried to join her and they proceeded to chase each other from window to window again.

For some reason, everything suddenly struck them as funny. They roared with laughter as they watched two hack drivers argue following an accident. They were practically rolling on the floor upon spotting a man being chased down the street by a woman brandishing what appeared to be a rolling pin.

When at last the theaters grew dark and the crowds had returned home, leaving the streets deserted except for an occasional drunk or policeman on horseback, Damian cupped her chin and tilted her face upward. "Thank you," he whispered, "for the most spectacular night of my life."

She gazed up at him, no longer able to ignore the smoldering flames in his eyes. Nor could she hide her nervousness behind playful laughter. "It was wonderful for me, too," she said.

"So what happens now?" he asked.

"Happens?"

"Do you stay and let me have my way with you, or . . ." He arched an eyebrow. "Do you go?"

It was a tough question and she hated him for asking it. Why couldn't he just sweep her off her feet and make love to her? Why must he force the issue, make her think about it? Why? "I should—"

Surprised to find herself close to tears she looked away and squeezed her eyes tight. Dear God, she loved her father, but from the moment Damian had entered the building and she feared for his life, she knew—knew with the very depth of her being—that she loved him, too. She opened her eyes and looked at him, still not knowing whether to stay or go.

His eyes searched her face as if he were trying to reach into her very soul and she realized suddenly how very much her answer meant to him. It was all she needed to know. "I should go . . . but I'm going to stay."

He looked at her in astonishment as if he couldn't believe his ears. Then his mouth curved with tenderness and his face filled with the utmost joy. "Oh, Amanda. I was so afraid you'd . . ." He placed his free hand at the small of her back, and pulled her close, so close, she could hardly breathe.

She felt a shock to her senses as her body molded against his hard, lean form.

Her arms and legs tingled and heated flames coursed through her veins. Her lips ached with desire and she eagerly lifted her face to him. But his feathery kisses were more torturous than pleasurable, awakening a deep and painful need that had been throbbing inside her since the first time he'd kissed her, and now practically screamed for release.

Hearing her moan, he pulled away and, for a single heartbeat, held her in his heated gaze. He then recaptured her mouth, this time taking her breath away with the fiery possessiveness of his lips.

Currents of desire rushed through her body, all the way to her toes. Her need for him was almost too much to bear and she arched against him.

His mouth left hers, but only for the short time it took to deliver a path of delicious hot kisses down her neck. When once again he captured her mouth, he did so with a driving passion that left her breathless. He pressed her lips with his tongue and filled her mouth with liquid fire.

And even this wasn't enough. She stood on her tiptoes, working her fingers into his hair to deepen the kiss, her hands driven by frantic need.

"Amanda," he murmured between kisses. "Oh, my dear, sweet Amanda." He eased her down on the blanket and ran the palm of his hand over her breasts. She practically exploded at his touch, and it was all he could do to keep from ripping off her clothes.

Instead, he released the tiny pearl buttons on the front of her shirtwaist, surprised to find his hands trembling. The fabric parted to his touch, revealing the full beauty of her soft feminine curves. He traced her lovely slim neck with the tip of a finger before slipping his hand into her silky chemise.

She arched against him once more, surrendering herself to his touch, telling him in a hundred different ways that her need for him was every bit as great as his need for her.

"I want you so much," he whispered between kisses.

"I want you, too," she whispered back. "But . . ."

His heart thudded. "But?"

"Do . . . do you think it's safe to make love so high off the ground? Dr. Paine said . . ."

"To hell with Dr. Paine," Damian growled, capturing her lips again. Slowly, he undressed her, removing her clothes with the same tender care shown by an art lover unveiling a masterpiece. His fingers skimming her hips and thighs, he inched her bloomers downward, following the path of the fabric with his lips.

Trailing hot kisses down the length of her, he proceeded to undo her garters and, taking a ragged breath, gently, sensually, peeled away each of her stockings in turn.

Amanda opened her eyes to see him gaze adoringly at her naked body, and strangely enough, she felt more cherished than shy. It was as if all earthly feelings and inhibitions had been left on the ground below. She felt free as a cloud skimming across the sky.

Dr. Paine had been right about one thing; the altitude obviously affected the mind. What else could explain her responding so freely to his heated touch?

"You're beautiful," he whispered. He dropped a kiss upon the flesh of her naked thigh. "And I want you so much."

She tugged at his shirt impatiently until the buttons pulled free. She wanted to touch him as he touched her. "Then what are you waiting for?"

Her hands on his broad chest, she ran her fingers down the length of him, feeling his heated body shiver in response. Impatiently, he pulled off his pants and tossed them aside.

She gazed at his bold, manly shaft in amazement. Glory be, she'd never seen anything like it. Feeling suddenly inadequate, she looked up at him in alarm.

He laughed at her expression. "I warned you there'd be a next time."

"But it's so . . ."

His eyes blazed. "It's the altitude," he said.

"But . . . I've never . . ."

"Don't worry, Amanda. We'll go slow." He pressed his forehead next to hers, then captured her lips. "We've got all night."

He lowered his body on top of hers, gathering her close until each of her womanly curves conformed to his contours.

She wondered how a body that was as hard as his could feel so utterly delicious. Her breasts pressed against his chest, she melted against him until their bodies moved as one.

She trailed her fingers up and down his back, pressing him as close as humanly possible. Heaven, that's what it felt like, his hard body on top of hers, his hands skimming down her hips to her thighs, his hot tongue exploring the rosy peaks of her breasts. It felt like Heaven.

She adjusted her hips, opening to him in every way possible, opening to him and for him, and absorbing his every essence into her heart. The heat of his body coursed down the length of hers. He pressed between her legs, teasing her with the tip of his male organ until she practically begged for release.

He plunged inside her and the exquisite pain brought tears to her eyes. He kept his body still, and holding her face in his hands, he kissed her until the pain had faded away. Then, moving his hips, he rocked back and forth ever so gently until she was newly aroused.

"Ready?" he asked.

She bit his ear in response and a smile curved his mouth as he moved his body faster. Soon it seemed as if the very air sizzled in an erotic tempo.

Higher and higher she soared, until suddenly the world shattered into a million pieces and wave after wave of spiraling sensations washed over her. His body shuddering next to hers, he cried out her name.

Gasping for air, they clung to each other until the last shivering waves had faded away. His bronzed body glistening with dampness, he rolled off her, still breathing hard.

Leaning on her elbow, she faced him and ran a finger across his chest, not willing to let him go, even now that her body was sated.

"Damian," she whispered after their breathing had returned to normal and she was able to have a sane thought. "I think I know why Mrs. Swanson fainted on her wedding night."

Chapter 31

Amanda was awakened by a ray of golden light. The sun poured through the bare window over her head, spilling over their naked bodies like warm melted honey.

She'd spent the night cradled in Damian's arms, but sleep had been sporadic at best. It seemed as if she had just sunk into a sweet dreamless sleep when Damian awakened her with his kisses. They made love repeatedly, and each time she discovered something new about herself, new about Damian.

Her love for him was all consuming, touching her on every level. She loved him with her heart and soul. And, yes, she loved him physically, and as shocking as that might seem, it was the truth. She loved him with everything she had.

The extent of her feelings dawned on her slowly during the course of the night. They had made love in a dozen different ways—sometimes with a passion that seemed to shake the very earth. At other times they made love with a gentleness that took them to unexplored heights.

Just thinking about the intimacy they shared filled her heart to overflowing. She sighed and pressed her head closer to his chest, the sound of his heartbeat filling her ears with what surely must be the music of Heaven.

She was tempted to touch him again, to stroke him down below until he grew ready for her, to caress him until his body once again burned with the need it gave her such pleasure to satisfy. But her body was sore and she decided it was best to let him sleep, at least for now.

She gazed lovingly at his face. His jaw was dark with whiskers and the curve of his mouth turned upward. She traced his upturned lips with her fingertip. *You'd better be dreaming of me, my love.*

Surprised to find herself suddenly possessive of him, she smiled to herself. Romantic love was unlike anything else she'd ever experienced.

Aware she had no clothes on, she moved from his arms, careful not to wake him, and reached for her bloomers and chemise.

He stirred awake and blinked his eyes just as she'd finished fastening the buttons of her shirtwaist and was trying to decide what to do with the tangled mass of curls that fell around her shoulders.

He peered up at her, his face curved in a boyish grin that completely contradicted the manly splendor of his naked body. "I'd ask you to come over here, but I don't think I have the strength."

She laughed and tossed him his trousers. "You better get dressed, then, or you might not have any choice in the matter."

While he donned his clothes, she occupied herself by gazing out the windows. "Oh! You're right, Damian. It really does look the way I imagined Paris to look." It was incredible. The light from the rising sun spilled from the east, casting the city in a rich golden glow.

Horse-drawn milk wagons rolled down residential streets, the milkmen leaving fresh dairy products on the stoop of each brownstone row house. The milkmen were followed by ice vendors and produce carts, street sprinklers and numerous horse-drawn street cleaners followed by men dressed in white uniforms carrying brooms.

Next came the farmers, driving their wagons along the cobbled streets on their way to Washington Market. On every corner stood carts filled with bright colorful flowers and newsboys yelling out the latest headlines.

She never realized how many trees grew on Manhattan—not just in Central Park, but everywhere! Paddle wheel boats and graceful tall ships glided along the sparkling waters of the North river, along with cargo schooners and oyster barges.

Ferryboats crisscrossed both rivers, carrying passengers to and from the Jersey and Brooklyn shores. Looking in the same direction, she could make out the tall towers of the Roebling Bridge, and almost everywhere she looked, she saw an amazing number of church steeples.

Damian joined her, the buttons on his shirt unfastened.

"Oh, look, over there," she exclaimed. A tall ship moved slowly down the North River, its full white sails billowing in the wind. The elevator trains wound along miles of steel track like snakes, stopping to absorb the throngs of people that waited on the platforms.

"Isn't that the—" She stopped.

He followed her gaze to Broadway. He'd forgotten how distinctive the Continental Theater with its wraparound marquee looked during the day. The building had been boarded up following the collapse of the balcony, and though the theater had been gutted by a mysterious fire shortly thereafter, its outer walls were a constant reminder of what had happened on that long-ago night.

"The Continental Theater. That's what you were going to say, isn't it?"

"It doesn't matter—"

"Say it!"

She glanced at him surprise. "Why? Why must I say it? I never meant to mention it. I was just startled to see it. I thought after the fire . . ."

"Say it, Amanda. If we can't talk about this, we can't talk about anything."

"All right, then!" she said, her eyes flashing. "The Continental Theater! There, I said it! Are you satisfied?" She turned. "Oh, look over there! Smoke. Do you suppose there's a fire?"

Aware of the dark cloud that had settled between

them, the sudden tenseness, the gradual pulling away, he stroked her hair, his fingers playing with the tangled curls. "Don't do this to me, Amanda."

"Do what, Damian? Oh, look, it *is* a fire. I see the hook and—"

He grabbed her by the arm and spun her around. "Pull away from me."

Her eyes held a sadness that practically tore him to pieces. "I don't want to talk about this," she said. "It will only ruin things between us."

"Will it, Amanda? Is what we have really that fragile?" His hands trailing down her arms, he pressed his forehead next to hers. "Talk to me, please." He drew back, gazing at her beseechingly.

She closed her eyes. "I'll never forget that night as long as I live. I still see his face in my dreams just before—"

"His face?"

As if startled by the intensity of his voice, Amanda's eyes flew open.

"If you saw his face, then you must have been at the theater that night."

"I was there." She paused for a moment. "I thought you knew."

He shook his head and turned away, placing the palms of his hands on a windowsill. He couldn't bear to think of her there, at the theater, on that long-ago night, witnessing with her own eyes such unspeakable horror. "Were you hurt?"

"No. I was standing by the stage. My father had left to check the lighting in the back of the theater. He saw flashes of light or something. He thought there was a short in the electrical wires." She squeezed her eyes tight. "He was so proud to be part of the theater."

Damian rubbed his palm over his prickly whiskers. The theater had been packed that night. That would explain why he hadn't noticed her prior to the collapse of the balcony. Afterward, it was bedlam.

Many people suffered injuries in the panic that followed. It was all he could do to pull Christopher from the path of the stampeding mob.

Moving his son had been a mistake, of course, possibly causing more damage to his already injured spinal column. But had Damian not moved him, Christopher would surely have been crushed beneath the mass of running feet.

Wanting to erase the painful memories, he pulled Amanda into his arms, burying his nose deep in her fragrant hair. He held her so tight it was as if their hearts beat as open. "Whoever is responsible for your father's death, I swear, I *swear*, Amanda, I'll find him and make him pay. And when I do . . ."

He tipped her chin upward so that he could gaze into her eyes. "I want us to be a family." No sooner had the words left his lips than he saw her expression change. It wasn't love he saw in her eyes, not the deep, all-encompassing love he had seen shining in their depths during the passion of the night. What he saw was doubt and suspicion, and he felt like someone had suddenly stomped on his heart.

Telling himself he was imagining things, he kept talking, hoping it was possible to say something that would erase the doubts. "Marry me, Amanda. Then we can be a family. You and me, Christopher and Donny." Just saying the words made him feel as carefree as Big Pete had acted since meeting that Porterville woman. "We can do this, Amanda. If only you'll let it happen. I think Donny would call it a perfect match."

"And he would be right," she said, and her pretty pink mouth curved into an uncertain smile.

He rubbed her nose with his own, then kissed her on the lips. Sensing that things were still strained between them, he tilted her head back. "Amanda?"

The doubt was no longer confined to her eyes; it had spilled over her lashes to cloud her face. "You said we have to talk. About everything. Did you mean it?"

He took a deep breath. "Of course I meant it."

"Does that mean we can talk about your father?" she asked.

It surprised him to discover himself torn between his love for his father and his love for Amanda. It was crazy. Somehow he felt that by loving them both, he could love neither one enough. "What about him, Amanda?"

"I want you to know, I no longer hate him."

"But you still think he's guilty. Even after everything I've told you."

She pulled her hands away. "I . . . I don't know what to think. I want so much to believe he's innocent. For your sake."

"But you don't."

She picked up her cape from the floor and twisted the fabric in her hands. "You love your father. It's only natural you would want to believe—"

"He's innocent—"

She whirled around to face him. "What if he's not, Damian? It's been three years. You said yourself you have nothing to go on. How long do you plan to keep banging your head against the wall? Five years? Ten?"

"However long it takes."

Her knuckles whitened. "But the evidence shows—"

"I don't give a damn about the evidence!"

"Damian, I was wrong to blame you for what happened. I know that now. We can't be responsible for our parents' actions."

"Why can't you believe me, Amanda? Or at least consider the possibility I might be right."

Her eyes darkened with pain. "Because I know love can be blind. I spent years believing Donny was normal. It was a mistake I'll always regret. By not accepting the truth, I did him a lot of harm. Had I taken him to the proper doctors earlier—"

"It wouldn't have made any difference."

"We'll never know for sure. In any case, I can no longer let love blind me to the truth, Damian. Not even for you."

It hurt to hear her say that. It hurt a lot. No one

believed in his father's innocence, not even that fool detective, Grape. But he expected more from the woman he loved. A lot more. Obviously he expected too much.

"My father is a good man. A kind man. He should not be in prison."

"And my father should not be dead," she said quietly. "Nor should Christopher be in that wheelchair." Immediately regretting her words, she covered her mouth with her hand. "I'm sorry, Damian, I didn't mean . . ."

"Christopher's one of the reasons I have to uncover the truth. I can't have him growing up thinking his own grandfather made him a cripple. And I surely can't have my wife cringing every time my father's name comes up."

"That's not going to happen. I loved my father more than words can say, but I love you, too, Damian. Maybe it's time to put the past behind us—"

He looked incredulous. "Give up the investigation? Is that what you're asking me to do?"

"I'm not asking for myself. I see what it's doing to you. How it's tearing you apart. And I'm afraid of what would happen if you found out—"

"Found out what, Amanda? That my father's guilty?"

"Please believe me, Damian. I'd do anything for you. If I honestly thought—" she looked away from him. "I'm even willing to live with the guilt, just so we can be together."

"Guilt?" His eyes glittered with hurt "You feel *guilty* for loving me?"

"Sometimes," she admitted. "But it doesn't matter. None of this matters. I love you with all my heart and soul, and I want us to be together." She asked him beseechingly, "Isn't that enough for you?"

He took her hands in his, but it was a long while before he spoke. "Have you any idea what it does to me to hear you say you feel guilty for loving me? I knew you felt disloyal and had doubts, but . . . Damn it, Amanda, guilt?"

His reaction surprised her, frightened her. "Forget what I said, Damian, please! It's not important. I can live with the guilt."

"Maybe you can live with it, but I can't. It kills me to know that every time I touch you, you must choose between your loyalty to your father and your love for me."

"It's not like that."

"Yes, it is, Amanda. I've tried to ignore it. Tell myself it wasn't true. But at times I see self-loathing in your eyes and I hear it in your voice and it pains me to know I'm responsible."

"It's not your fault," she whispered.

He pushed a lock of hair away from her face. "I live with guilt every day of my life. I can't live with yours, too."

She moved away from him, to the center of the room, but only because she couldn't think clearly when they were close. What Damian said was true. To marry a Newcastle would be disloyal to the memory of her father, no matter how much she tried to justify it. She had tried discounting it, ignoring it, and even denying it, but the guilt refused to be silenced. Now she knew it would eventually tear them apart—had already created a chasm between them.

As much as she hated to think it, she couldn't marry him, not while the issue of his father remained unresolved. But she was afraid, so utterly and completely afraid. What if Damian never found the proof he was looking for?

Worse yet, what would happen if he uncovered the truth and it was not what he hoped for? What then?

"You said you can't live with my guilt. Well, I can't stand by and watch you destroy yourself." The vision of him grew blurred behind her tears. "I won't . . ."

Chapter 32

It was over.

Three words, only three words, and she felt like her whole world had crashed around her feet in a million tiny pieces. *It was over.*

Over before it had really begun.

God, the pain was incredible. Who would ever think that need and want could fester inside like an infected wound? "I don't care a fig what your father did or didn't do," she shouted into the empty void of her apartment.

Oh, but she did care, she did! No matter how much she tried to deny it, she knew it was true. To pretend otherwise only filled her with unspeakable guilt.

But she needed Damian. How she needed him! She needed to feel his arms around her, feel his torrid kisses. She needed to touch him and be touched by him. She needed to love him. Talk to him. Especially now that the hearing for Donny's custody was only weeks away.

Dear God, she'd lost Damian. How could she possibly bear to lose Donny?

A week later, Damian's housekeeper knocked on his bedroom door, waking him a little after dawn. He'd had a restless night. In fact, he'd had a week of restless nights. He hadn't slept worth a damn since Amanda had walked out of his life. Hell, she didn't just walk out, she took his heart and soul and a whole lot more!

Aware of the urgency in his housekeeper's voice when she called his name a second time, he sat up and rubbed his eyes. "What is it, Mrs. Winkle?"

"Mr. White is here to see you, sir. Says it's of the utmost importance."

At the mention of Caleb's name, he swung his legs off the bed and reached for his robe. "It sure as hell better be important."

He found Caleb in the parlor, looking pale and shaken.

"I'm sorry to awaken you but something terrible has happened. The building . . ."

"Go on," Damian said impatiently. "What about the building?"

"It's gone."

Not sure he'd heard right, Damian stared at him. "What do you mean, gone? Are you trying to tell me someone walked off with a twenty-story building?"

"Not exactly."

"Then what?"

"It collapsed, sir. The whole damn thing collapsed."

New York was in a panic. The entire area from Eighty-first Street to Fifty-eighth was closed to traffic, forcing Damian to leave his horse outside the police barriers and cover the remaining distance on foot.

Nothing prepared him for the destruction that awaited him. All that remained of his magnificent building was a pile of rubble. He stared in disbelief and horror, his body numb. Everything he'd worked for—gone!

Officer Thorndike rode over to him. "Sorry, sir. It's a terrible, terrible thing."

Damian acknowledged the policeman with a nod of his head. "Was anyone hurt?"

"Not that we know of. Unless your men . . ."

"No one was scheduled to work for another hour."

"Then we're lucky. Had it happened later in the day—" The policeman shook his head as if to ward off the thought. He then galloped away to chase off a couple of curious youths.

Dazed, Damian stared at the rubble, oblivious to the confusion around him. Caleb tried to pull him away, but Damian resisted. One by one, the workmen arrived. Big Pete took one look and began bawling like a baby.

Blade patted Damian on the shoulder. "It's a sad day, indeed."

Chipper and the others hovered around, looking like lost souls. "I can't believe this happened," Chipper kept saying.

Moose joined the group of men, his eyes moist. "I don't know what Miz Mandy's gonna do now that her school is gone."

Damian spun around to see for himself. What Moose said was true. All but one wall of the brick building had been leveled by the falling debris. Damn! How could this have happened? The high-rise had collapsed, just like the balcony of the Continental had collapsed, though this time the damage was far more extensive and inclusive. Hardly anything remained standing but the iron framework.

He was so certain he'd done everything right this time. The design. Something had to be wrong with the design.

"Damian!"

His heart skipped a beat at the sound of Amanda's voice, and wanting to protect her from the destruction, he turned, ready to take her in his arms and block out her vision. But it was too late; the horror on her face was worse than even the crumbled building, and his mouth turned dry with sorrow. She ran into his arms, her face streaked with tears, and clung to him.

His eyes shut tight, he wrapped her in his arms, holding her close. She sobbed uncontrollably, her body shaking so hard it was all he could do to hold her. "It's all right, Amanda. I'll build you a new school. Don't worry . . ."

She pulled away from him, her face twisted in pain and anguish and fear. "Donny—"

A cold chill gripped him. "What . . . what about Donny?"

"I can't find him anywhere!" she sobbed. "Oh, Damian! No one has seen him."

He fought to control the panic that coursed through him like hot molten steel, fought to control his voice, to make sense of a world that had suddenly gone mad. "How long has he been gone?"

"I'm not sure. He generally waits outside every morning for the milkman. He was missing when I woke up." She covered her mouth with her hand, her body wracked by sobs. "What if he came here?" She stared at the destruction behind them, her eyes round with horror. "Oh, God!" She collapsed against him.

He held her steady. "He wouldn't come here. Not by himself."

"I've searched everywhere."

"We'll find him. I swear."

She pulled away from him and stumbled toward the demolished school. "Donny!" Her cries pierced his heart. "Donny!"

She suddenly fell to her knees and began digging with her hands. Fearing she had lost her mind, he raced to her side and dropped to the ground next to her.

Donny's beloved button box lay half-hidden in the dirt, the bright colored buttons spilling from it. The implication made him turn cold with horror.

"He was here," she sobbed.

Damian didn't want to believe it. He couldn't. There had to be some other explanation. "Amanda, stop!"

She fought him like a madwoman before pulling away and running toward the collapsed school building.

"Donny!" Her anguished cries devastated him. Never had he felt so utterly helpless. "Dooooonny!"

He started after her, but Caleb stopped him. "May I speak to you for a moment, sir?"

"Later."

"I need you to look at something. It can't wait."

Something in Caleb's voice alerted him. Reluctantly, he pulled his gaze away from Amanda and followed Caleb around the mountain of brick and mortar to the back of the property. "Look there." Caleb pointed to something beneath the tons of rubble.

At first he thought it was Donny, and for that reason, he was afraid to look.

"Sir?"

Sick with dread, Damian forced himself to follow Caleb's finger. A red cylinder stuck out of the rubble.

"It's dynamite," Caleb said. "The building didn't just collapse of its own accord. Someone blew it up."

Donny! Amanda stared at the tin box on her lap in stony silence. It had been hours since she'd found Donny's buttons. She and Damian had joined the search, which covered the entire area between the Harlem suburbs north of the park all the way to the Manhattan toe.

She'd sat next to Damian as he drove the carriage up and down more narrow streets and unpaved alleys than she knew existed. She blew her whistle intermittently, thinking Donny would recognize the sound. She called his name until her voice was hoarse.

Not one person they stopped to question recalled seeing anyone fitting Donny's description.

Growing more discouraged by the moment, she and Damian had knocked on the door of every apartment in Amanda's tenement and searched the roof and basement. Their fears growing with each passing hour, they'd returned to the park by way of Riverside Drive, calling Donny's name all the way.

Now she sat in a police wagon that was parked a short distance from the roped-off area, feeling numb and oddly removed from the confusion around her. *Donny, dear God, where are you?*

Policemen and firemen swarmed about, their voices hushed as they stopped on occasion to assure her that everything was being done to find the missing boy. Moose was beside himself, and tears rolled down his cheeks as he searched for Donny beneath the tangle of bicycles buried in the rubble of the school.

One by one, her students arrived, staring in disbelief at the destruction left in the wake of the blast and offering words of encouragement.

Miss Quackenbush climbed onto the seat next to Amanda and patted her on the leg. "The members of the Knickerbocker Ladies' Cycling Club have scoured the park. Luckily, that fool sparrow cop hasn't given us any problems."

"Officer Thorndike has been very kind."

"Yes, well, you can rest assured that we won't stop looking until Donny is found."

"We?" Mrs. Brewer stood by the police wagon, her hands on her waist, and glared up at the club's president. "Where do you get this 'we' business? You've done nothing but boss the rest of us around. The least you can do is get on your bicycle and help us search."

Miss Quackenbush glared back. "Someone's got to coordinate things and that someone is me." She reached for her whistle and practically blasted Amanda out of her seat. "Take the others and cycle out to the reservoir."

"Very well, Miss Quackenbush, but if I don't see you on your bicycle doing your fair share, I'll see to it that we get ourselves a new club president!"

No sooner had Mrs. Brewer flounced off than Lockhammer rode his cycle over to Amanda. "I want you to know the wheelmen have done a street-by-street search." He sounded uncommonly kind and Amanda warmed to him. He gave the mayor a friendly slap on the back and no one would have ever guessed the two were political foes. "The mayor here has ordered a complete investigation into the matter, Miss Blackwell, and he has my full support."

Mayor Ledbetter looked pleased that Lockhammer

gave him credit. "We're going to find your brother and then we're going to track down the person who blew up Mr. Newcastle's building and damaged your school. That's a promise."

Summerset rode up on his high-wheeler and stopped to hold up his wind device. "There's no rain in sight for at least three days," he said.

"Damn it, Summerset!" the mayor exploded. "Why the hell would Miss Blackwell care about the weather? She has other things on her mind."

Summerset looked insulted. "I just thought it would make her feel better, knowing her boy wasn't going to get rained on."

Amanda forced a smile. "Thank you, Mr. Summerset, it does help knowing that." She glanced at the earnest faces around her. "I appreciate what all of you are doing."

Dr. Paine rolled his high-wheel bicycle closer to the wagon. Damian had summoned him to Amanda's side earlier, but she had refused to take anything to help her relax. "Officer Thorndike said we could ride our bicycles through the park even though it's against the rules. Maybe we ought to check the children's area again."

"With God's help we'll find him," Reverend Jesse James said, and seeing the others pedaling away, waved his arm, calling, "Wait for me!"

Meanwhile, a crew of men continued to sift through the still-smoking rubble. It seemed like the wait would never end. Even Old Thorny took pity on her and brought her a cup of hot coffee.

"You better have some nourishment," he said.

"Thank you," Amanda said. She took the coffee, but refused the bread and cheese he offered her.

Damian joined her, and taking her hand, pulled her away from the watchful eyes of the crowd. "Let me take you home, Amanda."

She shook her head. "I can't leave."

"There's nothing you can do here."

"I have to stay."

He pulled her into his arms and she clung to him, grateful. "We'll find him," he promised. "You've got to believe that."

"Stop it!" She pulled away from him, anger flaring like a firestorm inside. "Why do you always refuse to accept the truth?" Despite the evidence, he continued to believe in his father's innocence. How she resented this, resented the way his stubbornness kept them apart. Now he wanted to fill her with false hope about Donny.

"Why are you so willing to believe the worst?" He threw up his hands and suddenly she saw the same fear in his eyes that kept her heart frozen in ice. "I can't bear to think . . ." His voice broke. "If something happened to Donny, it would be like losing my own son. I'll never forgive myself—"

"Don't, Damian." She stood on tiptoe and pressed her fingers to his lips, her already broken heart shattering into even smaller pieces. Lord, how could she blame him for choosing to believe the impossible when the alternative was so terribly, terribly painful? "It's not your fault."

"But if I hadn't built—"

"If anyone's to blame, it's me. Maybe my uncle is right. Maybe Donny would be better off—"

"Don't think that way, Amanda. No one could love Donny more than you do."

"Please, Damian, I need you. Just hold me."

He slid his arms around her and held her, held her so tight she could almost believe that nothing existed outside the realm of the safe circle he created around her. Her cheek pressed against his face, she felt his hot tears mingle with hers.

Late that afternoon, an elegant barouche drawn by two black horses with braided manes and shiny harnesses drove up to the police barricade. The driver was dressed in white trousers and a maroon jacket that matched the color of the lacquered coach.

No sooner had the barouche stopped when the door

flew open and Amanda recognized the fashionably dressed man as her uncle. He stood for a moment, looking around, then spotting her, limped to her side, his gloves and walking cane in his hand. "Amanda." He doffed his hat.

"Uncle Randall."

"I heard about Donald. I'm sure this must be a terrible time for you. If there's anything I can do . . ."

"There's nothing."

"I know that you and I haven't always seen eye to eye—"

"You're trying to take Donny away from me. I'll never forgive you for that."

"I'm only doing what I believe is right. I think this is best for you as well as Donny."

"How could you think that? You know nothing about me."

"I know that you have no future ahead of you. No man would marry a woman saddled with a simple-minded brother."

"That shows how little you know." Damian stepped up from behind her uncle and stood next to Amanda.

Uncle Randall glowered at Damian. "This is a private conversation and is of no concern to you."

"On the contrary. I care for Amanda and Donny very much."

Randall regarded Damian with an icy stare. "Do you, now?"

"Yes. Let me introduce myself." Damian held out his hand, but her uncle refused to shake it.

"I know who you are. You're the man responsible for this atrocity. If something has happened to my nephew, I shall personally hold you liable. Do I make myself clear?"

Damian let his hand fall to his side. "Perfectly."

"If you'll excuse us, I have matters to discuss with my niece."

"Any conversation you have with Amanda concerns me. You see, it's my fervent hope that one day your niece and I shall be married. I suppose that blows your theory out of the water, doesn't it? You know, the one about no man wishing to marry her because of her brother."

Uncle Randall's eyes gleamed with malice. "You might have disproved my theory, but you've helped my custody case enormously. I'm sure the court will question the sanity of a woman wishing to marry Phillip Newcastle's son."

Damian took a step forward, a dangerous look in his eyes, his body seeming to seethe with anger. Fearing he was about to hit her uncle, Amanda grabbed hold of his arm. "Don't, Damian, please!"

She felt the tension drain from his body. "I think you better go," she said to her uncle, her voice thin.

Her uncle looked about to argue, but obviously thought better of it. "Very well, then. Just remember, Amanda, the offer still holds. If you need anything, you know where to find me." He replaced his hat and walked the short distance back to his coach.

Damian glared after the departing barouche. "I wish I'd given in to my impulses and smashed his bloody face in."

"It wouldn't have helped and it might have made matters worse," Amanda said.

He doubted matters could be much worse than they already were. He took her hand in his and pressed it to his mouth. "Amanda, we'll find a way to fight him. I swear. I'll do everything in my power to help you. He's not going to take Donny away. I won't let him."

She gazed at him with tear-filled eyes. "If we don't find Donny—"

"I know." The custody suit was the least of her problems at the moment. Crushing her to him, his gaze traveled over her head to the mountainous pile of smoking rubble. Damn it, where was he? Where was Donny?

Later, he led her to the bonfire that someone had built in the center of the street. The area was still roped off to traffic and a small knot of local residents stood on the curb talking to a reporter from the *New York Times.*

The sun disappeared behind the low-riding clouds, and the air grew noticeably colder. Though the workers were still digging through the rubble, most of the onlookers had gone home. Only a few stragglers remained.

A kindly woman from one of the nearby farms wrapped a red woolen shawl around Amanda's shoulders and covered her legs with a threadbare blanket. Food and drink were spread across the flatbed of a dray and the exhausted workers took turns helping themselves.

Damian brought her a plate of food, but she had no desire to eat. When he insisted, she relented and accepted a cup of hot tea.

No sooner had darkness settled over them than huge gasoline torches were lit, flooding the area with glaring white lights. The search for Donny would continue through the night, if necessary.

Amanda's legs grew numb but she hardly noticed. She held Donny's button box on her lap, running her fingers across the smooth metal lid. She rocked back and forth and thought about all the times she had rocked Donny in her arms.

Where are you, Donny? Even though she continued to ask herself the question, she feared the answer.

Damian walked over to the fire and sat on the ground next to her, holding another cup of tea. He'd hardly left her side all day, except to check on the progress of the workmen. Despite the hours that had passed since the blast and the number of men who had volunteered to dig through the rubble, it seemed little progress had been made. What was taking so long?

He handed her the cup and shook his head at her silent question. She felt a little something die inside her each time he gave her the news. "Nothing."

And so the wait continued.

*　　*　　*

Dawn broke in a hazy gray mist, and the exhausted workers huddled around the fire, drinking newly brewed coffee and munching on freshly baked rolls, their hushed voices muffled in the collars of their coats.

Amanda had slept on and off through the night, her head resting on Damian's shoulder.

Hearing someone shout, Amanda opened her eyes. To her horror, Miss Quackenbush was perched on a high-wheel bicycle, heading straight for her. Amanda dived out of the way, but not a moment too soon.

Miss Quackenbush zoomed by, missing the fire by less than an inch. She zigged and zagged recklessly through the roped-off site, sending workers scattering in every direction.

"Good heavens!" the mayor cried out.

"Lawdy mussy!" Moose muttered.

Lockhammer clamped down on his cigar. "As soon as I take office, I'll see to it that women cyclists are banned from the streets forever, along with high-rise buildings." He glared at the members of the Knicker-bocker Ladies' Cycling Club, who watched their president's shocking wild ride with wide-eyed disbelief.

"Oh, no!" Amanda cried out. She pressed the knuckles of her hand against her mouth. "I think Miss Quackenbush's dress is caught."

Miss Quackenbush's bicycle wobbled, then made a sharp turn and plowed into Vincent's button cart.

Vincent leaped out of the way just seconds before the collision. The cart turned over on its side, spilling buttons everywhere. Miss Quackenbush shot over the handlebars, head over heels, and landed on a patch of grass in a shocking display of feminine apparel.

Amanda reach the poor woman's side behind Vincent. "Miss Quackenbush! Are you all right?"

Vincent cradled Miss Quackenbush's head in his arms, though he clucked his tongue in disgust. "You crazy fool. Now look what you've gone and done!"

Miss Quackenbush didn't look the least bit apologetic for the havoc she'd created. She was too busy gazing up at Vincent and swooning. "Oh, what male properties."

Vincent looked startled and his face turned scarlet. "Well, now .."

Meanwhile, Officer Thorny galloped toward them on his horse, but for once he didn't scold Amanda for blowing her whistle without regard for moderation. He did, however, recite park rules forbidding indecent exposure. "Now, perhaps you'll be kind enough to explain what in tarnation happened this time."

"Yes, do tell," Mrs. Brewer demanded. "How is it that our president made a fool of herself on her bicycle?"

Amanda quickly jumped to Miss Quackenbush's defense. "She's distraught over Donny and didn't see Vincent's button cart."

Mrs. Winston folded her arms across her ample chest. "How could she not see something as clear as the nose on her face?"

"Those dang bicycles are going to be the ruin of this city." Muttering to himself, Officer Thorndike tugged on the reins of his horse and rode off to direct emergency vehicles around the overturned button cart.

"Don't go riding over my buttons!" Vincent yelled.

"I'll take care of things." Damian strolled toward the cart, stooping over to pick up buttons along the way.

Meanwhile, Mrs. Winston took it upon herself to restore Miss Quackenbush's modesty. "I must say, Miss Quackenbush, I quite agree with Mrs. Brewer. How does it look for the president of the Knicker-bocker Ladies' Cycling Club to ride like a rank beginner? That's what gives us women a bad reputation."

"I quite agree!" Mrs. Blankenship sniffed.

"Now, hold your horses," Vincent said. "Miss Quackenbush was trying to do a goodly deed by looking for Mandy's brother. She just got herself in an emotional upheaval is all. It could happen to anyone."

"Oh," Miss Quackenbush giggled. "You really do have male properties."

"Amanda! Come quick!" At the sound of Damian's voice, Amanda spun around. "Hurry!" he called, beckoning with his arm. "I found Donny!"

Not sure she'd heard right, Amanda raced toward the overturned cart as fast as her legs could carry her. Then she saw him—her dear, sweet Donny—and she almost fainted with relief.

Chapter 33

Donny's safe! The news traveled like wildfire, bringing everyone on the run. Workmen, weary and covered in dirt, shouted in delight and threw their hard hats in the air. The wheelmen slapped each other on the back and passed out cigars.

The members of the Knickerbocker Ladies' Cycling Club hugged each other and seemingly forgot their president's shocking display of poor cycling skills.

Vincent, his face beaming, grabbed Miss Quackenbush clear off her feet and swung her around. "Donny's safe."

Everyone talked at the same time—everyone, that is, but Donny, who looked bewildered by all the commotion around him.

Amanda cried and laughed and even hugged Old Thorny, who for once didn't feel obliged to recite park rules regarding decorous behavior.

During the entire celebration that followed, Amanda couldn't take her eyes off Donny, not for a moment.

Not a dry eye could be seen anywhere. Even Vincent had a suspicious gleam in his eyes, though he tried hard not to show it.

"What I want to know is where you found him," the mayor said.

"Right here," Damian explained. He pointed to the space inside the cart that was normally hidden by the button trays.

"You mean he's been there the whole time?" Vincent asked, pushing his hat back. "Well, I'll be."

"But why didn't you notice him?" Mrs. Winston asked.

"I didn't open up the shutters on my cart," Vincent explained. "Not since the building blew up. Poor little guy. He must have heard the explosion and hidden in fear." He turned and gazed at Miss Quackenbush. "If it wasn't for Harriet here, I daresay it would have been days before we found him."

"You're right," Mrs. Brewer said. "This just proves that women cyclists have every right to be on the street."

"Yeah," the mayor agreed. "Even if they can't ride worth a damn."

Donny suddenly noticed the buttons that had spilled across the street. "Buttooooons!" he called, stooping over to pick up a brass one. "Come and git your buttooooons!"

Amanda could hardly see his grinning face for the tears. "Oh, Donny, you scared me so much." She planted a kiss on his forehead.

Donny had survived the ordeal better than any of them, and except for some rather odd red marks on both wrists, looked much the same as always. But he ate hungrily from the food wagon and couldn't seem to get enough to drink.

It wasn't until the crowd began to drift away that Donny first noticed the destruction left behind by the dynamite blast. Suddenly, his entire demeanor changed and he held on tight to his tin of buttons. "Give the signal!" he cried. "Give the signal."

"We better take him home," Damian said.

Amanda nodded, and after she personally thanked everyone who had helped in the search and hugged Miss Quackenbush, she climbed into the waiting hack next to Damian and Donny.

Donny could hardly keep his eyes open during the drive home, though once in bed, he insisted upon his usual story, and looked distressed to discover his sail-boat button missing.

"I'll tell you the story of this button," she said, pick-ing out the one with a rainbow. "Once upon a time," she began, but already he'd fallen asleep. "The prin-cess in the land of Nod fell in love with a handsome prince who promised her a rainbow." She sighed and dropped the button back into the tin box. "Only the princess didn't believe in rainbows. Not until the day her long-lost brother returned . . ."

Amanda sat on the bed, gazing at the sleeping boy. She leaned over and pressed her lips to his forehead. *Thank you, God,* she whispered. *Thank you!*

Damian was waiting for her in the other room, and after she had tiptoed from the bedroom, she fell into his arms. "Hold me," she whispered. "Hold me tight."

He gathered her in his arms and rocked her back and forth, restoring more of her soul with every sooth-ing word he uttered. "I missed you so much," she whispered back. They'd only been separated a week, but it had seemed forever.

He grinned. "I bet you never thought the day would come when you'd say that."

She returned his smile. "No, I never did." He looked tired, his face etched with deep lines of exhaus-tion. "Go home and get some sleep," she whispered. "Christopher will wonder where you are."

His eyes held hers. "I don't want to leave you. It could be dangerous."

She pulled away in surprise. "Dangerous?" Not sure she'd heard him right, she searched his face. "Danger-ous, how?" He hesitated to explain, but she wouldn't leave him alone until he did. "Tell me, Damian. I have to know. Is Donny in some kind of danger?"

"Donny didn't go to the site by himself."

"That's what I thought at first," she said slowly. "But I suppose it's possible. None of us really know, what he's capable of doing. He could have walked there. It's possible."

"But not likely. Besides, why would he?"

"Donny doesn't always need a reason for doing things. You know that."

"I'm not so sure, Amanda. I'm beginning to think Donny has a reason for doing everything he does. You said yourself you thought he understood more than doctors give him credit for."

"That's true, but there are still things he does or says that make no sense."

"There's more. The marks on his wrists. I'm willing to bet those marks are rope burns."

"Rope?" A sudden chill shot down her spine. "But that would mean—"

"That someone tied his hands."

"But who? And why?"

"I don't know. But it's entirely possible Donny's life is in danger."

She stared at him in utter disbelief. "You think someone tried to . . ." She could hardly get the words out. ". . . to kill him?"

"It's a real possibility. My guess is that someone tied him up and left him inside the building to die. Judging by the extent of the burns, I'd say the rope broke during one of Donny's fits."

It was possible. Donny was capable of amazing strength during his attacks. "But none of this makes sense. Unless . . ."

Damian's gaze sharpened. "Unless what?"

"Unless my uncle's behind this."

"Your uncle?"

"Maybe he was trying to prove Donny's not safe in my care."

Damian thought for a moment before replying. "That would mean your uncle blew up my building. That seems a bit extreme. Besides, I doubt your uncle wants to see Donny dead. In any case, if he wanted to prove you unfit, I daresay he would have simply abducted Donny and left him somewhere."

Damian was right, of course. Her uncle was many things, but she seriously doubted he was capable of murder. Nor was it conceivable he would blow up a building, especially since the odds that the court would rule in his favor were clearly on his side.

She rubbed her wrists, thinking about the burns on Donny. Anger and rage replaced her earlier fear. If she ever got her hands on the man who tried to harm Donny, she wouldn't be responsible for her actions. "But if it's not my uncle, then who?"

"Maybe—" Damian rubbed the back of his neck. "The day Christopher was kidnapped . . . are you certain he was the original target?"

"Of course I—" She stopped, surprised. "Surely you don't think there's a connection between this incident and the kidnapping?"

"I don't know. Think, Amanda. Tell me everything that happened the day Christopher was kidnapped."

"I told you. It all happened so fast." She related everything she could remember.

Damian listened intently, stopping her on occasion to ask questions or to clarify a point. "All right; you said one of the men grabbed Donny."

"Yes, that's right."

"Where was Christopher?"

"Several yards ahead."

"Then what happened?"

"Donny fell to the ground in a fit."

Damian frowned. "So we don't have any way of knowing if the kidnappers meant to take Christopher or Donny."

"I just assumed it was Christopher."

"Then why bother with Donny? Why not just take Christopher and run?"

"I don't know." It had never occurred to her that Donny might have been the intended victim. "Maybe . . . Donny was a witness. He was the only one besides Christopher who saw the kidnappers up close."

"That's true. But it's also quite possible they wanted Donny, not Christopher."

"Then why send you to Philadelphia?"

"To make me think Christopher was the intended

victim. Think about it, Amanda. I couldn't have prevented the kidnapping even if I'd been in town. Had they succeeded in taking Donny, we would have assumed they had taken the wrong boy by mistake."

"But why, Damian? What could they possibly want with Donny? They must know I don't have money. So it couldn't have been for ransom. It doesn't make sense."

"Hell, none of this makes sense. But I always thought it strange the men left Christopher behind when they made their escape. Why didn't they take him and run. The alley was blocked. None of the wheelmen could get through. Why go to all the bother of kidnapping him only to leave him? And why send me out of town?"

"I don't know, Damian. The idea that they took Christopher to throw us off the track . . . it all seems far-fetched."

"It worked, didn't it? I hired guards for Christopher, but Donny was left unprotected. That's what they counted on."

She held her head, her mind in a turmoil. No one would want to harm Donny, would they? Not her dear, sweet brother, who had never harmed so much as a fly in his entire life.

Donny cried out in the other room and Damian followed her into the bedroom. She sat on the bed. "It's all right, sweetie," she whispered. Donny's forehead felt damp. "You're just having a nightmare."

"Give the signal," Donny shouted. "Give the signal."

"Hush, now," she said softly. She settled him back among the pillows and drew the blanket over his shoulders. "You're home now and Damian and I won't let anyone hurt you. Not ever again." If only he could tell her what had happened. Lord, if Damian was right and Donny's life really was in danger, she didn't know what she would do. "There, now . . ."

Damian watched from the doorway while she rubbed Donny's back. Soon, Donny's eyes drifted shut and his even breathing told her he was asleep. She stood and followed Damian into the parlor.

"Does he have a lot of nightmares?" Damian asked.

"He hasn't really had any for a long time. He had them every night for months following my father's death."

"Was Donny at the theater the night the balcony collapsed?"

"Yes."

"He was?" Damian looked surprised.

"My father insisted upon taking him. He said it was a special night for the Blackwell family and we should all be together. What does it matter at this point?" Suddenly something occurred to her. "You don't think the dynamite blast is connected to what happened to the theater?"

"I don't know what to think at this point. It's possible someone blew up the balcony. Caleb tells me that if a series of small charges were set to go off in strategic parts, the balcony would have fallen. You said your father thought there was a short in the electricity. Maybe what he saw was something else."

"Dynamite charges!" She gasped in shock. "You think that's what he saw?"

"Maybe. If only that fire hadn't gutted the theater before we had a chance to investigate more thoroughly."

"But wouldn't we have heard an explosion or something?"

"Don't forget, the orchestra was playing. And if the charges were small enough and staggered, there wouldn't have been a loud explosion."

"But it makes no sense, Damian. Even if there is a connection, what possible reason would the perpetrator have for harming Donny?"

"I don't know. Unless—" His eyes narrowed.

She felt fingers of ice touch her heart. "Unless what?"

"Unless he saw or heard something that night at the theater."

"But why would anyone wait three years before going after him?"

Damian paced around the floor, his hands behind his back. "All right, let's say Donny heard something, saw something—whatever—at the theater. But no one knew it at the time."

"I suppose it's possible," Amanda said. "But if no one knew it then, how could they know it now? Donny's not capable of telling us what happened to him. How could anyone feel threatened by him?"

"I've been thinking about that. Donny tends to imitate expressions he hears."

"Yes, he does." At times he drove her crazy with his repetitive sayings.

"It seems to me he manages to use them in a way that makes sense."

"Most of the time," she agreed. "He can't put words together on his own, but he can memorize phrases, and he seems to know when to use them for the most part."

"What about the phrase *Give the signal*? He repeated that phrase all the way home today. And he woke up from a nightmare saying it. What does it mean?"

"I don't know. I've always assumed he wants me to blow my whistle. He's aware I use my whistle to warn my students of danger. Naturally, when he saw the destruction done to your building and the school, he wanted me to blow my whistle."

"But I've heard him use the expression at times when no danger was imminent." He thought for a moment. "For example, he used it during our outing in the park."

"Yes, he did. But you have to remember that Donny sometimes perceives danger when none exists."

"But the term itself, *Give the signal*. Is that something you say?"

"I've never used that expression."

"Interesting. Do you know who does use it?"

"I can't think of anyone. Is it important?"

"I don't know. Maybe not. But he must have heard the expression from someone. He used it today and during the parade. Can you think of any other times?"

She thought for a minute. "I've heard him use it during my cycling classes. Once he kept chanting it so loudly, Moose had to take him away."

"Does he say it during every class or just some?"

Amanda tried to think, but the truth was she was so exhausted, nothing was making sense. Finally, she shook her head. "I can't remember. I know the wheelmen get pretty irritated with him."

Damian's face darkened. "The Wheelers' Cycling Club?"

"Yes. I remember one day in particular. They were practicing their routine and Donny kept shouting those words over and over. He can be very distracting."

"That's odd. I seem to recall the wheelmen were in the park when Donny started chanting."

"But the wheelmen weren't around when Donny said it today. It was just you and me."

"I know." *Give the signal.* The words kept running through his mind. What was Donny trying to tell them? And why did Damian have the feeling it was something important?

Damn, he was close to something. But hell if he knew what it was. All these weeks he'd been convinced he was being watched . . . wasn't it possible that it was really Amanda who was being watched, instead?

If he was right, then he might also be right about someone wanting Donny dead. The questions was why.

"Amanda, I know you're exhausted, but try to think. Do you remember when Donny first used the phrase?"

"I don't know. He's used it for years."

"Think, Amanda.

She walked around the room, hands on her head.

"Wait." She swung around to face him. "I'm not sure about this, but it seems to me I first heard him say it during my father's funeral. I remember he stood by my side as the casket was lowered into the grave. I think that's the first time I heard him say it, but I can't be sure. Damian, what does this mean?"

"I don't know. Were any of the wheelmen at the funeral?"

"Only Dr. Paine," she said. "We didn't know any of the others at the time." She shivered and ran her hands up her arms.

"Are you all right?" He regretted having to worry her, but if Donny was truly in danger, she had the right to know.

Her lips trembled, but she nodded. "I can't bear the thought of someone trying to harm Donny. What possible reason could there be?"

"I don't know, Amanda. I just don't know."

"Maybe it *is* my uncle. Do you think that's possible?"

"That's what I intend to find out."

"Oh, Damian, hold me!" She was in his arms again, her head on his shoulder.

He chuckled in her ear. "I love it when you beg."

"I didn't beg," she said. "Well, maybe just a little."

"Everything's going to be all right, Amanda. I swear. Trust me."

She gazed up at him. "I do trust you. Oh, Damian, I realize I've wasted so much time worrying about things that don't matter. Instead of cherishing Donny for the person he is, I've grieved for the person he'll never become. I'll never do that again, not ever. Nor will I ever let the past interfere with my future."

"You don't know how happy I am to hear you say that," he whispered. "Stay with me, Amanda, please. Come to the farm. Donny will be safe there. And we'll hire the best lawyers possible to fight your uncle."

What he offered her was Heaven and she was tempted to accept, but she couldn't. Swallowing hard, she pulled away from him, and for the longest while they stood staring at each other, he puzzled and confused, she trying to brace herself for what she must now do.

"Amanda?"

"I can't come to the farm, Damian. I can't see you for a while. Not after tonight."

He turned ashen, as if someone had suddenly stabbed him from behind.

"Please try to understand," she pleaded. "I have no choice. My uncle will use you against me in court."

"Let him!"

"I can't jeopardize what little chance I have of keeping Donny."

"Since when have you let someone dictate what you can and cannot do?" He was angry and hurt and made no effort to hide it.

"You don't know my uncle."

"I know you.'"

"Please, Damian, if you really care for me, you'll honor my wishes."

"Care for you? Hell, I don't just *care* for you. I love you!"

His declaration of love, even when shouted in anger, made her heart race. "Then you'll do as I ask."

"No!"

"Please, Damian. You're a Newcastle. My father was killed—"

His eyes narrowed as he watched her. "Go on, say it. Your father was killed by my father."

"That's what my uncle will testify to in court. How would it look if it's known that I—"

"That you what? Love me, a Newcastle, a dirty, scheming Newcastle!"

"Yes," she whispered softly. "I do love you." Her mouth twitched upward. "See? I do change my mind on occasion."

He smiled, but the frown remained on his brow. "You didn't change your mind," he growled softly. "It was love at first sight and you know it."

"I know nothing of the kind," she said hotly, though

it was entirely possible he was right. "Please, Damian, don't make this any more difficult than it already is. It's only until after the trial."

He shook his head vehemently, then spoke in a quiet voice that was frightening in its intensity. "Nothing will change after the trial. This thing with my father will always come between us whether we want it to or not."

"That's not true—"

"It's come between us before and it's coming between us now."

"But only because of what my uncle threatens to do."

"It was there between us from the start, Amanda." He took his hat from the table and pressed it onto his head. "Old habits are hard to break." He shook his head, his eyes filled with a finality that turned her blood cold.

"Things will change, Damian. I promise. Just let me get through the trial. . . ."

"Then what?"

"Then we can be together."

"Even if I continue to work on my father's case?"

"Even then," she whispered softly, but though she said the words in her heart, she knew that all the love in the world couldn't erase the guilt in her soul.

Even worse, Damian knew it, too.

Chapter 34

The courtroom was packed that second day in November. Donny sat next to Amanda, dressed in a gray tweed jacket trimmed in black silk braid, vest, pantaloons, and matching knee-high spats, his neatly combed hair hidden beneath his floppy straw hat. He held his tin button box tightly clutched in his hands and kept his eyes downcast.

Amanda wished the butterflies in her stomach would go away. She was so nervous, she could hardly sit still. Though she taken her attorney's advice and exchanged her usual bloomers and Turkish trousers for a more sedate plum-colored suit with a modified bustle and wide-flounced hem, she felt strangely conspicuous and out of place. Lordy, it would be a miracle if she survived this day!

The last few weeks had been extremely difficult. Damian had respected her wishes and stayed away. But the separation had cost her dearly. Without Damian, she felt lost and alone—more alone than she'd ever felt in her entire life.

Last night she had been tempted to throw caution to the wind and go to Damian. Wouldn't that have been something? Would Damian have welcomed her with open arms? Or would he have turned her away?

Irritated at herself for caring so deeply, she pushed her thoughts away. What possible good could come of wishing for things that could never be? That was Damian's way, not hers. Right now, she had to concentrate on the problem at hand.

She patted Donny's leg and her heart went out to him. If only she knew how to reach him, how to make him understand what was happening and why she had all but locked him up in recent weeks. He'd looked so solemn lately; his usual quick smile had all but vanished. He missed Christopher. They both did.

She didn't dare let her brother out of her sight, not for a single moment. Now that she suspected someone meant to harm him, she never went anywhere without him.

Moose took his place next to Amanda and squeezed her arm. "It's gonna be all right, Miz Mandy. Yessiree, you wait and see."

She forced a smile in an effort to relieve his worry. He had been telling her this for weeks now, ever since she'd first told him of Damian's suspicions. Moose had been outraged. "Now who would want to go and hurt our boy?"

If only she knew.

The weeks following the explosion had been filled with uncertainty and fear. An official investigation had been conducted and there was speculation that someone had dynamited Damian's building to protest what many considered an eyesore.

An eyesore, indeed! It infuriated Amanda that the police didn't take the destruction of the building more seriously.

She was willing to bet buttons to dollars that had it been a crime against anyone other than a Newcastle, the police would have found the culprit by now and brought him to justice.

Oh, Lord, how she missed Damian! Even now, she searched the courtroom, hoping against hope he might have come even as she prayed to God he wouldn't.

Her uncle stood watching her from the back of the courtroom; he'd watched her for months now, she was certain of it. Watched and waited for her to do something—anything—he could use against her in court.

Now he met her gaze with a curt nod of his head, then limped up the aisle with his cane and sat at the plaintiff table, surrounded by three of New York's best attorneys.

The attorney representing Amanda was a short, compact man by the name of Mr. Quinton. The man squinted through his pince-nez spectacles and had a stutter, but he was the only attorney she could persuade to take her case. The attorney had not yet arrived. Donny's life hung in the balance and her attorney was late!

"Don't you go worryin' none, Miz Mandy," Moose whispered. "He's won a lot of important cases."

"He's not going to win this one if he's not here," Amanda whispered back.

Donny grew restless. He turned in his seat, and spotting Vincent in the back row, sitting next to Miss Quackenbush, called out the vendor's refrain. "Buttooooooooooons!"

"Shhh." Amanda put her arm around Donny's shoulder. "You mustn't talk out loud."

Uncle Randall and his lawyers glanced at Donny following his outburst and hastily put their heads together in a whispered exchange.

Feeling her already low spirits plummet even lower, she glanced at the rows of seats behind her.

It surprised her to discover half the tenants in her apartment house were in the courtroom. Carolyn and Arthur Webber sat two rows back, gazing at each other like newlyweds. Mrs. Aviary and Ellie-May sat across the aisle from Mrs. Brook. A raspy cough helped her pick out her father's old friend, David Ludwick, who looked even more sickly than when she had last seen him.

Many of Amanda's cycling students were scattered about the room. The members of the Knickerbocker Ladies' Cycling Club took up an entire row. Wearing enormous feather hats, the women looked like a flock of birds sitting on a telegraph wire.

The members of the New York Wheelers' Cycling Club sat farther back, and Sergeant Summerset walked up to Amanda to give her a three-day weather report. "We're due for some snow flurries Tuesday night," he said worriedly. "I was hoping for sunny skies until this trial is over."

"It's all right," Amanda said, knowing how the weatherman took full responsibility for any inclement weather.

Summerset brightened. "Of course, the wind can always change."

Mr. Quinton hurried up the aisle, a leather portfolio in hand, and took his place next to Amanda.

"Wind can change," Donny said.

Moose glowered at the attorney. "Not nearly as much as we hope for."

No sooner was Quinton seated than the judge, dressed in a flowing black robe, walked into the courtroom and took his place at the bench.

Mr. Liversworth spoke first. If Amanda were the type to judge by appearances alone, she would say he was everything her own attorney was not. His long frock coat emphasized a straight back and rigid square shoulders. His beard, trimmed to a sharp point beneath the chin, was the same salt-and-pepper shade as his neatly combed hair. His habit of standing with his hand behind his waist, orator style, contributed to his commanding presence. His opening remarks were eloquent and disturbingly persuasive.

"We are here today to determine the future of Donald Blackwell, a young man with special needs. Needs that Mr. Randall Compton is prepared to provide." He explained at great length the extent of Mr. Compton's financial resources and standing in the community. Lord, if he didn't make her uncle sound like a living saint!

Liversworth's voice grew slightly cynical. "We will show the court that Donald Blackwell's present caretaker, Miss Amanda Blackwell, isn't fit to raise a child. Especially an idiot child."

Amanda held herself rigid, but she couldn't hold back the angry tears. "He's not an idiot!" she whispered, and Moose laid one enormous hand on her arm.

"Now, Miz Mandy, you'll get your chance to dispute him," he whispered back.

"Miss Blackwell's reputation precedes her." Liversworth picked up a stack of old newspaper clippings and read the headlines regarding her colorful and often controversial activities during the time she was trying to open her cycling school. In retrospect, the activities and speeches seemed bold, even shocking, especially her much-quoted opinion regarding men who insist women ride sidesaddle.

Well, they *were* misogynistic billy goats! Though perhaps she should have found a different way of saying half-cocked and half-arsed. But how could she possibly know her every word would be quoted in newspapers and later repeated in a court of law?

"Does it really come as a surprise that a woman who consistently flaunts convention would allow her own brother to run wild?" Liversworth pulled a sheet of paper from his portfolio and proceeded to cite the many incidents that had occurred in recent months to support his disturbing claims.

"Donald Blackwell was seen on the roof of his apartment building and then climbed to the fourth floor of the Newcastle building while it was still under construction."

He paused for effect, then continued. "He was kidnapped and nearly killed in an explosion. I have witnesses who will testify this young man has little or no supervision. I'm convinced that after I've presented the facts in this case, you will rule in favor of Mr. Randall Compton, who has proven without a doubt to be a pillar of society and a member in good standing of his church. Mr. Compton has nothing to gain by taking Donald Blackwell away from his sister. He only wishes to do what is best for the boy." His opening statement completed, he sat down.

Amanda glared at him. Best for the boy, indeed! It was all Amanda could do to keep from jumping up and demanding Liversworth explain why her uncle showed no concern for Donny's welfare during the last twelve years. Let him try to weasel out of that one! Still, she had to give Liversworth credit; it took him less than twenty minutes to do his damage.

Amanda's attorney stood, dropped his glasses, and had to scramble on the floor after them. He then took his time before beginning his opening statement, shuffling through papers and clearing his throat repeatedly before uttering a single word. She tried not to panic, though her foot tapped impatiently beneath the hem of her skirt.

When at last he began, he proceeded to contradict everything Liversworth had said, but he stuttered and stammered so much, no one, including the judge, seemed to be paying much attention.

Amanda was so frustrated she was tempted to stand up and complete the opening argument herself. Indeed, had Moose not been holding her down, that's exactly what she would have done.

As hard as it was to believe, things got worse as the day progressed.

"There's no chance Donald Blackwell will ever lead a productive life," one noted physician declared under oath.

"I saw it with my own eyes," a horsecar driver said. "I swear to God. The boy jumped out of the window of my vehicle, he did. Like to scare the shit out of me."

"The witness will stick to the facts," the judge admonished.

"Those are the facts," the driver argued.

"Were you moving at the time?" Liversworth asked.

"Yes, sir."

Liversworth turned to Amanda's attorney. "Your witness."

Quinton stood. "C-c-could you p-p-please t-tell the c-c-ourt what Miss Blackwell did after her brother jumped out the w-window?"

"Yes, sir. She jumped out after him."

Amanda gave a satisfied nod. Of course she jumped out after him. Wouldn't anyone? Convinced the testimony could only help her, she glanced at the judge, who was shuffling paper. "This is important testimony," she called out.

The judge banged his gavel and glared at her. "I'll tolerate no more outbursts in this court." He adjourned for the day and Moose whisked Amanda and Donny out of the courtroom and drove them home in his carriage.

"I'm going to lose Donny, Moose."

"Now, Miz Mandy. You haven't presented your case yet. You can't give up hope."

"Now you sound like Damian."

"I hope so, Miz Mandy. I sure do hope so."

By the following morning, Amanda's nerves were completely frazzled. As if things weren't bad enough, Donny refused to cooperate. The moment she laid out his good suit, he started acting up. He refused to dress himself and wouldn't even stand still while she combed his hair.

Obviously, he knew they were going to court again, and if she didn't know better, she'd think he was telling her he didn't want to go.

There she went again, thinking he understood more than he did. But it was growing increasingly more difficult lately to believe what the doctors had told her was true. What if Donny wasn't only reacting to her nervousness, as they said? What if he knew his entire future was at stake?

Now *she* was beginning to sound like Damian!

She drew a deep breath. "It'll be all right Donny," she said more for her own benefit than his.

Despite her efforts to remain calm, Donny continued acting up, and after he was finally dressed, he ran out of the apartment.

"Donny!"

Afraid to let him out of her sight, she ran after him, practically falling down the stairs in her haste.

Donny was waiting on the ground floor, the scruff of his neck held by old man Adams. Or at least that's what she thought at first glance. But a closer look revealed it wasn't the doorman hired by Carolyn but a stranger dressed in Adams's uniform.

Alarmed, she pulled Donny away from him. "Who . . . who are you?"

"I'm sorry, ma'am, I didn't mean to frighten you. I didn't think you'd want your brother running outside by himself."

"Who are you?" she asked again. "And where's Mr. Adams?"

"I'm . . . taking his place."

"Did Mrs. Webber hire you?"

"Oh, no, ma'am. It's Mr. Newcastle I work for."

"Damian?" Her heart skipped a beat. "Damian hired you? Why?"

"It's my job to make certain no harm comes to the boy. I've been sitting here for weeks now, pretending I'm in a stupor, just like your last doorman. No one even suspected. . . ."

It took her a moment to absorb his meaning. Damian hired him? Just to watch Donny? She couldn't believe it! "Thank you," she whispered, her heart in her throat. For weeks she had thought she was all alone, and all this time, Damian had been looking after her interests. "Thank you so much."

"My pleasure, ma'am." He settled on the floor by her feet, pulled his hat down over his face, and the transformation was complete. No one would guess the man beneath the beaked cap wasn't old man Adams in one of his stupors.

She was teary-eyed all the way to the courthouse. Donny sat next to her in the horsecar, looking worried. "Baby's hungry," he said, repeating the phrase she'd used on numerous occasions to explain why the Fennessy baby cried.

She smiled through her tears. When Damian refused to stop working on his father's case, she'd thought he didn't love her enough. But that wasn't true. He *did* love her. He did! "Babies don't cry only when they're hungry, Donny." She gazed out the window with a deep sense of longing. "Sometimes they cry when they want to be held."

Chapter 35

Ignoring the clamor of reporters outside the courtroom, she walked through the double doors and froze in her tracks. Damian sat in the back row, next to Christopher. Nothing had prepared her for the rush of emotions that suddenly overwhelmed her. She felt all at once euphoric and fearful. She was torn between wanting to rush into his arms and asking him to leave before her uncle spotted him.

As if he sensed her presence, Damian turned and their gazes collided. Caught in a whirlpool of conflicting emotions, she looked away quickly, but her gaze soon found its way back to him and this time she didn't turn away.

Donny tugged on her hand, but she held on tight. "Hello yourself," he called to Christopher.

Reminded how her uncle had threatened to use Damian against her, she started down the aisle, her lips wooden. "We can't talk to Christopher. Not now."

Walking past Damian at that moment without so much as a word of acknowledgment was one of the hardest things she'd ever had to do. It was also the most necessary.

She took her place next to Moose. At least Quinton was on time today, and his papers were already spread on the table before him.

Testimony resumed at precisely nine a.m. and by noon her uncle's attorney rested his case.

Following midday recess, Quinton called his first witness to testify on Amanda's behalf.

Miss Quackenbush testified that Amanda had more patience than a churchful of saints. "And she's only been in jail once that I know of."

Miss Quackenbush was trying to be helpful, but Liversworth jumped on her testimony quicker than a frog going after a fly. "Miss Blackwell was in jail?"

"Yes, but only because the sparrow cop insisted upon making us obey those ridiculous rules."

"Does Miss Blackwell have difficulty obeying rules?"

"Oh, no, sir." Miss Quackenbush gave a self-righteous mew. "Only the ones that apply to cycling."

Moose took the stand next. "There ain't no better than Miz Mandy," he said, glaring at the prosecuting attorney. "When Master Christ'pher was kidnapped, Miz Mandy didn't let nothin' stop her. Not even a bunch of ole hogs."

Amanda covered her face as Moose described how a hog had pulled off her bloomers. "And what did Miz Mandy do? Why, she kept going, that's what. Did she care that her legs were exposed? She did not!"

Liversworth could hardly wait to cross-examine. "How often does Miss Blackwell appear in public in a state of undress?"

"Oh, Miz Mandy don't never appear in public undressed," Moose said, looking at the judge. "Not unless she's got good reason."

Mrs. Aviary's testimony was less damaging. "All the time I've lived in the same apartment building, I've never once seen a strange man's underwear hanging from her clothesline." She glared at Mrs. Brook. "Not like some people I know."

But no matter how complimentary the testimony, Liversworth managed to discredit the witness. Now he faced Mrs. Aviary and leveled his steely gray eyes at her. 'How would you describe yourself, Mrs. Aviary?"

"Describe myself?" She looked around the courtroom. "I know it's not considered proper to think too highly of oneself, but I would have to say I'm a lady."

"Would you, now? And what were you before you were a lady?"

Quinton objected, but Liversworth had skillfully managed to cast doubt on Mrs. Aviary's moral character.

But the witness who did Amanda the most damage was Mrs. Brook. After Quinton had questioned her about taking care of Donny, he turned her over to Liversworth.

Liversworth worked her over as smoothly as a con man bilking a gullible victim. "Your husband died how long ago?"

"A little over a year ago."

"And who is the man living with you now?"

Mrs. Brook turned red. "I don't think that's any of your business."

"Ah, then you do have a man living with you?"

"No."

"No, Mrs. Brook? Are you aware of the penalty for lying under oath? Now I ask you again. Do you or do you not have a man living with you?"

"Well, he's not actually living with me—"

Her shocking confession was met with a loud murmur. Mrs. Aviary nudged Ellie-May, who covered her mouth and tittered.

Amanda stole a glance at her uncle. The pompous old fool. Look at him. He looked as if he didn't have a care in the world.

Liversworth never missed a beat. "So am I to understand that Miss Blackwell left Donny in your care even though it was common knowledge you have a man living with you?"

"I told you, he's not living with me. Besides, I took good care of the boy," Mrs. Brook insisted. "I love him like he was my own flesh and blood. I do."

"I have no more questions of this witness."

Quinton looked like someone had drained the blood from his body, and even Dr. Paine's testimony regarding Donny's ability to type couldn't offset the damage caused by Mrs. Brook. "I have no further witnesses, your honor."

Suddenly a tiny voice traveled from the rear of the courtroom. "I want to be a witness." Amanda turned at the sound of Christopher's voice. Damian looked as surprised as anyone.

A buzz of whispered voices swept from the front of the courtroom to the rear. The judge banged his gavel. "Quiet!" He then leveled his eyes on the back row. "What is your name, son?"

"Christopher Jacobs Newcastle. I'm Donny's friend."

"His friend, eh? Very well. Let's hear what you have to say."

Liversworth jumped to his feet. "I object, your honor. I don't think we should waste our time on the testimony of a mere child."

The judge dismissed Liversworth's objection with a wave of his hand. "We've heard testimony from firemen, policemen, cyclists, vendors, and horsecar drivers, to name a few. But I've not heard testimony from any of Donald Blackwell's friends. Indeed, Mr. Liversworth, you've given us the impression that this young man is incapable of making friends. Overruled!"

Damian wheeled Christopher's wheelchair down the aisle and parked it next to the witness stand.

"Do you understand what it means to take an oath?" the judge asked.

Christopher nodded solemnly. "It means I have to tell the whole truth."

"Very well," the judge said. "Let's get started."

Christopher placed his hand on the Bible and took his oath and Amanda's heart went out to the small earnest boy who was trying to help his friend.

Quinton began. "W-w-would you explain your friendship with D-d-onny?"

"That's easy. He's my bestest friend in the whole wide world."

"Do you boys t-t-t-alk to each other?"

"Oh, yes, sir. All the time. Donny wants to stay with his family. He told me so."

"B-b-but doctors have t-t-testified that D-Donny can't t-talk."

"That's a lie," Christopher said. "You can talk, can't you, Donny?"

"I have no more q-q-questions."

Liversworth stood and Amanda felt sick to her stomach. She leaned over to whisper in her attorney's ear. "He'll tear Christopher apart. We can't let him—"

"Order!" the judge glared at her.

"Order!" Donny said and Amanda hushed him.

Liversworth directed his remarks to the judge. "I have no questions of this witness. However, with the court's permission, I would like to ask that Donald Blackwell be allowed to take the stand. If he can talk, as his young friend insists, then perhaps he can tell us who he wants to live with."

Gasping, Amanda covered her mouth with her hand. Dear God, no! Desperate, she turned to Quinton, but already he had jumped to his feet faster than Amanda had ever seen him move. "O-o-objection!"

The two attorneys approached the bench, and after a long whispered discussion the judge ruled that Donny would take the stand.

Amanda turned to Quinton. "He can't do this."

"W-w-we have n-no choice!"

She took a deep breath. "Be gentle with him, please."

She turned to Donny and quickly explained that he had to go up front. Dear God, if there was the slightest chance in the world Donny understood anything, let it be this. "Let Moose hold your buttons." She practically had to pry the tin box loose. She then took Donny by the hand and led him to the stand.

The judge nodded. "Thank you, Miss Blackwell. Please return to your seat."

Quinton approached the witness stand. "That's a b-b-boy."

"Hello yourself," Donny said, and nervous laughter rippled among the spectators.

The bailiff held a Bible in front of Donny and made him put his hand on top. "I swear to tell the truth . . ."

Donny stared at the Bible, but said nothing.

After several attempts to get Donny to repeat the oath, the bailiff turned to the judge and shrugged.

Quinton stood and argued that since lying took a certain amount of intelligence, Donald Blackwell was incapable of speaking anything but the truth. Therefore the oath should be omitted. Since Quinton's argument could only help his client, Liversworth had no objection.

The judge waved the bailiff away and signaled for Quinton to begin.

Amanda was so nervous, she could hardly stand it. Donny looked especially young and vulnerable sitting in the witness box, his eyes fixed on Quinton.

Quinton began. "W-would you p-please state your name."

When Donny remained silent, Quinton tried again. "My name is Claude Quinton. Now what's yours?"

"Hello yourself," Donny repeated.

"W-w-would the record p-p-please show that the w-w-witness's name is D-d-donald B-b-blackwell."

"Objection!"

Quinton glanced at Liversworth before turning to face the judge. "The question in front of the c-c-court is not whether this young m-man can state his name or repeat an oath. But whether he is c-c-capable of expressing his wishes as to where he wants to live."

"Overruled."

Quinton resumed his questioning. "D-d-donny." He spoke very slowly. "T-tell us w-where you want to live."

"Hello yourself," Donny said.

"W-w-w-where d-do you want to live, D-d-donny. T-t-tell us where."

Amanda twisted her hands together. This was sheer torture. Dear God, don't let him have one of his attacks.

Donny fingered his straw hat and looked confused, but so far showed no sign of losing control.

Quinton tried rewording the question. "D-d-do you w-want t-to live with your uncle?" He pointed to Donny's uncle Randall. "Or do you want to live with your s-s-sister, Amanda?"

Donny's lower lip quivered and Amanda's stomach knotted. Dear God! She was going to be sick.

Liversworth rose to his feet. "Your *honor*," he began in an exasperated voice. "I think we can all conclude that Donny Blackwell does not know his own mind and therefore would be better off in an institution."

"No!" Amanda covered her face with her hands. "No, no no!"

The judge pounded his gavel. "Order!"

She tried, tried with all her heart to remain calm, but watching Donny on the stand looking lost and confused was more than she could bear. She felt her stomach churn and she was afraid she was going to be sick. Thinking some fresh air might help, she stood and raced to the back of the courtroom. Her tears blinding her, she ran straight into Damian.

"Amanda!" he said, his voice low. He took her by the arm and hastily led her through the double doors and outside the courtroom. "Where do you think you're going?"

It was cooler there than inside and she drew a deep breath. "They're going to take Donny away from me," she murmured. "I'm going to lose him, Damian."

His hands on her shoulders, he shook her gently. "Maybe not."

"Don't, Damian. Even you have to see what a hopeless battle I'm fighting."

"Let me testify."

"You?" She stared at him through her tears. "Don't

you understand that's the worst thing you could do? My uncle will use you against me."

"Let him."

"But what could you possibly say?"

He lifted her chin and kissed her tenderly on the lips. He then gently wiped away her tears with his handkerchief. "I think it's time the court heard about the little girl who found her baby brother and saved his life. It's time they knew how she's loved him and cared for him all these years, against the most incredible odds. How she's always put his needs before her own. I want to do this, Amanda. Please let me do this."

Her mind raced. "Liversworth will—"

"Turn me into mincemeat? Let him. He won't be the first. Just do me a favor. When we get to that point, have Moose take Christopher outside."

"Oh, Damian. Do you think this will work?"

"We won't know till we try. Now where's that fighting spirit of yours? Heaven knows you've used it on me enough times. How about a smile?"

As incredible as it seemed, she did smile. For the first time since this whole mess began, she felt hope, not much, but a little, and that was something she hadn't felt in a very long time.

Chapter 36

Together Amanda and Damian walked back into the courtroom. He followed her to her seat and sat next to her, taking her hand in his.

Donny was still on the witness stand, looking more sullen and withdrawn than before. It nearly broke Amanda's heart to see him there, all alone.

Sensing her distress, Damian slid an arm around her shoulders. She smiled up at him through her tears, grateful to have him by her side. If his plan worked—dear God, if it worked—this whole nightmare would soon be over. But that was a mighty big if. She squeezed Damian's hand tight, and somehow that simple gesture renewed her hope.

Quinton had apparently not had any luck with Donny during her absence, and the lawyer looked more befuddled than before. Quinton turned toward Amanda and shrugged in defeat.

Amanda motioned Quinton over and informed him of Damian's decision to testify. Much to her dismay, Quinton didn't look the least bit happy.

"T-that could be a b-b-big m-mistake. Your uncle's attorney k-knows you spent the night with Mr. Newcastle on the top of his b-b-building. By putting him on the stand, Liversworth will be free to use that information in his cross-examination."

Amanda was shocked. "But how would he know such a thing?"

"A newspaper reporter spent the night across from the building, hoping the wind would topple it, no doubt. He s-s-saw you go inside. W-w-we can't put Mr. Newcastle on the s-s-stand."

Stunned, she stared at Quinton, speechless. The last of her hopes shattered, she felt crushed, devastated. One night! One glorious, ecstasy-filled night spent in Damian's arms, and her uncle planned to turn it into an ugly weapon against her.

"I'm sorry," Damian whispered, his voice choked. "I'm so sorry." He tightened his hold on her, his head next to hers. "I never meant to hurt you."

"Don't," she whispered. "I came to you that night." She lifted her hand to his face and pressed her cheek next to his. "And I would probably do it again if given a chance."

Her uncle turned to look at her, a satisfied gleam in his eye upon seeing her in Damian's arms. He turned to his attorney and she could well guess what he said.

But someone else was watching, too. Someone else noticed Amanda in Damian's arms, saw Damian drop a kiss on her forehead, saw her lift her hand to his face.

Donny.

Donny watched his sister as Quinton helped him step down from the witness stand and something flickered deep in his eyes, like a burning candle. Suddenly he spoke, his voice loud enough for all to hear. "Good match!"

Silence followed his words until Moose jumped to his feet. "Donny's right! He and his sister make a mighty good match! Yes, sir, mighty good."

The spectators went wild. Vincent rose to his feet, waving his hat. The members of the Knickerbocker Ladies' Cycling Club hugged each other and Miss Quackenbush unabashedly threw her arms around Vincent's neck.

Moose grinned from ear to ear and took it upon himself to shake everyone's hand. Even Old Thorny looked pleased.

It took some doing, but the judge finally managed to restore order.

"See I told you he could talk," Christopher said.

The judge looked directly at Christopher. "It looks like you might be right," he said. A hush fell over the courtroom as the judge flipped through his notes. Amanda leaned forward, her hands pressed to her chest. Did the judge really believe Donny knew what he was saying? Dear God, she hoped so. Next to her Damian shifted and squeezed her arm. The waiting was agony.

Finally, the judge folded his hands in front of him and cleared his throat. "I think we can conclude that this young man does, indeed, know his own mind. I see no reason why he can't remain in his sister's care." He banged his gavel down. "Case dismissed."

Pandemonium broke loose for a second time. Damian lifted her to her feet and they literally fell into each other's arms. Cheers filled the courtroom and the mob of people rushed forward to congratulate Amanda and to praise Donny.

For his part, Donny ignored all the confusion around him except to ask "Where's your pride?" when a group of spectators stood clapping their hands.

He made his way through the crowd to Christopher, grabbed hold of the wheelchair, and pushed it down the aisle and out the double door in back.

Damian followed close behind and took over the chore of lowering the wheelchair down the courtroom steps.

Amanda's neighbors and friends were gathered in front of the courthouse and everyone started talking at once the moment she and Damian arrived.

"This is so exciting," Mrs. Aviary bubbled.

"Did you see the face on that attorney when the judge ruled against him?" Ellie-May added.

"I'll tell you something, Amanda," Mrs. Aviary said. "Donny was right. You and your brother are a perfect match."

"I think Donny was referring to Damian and Amanda," Priscilla said quietly from Caleb's side.

Damian looked in one direction, Amanda in another.

"They do make a good match," Moose said. "Just like a horse and saddle." He laughed at his own joke. "Maybe it's time they did somethin' about it."

Amanda gave Moose a meaningful look, signaling him to drop the subject. But either he had suddenly gone blind or was just being ornery, for he promptly began soliciting everyone's opinion on the subject.

Miss Quackenbush expressed her views. "Of course the two are meant for each other. And trust me, Amanda, you won't find better male properties anywhere."

Vincent looked insulted. "You said that about me."

"Yes, but you're spoken for, so it doesn't count," Miss Quackenbush said.

Vincent blinked. "Spoken for? Me?" The others laughed, and Vincent finally shrugged his shoulders and laughed, too.

Then everyone started in on Amanda and Damian. Amanda couldn't believe it, the way they carried on. Lord almighty, when did matchmaking become a national pastime? "Wait!" Amanda pleaded. "It's not that simple."

Carolyn Webber lifted her voice to be heard. "You always said that if two people love each other, nothing else matters. That's what you told me."

"But Damian is trying to prove his father's innocent. He can't possibly take on a wife."

"That's ridiculous," Caleb said. He turned to his employer. "How much investigating have you done since you two stopped seeing each other?"

Damian raked his fingers through his hair. "None," he admitted, looking uncharacteristically sheepish. "But I've had a lot on my mind, what with having to rebuild."

"Pshew!" Big Pete spit out a wad of tobacco. "There ain't nothin' that gits done when a woman crowds the mind." He sidled up to Miss Porterville. "I know that for a fact."

"Wait, please, everyone, stop!" Amanda pleaded.

"It's all right, Amanda," Damian said, slowly, quietly. "They're right, you know. I can't do anything when you're not around."

Caleb's wife giggled. "That sounds like a proposal to me." She slipped her arm through Caleb's. "We couldn't be happier for you, could we?"

"Now wait a minute," Damian protested. "It's not a proposal till I say it's a proposal."

"What are you waitin' for?" Moose asked.

"All right. Get ready, Amanda." Damian lowered himself on one knee in front of Amanda and, gazing up at her, took her hand in his. His expression grew serious, but his eyes danced with warm, loving lights. "Miss Amanda Blackwell, I know that loving me seems disloyal to your father and I don't know what to do to change that. All I know is that I love you more than life itself, and if you can find it in your heart to be my wife, I would be the happiest man alive."

Amanda wanted so much to say yes—yes, she would marry him, yes, she would be his wife, yes, she would spend the rest of her life with him—but the word stuck in her throat, and much to her horror, she recalled her father's fear-filled face.

Unable to speak, she shook her head. "I can't—"

"I have something to say." David Ludwick stepped forward, then kept everybody in suspense while he succumbed to a coughing spell. "Excuse me for interrupting," he said at last, forcing everyone to move closer to hear his weak voice. "Amanda, I knew your father for a good many years. I promised him that if anything ever happened to him, I would give you away at your wedding."

"I know that, Mr. Ludwick."

"Yes, I guess you do." He coughed once before continuing. "Your father's greatest dream was for you to find a man to love and cherish you. A man willing to let your spirit run as wild as the wind. What I've seen here, today, convinces me that Damian Newcastle is exactly the kind of man your father had in mind. Since you father entrusted the job to me, I want to be the first to give my blessing to you both."

Amanda gazed at Mr. Ludwick and saw reflected in his eyes the face of her father—not the face that had haunted her since the night he'd died, but the kind and gentle face she had tried desperately to recapture in recent years and couldn't.

And because she could so clearly see her father's face, see the kind of man he was, she knew Mr. Ludwick had spoken the truth. Her father would approve of Damian, would approve of their love for each other. She knew that now.

Shaken by the sudden realization, she turned to Damian. Her cheeks flushed with joy, her heart was so full of love there was no room left for the bleak memories or guilt that had separated her from Damian and even her father.

"Then it's settled," Moose said.

"Let her speak for herself," Priscilla said.

Miss Quackenbush folded her arms across her chest. "Take your time, Amanda. Don't let anyone push you into doing something you don't want to do."

The weatherman glanced anxiously at the sky. "You better make up your mind before those snow flurries start to fall."

"Come on, Amanda," Damian said. "This is no time to be stubborn. Do you or don't you want to be my wife?"

"I'm not being stubborn," she said. "I'm being practical. Now that we know about my father, what about yours?"

"I'll continue to work on his case. You know I will. I have to, Amanda." The look on his face filled her with the greatest joy and happiness. "But I'm not about to let anything come between us again."

It seemed to her they were the only two people in the world. She lifted her hand to his cheek, and gazing at the love in his eyes, she knew that nothing was impossible as long as they were together. "Oh, Damian, I had no right to ask you to give up your search." The burning look of love he gave her grew more intense. "I'm going to help you prove your father's innocence. I'll type letters—anything."

He chuckled softly. "I've seen your typing and I think we'll both be happier if I hire a typist. Just say you'll marry me, Amanda. That's all I ask." When she didn't immediately reply, he prompted her with a frown. "Well? What happened to the woman I know who made up her mind on a dime and never changed it unless threatened with death?"

"I change my mind all the time," she assured him. "But I'm not changing my mind about this." She took a deep breath, wanting to savor the moment. "Yes, I'll marry you," she whispered. then, her voice growing louder, she repeated, "Yes, yes, YES!"

The small gathering went wild. Grinning from ear to ear, Damian picked her up and twirled her around the courthouse square. "See? I always told you you loved me," he said, putting her down.

"You never told me I was going to marry you."

"That's because I wanted to surprise you."

Lifting her hand in his, he turned to face the crowd. Moose beamed and Mrs. Aviary sniffled. The weatherman stared worriedly at the sky and the mayor scratched his head, no doubt trying to think of how he might use this to gain votes. "What do you think about a bicycle parade for the wedding?" he asked.

Miss Quackenbush brightened. "And I'll lead it off."

The mayor turned white at the thought and everyone groaned. Damian set Amanda down, but he kept his hands placed firmly around her waist.

"I have a better idea, Harriet," Vincent said grandly. "How about riding tandem with me?"

Miss Quackenbush grew pink, then red, and finally, purple.

Damian grinned. "That sounds like a proposal to me."

"Me, too," Amanda said.

"Absolutely," Moose agreed.

No one looked more surprised than Vincent. "It did?" He looked at Miss Quackenbush and she looked at him. "Well, what do you know?" he said, grinning.

Summerset looked worried. "This wedding thing is evidently contagious. I'm getting out of here before I find myself proposing, too." And with that Summerset sprinted away amid good-natured laughter. But thinking he might have a point, the unmarried women glanced around with hopeful looks on their faces, and the single men began backing away. All except Big Pete, who looked like he was hoping Miss Porterville would take the bull by the horns and propose to him.

Later, after all the excitement had died down, Mrs. Brook hugged Amanda. "I'm so happy for you. Donny's a fine boy and I'm going to miss you both."

"We'll come and visit you, I promise," Amanda said. She hesitated for a moment. "What happened in the courtroom . . . I'm so sorry."

"You have nothing to be sorry for, Amanda. You got Donny and that nice Mr. Newcastle and it does my heart good."

"Thank you." The two hugged again and this time Amanda happened to notice Old Thorny watching from atop his horse.

Mrs. Brook followed Amanda's gaze and blushed. "Go along with you, now. Your family is waiting for you." She climbed into the driver's seat of her wagon.

"Mrs. Brook . . ." Amanda lowered her voice. "The man you've been seeing . . . it's not Officer Thorndike, is it?"

"Why, Amanda, where did you ever get an idea like that?" She grabbed hold of the reins and kept her eyes focused on the horse. "Why, something like that would get him drummed out of the police so fast he wouldn't know what hit him." She looked left and right to make certain no one was eavesdropping. "You won't tell anyone, will you?"

It was all Amanda could do to keep from laughing out loud. "Don't worry, Mrs. Brook. No one would believe me, anyway."

So it was Old Thorny's long johns that dangled from Mrs. Brook's clothesline from time to time! Oh, glorious day. She'd always thought the two would make a good match.

She was still smiling to herself when she returned to Damian's side. He gazed at her with suspicion. "Now who have you matched up? Not Chipper?"

"No, not Chipper," she said softly, although she intended to find him a wife before long.

"Then who? Come on, Amanda, confess."

Their good-natured sparring was interrupted by Christopher, who tugged on his father's coattails. "Where's Donny?"

"Don—" Amanda quickly scanned the area.

"He was here a minute ago," Damian said, looking all around.

"Donny!" Amanda cried. Cold, black fear swept through her. The relief of winning the lawsuit and the excitement of Damian's proposal combined with the happiness of being surrounded by friends had lulled her into a feeling of false security. That was a mistake. Donny's life could still be in danger.

Feeling as if her breath had been cut off, she frantically ran up the steps of the courthouse and bumped into Quinton.

"Have you seen Donny?"

Quinton shook his head. "H-h-he's not inside."

"Dear God!" She raced back down the steps. Where was he? She shaded her eyes against the sun. Then she saw him, standing inside a cabriolet parked in front of the courthouse. Feeling almost faint with relief, she cupped her mouth. "Damian!" she called, pointing toward the street. "He's over there."

Damian reached the cabriolet first and had already

helped Donny to the ground by the time Amanda reached them.

Amanda grabbed Donny and hugged him. "You mustn't get in other people's carriages." Still holding on to him, she lifted his face upward to hers to make certain she had his full attention. "No carriage."

"Show Amanda your button," Damian said, his voice strangely quiet.

Puzzled, Amanda dropped her arms to her side and studied Damian for a moment before turning to look at Donny's open palm. Donny grinned as he showed her his favorite button. It was the one with the little sailboat that had been missing for weeks.

"That's the button you lost," Amanda said. "Where did you find it?"

"Once upon a time," Donny said.

"He found it in the cabriolet," Damian explained.

"But I don't—" Before she could complete her sentence, Damian sprinted into the street.

"Lockhammer!"

Amanda watched in bewilderment as Damian chased Lockhammer, darting around a horsecar and tackling the politician onto the sidewalk.

"Oh, dear me." Mayor Ledbetter looked aghast. "I know Lockhammer can be annoying at times, but even I've never hit him."

Passersby stopped to watch. Christopher tugged on Amanda's arm and Donny held on tight to his button box.

"Give the signal," Donny said.

"Good idea, Donny." Amanda glanced around, and seeing Officer Thorndike a distance away on his horse talking to Mrs. Brook, she blew her whistle to get his attention. The policeman galloped toward the battling duo.

"All right, you two. Break it up!"

Amanda turned to Moose. "Watch the boys for me."

"Will do, Miz Mandy. Will do."

Dodging traffic, Amanda ran across the street, but

the fight was over almost as quickly as it had begun. Damian was on his feet, his lip bloodied. He grabbed Lockhammer by the scruff of his neck and shoved him toward Thorndike. "Arrest him."

Officer Thorndike looked confused, but he pulled out his handcuffs just the same. "On what charges?"

"Kidnapping and murder."

Epilogue

The trees in Central Park were bare except for a few red leaves that trembled beneath the gray skies of that dull November day. For Amanda, it felt like spring, despite the cool breeze and Summerset's yet unfulfilled promise of snow.

Soon the pond would freeze and she would have to think about signing up students for skating lessons.

This was the first time since the end of the trial five days ago that Amanda had Damian to herself. He had greeted her earlier with the astounding news that his father would be released from prison the first thing Monday morning. He'd promised to fill her in on all the details and she could barely contain her curiosity.

She could feel Damian's excitement as together they strolled along the promenade mall. She waited until Donny had pushed Christopher's wheelchair a short distance ahead before turning to Damian and bombarding him with questions.

"How long are you going to keep me in suspense, Damian? What's this about your father?"

His mouth twitched in amusement. "I was wondering how long before curiosity got the best of you. It's true. My father was not responsible for what happened at the Continental Theater."

"Oh, Damian!" She stared at him in total wonder and disbelief. All along he'd maintained his father's innocence, and now it turned out he was right. She couldn't be happier.

"Do you know what this means? Now that the truth

is out, we can all start living a normal life again. I no longer have to protect Christopher from gossip. He can go to school and even ride one of your confounded tricycles, if he wants."

Amanda clapped her hands in delight. "This is wonderful news! But how did it happen? And what's any of this got to do with Donny? Why would Lockhammer kidnap Donny? And how did you know it was him? And what was all that about murder? And—"

Damian laughed at her impatience. "Hold it, my darling. Only one question at a time. It's true. Lockhammer kidnapped Donny and intended for him to die. Donny, as you know, had other ideas."

Amanda shuddered. "Thank God." How she hated realizing someone she knew—one of her very own students—was capable of such a heinous crime. Suddenly feeling overwhelmed, she sat on a park bench. "But why?"

Damian glanced at the boys before sitting on the bench next to her. "Lockhammer didn't want Donny to reveal the truth."

Now she was really confused. "What truth?"

"That Lockhammer was responsible for the collapse of the balcony."

"What?"

Damian nodded. "It's true, Amanda. It all started when my father was told he'd gone over budget in building the theater. Naturally, he asked for an accounting of all the money paid out. That's when he discovered the unexplained expenditures."

"Lockhammer?"

"Yes, but my father had no way of knowing it at the time. He decided to do some checking on his own."

"And Lockhammer found out about it."

"Lockhammer knew his political aspirations were over unless he could find a way to keep my father from discovering he had embezzled money from City Hall."

"But how could he know that your father would be sent to prison for manslaughter?"

"He didn't. His original intent was to make it look as if the Newcastle Building Company was doing shoddy work and using cheap materials, thus destroying my father's credibility. He was then going to insist upon an audit, and when it was discovered that funds were missing, he would simply point the finger at my father."

She listened in astonishment. "I never much cared for Lockhammer, but I had no idea he was capable of such a devious plan."

"It's my guess he's been getting away with this kind of thing for years."

Sickened, she shivered. "But to kill all those people—"

"I don't think that was ever Lockhammer's intention. I think he simply wanted to make the balcony sag just enough to prove his point. Lockhammer didn't count on the balcony actually collapsing." Damian reached for her arm. "I'm sorry, Amanda."

She shook her head. "I'm the one who's sorry. You told me your father was innocent and I . . . Oh, Damian, I wanted to believe you," she whispered. "I truly did."

"I know."

"What I don't understand is why Lockhammer wanted to hurt Donny."

"This is where it gets interesting," Damian explained. "I found out why Donny keeps saying 'Give the signal.' Donny heard Lockhammer tell his two assistants to 'give the signal' when it was time to light the dynamite charges."

Amanda shook her head in disbelief. "But if the balcony had been blown up with dynamite, why didn't the police know this?"

"They weren't looking for it. Remember how your father thought he had an electrical problem?"

"Yes, that's why he went back to check. So you think it really was dynamite charges he saw?"

"I'd bet my life on it. As for the police, don't forget Lockhammer has a lot of friends in high places. He was pretty much able to manipulate the investigation. Once he dropped the idea of graft in the ears of the right people, nothing else was considered. And to make certain no one got any ideas down the line, Lockhammer arranged for the theater to catch fire."

"But why did Lockhammer wait so long before he went after Donny?"

"He didn't know Donny could hurt him until that day he saw us in Central Park. When Donny saw Lockhammer, he tried to tell you what had happened by repeating the phrase he heard Lockhammer use that night."

"And I didn't understand."

"No, but Lockhammer did and he realized he had a problem."

"And the kidnapping?"

"Lockhammer again. Only his assistants panicked when Donny had one of his fits. It was just as I suspected. They took Christopher instead, just to throw us off. And that was why Lockhammer sent me out of town on that wild-goose chase."

"But why blow up your building? There were other ways he could have gotten rid of Donny."

"Yes, but none that would better suit his purposes. The mayor approached me with the idea of building a twenty-five-story office building for the city. I told him the only way I would consider taking on the job was if he saw to it that my father's case was reopened. That's the last thing Lockhammer wanted."

"So he destroyed your building," she said.

"Yes, and had Caleb not spotted dynamite beneath the rubble, he might have gotten away with it. In any case, another company would have been hired and Lockhammer would have kept stealing money."

Amanda shook her head, incredulous. "But how did you figure out it was Lockhammer?"

"I suspected Donny was trying to tell us who had tied him up when he kept repeating that phrase 'Give the signal.' Then when you told me he kept saying that same phrase during your father's funeral I decided there had to be a connection."

Amanda caught her breath. "You mean he was trying to tell me who was responsible for my father's death?"

"That's exactly what he was trying to do."

"But that still doesn't explain how you knew it was Lockhammer."

"I didn't. Not until I saw Donny reach under the seat of Lockhammer's cabriolet and retrieve the button he'd dropped the day Lockhammer kidnapped him."

Amanda couldn't believe it. "You mean Donny led you to Lockhammer?"

"Do you still think he doesn't understand what's going on around him?"

"Oh, Damian." She sat back in wonder. "This is all so overwhelming."

"I know."

"When I think how close I was to losing Donny. Not just to my uncle but to Lockhammer . . ."

"Donny's safe now." He slipped his arms around her waist and kissed her tenderly.

Amanda's heart was filled to overflowing with happiness and love.

"Look at the boats!" Christopher called. "Hurry, Papa. Hurry, Amanda."

"Hurry, Papa. Hurry, Amanda," Donny echoed.

Damian grinned. "Our boys are calling us." He stood and, taking her hand, pulled her along the path. He stopped to smile at an infant in a baby carriage. "Hello, little Amanda," he said.

The baby cooed and the proud parents, whom Amanda had introduced to each other a year earlier, grinned happily.

"Hello, Amanda," he called after an eighteen-month-old toddler who was trying to outrun her nanny. "Hello, Amanda," he said, tousling the golden curls of an adorable little girl dressed in a ruffled apron.

Carolyn and Arthur Webber strolled by, hand in hand, Carolyn's middle already swelling with the new life expected in the late spring, a month before Caleb and Priscilla's little bundle was due.

A bicycle horn sounded and Damian and Amanda stepped out of the path of a tandem bicycle. Vincent sat in front, pedaling hard, his face red with exertion. On the seat behind him sat Miss Quackenbush, her legs held out like a pair of clippers.

She'd recently resigned as the president of the Knickerbocker Ladies' Cycling Club. "I've got more important things to do with my time," she'd said mysteriously, and Amanda could well guess what those things might be.

"Buttoooons!" Donny called after them.

Vincent huffed and puffed. "For God's sake, Harriet. Pedal!"

Amanda saw a pretty young nanny, with skin the color of golden oak. "What do you think about her?" she whispered to Damian. "Moose would think her mighty pretty and—"

She was stopped midsentence by Damian's warm, probing lips. He moaned in delight. "You taste so good," he whispered.

"Do you mean that?" she asked teasingly. "You're not just saying that because you're a gentleman, now, are you?"

He chuckled softly. "A gentleman? Me? Never!" Taking the precaution of pulling her behind the trunk of a red maple tree, he proceeded to break every rule in the park forbidding all but the most decorous behavior. They were safe from Old Thorny's prying eyes. But not Donny's.

Spotting his sister in Damian's arms, Donny promptly turned Christopher's wheelchair so his soon-to-be "brother" could see them, too. "Good match," Donny said.

Christopher couldn't agree more. "Good match."

Author's Note

I've always admired those brave souls who risked life and limb for the benefit of mankind. We all know the names of the adventurers who first sailed around the world and flew to the moon. But what about the courageous and, for the most part, unknown pioneers whose job it was to determine if, for example, artichokes or mushrooms were safe to eat? You have to admire the first warrior to go into battle wearing a suit of armor. Or the first woman to stuff herself into a corset. But what about the first person to sit in a dental chair? Test out an elevator? Eat with a fork?

Then there was New York architect Bradford Lee Gilbert, who, like the hero in my book, climbed to the tenth floor of his thirteen-story superstructure during a gale wind in 1885 to prove to the panicked crowd that the forerunner of skyscrapers would not topple. It's questionable whether Mr. Gilbert enjoyed himself as much as my hero, but he certainly was an inspiration.